When the Stars Fell from the Sky

David Spell

Volume Three of the Zombie Terror War Series

This is a work of fiction. Any similarities to events or persons, living, dead, or fictitious are purely coincidental. Some actual locations are used in a fictitious way and the descriptions included here are not meant to be accurate. No part of this publication can be reproduced or transmitted in any form or by any means, electronic or mechanical, without permission in writing from the author.

ISBN: 9781980469582

To my daughters: Sarah and Rachel. I could not be prouder of the amazing people that you are. You are wonderful wives, mothers, friends, and incredible servants of our God!

"I watched as the Lamb broke the sixth seal, and there was a great earthquake. The sun became as dark as black cloth, and the moon became as red as blood. Then the stars of the sky fell to the earth like green figs falling from a tree shaken by a strong wind." (Revelation 6:12-13)

"They surrounded me on every side, but in the name of the Lord I cut them down." Psalm 118:11

"The art of war is simple enough. Find out where your enemy is. Get at him as soon as you can. Strike him as hard as you can, and keep moving on." General Ulysses S. Grant

"All right, they're on our left, they're on our right, they're in front of us, they're behind us…they can't get away this time." Marine Lieutenant General Lewis "Chesty" Puller

Table of Contents

Prologue

Interstate 95 Northbound, Virginia, Wednesday, 1600 hours

Terrell Hill tried to stay with the flow of traffic. The last thing he needed was to get stopped for speeding. He wasn't afraid of the cops but he had finally heard from the mystery man in Washington, D.C. Hill had an appointment with him on Thursday.

Terrell had tried to call his boss, Amir al-Razi, but there had been no answer. He called the other number that Amir had given him and the accented voice who answered said they wanted to have a face-to-face talk with Terrell.

Hill didn't know what to expect from this meeting. He figured the dude would want to recruit him for some more jobs. That was fine with Terrell, as long as they paid him. The man on the phone's accent had sounded similar to Amir's and he had given Hill some instructions about avoiding detection from the authorities. He sounded like he knew what he was talking about. Spy stuff.

The Iranian terrorist, Amir al-Razi, had recruited Terrell to be the inside man at Sanford Stadium the previous Saturday. Hill was working at a concession stand inside the location to make extra money during football season. He jumped at the chance to strike back at the University of Georgia.

The school had withdrawn their football scholarship when Terrell had been arrested for armed robbery and aggravated assault. His access and his anger made him the perfect recruit for Amir. The terror cell leader had given Hill two vials of the zombie virus, three thousand dollars, and a pistol.

Terrell had poured the vials of the poison onto two pizzas that had quickly been sold to the hungry football fans. He had then murdered his supervisor, Richard, stolen the cash generated that day from the concessions stand, and fled the scene in Richard's Ford Explorer.

Hill was feeling really good. He had spent the last three nights at a Travel Lodge motel, just off the interstate, south of Petersburg, He watched the news closely, expecting to see his own face. Instead, there had been no mention of him at all. I might just have gotten away with the biggest mass murder in American history, he thought, smiling to himself.

There was plenty of talk on the news about the terrorist attacks in Athens, Georgia. Looking back, Terrell was impressed with the depth of Amir's planning. Georgia Square Mall was infected first on Saturday morning with the bio-terror virus. This attack served to pull police and first responders away from the UGA campus. Then, the chemical was spread simultaneously inside Sanford Stadium and the packed Tate Student Center across the street.

The reporters said that the death toll was estimated in the thousands and that the university and the city of Athens were still not secure. It's a good thing I got out as quick as I did, Terrell thought. If I had tried to leave the stadium ten or fifteen minutes later, it might have been a different story.

Yeah, he hoped this guy that he was meeting had some more work for him. He definitely needed the cash. Hill knew that he would need to dump his vehicle pretty soon. This new ride was definitely a step up from Richard's but he couldn't keep it too long. He could steal another car but buying one would be better. The goal was to avoid getting arrested.

I'm pretty good at this stuff, he smiled to himself. Maybe I'll become an international assassin or something. Those guys make a lot of green and get a lot of girls. He turned the radio on and sang along to a rap song about killing all the cops.

Alexandria, Virginia, Wednesday, 1700 hours

Imam Ruhollah Ali Bukhari sat across from the three young men in the living room of the safe house. It was time to strike the Great

Satan again. Over the last several weeks, there had been many powerful blows throughout America utilizing the zombie virus.

Several key cities had been attacked and many infidels had been infected. The death count nationwide was almost thirty thousand. And this did not include the attack from the University of Georgia the previous weekend. Ruhollah had not been able to reach Amir al-Razi, his agent behind that strike. He had to presume that al-Razi was dead or in custody.

It was a brilliant move by Amir to somehow spread the virus inside the stadium at UGA's home opener football game. News reports had reported the crowd at ninety-one thousand people in attendance. There had not been an official estimate of casualties in the bio-terror attack but Bukhari knew it had to be in the tens of thousands. And, the university campus was still not secure. The news was reporting that the National Guard was working to clear the area of zombies and rescue any survivors but they still had a long way to go.

In spite of Amir's success, however, the imam was still disappointed. His instructions had been clear. "Cripple the city of Atlanta."

Al-Razi had launched multiple strikes but they had been on the periphery of the city. The media had also reported, and Bukhari's own sources confirmed, that Somalian terrorist, Mohamud Ahmed, had been shot and killed by Centers for Disease Control enforcement officers in the heart of the city, before he could launch his deadly attack near Georgia State University.

The President of the United States had struck back harder than the leadership in Iran had expected. Once he was satisfied that Iran was behind the bio-terror attacks on America soil, the President had unleashed the full fury of the American military.

The Iranian air force, army, and navy had been destroyed in less than a month. Tehran and many other cities had been completely destroyed by the infidel forces. Ruhollah had to presume his children and their families were dead. He had had no contact with them in weeks.

Now, he was sitting with three more young jihadists. Three martyrs for three more crippling blows inside America. Ali, Hassan, and Ramzi were being sent out as the warriors of Allah that they were. This was their last briefing before they started driving towards their targets.

Washington, D.C., New York, and Atlanta were going to be struck again. These three cities were hit hard in the initial stages of the jihad. The imam's area of responsibility was the east coast. He had been told to do as much damage as possible and to cripple the most important cities.

New York City represented America and had been the target of terrorists since the first World Trade Center bombing in 1993. Washington, D.C., was the seat of American power. Atlanta was the major southern city and, while attacked by Amir's men, had not suffered the crippling blow that Bukhari envisioned.

Ruhollah would pray with the three young martyrs and send them on their way. The coded message on the Islamic internet message board ordered that the new offensive begin on Friday at 1700 hours. Ali, Hassan, and Ramzi had forty-eight hours to reach their targets and to launch their attacks.

Bukhari's bomb maker and lieutenant, Usama, would start the timers as the soldiers of Allah left the safe house. They would merely need to park their vehicles in a populated area near their targets and walk away. They would then find another location to activate the suicide vests each would be wearing.

The imam knew there were other assets in place, cells that had been in existence for years. He had no idea who or where they all were. The American intelligence machine was good and it was better to keep different groups and agents compartmentalized.

Most of these sleeper cells had been activated during the initial attacks, weeks earlier. These were soldiers who had been waiting for their chance to become martyrs, as well. The imam knew that these other groups of Allah's soldiers had received the same orders he had.

This should be a very interesting weekend.

After Ali, Hassan, and Ramzi drove away, Ruhollah sat in the kitchen sipping a cup of tea that Usama had prepared for him. Now, he had to decide what to do with Terrell Hill. He had clearly proven himself useful to Amir and had been responsible for the deaths of many thousands of infidels.

He was not a true believer, though. The imam knew that. Prison converts seldom were. That did not mean that he could not serve a purpose. It just meant that Hill's motives were not as pure as the three men they had just sent out. And, he was clearly not a professional.

Bukhari had had Usama call Terrell earlier that day. He'd been surprised to hear that the killer was still driving the same stolen car and was still using the same cell phone. Didn't the fool know that the Americans, infidels that they were, had a very long reach? The imam did not even have a cell phone and Usama had returned Hill's call using a pay phone down the street.

Usama told Hill to get rid of the car he was using and to steal another one. He also told Terrell to buy two or three cheap, prepaid phones. Usama gave Hill the address for a mall a few miles away from the safe house. They would meet in the food court during the lunch rush tomorrow and, if Hill was free of a tail, he would be brought back to meet the imam.

And that brought him back to his original question. What do I do with Terrell Hill? He clearly has no qualms about killing people. There must be some way to use a man like that, even if he lacked the operational skills that most operatives possessed. I'm sure I can find some role for him in this Holy War.

Chapter One

Chasing Shadows

The hallway was almost completely dark but he knew he was running in the right direction. He had been here before. Behind him, the footsteps were getting closer. Ahead, she was waiting for him. He had to get to her. He had to save her.

Chuck McCain turned the corner and saw the large room in front of him. The flickering fluorescent lights ahead of him caused him to slow down. He didn't want to get jumped as he entered the big room. Behind him, the sounds of growling and the pounding of footsteps were drawing nearer.

McCain reached for his pistol but the holster was empty. He felt a stab of fear. Where was his gun? How could he have lost his gun? The lights continued to flicker as he peered cautiously into the room. Empty. She had to be there. He knew that she was in this room.

He stepped inside and looked around again. There she was, lying on the floor in a corner. Why was she on the floor? McCain rushed over to her side and saw the blood. So much blood. They were getting closer. He only had seconds.

"Rebecca, wake up. Let's get out of here."

There was no response but he knew that he could save her if he could just get her out of there. He scooped her up in his arms and ran for the door on the far side of the room. He glanced behind him and saw that they were in the room now, closing on him and growling loudly, snapping their teeth at him.

McCain got to the metal door, turned the knob, and was in the next hallway, still carrying her. Chuck threw his body against the door to close it. A second later, the slam of bodies from the other side echoed down the corridor.

This should be the last hallway. The exit was just ahead and he could get Rebecca some help. She was going to be fine. As he got to the last door and pushed it open, he felt her stir in his arms. Chuck stepped into the sunlight as it reflected off of her blonde hair.

He smiled at the beautiful woman he was carrying. "I knew you were going to be OK."

Rebecca's eyes opened and her hands that had been laying lifeless, reached up and around his neck. He felt her pulling him closer. He started to kiss her. Suddenly, a low growl came from her throat and McCain felt her teeth sinking into his neck.

"No!" he screamed and sat up in his bed, the sweat pouring off of his muscular body. His heart was racing and he felt like he had just sprinted around the block. A large figure stood in his doorway, watching. He walked over to Chuck, handing him a bottle of water.

McCain took it and drained half of it. "Thanks. Sorry if I woke you up."

"Sleep's overrated," said Scotty Smith. "You want to talk about it?"

Chuck shook his head. "Same dream. I keep hoping for a different ending."

The red numbers on the clock beside his bed showed 0350 hours. The big man knew he wouldn't be able to go back to sleep and he reached for the cargo pants on the floor, standing, and slipping them on.

"I'll be OK. I'm going to make some coffee and read for a while. Go back to bed. You need your beauty sleep."

Scotty chuckled. "Sure, Chuck. And, for what it's worth, I've been there, too, with the bad dreams. When I got blown up in Iraq and Alex and TJ got killed, I woke up every night in the middle of a nightmare."

"How long did it last?"

"A few weeks."

McCain nodded. That was what he expected. He had had nightmares before. It was nothing like this, though. He had never lost someone that he had loved as much as he had loved her.

Centers for Disease Control Headquarters, Atlanta, Wednesday, 0600 hours

He had sat in his living room, sipping coffee and reading a few of the Psalms. David was a guy he could relate to. He was one of the greatest warriors and leaders in history. He had made some really bad personal decisions along the way but he never completely walked away from God. He wrote about his own pain and grief from losses that he had suffered and Chuck always found comfort in David's words.

After McCain could hear Scotty snoring in the guest bedroom, he finished dressing, let himself out of the house, and drove to work. When he stepped through the secure basement entrance at CDC headquarters, a short African-American man with gray hair, wearing a security guard uniform, was waiting for him.

"I saw you pulling in on the security cameras, Mr. McCain. I just wanted to tell you how sorry I am about Ms. Johnson. She was a fine person and a good cop."

"Thanks, Darrell. That means a lot coming from you. We're all going to miss her."

The security supervisor stuck out his hand and Chuck shook it, noticing the tears in the man's eyes. Darrell was a former City of Baltimore police officer. He had retired as a sergeant and after relaxing for a year had taken the security job at the Centers for

Disease Control. He was now one of the supervisors. The security staff and the CDC Enforcement Unit that Chuck headed had a good relationship. Most of the security officers were retired law enforcement or military so they all got along well.

McCain walked into the locker room and changed into his workout clothes. The fitness center was empty at this early hour, exactly how he liked it. Today was chest day and the flat bench was a good place to exert himself.

After a few warm up sets, he put two hundred and twenty-five pounds on the bar. He got an easy twelve reps so he added another fifty pounds. This time, he only managed eight reps. He did two more sets at two seventy-five and then bumped it up to three hundred and fifteen pounds.

At six feet two inches tall and two hundred and twenty pounds, Chuck was strong but he also knew that his long arms meant that a heavy bench press was always going to be a challenge. He had friends who were moving four and five hundred pounds but they also had short arms. His long arms were good for fighting, though, and his reach had saved him on more than one occasion.

McCain heard the door open as he was about to lift the bar off the bench.

"You need a spot?" a familiar voice asked. "Not that you're doing that much weight, but I know how easy it is for you old guys to hurt yourselves. And don't forget, you can't sneak away from me. I'm a Ranger. I sleep with one eye open."

Chuck closed his eyes in resignation. Scotty Smith had become McCain's designated shadow since the events of the previous weekend. He had spent every night except one at Chuck's house. Smith was a big, bearded six foot five and a muscular two hundred and fifty pounds.

After spending twelve years in the army as a Ranger, he had taken a discharge after his humvee had hit an improvised explosive device. His injuries had not been serious but his two best friends had been killed. Smith had always dreamed of becoming a fireman so after getting out of the army, he applied and was accepted at one of metro Atlanta's fire departments. He was trained as a paramedic as well as a firefighter.

After two years, though, Scotty had gotten bored and applied to a security contracting company to go back to Iraq. It was at that point that Rebecca Johnson, the head of the Centers for Disease Control Enforcement Unit in Atlanta, was able to recruit him to come apply his talents and skills there. His training as an Army Ranger Sniper and as a paramedic had made him a vital part of Chuck's team.

He helped Chuck lift the bar off the rack and watched him closely as he got four repetitions. Smith set up on the flat bench next to McCain's and started his own warm ups. He spotted Chuck for another set of five and then six repetitions at three hundred and fifteen pounds.

Scotty put a twenty-five on either side of McCain's bar for a total of three hundred and sixty-five pounds. Chuck managed to get two reps. Smith already had four hundred and five pounds on his own bar and positioned himself under it. McCain stayed close to spot him as he got six repetitions.

After lifting weights for an hour, Chuck walked over to the hanging heavy bag. He pulled the wraps out of his bag and deftly wrapped his hands. He set the timer on his phone for ten three minute rounds, slipped on the twelve-ounce boxing gloves he carried in his gym bag, and went to work.

Scotty had moved to the incline bench press and was about to lift three hundred and fifteen pounds. He watched his friend pounding on the heavy bag, the noise of his punches and kicks exploding throughout the room. It just sounds different when that man hits the bag, Scotty thought.

He remembered back to when he had asked to spar with him a few months earlier. Chuck had tried to dissuade him. Smith knew that McCain had been a part-time professional mixed martial arts fighter but he also knew that he had the size, weight, and age advantage. Scotty was three inches taller, thirty pounds heavier, and eleven years younger.

While Smith had never been an MMA fighter, he had wrestled in high school and played football. He had learned to box in the army and had never lost a fight. He still lived in the gym and knew he was the strongest of his CDC teammates. Scotty had never lacked for confidence and he thought he would be able to hold his own against his boss. He had never been so wrong.

Chuck eventually agreed to spar with him and told him to wear a cup and bring a mouth guard. McCain brought in some MMA practice gloves. These weigh seven ounces, as opposed to the four-ounce competition gloves.

Somehow, word had gotten around about the sparring match and the CDC weight room was full. Chuck asked Luis García to serve as the referee. Luis was a former bouncer, Miami Police Officer, Secret Service Agent, bodyguard, and current CDC Enforcement Officer assigned to Chuck's team. He also held a black belt in Brazilian Jiu-Jitsu and had taught martial arts for years.

In one corner of the CDC fitness center there were mats that were used for core and defensive tactics training. Scotty, Chuck, and Luis met on the mats. Smith looked relaxed as McCain handed him a pair of MMA gloves.

As he put his own gloves on, Chuck asked, "So, what do you want to do, Scotty? Full MMA rules or just boxing?"

"Let's do MMA. I'll try not to hurt you," Smith answered, smiling broadly.

Chuck nodded and looked at García. "One five minute round, Luis. It shouldn't take that long," he said, slipping in his mouth guard.

"Amigos, this is just a friendly sparring match," cautioned Luis, a concerned look on his face. He looked at McCain. "We need him, Chuck, so please don't break anything."

Scotty just laughed at this. "I'll try not to hurt the old man, Luis."

The assistant Team Two leader, Jimmy Jones, was standing next to his team leader, Eddie Marshall. The other team members were gathered around.

"What do you think, Eddie?"

"I think Scotty is about to get educated," the Team Two leader said.

"I don't know, man. Scotty's a big boy. I wouldn't want him punching on me."

Eddie shook his head. "I'll be surprised if Scotty even lands a punch and from what I've heard, not many people punch as hard as Chuck."

The two fighters touched gloves and García motioned for them to fight. Smith came out in a traditional stance, leading with his left leg and left hand. His fists were held high in a tight guard. McCain started in his normal southpaw stance with his right leg and right hand forward. His hands were also high but more relaxed.

Scotty threw a left jab that Chuck easily avoided. McCain had already seen something that he could use and stepped back into the range of Smith's jab. When Scotty threw it again with a straight right behind it, the southpaw ducked under it and fired a hard straight left into the bigger man's body. The breath left him and he grunted in pain.

Always aggressive, though, Scotty launched another right cross at Chuck's head. McCain stepped to the right, slipping the punch, and landed a thudding thigh kick to the bearded man's front leg. It knocked him off balance and Chuck moved in with a quick right jab, left cross combination to Smith's head. These weren't heavy punches. Chuck purposefully held back because he didn't want to hurt his friend, but they were still strong enough to snap Scotty's head back.

Instead of pressing his advantage, McCain took a step back to let Smith recover. Chuck shifted into an orthodox stance, now leading with his left. Early in his martial arts training, he had learned to work both sides. Changing stances in a fight would often confuse his opponents and give him an advantage.

As the sage Mike Tyson once said, "Everybody has a plan until they get punched in the mouth." Chuck's strikes had not hurt him badly but they had stirred up Smith's naturally combative personality. He charged McCain, throwing hard, wild punches at his head.

Scotty was told later, and smart phone video confirmed, that Chuck had side-stepped the rush and hit him with a left hook to the point of his chin that dropped him unconscious on his face. The total time of the sparring match was twenty-nine seconds.

After a shower, Chuck stopped by Scotty's cubicle. The bearded man was watching the video of the fight that someone had sent him on his computer. He looked up at his boss with a sheepish grin and shook his head.

"You OK?" McCain asked.

He laughed. "My ego is shattered beyond repair. Everything else will heal."

Smith held out his hand. McCain shook it. "You're a tough guy, Scotty. I'm glad you're on my team."

"Thanks for not killing me."

"Remember, I've trained my whole life and I used to do this for money. Not much money, but I did get paid for it. It was always awkward after a tough fight to put on my police uniform the next day and go back to work with my face cut, swollen, and bruised."

"Did you ever get knocked out?"

"No, I lost a few times by decision but I never got submitted or knocked out."

"Well, today was my first time getting KOed."

"If you ever want to train together, punch the pads and work on your technique, I'd love to help you."

Smith had taken advantage of McCain's offer. Chuck helped him to sharpen his technique and hone his skills. Scotty felt he was punching cleaner and harder than he ever had in his life after working with McCain for a few months.

The downside of it was when he held the punching pads for Chuck. Smith would never admit it, but his shoulders would be sore for two or three days afterwards. He could not imagine what it would feel like in a real fight, with four-ounce gloves, to have that man hitting you as hard as he could for fifteen minutes.

CDC HQ, Wednesday, 0900 hours

Chuck carried the cardboard box into the office and sat down behind his new desk. Her scent still hung in the air. The emotion hit him in the chest and he closed his eyes.

He didn't want to move into her office but Admiral Jonathan Williams, the Assistant Director of Operations for the CIA, had insisted. Up until this past Saturday, Rebecca Johnson had been the Officer in Charge of the Atlanta Office for the CDC Enforcement Unit. She and Chuck had recently begun dating and were spending the day with Chuck's daughter, Melanie, and her boyfriend, Brian, on the University of Georgia campus when the bio-terror virus had been unleashed in the packed football stadium and in the Tate Student Center.

McCain and Johnson had gotten into a shootout with the Iranian terrorist, Amir al-Razi. Chuck had killed him, but not before he had managed to squeeze off two shots from his pistol. One of those 9mm rounds had struck and mortally wounded Rebecca.

There was nothing that Chuck or anyone else could have done. She had died within a minute. McCain had almost lost his life as well, due to the fact that the terrorist had been infected by the same zombie virus that he had been spreading. Even though Chuck was able to finish off al-Razi for good, the damage had been done. Rebecca was dead and the virus had been released at the university.

Chuck, Melanie, and Brian were able to escape but many

thousands of students, parents, faculty, police officers, and others were not so fortunate. McCain returned later with the rest of the CDC officers, rescuing a number of survivors and killing hundreds of infected people.

Rebecca had been the CIA agent to uncover the Iranian plot to use the zombie virus on American soil. She had also been the first agent to follow up on reports of the chemical weapon being tested in remote Afghanistan, near the Iranian border. Johnson and her Army Special Forces escorts had witnessed an entire village that had been infected. They'd had to fight for their lives against over sixty zombies intent on killing and eating them.

Rebecca was then sent back to the United States to recruit both federal and local police officers and military personnel to come to work for the CDC. Most had SWAT or Special Operations experience. Chuck, for example, had been a police officer in the metro-Atlanta area for twenty years, much of that time serving on the SWAT team. After taking an early retirement, he had two one-year contracts as a police liaison officer with a team of Green Berets in Afghanistan.

The new personnel for the CDC Enforcement Unit had been screened by the CIA's proprietary software that evaluated potential agents for their intelligence and how well they processed traumatic incidents and dealt with stress. Their training had been heavy on shooting and tactics. The CDC teams quickly became the tip of the spear throughout the country in this new war on terrorism.

The Central Intelligence Agency was forbidden by law from operating on American soil but none of the other federal agencies had taken the threat of the zombie virus seriously. The CIA director was able to convince the President to sign an executive order creating an enforcement branch for the Centers for Disease Control. It was funded by the CIA and they provided most of the intelligence. This arrangement allowed the CIA to stay at the front of the war against the bio-terror virus.

Chuck had been the only officer to put the pieces of the puzzle together and correctly guess about the involvement of the CIA with the new law enforcement branch of the CDC. Rebecca had sworn him to secrecy but that was about to change. He had gotten approval from Admiral Williams to brief his two team leaders so they would be able to function if something happened to McCain.

"Close the door, Andy," said Chuck.

Andy Fleming and Eddie Marshall sat across from McCain. Andy had replaced Chuck as the Team One leader after Rebecca's death and Chuck's subsequent promotion to Supervisory Agent in Charge. Fleming had been a staff sergeant in the Marine Corps Forces Special Operations Command. MARSOC is the Marine Corps' answer to the Army Special Forces. Andy had been an elite operator in MARSOC until family problems forced him to take an honorable discharge. Rebecca had to work hard to persuade Andy to come work for the CDC, but now he could not imagine doing anything else.

Eddie was built like a football player and had, in fact, played linebacker at Notre Dame before graduating and getting hired by the Chicago Police Department. He had attained the rank of sergeant but eventually decided to go federal, taking a job as a United States Marshal. He had tracked down bank robbers, murderers, mobsters, cartel leaders, and many other fugitives before Rebecca had convinced him to come work for the CDC. Like Andy, he was glad he had made the switch. The zombie bio-terror virus was the biggest threat that America had ever faced and he was right in the middle of the fight.

"How ya doin', Chuck?" Eddie asked.

McCain sighed. "I'll be OK. I spent Monday with Rebecca's mom and step-father. Good people. Danny, her step-dad, is a retired SF guy."

"That explains a lot," nodded Andy. "She was one of the toughest women I've ever met. I'm a Marine. We're known for taking young men and women and turning them into warriors. But

Rebecca was like a Marine, a SEAL, and a SF soldier all rolled into one."

"Don't forget the Rangers," said Eddie, smiling. "Scotty would take offense."

"And a Ranger," agreed Andy.

In spite of himself, Chuck grinned along with his friends.

"When I was in Afghanistan, I overheard one of the SF guys talking. He was telling some of the other guys on the team, 'She looks like a model but is as tough as nails and pretty good in a firefight.'

"I didn't know who he was talking about at the time, but I found out later he was talking about Rebecca. I'm going to tell you guys some things that are classified. They're for your ears only and I need you to sign these disclosure agreements."

He slid a form over to each man. They both glanced at the forms, signed them, and slid them back.

"Rebecca was not all that she appeared to be," Chuck said. "Not only was she the officer in charge of us, she was actually a CIA field agent. She was serving in Afghanistan when reports of a new chemical terror weapon started coming in. None of the other agents took the reports seriously but she began following up on them and got some of the Special Forces operators in the area to help her.

"She convinced six of the SF guys I was embedded with to take her to a remote village near the Iranian border where the zombie virus was supposedly being tested. As it turned out, the entire village had been infected and the good guys barely got out alive. Sound familiar?"

Eddie and Andy both nodded grimly. They had all been in similar situations over the last few months.

"They killed over sixty Zs but, more importantly, this was the first tangible evidence of the virus. Rebecca got some video and some DNA samples. Of course, we're talking about the government here and the former President didn't seem to be too concerned. 'Just keep watching and gathering intelligence,' was what the CIA was told to do.

"After the last election, the Director of the CIA went to the new President and showed him the intelligence that Rebecca had gathered. At this point, there were already reports of Iranian agents slipping into the US through Mexico. The new President asked the CIA Director what he needed and here we are.

"The President signed an executive order calling for the CDC to have an enforcement branch. We're legit but in a real sense, we're a front for the CIA. The Agency provides most of our funding and intelligence."

"So, when did you find all this out, Chuck?" Eddie asked, trying to take it all in.

"After the first attacks here in Atlanta, I confronted her about it. I'd had my suspicions. I'd even talked to Andy about it."

Fleming nodded. "I had my suspicions as well but I kept them to myself. The intelligence we received was better than anything the FBI would have given us and they're paying us more than is normal for federal cops. I figured the money was coming from some place like the CIA."

"But why the secrecy?" Marshall wondered.

McCain shrugged. "We all know the CIA can't work inside the US. This gives them a legitimate way to stay in the fight. And if the media ever got hold of this, we'd be shut down immediately. Then who's going to do what we do? The local cops? The FBI? No, we're leading the way.

"I'm telling you guys this so if something were to happen to me, you'd know where to turn. Because Rebecca had cleared me, I was able to get that helicopter to help us this past weekend. What would we have done without that Blackhawk and the door gunner's mini-gun covering us?"

Andy grunted. "We wouldn't have lasted ten minutes on that campus without that air support."

"Definitely," agreed Chuck. "Now, nothing changes in how we're doing business. I was able to get Admiral Williams, the

Assistant Director of Operations for the CIA, to assign that helicopter to us. We also get priority use of that small Department of Homeland Security jet. And, he authorized me to make decisions on hiring and recruiting like Rebecca did. In other words, we have the freedom, in certain cases, to bring guys on without making them go through the whole training process that we went through.

"I'll give you guys some contact info about who to turn to if you ever can't reach me. Any questions on that? Remember, you can't talk about this. I trust our guys completely but they don't need to know.

"Next thing. Eddie, I understand that you were pretty good at tracking down fugitives when you were with the Marshal's Service?"

"I did OK."

McCain slid a manila folder across the desk to the Team Two Leader. Eddie flipped it open and pulled out the eight by ten photos of a slim black man with long dreadlocks. There were several photos, including some from the Department of Corrections.

"I want you and your team to find this guy."

"Terrell Hill," Eddie read off one of the pages in the folder. "Wanted for multiple counts of Murder, Armed Robbery, Motor Vehicle Theft, and violation of the Bio-Terror Act. So, this is a bad dude. Where does he fit into all of this?"

"It's all in the folder, but he was inside Sanford Stadium Saturday and is believed to have been the guy who somehow spread the virus in there. He's an ex-con. Armed Robbery and Agg Assault. He works at one of the concession stands on game days. Maybe he put the virus in some food or drinks that he sold. We don't know.

"But once the infection started spreading, he shot his boss in the head, stole his car, and took off. It looks like he's heading north, up I-85. He was still using stolen credit cards up until yesterday in southern Virginia. The way he's going, he might be heading for DC to cause some more damage.

"That's everything we have on him. Read it, make a plan, tell me what you need, and then go get him. If you can take him alive, great. If not, oh well," Chuck shrugged. "He's responsible for thousands of people's deaths. I actually hope he wants to go out in a blaze of glory."

Eddie and Andy glanced at each other. Chuck was a straight shooter and a good cop. They were not soldiers, though. They were federal police officers and had to follow the law. While not actually telling Eddie to track down and kill Terrell Hill, it was easy to read between the lines.

"No problem, Chuck. We'll get him, one way or the other," Marshall said, confidently.

"We get first crack at trying to find him," added McCain. "This information will be released to the FBI and made public in two weeks. I was also informed that there's the possibility of a mole in the Justice Department, which probably means the leak is in the FBI. Use your best judgment on what you tell to whom."

"What about us? What do you want us working on?" asked Andy.

"How's Luis?"

Luis García had twisted his ankle and severely sprained it on Saturday during the fighting at UGA.

"The doctor said it'll take a few weeks to heal completely. He's a tough little guy, though. They gave him a crutch to use and he'll come back to work Monday. We'll have to find some things for him to do in the office. Any chance of us getting another guy to fill the team out? With you taking this position, we're one guy down now. And with Luis hurt, it's just me and Scotty that are active."

"Let me think about it."

Chuck slid a second manila folder to Andy. "For now, take a look at this. It's the most current intel speculating on the next wave of bio-terror attacks. I'd love for you and Scotty to begin working on some of the leads that are mentioned in there."

CDC HQ, Wednesday, 1030 hours

McCain sat at his desk, reading over recent police reports concerning the zombie virus. It continued to spread up and down the east coast. It was spreading into other parts of the country, as well, but for now, he was concerned with his own areas of responsibility.

The pattern seemed to be that the incidents followed the interstates. People were leaving the cities where most of the infections had started. In some cases, however, some of the fleeing people were also infected and turned during their journey.

Many other people had contracted the bio-terror virus through the tainted medicine that was still floating around. Part of the original attacks from over a month earlier had involved Iranian agents who had managed to get jobs at different drug distribution warehouses. They had been able to add the virus to hundreds of packages of medicines that were sent all over the country. The CDC and the FBI had been able to intercept some of the packages but many others had been received and used by the person who had ordered them.

Chuck noticed that there had been four zombie infections on the I-85 corridor, between Atlanta and the South Carolina line. The local police had been able to contain each of the incidents. The four infections were spread out and did not seem to be related. In these four situations, thirteen people had been infected and had turned into zombies, including two police officers and three firemen.

One of the incidents took place near Hartwell, not far from where Melanie was staying. The police had responded to an aggravated domestic call at a home. Two officers had ended up shooting three people who had turned into zombies. They found that three other family members had been ripped apart and eaten. McCain checked the map and saw that was only a few miles from Brian's parent's house.

He had not talked to his daughter since the weekend. When the attack took place at the university on Saturday, Chuck had barely managed to escape with Melanie and her boyfriend, Brian Mitchell. He had asked Brian to take her someplace safe.

The campus was on the verge of being overrun and he needed to meet up with his team. He could not function if he had to worry about Melanie. Chuck had already lost Rebecca. He wanted to know that Mel was someplace safe.

Brian's family lived about an hour away, near the South Carolina border. Chuck had called Melanie on Sunday but they weren't able to have much of a conversation. The wound was still too painful. They both had just cried into the phone.

Melanie and Brian had met Rebecca for the first time last Saturday. And, they had watched her die a horrific death. Chuck needed to talk to Mel and make sure she was OK.

She answered on the first ring.

"Hey, Daddy. How are you?"

"Hey, Mel. I'm better but I'm still hurting. I spent the day with Rebecca's family on Monday. They're great people. I think they comforted me as much as I tried to comfort them. How about you? How are Brian's parents?"

"They're so sweet and are taking good care of me. His parents are lay pastors at their church and Brian's mom has prayed with me and let me cry on her shoulder."

"That makes me feel so much better, Sweetheart. I've been worried about you. No one should have to see all the terrible things you saw on Saturday."

"Yeah, but you see it all the time, Daddy. I don't know how you do it."

"Somebody has to try and stop this, so lucky me," he managed to smile into the phone.

"How long do you think I should stay here? There hasn't been much on the news about when the university was going to open back up."

He hesitated. "Honey, it might be six months or a year before the school reopens. The National Guard are pulling their weight on this one but still haven't declared Athens safe."

Chuck could hear her crying. "I've tried to call or text all my friends," she sobbed. "I've only heard back from three of them.

"Two were at the game but managed to get out of the stadium and get to their car when things went crazy. They're both married and live off campus. The other one didn't go to the game. She locked herself in her dorm when she heard what was happening. She just got rescued last night by the soldiers."

"I'm so sorry. We were able to rescue some people on Saturday but not many. Did you hear anything about an incident near where you're staying? Some people were infected in Hartwell Monday and the police had to shoot them."

"Brian's dad, Tommy, told us about it last night. It's all word of mouth. There hasn't been anything on the news. What do you know?"

Chuck related the little he knew. He understood that news outlets were being asked not to publish every zombie story they came across. The nation had taken several big hits. They did not need any more panic than was already being felt.

"Mel, listen to me carefully. Do Brian's parents have a fallback plan? Where will they go if this thing spreads up that way?"

"Brian told me that his grandparents have a farm a couple of hours from here, near Hendersonville, North Carolina."

"Okay, that's good to hear. I just want to know that you are going to be alright."

"I'm worried about you, Daddy. I don't want what happened to Rebecca…"

He heard her crying into the phone and he felt his own emotions coming to the surface again. "I know. I'm going to be careful but you know this is where I need to be."

Thirty minutes after disconnecting with Melanie, the phone on his desk rang. Chuck was staring at the computer screen and familiarizing himself with some of the administrative duties that came with his new position. He pushed the speakerphone button.

"McCain."

"Chuck, you'll want to talk to this young man," his administrative aide, Vanessa, told him. "He said you know him."

"Thanks, Vanessa. Put him through."

"This is Chuck McCain."

"Mr. McCain, this is Terrence Matthews. You may not remember me but…"

"Of course, I remember you, Terrence. You really helped us out that night at Six Flags. That was when all this craziness started. How's everything going?"

When the initial bio-terror attacks were launched in Atlanta, one of the targets was the popular Six Flags Over Georgia amusement park. Matthews was a local SWAT officer who volunteered to help Chuck and Luis clear the large park of zombies.

There was a silence on the other end of the phone after McCain's question. "Are you still there, Terrence?"

"Yes, sir. I'm sorry. I'm…" he cleared his throat. Chuck realized the young man was crying.

"What's wrong, Terrence?"

Matthews took a deep breath. "Its my little sister, sir. She's a freshman at UGA. We haven't heard from her. Nothing. She told us she was going to the game this past Saturday. She even texted me a selfie of her and her friends laughing inside the stadium right before everything happened. That was our last contact with her."

McCain felt his pain. "I'm sorry, Terrence."

"Were you guys at UGA on Saturday, Mr. McCain?"

"We were there, but it took us some time to get organized and get everybody out to Athens. The attacks had been going a while by the time we arrived. It was really bad, Terrence."

"Did y'all go inside the stadium?"

"We made one trip in and almost got overrun. All together, we managed to rescue about sixty people. That's it. And we lost an officer."

"I'm sorry," said Matthews.

"And I'm sorry about your sister," answered McCain. "I wish I could offer you some better news."

"Maybe you can. Is that job offer still on the table?"

"I thought you were happy where you were at?"

"I've thought about it a lot. This virus has to be stopped. If you guys have an opening, I'd like to do my part to fight this thing."

They talked a while longer and by the end of the conversation, McCain knew he had found the officer to fill the hole in Team One.

Chapter Two

Virginia Highlands Hell

Virginia Highlands, Atlanta, Thursday, 1400 hours

The Atlanta Police cruiser stopped one house down from the address they were responding to for a 'Make Contact with Resident' call. Rookie Demetrius Howard was driving. He pushed the "Onscene" key on the computer next to him and then pushed the transmit button on his police radio.

"113 onscene."

"10-4, 113," the dispatcher acknowledged.

"You could've gotten us a little closer, Rookie," observed Field Training Officer, Dexter Long.

"Sorry, sir. They told us in the police academy not to pull right up in front of a location. They said if we stop a house or two down, we can make a more tactical approach."

"Those clowns in the police academy haven't worked the street since Jesus was a private. They don't know what works in the real world and what doesn't. Well, let's go check on these people and then get caught up on our reports. It's almost time to go home."

As the two officers walked up the sidewalk in the upscale neighborhood, Long continued to grumble. His shirttail was untucked and his leather gear looked every bit of its twenty years of age. That was how long Dexter had worked for APD.

Both men were African-American but the FTO was short and round while the rookie was tall and trim. He had just graduated from the police academy two months before and was still in great shape from the physical training that the recruits had to participate in.

Long had learned early on in his police career that it was good to be a field training officer. It had nothing to do with him wanting to train young officers and everything to do with having someone who would handle all the paperwork for him.

"I have a driver and a secretary," he would joke with other veteran officers.

In a perfect world, good sergeants and lieutenants would never allow someone like Dexter Long be a field training officer. He had a reputation for being lazy, or the more politically correct version, unmotivated. The problem was that Dexter had been around long enough to know where all the bodies were buried.

He had dirt on his sergeants, lieutenants, a few majors, and several other patrolmen. He even had evidence. Long had snapped some photos of cars parked at girlfriend's houses and strip clubs and even had pics of his lieutenant standing in an apartment doorway, kissing his girlfriend goodbye after a little on-duty action.

Dexter wasn't malicious. He could care less who did what with whom. As long as the brass left him alone and kept giving him rookies to drive him around and do his reports, he would keep his mouth shut and his photos to himself.

"So, what do you think this call is, Officer Long?" Demetrius asked.

"Probably nothing. It came in from out of state. Family says they haven't been able to contact them in a week. They probably just don't want to talk. But, sometimes on a call like this you might find a dead body where someone elderly has passed away."

There were five newer cars in the driveway of the large brick house. Officer Howard saw that neither the glass storm door nor the front door was closed all the way. There have to be people here, he thought. The cars in the driveway and the doors of the residence partially open seemed to say that someone was here. The FTO is probably right and there is nothing to this.

Demetrius started to ring the doorbell. His FTO waited for him at the bottom of the steps. Make contact with the residents. Make sure they were okay, tell them to contact their concerned relatives, and then go catch up on their reports.

An odor coming from the partially open doors made the young officer stop, his finger hovering over the doorbell. He could not see inside. The front door was only open about three inches. The smell was strong, though. Something rotten. Something…dead? Howard backed up and joined his FTO at the bottom of the steps.

"Officer Long, there's something going on here. Can you smell that?"

Dexter sniffed the air. "No, what am I supposed to be smelling?"

"I don't know, sir. It smells like something bad. You can smell it real strong by the door."

The FTO took a deep breath. They should have already been done with this call and he should already be holding his afternoon cup of coffee while the rookie typed reports. He pulled his heavy body up the stairs and stood by the door. His nose did pick up something but his twenty-five years of chain smoking had dulled his sense of smell.

"Let's do it like this," he told the younger police officer.

Long slowly and quietly pulled open the storm door. He set the catch at the bottom so that it would stay open and not slam into him. Then he eased the front door open, a little at a time. He heard himself gasp when he saw a set of legs stretched out on the floor, just inside the opening. When he realized that the rest of the body was mangled beyond recognition, he recoiled backwards, leaving the front door standing open.

Dexter drew his Smith & Wesson M & P 9mm pistol and motioned with his head for Recruit Howard to take a look. The FTO turned his back to the door to call the dispatcher. Demetrius also drew his pistol and took a step into the house to get a better view.

The smell of decaying flesh hit the young officer in the face.

"What do you think did this, sir?" he asked the older officer.

Officer Long was still talking animatedly on the radio requesting additional officers and a supervisor. This was going to be a crime scene, Howard suddenly realized. I need to get out of here so I don't contaminate it.

As he turned to exit, he heard footsteps and then the sound of growling coming from down the hallway. We didn't check the house, he suddenly realized. The killer is still here. The stench of death was even stronger inside.

Demetrius tried to spin and confront the threat but a man and two teenage boy zombies hit him, knocking him out the front door and down the steps, just missing Dexter. The back of Howard's head hit the edge of the bottom step, fracturing his skull and killing him instantly. The zombies began biting and ripping at the police officer's flesh.

The older officer raised his pistol to shoot but he couldn't fire because he would hit his recruit. Help was on the way but he knew he had to do something now to help Howard. There was a growl from behind him. A teenage girl zombie charged out the front door, grabbing Long and sinking her teeth into the side of his neck, biting and tearing at his flesh.

The FTO saw his own blood spurting into the air. He fired his pistol point-blank into the girl's body. Once, twice, a third time. The gun fell from his grip and he collapsed onto the front porch.

CDC HQ, Thursday, 1445 hours

The offices were quiet. Eddie and his team had left that morning for Virginia. Team Two had a lead on Terrell Hill and Chuck had arranged for them to fly, utilizing the Department of Homeland Security's Lear jet. One of the CDC enforcement teams from Washington, D.C., had met them and would be supporting them on this mission.

Chuck found Andy and Scotty staring at an aerial map on a computer screen.

"We may have something here, Chuck," said Andy. "There are a few addresses in that intel you gave me. This one might be worth pursuing. It's about two hours from here and looks like it could be an actual terrorist training location."

"We were just getting ready to head out there and do a little nighttime recon," said Scotty. "The Marine Spec Ops guys aren't quite as good at those as us Rangers, but I think I can bring Andy up to speed."

McCain smiled at the banter. "Put that on hold and suit up. Atlanta PD just called requesting some help. They have at least four officers down and a minimum of six zombies terrorizing the Virginia Highlands area off of Virginia Avenue. Three of the Zs are cops."

"No!" said Smith. "That's one of my favorite areas. That's where Emily and I had our first date, at a little pizza place over there."

"APD has no idea how these people got infected," Chuck continued. "They responded to a 911 call to do a welfare check. It was a two-man car. They told the dispatcher they were onscene and a few minutes later, one of the cops called in a possible homicide. He said there was a chewed up body lying inside the house. That was the last contact.

"When the sergeant and other backup units got there, they were attacked. It sounds like they were able to put one of the Zs down but the other three attacked the cops and infected two more. One officer managed to survive and watched the three zombies run down towards all the restaurants, bars, and businesses.

"Then, he saw one of the original officers reanimate and a few minutes later, the sergeant and one of the patrolman turned into Zs, too. Now, they're getting all kinds of 911 calls from down there. And, of course, the responding cops are paranoid since most of them can't shoot. They're throwing up a perimeter and asking for us."

Both men were on their feet and grabbing for their equipment.

Chuck went back to his office to finish getting dressed. The normal uniform for the CDC Enforcement Unit was gray cargo pants and a black polo shirt with "POLICE" in yellow letters across the back and a sewn-on badge on the front. They wore soft body armor under their polo shirts, capable of stopping handgun rounds.

For incidents like this one, they all put on their black kevlar lined pants. Their nylon duty belts held a 9mm Glock 17 pistol, two extra handgun magazines, handcuffs, a screw-on suppressor for their pistols and a flashlight. They had black kevlar-lined jackets that were also marked "POLICE" on the back. The kevlar-lined uniforms would not stop bullets but had protected them more than once from getting infected by zombie teeth.

Next came their heavy body armor and web gear. This armor would stop rifle rounds and give more protection against zombie bites. Attached to their web gear were pouches of rifle and extra pistol magazines, a first-aid kit, and a radio. When they got to the location, they would be carrying suppressed Colt M4 rifles and would also be wearing black kevlar helmets and kevlar-lined gloves.

Chuck sat in the passenger seat of the black Ford Interceptor and Andy sat behind him. Scotty was driving as fast as he could in the Atlanta traffic. Even with the blue lights and siren activated, it was still a slow go. The massive, bearded man was munching on a protein bar as he cut around cars and yelled at the ones he couldn't get around.

"Andy, you're the team leader now. You run the op," said Chuck, looking behind him.

"Roger that," he answered, studying a map of the area on his tablet.

McCain called Dr. Charles Martin, the Assistant Director of the Office of Public Health Preparedness and Response. On paper, the federal agents reported to him and he was responsible for getting resources moving to areas where bio-terror attacks occurred. Chuck let Dr. Martin know what kind of call they were responding to, promising to update him when he had more information. McCain also sent a secure text to Admiral Williams at the CIA. Hopefully, they would be able to get this incident under control before the virus spread anymore.

Virginia Highlands, Atlanta, Thursday, 1540 hours

Scotty parked half a block from the crime scene. Both marked and unmarked police cars filled the street with flashing blue lights. The three men dressed in black with rifles slung across their chests approached the command post. APD's SWAT team was also onscene and waiting for some direction. A police major was the officer in charge of the incident.

Andy introduced himself, Scotty, and Chuck in the CP.

"I'm Major Thomas," the tall African-American man, with a graying afro, said, shaking their hands. He gave them a quick breakdown of what was happening. "When will the rest of your people get here?" he asked.

"This is it," McCain told him. "We try and work with the local SWAT or tactical teams on an incident like this."

"Okay," the major said, clearly not sure that only three men were going to be the answer to this problem. "We were just getting ready to send our SWAT team in to clear the house."

"We'll handle that," said Fleming. "Then we'll have our forensics team come and assist yours in processing the scene and securing the bodies. One of our goals will be to try and determine how this infection started. Like Chuck said, we'll also need your SWAT guys to help us clear the neighborhood and track these infected people down and eliminate them.

The major nodded. "I'll talk to them while you deal with the house."

Fleming pointed up the street to the intersection a block away. An APD cruiser was driving slowly up the street, the officer probably trying to find the zombies.

"The infected were seen moving that way?"

"That's right. All of them," Major Thomas answered.

From down the street, they all watched the police car turn right into a parking lot. A few seconds later, the sound of gunshots and a loud scream rang out. The three CDC officers shook their heads.

Andy said, "I'm sorry, but if they can't raise that officer on the radio, please don't send any backup to him. They're not going to be able to help him. We need to check the house and make sure no more of them are inside. Then, we'll go and see about him. My guess is, you just lost another officer. It would be best if you could have the uniform guys pull back, stay out of that area, and set up a good perimeter four or five blocks back."

Chuck notified one of the CDC Clean Up Teams to respond. These were specially trained forensic teams with both local and federal law enforcement experience. They were part of the CDC Enforcement Unit's support team.

As the three men approached the house, they stopped at a sheet-covered body lying near the street, next to a police car. Scotty pulled the sheet back and saw a decomposing teenage girl. She had a bullet hole in her forehead and three other gunshot wounds to her chest and abdomen. She had bite marks on both of her forearms.

"Look at the decomposition on this one," noted Smith. "She's been dead for a while, maybe a couple of weeks. Of course, the virus kept her going until today."

When they got to the front of the house, Chuck pulled the sheet aside from the body lying at the bottom of the stairs leading up to the front door. A young police officer stared back at him through lifeless eyes. The flesh from his face, neck, and arms had been ripped off, leaving jagged wounds. They could see the open fracture to the back of his skull where he had landed and the corresponding blood and brain splatter on the brick stairs. At least he would not be returning as a Z with that head wound, McCain thought.

Andy took the point, put Scotty behind him, and had Chuck bringing up the rear in their building-clearing stack. They searched the house quickly but thoroughly. They only found the one body lying just inside the front entrance. It was a large house and they did not have time to look for other evidence. The Clean Up Team would take care of that. Now, it was time to track down the Zs.

Virginia Highlands, Atlanta, Thursday, 1600 hours

A block from where the incident started, Virginia Avenue crossed North Highland Avenue. This was an area that contained restaurants, banks, convenience stores, coffee shops and the Highland Hardware Store. The six zombies, drawn to the noise and movement of the busy intersection, were making their presence known.

The three original zombies from the house saw several potential victims in the parking lot of Marie's American Diner. The early eating crowd was just starting to arrive. The infected middle-aged man and his two infected sons pounced on a couple who had just parked and were walking towards the restaurant.

The three zombies had them on the ground before they had a chance to react. A younger couple was coming out of Marie's and saw the life and death struggle taking place in the parking lot. The young man saw the spurting blood and wanted to run away but his girlfriend prodded him.

"Do something."

He didn't know where to start but he balled his hands into fists and walked towards the smallest of the teenage zombies. The three Zs had ripped open the throats of the husband and wife and were bent over, chewing like buzzards on the side of the road. The Good Samaritan aimed a kick at one of the zombie's ribs and yelled for them to stop.

Without hesitation, the teenage zombie launched himself at the young man, easily knocking him down and biting his face and neck, tearing open the skin. The girlfriend quickly dialed 911, but started screaming as she watched her boyfriend die. The other two zombies left their victims and went after her. She was soon on the asphalt, as well, her lifeblood pumping out of her, the phone falling from her hand.

A 911 operator answered the emergency call from the now dead girl's phone, "911, what's your emergency?"

The girl's final gasp, accompanied by the growling and snarling of the zombies was the only answer to the police dispatcher.

Officer Tyrone Woodson was driving slowly, looking for signs of the infected. He had known and liked Officer Demetrius Howard. The young rookie had had the makings of a good cop, but was now lying a block away, covered with a white sheet. Tyrone was angry, wanting someone to pay.

There, in the parking lot of Marie's Diner, he saw them. Five people were bent over several bodies and ripping at them with their teeth and hands. Woodson turned in and sprung out of the cruiser, drawing his pistol. A group of bloody, growling people, both men and women, got to their feet and started walking towards him.

The officer raised the Smith & Wesson 9mm and ordered, "Stop! Get down on the ground, now!"

They kept coming, straight towards him, snapping their teeth open and closed. He sighted in on the closest one, a middle-aged man covered with blood. Head shots. They told us we have to make head shots on the zombies. He shot and missed. He fired again and missed again. In his frustration, he resorted to what he knew best. He lowered the sights to the man's chest and fired three times, making good hits but not stopping him.

Suddenly, Tyrone felt hands grabbing him. He never saw the two that had came up from behind. He felt teeth biting at his arm and neck. He shoved one of them away but by now, the rest of the group was on top of him, forcing him to the pavement. The officer screamed as hands and teeth ended his life.

Additional screams erupted from the other side of the street as the three police zombies converged on Poncho's Tacos Mexican Restaurant. The open-air dining area was already full as people were enjoying a late afternoon margarita or beer with their chips and salsa. The infected uniformed officers tore into the crowd. They were able to bite several customers who managed to escape, but were now infected, as well. These did not make it far before the bio-terror virus claimed them, too.

It was a mad rush, as people tried to get out of the path of the crazed cops. People tripped over each other and knocked others down in their haste to get away. The zombie police officers fell on those victims who were not quite fast enough.

Billy Dixon had hoped to be finished by now as he pulled his Dodge Ram into the parking lot of the Highland Hardware Store. Mrs. Webb was one of his best customers, though, and he would work a little overtime to keep her happy. Billy's Renovations and Repairs had a reputation for quality work at reasonable prices. Word of mouth kept him supplied with plenty of business and he'd never had to advertise.

Billy also never minded coming to Highland Hardware. The hardware store was just the right size. It was not as large as one of the big chains but it had everything he needed. Plus, Sasha worked there. Billy had never been able to get up the nerve to ask her out but he always enjoyed talking to her.

As he was pulling open the door to the store, he heard yelling and saw people running out of the Mexican restaurant over to his left, on the other side of the intersection. Horns honked as people ran into the street, forcing cars to slam on their brakes. Maybe a fight or some people who've had a little too much Happy Hour, he thought with a chuckle, continuing inside the business.

This had been an easy assignment. Mrs. Webb just needed a new ceiling fan installed. It would normally be a thirty-minute job and he'd be on his way. The fan did not come with the extension pole, however, so he had to get one to finish up.

Billy chatted with Sasha for a few minutes and paid for the part. He knew it was time for the business to close, so he said goodbye and turned to leave. The front door suddenly burst open and an effeminate young black man ran inside.

"Somebody call 911! The police are attacking us! They got my friend and I think they killed him."

He started crying, holding his hand over a wound on his forearm as blood seeped between his fingers.

Sasha said, "Slow down. What do you mean? Why were the police attacking you? Was your friend resisting arrest or something? And how did you get hurt?"

The crying man looked behind him, making sure no one had followed him into the store, and said, "No, Jermaine and I were just eating at Poncho's and…"

There was a loud bang as a short, round police officer ran into the door and bounced off of the glass, leaving a smear of red. Billy saw the blood on the officer's face, neck, and uniform.

"That officer's hurt," said Billy. "What did you and your friend do to him?"

"Nothing," he sobbed. "He attacked us and bit my arm and…and…" He collapsed to the floor, let out a groan, and became motionless.

Billy and Sasha looked at each other. They had been the only two people in the store and Sasha was just about to close up for the night. She picked up the phone to call 911.

The injured officer continued to pound on the door. It sounded like he was making a growling sound. Billy saw his mouth opening and closing and noticed that the wound to his neck was a large, deep tear. Instantly, everything fell into place. Dixon had been following the zombie virus story on the news and reading as much as he could find on the internet, but this was his first contact.

The young man on the floor of the store started moving again and making noises. His eyes opened and he began trying to get to his feet. Billy looked around the store. He needed a weapon and fast.

"Sasha, I think this is the zombie virus. Stay back and don't open that door."

He saw what he was looking for, hanging on the far wall. Billy rushed over and pulled an axe down from the display. Sasha held the phone to her ear.

"The police have me on hold," she said. "What's happening?"

"I think he's infected and maybe that cop, too. I don't want to hurt him, but if he's got that disease, he can kill us both," Billy said, hefting the axe to a ready position.

The young man finally managed to get clumsily to his feet, shuffling towards Sasha. His eyes were glazed over and a low growl came from deep in his throat. Billy could now see the jagged wound to his left forearm, the blood slowly oozing out.

"You need to stop right there!" Dixon ordered, running to intercept him. "I don't want to hit you but I will!"

The infected young man was ten feet away and started moving faster towards his victim. Sasha backed up two feet but found herself against the counter. She opened her mouth to scream but nothing came out. The zombie reached for her, his growl getting more intense.

Billy ran up behind him, brought the axe up high, and then down. The blade impacted on top of his head and buried itself inside his skull. The zombie fell to his knees and then to his face, the blood pooling around his head. Billy jerked the axe free and prepared to strike again but there was no more movement from the body. Dixon was breathing hard and his hands were shaking from the adrenaline. He looked at Sasha.

"I'm sorry," he said, shaking his head. "I told him to stop. I didn't want him to hurt you."

Tears ran down her face. Her mouth was open and she tried to speak but had lost her voice.

After a moment, she managed to whisper, "I know. Thank you. You had to do it. But what now? Is he really dead?"

The banging at the front door continued. Now, they saw several other bloodied figures gathered around the door, trying to get in. Thankfully, the zombies had not figured out how to pull open a door. Just to be safe, Sasha ran over and turned the bolt, locking it.

Gunshots exploded from nearby. A long string of shots and then silence. The zombies at the door turned and moved in the direction of the shooting.

"Is there another way out of here?"

"My car's parked in the back," she said."

Virginia Highland, Atlanta, Thursday, 1615 hours

APD's SWAT Team had two six-man assault elements suited up and ready to go. Andy talked to the SWAT commander and asked him to split them into three four-man teams. He, Scotty, and Chuck would each lead one, allowing them to cover more ground.

Each of the CDC officers briefed their teams and went over their particular rules of engagement. In the normal law enforcement world, shooting unarmed people was not acceptable. In this new world where the zombie virus had been introduced, things had changed.

A bite, scratch, or even contact with the infected's bodily fluids would probably be fatal and lead to the creation of another Z. The rules of engagement for dealing with zombies were simple. Any violent or aggressive persons suspected of being infected were shot in the head.

Andy gave each team an area of responsibility. They would all move up to the intersection of Virginia Avenue and North Highland Avenue. Fleming's group would work to the right, onto North Highland, clearing businesses of infected and trying to locate survivors. Smith's group would continue straight across Virginia Avenue. McCain would take his team left onto North Highland Avenue, clearing out that area.

Initially, the teams would all be close enough to support each other if needed. Andy had asked the major to have any available prisoner transport vans standing by at the command post. They could help rescue people, and worst-case scenario, the officers.

Andy looked over at the other two teams of tactical officers led by Chuck and Scotty. He motioned with his hand and all three teams moved towards the intersection. Fleming and his four SWAT officers moved in single file up the right sidewalk. McCain's team was on the left sidewalk and Smith's group was in the middle of the street.

A news helicopter was suddenly hovering overhead. A second one quickly joined the first and they began circling the scene. I guess we're going to be on the news again, Andy thought.

As the officers approached Marie's Diner up ahead on the right, they could all hear the sounds of growling and snarling. A wall and several trees prevented them from seeing into the parking lot until they got closer. They could see the APD cruiser, or at least the back half of it. The growling got louder and the unmistakable sound of cracking bones carried down to the officers.

Rifle against his shoulder, Andy led the SWAT members up to the wall. He looked at the grim-faced Atlanta officers and said, "Let's get some payback."

They stepped around the corner and quickly surveyed the chaos in the parking lot. Three bodies were sprawled on the asphalt and had been ripped apart with six infected continuing to feed on them. There were several blood pools scattered around the location where others had gotten bit and had turned before they were completely consumed by the feeding zombies. There were also another five Zs on the far side of the parking lot moving away to look for other victims.

The movement of the officers coming around the corner got the attention of the closest infected who were feeding. They responded by climbing to their feet and charging the police. Andy's suppressed M4 exploded two heads. The SWAT officers began firing their unsuppressed rifles, the loud report echoing through the intersection. The first group of six went down quickly.

The infected on the far side of the parking lot turned and began moving towards Fleming's team. Two of the zombies started running. The SWAT officers tried to hit the running zombie's heads without any luck. Two of them made torso shots with no effect.

"Shoot the ones that are walking," he ordered, taking out the two runners, dropping them just ten feet from where the officers stood.

A momentary pause. Marie's parking lot was clear for the moment. The officers did quick reloads and then moved around the police car to look for the officer. The remains of Officer Woodson were still there. His head had been almost completely ripped from his body and flesh of both arms had been eaten to the bone. One of the SWAT officers turned and vomited behind the police car.

Scotty's men covered Andy's team as they killed the Zs. As soon as the parking lot of the restaurant was clear, he motioned for them to start moving again. Smith saw Chuck's group approaching Poncho's Tacos. The sound of shooting from Fleming's team brought a group of infected stumbling out of the open-air dining area.

McCain stepped up and began shooting before the Atlanta officers had processed what was happening. Chuck cut down six out of a group of eleven. SWAT soon added their firepower and made good head shots on the last five.

"Let's clear the restaurant," Chuck told them, as he conducted a tactical reload of his rifle. He directed two of his men to make entry through the exterior dining area. He and the other three would enter through the side door, where the main dining room was located.

The restaurant appeared to be empty, at least of living people. A petite Mexican girl wearing an apron rushed towards the police officers. Chuck saw bite marks on her face, neck, and arms. Blood was dripping from her growling mouth. He snapped a quick shot that hit her under the right eye. She collapsed to the floor at his feet.

“Look, it’s Saunders!” one of the SWAT officers exclaimed, as a figure wearing an APD uniform came around the corner.

Saunders was a tall, muscular white man who was clearly not himself anymore. Officer Saunders had responded as a backup officer on the initial call in which Howard and Long were killed. He had been the one who had managed to shoot and kill the teenage girl zombie. The problem was that he had shot her in the head after she had bitten his left forearm. The damage was done and within minutes Saunders was infected, dead, and then reanimated as a zombie, himself.

Now, Saunders looked at his colleagues through glazed eyes, growling at them and snapping his teeth. He raised bloody hands and reached for the closest officer. The Atlanta policemen raised their rifles but hesitated to shoot their comarade. Chuck fired a single 5.56mm round that hit Saunders in the side of the head, sending him facedown to the floor.

“Sorry, guys,” Chuck said. “We can mourn him later. If you hesitate, you’re dead, and we’ll have two funerals instead of one.”

The tactical officers glared at the big CDC agent but knew he was right. They found four employees and five customers hiding in the back who had not been infected. McCain had them lock themselves in the office and promised to send help when the area was secured.

They were about to leave Poncho’s Tacos and continue down the street when one of the SWAT officers gasped. A fat Mexican man had him in a vice grip and was biting his arm. The tactical officer’s rifle was pinned against his chest but his thick uniform jacket was protecting him for the moment.

Chuck quickly rushed over and grabbed the zombie’s head in his powerful hands. With a vicious twist, he broke its neck with a loud snap, and threw it to the floor. He fired a single shot into the back of the head just to be safe. McCain turned his attention to the officer who was holding his arm.

“Roll up your sleeve and let’s see. You other guys cover us.”

The three men formed a circle around Chuck and their comrade, pointing their rifles outward. The skin was not broken but it was already starting to bruise. McCain pulled a plastic bottle out of one of the pouches on his vest.

"Roll your sleeve back down and let me pour some of this on it. It kills the virus on contact."

Chuck doused the officer's jacket sleeve and his own gloved hands. The solution had been created by one of the teams at the CDC which was working on creating a vaccine. It was of no use to someone who had been infected but it worked perfectly for killing the virus on clothes, shoes, and skin.

Shots erupted from outside and McCain led his team out into the street.

As Andy's group continued inside Marie's Diner after clearing the parking lot and Chuck's team was cleaning out Poncho's, Scotty and his SWAT officers moved straight ahead. Smith saw a convenience store on the opposite corner of the intersection and the Highland Hardware Store next door to it.

A group of nine infected had heard the shots and were charging in their direction. Smith felt exposed standing out in the middle of the intersection but with growling zombies advancing towards them, it was not the time to run. One of the Zs coming towards them was a short, stocky APD officer. Even at sixty yards, they could see the large gaping wound on the side of his neck.

The virus played no favorites. There was an Asian girl in high heels, two black guys in suits, a big black girl, two skinny white guys, and two young white girls, all growling and all intent on killing and eating the five police officers standing in the roadway.

"We need to get out of the middle of the road," one of the SWAT officers said to Scotty.

"You think?" Scotty said, glancing at him. "Let's take out that group and then start clearing those businesses," motioning with his muzzle towards the area of the convenience and hardware stores.

He raised his M4 and started shooting when they were fifty yards away. The police zombie, Officer Dexter Long, fell dead onto his back when the bullet hit him in the nose and continued into his brain. Smith shot two more before the rest of his team got into the fight. Within seconds, all nine of the infected people were lying in the roadway with bullet holes in their heads.

Scotty started running towards the convenience store. There were several cars in the parking lot and he saw two mangled bodies lying next to vehicles parked near the gas pumps. Almost on cue, the closest one began stirring, a growl emanating from deep within her throat. She was an obese white woman, lying in a pool of blood from her wounds. Without slowing down, Smith fired one shot, hitting her in the side of the head and knocking her back to the asphalt.

The other body might have been a teenage girl but was too ripped apart for anyone to be sure. There wasn't a lot left to reanimate. Scotty cautiously approached the front of the small store.

"Two of you come with me to clear the inside. The rest of you, cover us."

There were beer posters and other advertising covering most of the windows but they could not see any movement inside the business. Smith carefully pulled the door open and listened. Quiet. The three officers entered the store, the muzzles of their rifles moving as they swiveled their heads looking for threats.

The retail area was empty. They still needed to clear the restroom, the walk-in cooler, and a room marked, "Private." The two Atlanta officers checked the restroom and the cooler and pronounced them clear.

"I think I hear something," one them said, softly, moving quietly to stand next to the private room.

Then, they could all hear a heavily accented Indian voice. "Look, I'm going to die. I don't know. They came from nowhere. This may be the end of the world.

"Please tell my parents I love them and I'm sorry I didn't send them more money. Tell our girls I love them and I'm sorry I got killed. If you can, get out of this crazy country and go back to India where it's safe."

The SWAT officer knocked on the office door. "Police Department. Can you open the door?"

"Oh, my God! The police are here. I may not die after all. Hang on."

The door opened a crack and a small Indian man, holding a cell phone, looked out at them. When he saw that it wasn't flesh-eating zombies, he threw the door open and fell down on his knees, crying.

"Thank you for coming. Thank you very much." He grabbed the closest officer and began hugging his legs.

"Well, this just got awkward," commented Scotty.

Ravi Patel did not want to be told that he had to stay in the store a while longer. He also did not want to be eaten by zombies in the street. He locked the front door of his convenience store and then locked himself back in his office. The Atlanta officers assured Ravi that they would send someone to get him after the area was secure.

"Team One Alpha to CDC One and Team One Charlie, status report," Andy requested.

"CDC One to Team One Alpha," Chuck answered. "We cleared the Mexican Restaurant. There are several survivors locked in the office inside. We're continuing up North Highland, clearing businesses on the same side of the street as the restaurant."

"Team One Charlie," Scotty transmitted, "we're at the convenience store on the corner. One survivor locked inside. There's a hardware store next door that we're about to clear. Then, I thought we'd go the same direction as CDC One, just on the other side of the street. There are a lot of businesses down that way."

"Team One Alpha clear. We left seven survivors locked in that first restaurant. There's a pizza place and a frozen yogurt shop in the same complex. They're clear. Two survivors at the pizza joint, none at the frozen yogurt place. Let's keep moving. Team One Alpha out."

There was a short alley between the convenience store and Highland Hardware Store and a wall on the far side of the hardware store, marking the end of their parking lot. A gray Dodge Ram pickup truck was the only vehicle parked in front of the business. Two APD officers went to check the front door while Scotty and the other two covered them. An officer pulled on the door of the hardware store and found that it was locked. They peered in the windows and then came back to report.

"It's locked. There's blood smeared on the door and we can see one body lying on the floor inside. We didn't see anyone else."

A scream and the sound of breaking glass came from the rear of the hardware store. Scotty motioned for the other officers to follow as he cautiously made his way down the alley. There was clearly a struggle taking place from the noises that were coming from around the corner.

Smith did a quick peek and saw a light-skinned black girl standing on top of a gold Toyota Corolla, holding a crow bar. A young white man with an axe was trying to fight off two zombies. Two others were sprawled on the pavement with their heads split open.

Scotty raised his rifle, putting the red dot of his EOTech sight on the side of the closest zombie's head and squeezed the trigger. The Z spun around and collapsed to the ground. The male with the axe held it horizontally and shoved the remaining zombie in the chest, knocking him backwards several feet. Smith quickly shot that one in the ear putting it on the pavement, as well. For the moment, the area was clear.

"Are you guys OK?" Smith asked, approaching cautiously. He didn't know if either one of them had gotten bit.

The girl was still holding the crow bar, standing on top of the car. Her eyes were big and she looked like she was about to go into shock. The man laid his axe against the vehicle and reached up to help her down. Billy turned toward the officers.

"We're OK, now. Thanks. We wouldn't have been in about another thirty seconds."

One of the Atlanta officers asked, "Do you guys work here?" motioning at the hardware store.

Sasha nodded and found her voice. "I do. Billy came in to buy something and then this other guy came in and…" She started crying.

"I'm Billy," he said, putting his arm protectively around Sasha's shoulder. "The guy that came in, he had some kind of an injury on his arm. He was talking crazy and then he collapsed. Within a minute, he was a full-blown zombie. He's still inside. I hit him with the axe. We thought it was safe to leave so we came out the back door and these guys came around the corner where y'all came from."

Scotty glanced over at the car. The driver side window was smashed out and the left front tire was flat. One of the dead Zs was lying next to it.

Dixon saw what Scotty was looking at. "I hit the one guy and knocked him down. Then, I went after the other one and he fell but was still moving. He was right next to that tire and when I swung again, I missed him and my blade punctured it. I finally got him, though.

"Sasha took a swing at one of them with that crow bar while she was standing on the car and missed. She almost got me, though," he smiled. "That's how the window got broken."

"This area's still not secure," an Atlanta SWAT officer said. "There are a lot these things wandering around. It would probably be better if you go back inside and wait until everything is safe."

Sasha shook her head. "There's a dead guy in there. No, I can't do it."

"My pickup truck is parked around front," Dixon said. "Can you walk us around there and we'll get the heck out of here? I know you probably need to interview us. I'll cooperate and I understand if you need to arrest me. I just want to get Sasha someplace safe. She didn't hit anybody. I killed the guy inside and these two out here."

Scotty cocked his head at Billy. "Why would we arrest you, sir?"

"I don't know. Manslaughter or something?" he answered, motioning at the zombie's bodies.

The CDC officer laughed. "I don't think so. As they say in Texas, 'Some people just need killing.'"

Scotty looked at the Atlanta officers. "Let's get these two around to his pickup truck so we can get back to work."

The cops shrugged and one of them said, "Sure, no problem. I'm glad you guys are safe," he said, nodding at Billy and Sasha. "When you leave, please take a right down Virginia Avenue and check in at the police command post down there. That way we can contact you later if we need to. And for what it's worth, I agree with him," nodding at Smith. "You don't have anything to worry about. You were acting in self-defense and in defense of the lady. You also probably kept these zombies from attacking anyone else."

The sound of footsteps coming down the alley snapped everyone back to attention. A loud growl preceded another zombie wearing an Atlanta Police uniform. Sergeant Terry Jenkins had been one of the first responders and one of the first infected at the original incident scene.

Jenkins' face was badly mangled and blood covered his hands, arms, and uniform. When he saw the group of officers, his teeth started snapping together in anticipation of a meal. The four Atlanta officers were between Scotty and the zombie and they would have to deal with the threat. Smith made sure that Billy and Sasha were behind his big body.

Two shots rang out and the sergeant's head recoiled, a bloody mist exploding outward, and he crumpled to the pavement.

"I'm sorry, Sarge," an APD officer said, quietly.

After waiting a few minutes, making sure the immediate area was safe, the officers walked Billy and Sasha to the front of Highland Hardware and within moments the two survivors were out of the kill zone.

Virginia Highland, Atlanta, Thursday, 1740 hours

After checking with Chuck and Scotty over the radio, Andy had declared the scene secure and the officers made their way back to the command post. Smith saw his two CDC teammates chatting next to the CP. As he walked by the SWAT officers who had been with McCain and Fleming, he heard them conversing animatedly. One of them had the sleeve on his tactical jacket rolled up and was showing them his bruised forearm.

"This fat Mexican zombie grabbed me and was chewing on my arm and had my rifle pinned against my chest. I couldn't shoot him and the smell from his breath was terrible. That big guy over there," he said, pointing at Chuck, "came over and grabbed its head and twisted it, breaking his neck. I've never heard a neck crack before, but he dropped the body on the floor, shot it in the head to make sure it was really dead, and then checked to see if I was OK."

Another officer picked the story up. "He saved me, too. Right before that, Saunders came around a corner and was just about to grab me and put the bite on me. I froze. I mean it was Joe Saunders. We used to work adjoining beats when we were rookies. But McCain put a bullet into his head and kept me from becoming a zombie, too."

"How'd the army do?" Andy asked the former Army Ranger as he walked up.

"We all survived. That's a pretty good day in my book. How about you guys?"

"I think we got all of them. Of course, some could've slipped through the cracks. But if they did, I'm sure we'll hear soon enough," Fleming answered.

The three teams had eliminated fifty-four infected and rescued thirty-one survivors. This wasn't the worst situation that the CDC officers had encountered, but part of the reason for that was their quick response time. The Atlanta SWAT officers had performed well in their first zombie encounter and that experience would serve them later on.

Scotty saw the media vans set up a block south of the command post. Officers were not allowing them to get any closer, telling them that there could still be infected people wandering around.

Andy gave Major Thomas the location of all the survivors who were waiting to be rescued inside of businesses. SWAT officers drove prisoner transport vans to those locations, loaded all of them up, and brought them back to the command post. It took a few trips but they did not encounter any more infected.

The FBI and APD detectives debriefed the CDC agents and the SWAT officers. The CDC Cleanup team would work with the Atlanta police and the FBI's CSI teams to process the different scenes and then remove the bodies.

Chuck stepped aside to make his notifications. He called Dr. Martin and gave him their status. McCain briefed Martin on the incident and asked for an emergency management team to respond. The federal response team would work with the Atlanta Police Department and Fire Department to clean up the scene and make sure all the necessary protocols were followed.

McCain's second phone call was to his boss at the CIA, Admiral Williams. "Hello, Mr. McCain. I've been watching you in action on the newsfeed. Well done. Who were all those officers with you? I know you don't have that many agents in the Atlanta office."

"That's correct, sir. Four of my men are in Virginia tracking down Terrell Hill. The three of us who responded to this incident split up. Atlanta SWAT gave us twelve men and we split them into four-man teams. We each led one of those teams. They performed very well and it allows us to stay in the shadows since APD can claim the credit."

"Very good. I'm still not a fan of you being on missions like that. You're now responsible for the entire Atlanta operation and I need you to support them and be available if I need you."

"I understand your concern, sir, but that was one of the

conditions of my taking the promotion. I won't be in on every operation that we're involved in, but I'm not going to stay in the office when I can use my skills and talents to keep my men alive. Plus, one of my agents, Luis García, is still injured from the fight in Athens. He screwed his ankle up."

Chuck heard the admiral sigh. "Alright. I understand. If I was a few years younger, I'd probably join you on an operation or two."

McCain smiled to himself. Williams was in his late seventies but had been a Navy SEAL in Vietnam. On his second tour of duty in Southeast Asia, he had gotten shot in the leg during an intense firefight. It was a serious wound that meant he would have to leave his beloved SEALs. Even though Williams still walked with a limp, he had stayed in the Navy, eventually rising to the rank of admiral. Soon after his retirement, he was offered the job at the CIA.

"I'd be honored to fight next to you, sir," Chuck said.

"Well, thank you for that and thank you for the update. Is there anything else I need to know?"

"No, sir. Not yet. My next call will be to my team in Virginia to see what kind of progress they're making."

"Chuck, before I let you go, can you please ask your man Smith not to make any more obscene gestures at the news helicopters? It's not very good PR."

"I wasn't aware that he'd done that, sir. I'll have a talk with him," McCain said, suppressing a laugh.

After they disconnected, Chuck felt his phone vibrate and saw that he had a text from Eddie.

Chapter Three

Tracking a Fugitive

Blackstone, Virginia, Thursday, 1300 hours

It had been a whirlwind of a day for Eddie and his team, and they were just getting started. Around 1100 hours, the DHS Lear jet dropped them off at the Blackstone Army Airfield in Blackstone, Virginia. Washington, D.C., CDC team leader, Jay Walker, and his men picked up the Atlanta officers, loading them and their equipment into two black Suburbans. The airbase at Blackstone was the closest one to Petersburg.

The first order of business had been to find some food and a quiet place so that Eddie could brief the agents from DC on their crucial mission. Surprisingly, the military base had few amenities so they had started driving towards Petersburg, their first and, hopefully, only mission stop. When Marshall spotted the Fiesta Mexican Grill in downtown Blackstone he knew it would work.

He asked Jay to pull into the parking lot where Eddie got out and walked over to the other Suburban that contained Alejandro and Chris.

"Hey, Hollywood, can you go in here and get us a private room? I figure you might be able to be a little more persuasive in Español."

Estrada smiled and said, "No problem, Boss. I'll be right back."

Eddie looked at the four men from the Washington office. Team leader Jay was not very tall, maybe five feet eight, but powerfully built, with close-cropped light brown hair. Definitely former military, Marshall thought.

Jay's assistant team leader was LeMarcus Wade. He was around Eddie's size, six feet three and two hundred and thirty muscular pounds. The number three guy was Terry Hunt. Eddie had not heard him speak yet. Terry was a six footer and weighed in at a hundred and eighty pounds. Like so many elite operators, Hunt exuded confidence and competence without having to open his mouth.

The last member of the DC team was an African-American version of Chris Rogers, the newest member of the Atlanta teams. Elbert Harris was probably older than he looked, but Eddie guessed he still got carded when he bought beer. Chris was twenty-eight but looked like he could still be in high school.

A few minutes later, Hollywood Estrada came out and waved the seven other officers into the restaurant. Alejandro had gotten his nickname because, prior to coming to work for the CDC, he had been with the Los Angeles Police Department. Before that he had served in the army as a military police officer for five years.

"We're set, Eddie. I got us a private room in the back."

"Nice. What'd you tell 'em?"

"I told them we worked for ICE but that we'd already met our quota for the month on Hispanics. I told them we were looking for illegal Bosnians and we needed to have an important meeting over lunch."

Eddie laughed. "Sounds good, Hollywood. The only problem is that it says, "CDC Enforcement Officer" on our badges."

"We'll just say that we're a secret division of ICE. They're just happy we aren't messing with them."

Over lunch, Eddie passed around pictures of Terrell Hill and told the other CDC officers of his role in the attacks the previous week that had killed thousands of innocent people. He saw the anger in the eyes of Jay and his men. Marshall knew they were locked in and would do what needed to be done to catch the terrorist.

"How'd this guy get hooked up with the Iranians?" LeMarcus asked, sticking half a taco into his mouth.

"He converted to Islam in prison," Eddie answered. "He was set for a full-ride scholarship to the University of Georgia to play football. He'd set a bunch of records as a high school wide receiver.

"The problem was, he earned his spending money by doing armed robberies. On the weekends, he and some of his friends would drive around looking for people to rob. They would do maybe ten of those over a weekend.

"They finally got caught when this Mexican guy didn't want to give up his cash. He tried to fight back, even with three guns pointed at him. Terrell shot him in the leg. Somebody was watching it happen and called 911.

"The police got there quick and got all four of them. Hill thought he could outrun the German Shepherd and ended up getting chewed on. He did almost six years at the state pen in Reidsville."

"So, what's he doing up this way?" Jay asked. "Has he got any family or friends in the area?"

"None that we know of. He has four brothers and three sisters, each with a different dad. They all live in Georgia or South Carolina. His mom died while he was in prison. Drug overdose. He didn't have any visitors for his entire incarceration.

"The intelligence we received was that somebody inside the joint gave him a local imam's name in Athens and the imam hooked Terrell up with the late Amir al-Razi. Amir was running the cell that orchestrated the attacks in Georgia. The FBI picked up that imam, by the way, and the future doesn't look too bright for him."

The Washington CDC officers had heard what had happened in Atlanta and Athens the week before. Jimmy and Alejandro had shot and killed Mohamud Ahmed the previous Friday before he could launch a bio-terror attack near the Georgia State University in downtown Atlanta. That next day, Saturday, was when al-Razi and

Hill initiated their zombie virus attacks in Athens. Chuck McCain had killed Amir but not before he had gotten off shots of his own, one of which had killed Rebecca Johnson.

"Now," Eddie continued, "we think that Terrell is going to meet up with another Muslim cleric, Imam Ruhollah Ali Bukhari. He's based in Alexandria."

"Alexandria is a long way from Petersburg," said Elbert Harris. "Why didn't we just start there?"

"Terrell is still using his cell phone and we...I mean, another government agency, has been tracking it," said Eddie. "It looks like he's staying put in the Travel Lodge Motel just south of Petersburg. It could be that Bukhari is coming to meet him there. That would be the perfect scenario."

Everyone around the table knew that Marshall's referral to "another government agency" was to the Central Intelligence Agency or the National Security Agency. It was common to get information from either of these agencies in the war on terrorism. No one else had access to their resources, and those two entities were often responsible for stopping terror attacks by forwarding good intelligence to the right agency.

"He's still using his cell phone?" Jay confirmed, surprised at that revelation.

"No one said he was a very smart terrorist," Jimmy answered.

Eddie nodded. "As of right now. We're still getting a signal from his phone at that motel. The FBI and local police are sitting on it. J. Edgar's boys, for once, are happy to play a supporting role. No one knows if Hill has any more of the virus. We have to assume that he does and that makes it our jurisdiction."

Jay smiled. "This is shaping up to be a good day. Is his car still there?"

"There's a black Ford Explorer like the one he stole backed into a parking space on the opposite side from where his room is. The FBI boys and girls didn't want to approach the car to confirm the tag. They're worried it might be booby-trapped."

The other CDC officers shook their heads. They were all familiar with these kinds of stories about their brothers and sisters from the Justice Department. Like all police departments, the Federal Bureau of Investigation had some very good officers and some not so good officers.

The FBI was finally starting to hire more people with local law enforcement experience. For years, however, their model had been to hire college graduates with law or accounting degrees. Those kind of agents were great for unraveling complicated money laundering schemes but not as good at taking down terrorists.

"We'd love to take Hill alive, along with the cleric, if he's there. But, these are real bad guys. Terrell's boss, the guy he stole that Ford from, was found with a bullet hole in his head so we know he's armed. Plus, he turned a stadium full of football fans into zombies. If we can arrest him, great, but none of us gets hurt. So, if you guys are done eating, let's go grab a terrorist."

Petersburg, Virginia, Thursday, 1400 hours

The FBI had seven agents in and around the Travel Lodge Motel. A male and female agent had checked into room 221 next door to Hill's. Two others were in a white surveillance van in the parking lot watching the terrorist's room. Another two-man team were in a gray Dodge Charger on the back side of the motel where they could keep an eye on the Ford Explorer. A pair of local, uniformed police officers were parked nearby in their marked cruisers, out of sight from the motel.

Only the CDC officers knew the identity of the person in room 223. The FBI's assistance had been requested by the Department of Homeland Security, but the only information that they had been given was that the suspect was a person of interest with possible terror links. Supervisory Special Agent Daniel Ward secured a key card for room 223 from the front desk and waving his FBI badge and

ID was enough for the clerk to promise not to rent out room 225. If there was gunfire, they did not want anyone in the surrounding rooms to get hurt.

Agent Ward parked his gray Dodge Durango on the side of the convenience store across the street from the motel. He had joined the FBI right after graduating from college. After serving his time in some of the smaller field offices, he had finally managed to get transferred to the DC office, where he had always dreamed of working. There was something intoxicating about being so close to the seat of power.

He had received orders that morning to drop everything and take his team and assist the CDC with whatever they were working on. It wasn't like he and his agents were lacking things to do. They all had full caseloads but when the Attorney General, or at least one of the Attorney General's subordinates, asks you to do something, you stop what you are doing and drive two hours south to Petersburg.

What aggravated Ward the most was that he had no idea what they were dealing with. They had only been told that a person of interest was hiding out in the Travel Lodge across the street. If the CDC Enforcement Unit was involved, that meant the zombie virus.

Special Agent Ward had no desire to get anywhere near someone who was infected with the virus or who might use it as a weapon. Those CDC agents were crazy to do what they did. He was perfectly satisfied to let them go in and deal with whoever or whatever was in that motel room. Ward just did not like to be kept in the dark.

The fact that he himself kept local police in the dark when working with them was different. He only gave out minimal amounts of information when working with state or city police departments, knowing that the locals had to do his bidding. If one of the cops started asking questions, Agent Ward loved to ask, "Officer, do you understand what 'need to know' means? You have no need to know any more than I'm telling you."

CDC team leader Jay Walker had called to let him know they would be arriving in twenty minutes and would give him more information then. Ward had tried to ask Walker some questions over the phone but the little prick had hung up on him. The two men had had contact on several occasions as the zombie virus had spread. The capital city had been one of the terrorists' early targets and sections of the city were still not completely secure.

Jay and his men had been in the thick of the fighting and in eliminating Zs in DC itself, Northern Virginia, and in Maryland. After one horrifying day of zombie attacks in the center of the city, Ward had made the mistake of asking Walker what was taking them so long to have the bio-terror threat under control.

The CDC team leader's eyes had flashed with anger as he walked over to Special Agent Ward and stopped right in front of him. Jay was shorter than Daniel and had to look up at him. The CDC agent was covered in sweat and grime and stood so close that the FBI agent could smell him. Daniel, after getting the call at 0400 hours to come and help with the aftermath of that particular incident, had taken the time to shower and put gel in his hair.

Walker, still holding his M4 rifle in his left hand, was clenching and unclenching his right fist. After staring at the taller man for a few seconds, he apparently made up his mind that the FBI agent was not worth his time. He turned and walked away. Ward realized that he had been holding his breath and exhaled.

After that encounter, he had done some digging on the CDC agent. Daniel learned that Jay had joined the Navy right after high school and gone to Basic Underwater Demolition Training/SEAL or BUD/S and come out a Navy SEAL. He had served on several SEAL teams during his twenty-two year career.

Agent Ward had called a friend at the Department of Defense for a little more background on Walker. The CDC team leader's military file was surprisingly thin for a SpecOp warrior who had over twenty years of service.

The contact at the DOD would not tell Daniel much except to say, "Just don't piss this Walker guy off. His last four years of service were in SEAL Team Six and he's probably killed more people than he can remember."

During the forty-minute drive from Blackstone to Petersburg, Jay asked Eddie about his background. "I was a Chicago cop for almost fifteen years. Then I got an itch to do something different, so I went federal, becoming a U.S. Marshal. That was the greatest job on the planet, or at least that's what I thought at the time. Now, I know I have the best job that a cop could have. What about you?"

"I was in the Navy for a while. Then, I got recruited to come work for the CDC."

Eddie laughed. "Yeah, we recruit a lot of Navy guys. Working on one of those big ships is a real help in fighting zombies. Were you a SEAL?"

Jay grinned and nodded. "For twenty-two years. It was a great gig but you're right. This is a good job. Not quite as good as the SEALs but pretty close. The pay is a lot better and I'm not having to dump sand out of my boots at the end of the day like I did in Afghanistan."

"Man, you have to tell me about your name. 'Jay Walker?' I thought black folks were the only ones to come up with crazy names."

Walker smiled again. "My parents actually named me Johnny Walker. They were both teetotalers and didn't realize that they had accidentally named me after one of the most famous scotches in the world.

"When I was two, we went to a family reunion and my drunk Uncle Joe, who's very good friends with Johnny Walker, laughed every time he saw me. He was always sipping on some of the amber liquid and he kept offering me a drink. My mom finally got tired of it and pushed old Joe into the pool. Thankfully, it was the shallow end, so he didn't drown.

"After that, mom and dad started calling me 'Jay.' As I got older, I realized what they'd done. I had gone from being a bottle of scotch to a pedestrian traffic violation."

"That's a good story," Eddie laughed.

"Hey, I'm sorry about Rebecca," Jay said, growing serious. "I met her once when we were first getting started. She was up here meeting with our boss. A really nice lady. And you guys lost another officer a while back, right?"

"We did. Marco Connolly was one of my guys. He got jumped by three Zs. My man, Hollywood, back there," pointing his thumb over his shoulder towards the other SUV, "got hurt trying to save him but they killed the zombies. The really sad part was that a little while later, Marco reanimated as a Z and Rebecca had to shoot him."

Walker shook his head. "Sorry, buddy. I lost a lot of friends in the Middle East fighting ISIS. So far, our CDC office hasn't taken any casualties."

The two SUVs pulled into the convenience store parking lot and stopped near Agent Ward's Durango. The eight CDC agents exited, ready for action. Jay and Eddie walked over to Ward's vehicle. The FBI agent was talking on the phone. He had seen the two men walk up but ignored them, continuing to talk on the phone.

Eddie glanced at Jay. "Yeah, he's one of those," Walker said. "Supervisory Special Agent Daniel Ward. He's pretty much a…well, I don't want to poison your opinion of him so I'll just shut up now."

Marshall chuckled. "Well, he doesn't have to be Mr. Personality as long as he and his people do what we need them to do."

After making them wait for a few minutes, Ward got out of his vehicle. He nodded at Jay and shook hands with Eddie as the formal introductions were made.

"Sorry to keep you waiting," said Ward, "but I was on the phone trying to get some more information about this operation."

"I told you that I'd fill you in when we got here," said Walker.

Daniel ignored him and looked up at the big agent from the Atlanta CDC office. "So, Marshall, tell me what all this is about. If you want our help, I need some answers."

Eddie nodded. "What did you find out from your phone call?"

"Nothing. No one knows anything about this mission. I'm not even sure this is a sanctioned project. I want to know everything right now," Ward demanded.

Eddie glanced over at Jay again and winked at him. "Special Agent Ward, do you know what the phrase, 'need to know,' means?"

The FBI agent's face flushed. "I have the highest security clearance in the FBI. Don't pull that 'need to know' crap on me!"

"I just did. All you need to know is that this is a matter of national security and your agents are here to provide support for our teams. If you do that, I'll let the Attorney General's office know that you did your job. If you don't, I'll let them know that, as well. And, I'll make sure to spell your name correctly when I pass that info on."

Special Agent Ward felt like he had just been slapped. Who was this CDC agent to speak to him like that? He took a deep breath. Fine, he thought to himself. Support whatever crazy mission this was and then get back to Washington.

Travel Lodge Motel, Petersburg, Virginia, Thursday, 1430 hours

The eight CDC agents were suited up in their tactical gear and ready to go. They performed one last weapons check and moved towards room 223. The Atlanta team would make entry into the motel room. The Washington team would wait outside on the breezeway as backup.

The men had done a quick walkthrough of a motel room on the first floor. The Indian clerk had assured him that all the floor plans were exactly the same. He begged them to be careful and not to do any damage to his rooms.

Jimmy put his arm around the man's shoulders. "You don't have anything to worry about, man. We're trained professionals. We only kill the people that need killing and we'll only blow up that one room. Everything will be fine." The Indian's eyes got big and he scurried away muttering in Hindi.

Eddie would be leading the way into the room. Jimmy was number two, with Alejandro and Chris following. Jay had a set of bolt cutters to cut through the privacy lock if it was engaged. Marshall obtained the key card from Agent Ward and handed it to Jones.

They stopped next to the motel room and listened for any noise from inside. Eddie readied a flash bang grenade by pulling the pin but keeping the charging handle depressed. He glanced at his men. Ready.

Jimmy slipped the key card into the lock. When it turned green, he pushed the door open and then let go. The privacy lock was not on and Eddie tossed the grenade into the room before the door closed automatically. He stuck his foot in the doorway to keep it from closing all the way.

The men turned away from the blast. Flash bangs are not designed to be lethal and are also known as 'stun grenades.' The device produces a blinding flash of light and a very loud bang. In a small hotel room, the concussive blast is multiplied even more and the result would be extreme disorientation for anyone inside.

Eddie was moving through the doorway as soon as the grenade detonated. The flashlight on his rifle illuminated the small room, dust and smoke filling the air. Marshall and Jones cleared the living area and moved to the bathroom. Empty.

Estrada and Rogers cleared the closet and checked under the bed. They also pulled the mattresses off the bed. As cops, they all knew of people hiding in unlikely locations.

When they were satisfied that the room was empty, they turned on the lights and opened the door to air it out. Marshall looked at the vacant room and cursed loudly. Then he took a deep breath and looked at his men.

"Sorry, guys. I was hoping he'd be here."

"You just said what we were all thinking, Boss. No problem," said Jones.

They were careful not to touch anything because the room would need to be processed. The officers could see that it was filled with empty beer cans, pizza boxes, and fast food bags. The cell phone was laying on the table next to the bed. That was why the NSA had alerted them to Hill's presence at that location. They had been tracking his phone. Now, it appeared that he had fled and left his phone and his vehicle behind as a ruse to make them think he was still there.

Next to the phone was a crude drawing on the motel stationery. It was picture of a hand with the middle finger extended. "Gotcha Pigs!" was written underneath it.

"I'm going to enjoy meeting this guy," muttered Eddie.

Eddie asked Jay and his men to do a visual inspection of the stolen Ford Explorer to make sure it wasn't booby-trapped or that the terrorist wasn't hiding in it. He called the local police department and requested their forensic team and one of their road sergeants respond to the scene.

Marshall walked over to where Special Agent Ward was standing with his agents. The FBI supervisor had a smirk on his face as Eddie approached.

"No luck, huh? That's too bad."

"Yeah, it is. But, you can still help us out."

"No, I think we're done. You guys dragged us down here on your wild goose chase and then you struck out. We're heading back to DC."

"Do you really want me to pull rank on you in front of your agents?" Eddie asked quietly.

Who is this guy? Daniel wondered, taking a deep breath. He looked around at his team.

"Give us just a minute," he said to them. "Let's plan to be on the road in ten."

The FBI agents had never heard their boss spoken to in that manner. Not that Eddie had been rude or condescending, but it was clear that he was in charge and Daniel Ward was not. They all wandered slowly toward their own vehicles, straining to hear the conversation over their shoulders.

"Agent Ward," Eddie said, when they were alone, "there's a very important piece of evidence in that motel room. The local police forensic team is going to come process the scene and I need you to get this item to your lab in DC ASAP.

"I know this isn't convenient and I know you and your agents have better things to do, but Homeland is very interested in this case and they're following our progress closely. I'm about to call in and let them know what we found. I'd like to be able to tell them how helpful Agent Ward and his team have been."

Homeland, huh? thought Ward. This might be bigger than I realized. The FBI did not fall under the DHS umbrella but the CDC enforcement unit did. The Federal Bureau of Investigation was a part of the Justice Department but it never hurt to be on good terms with the Department of Homeland Security.

"I understand," answered Ward. "I'd be happy to help out in any way I can. I'll cut my agents loose so they can get back to work and I'll stick around until forensics gets here and does their thing."

"Excellent!" said Eddie, smiling and patting the agent on the back with his massive arm. "I knew I could count on you."

Daniel managed to return the smile, even though he had not been hit that hard since his defensive tactics training in the academy.

A marked police cruiser pulled into the parking lot. "Probably just being nosy," said the FBI agent. "I already released the local police who were here."

"No, I called for one of their supervisors. There are some things that you can only learn from a street cop."

With that, Eddie turned his back on Ward and walked over to the police car.

A wiry, older white man, with a bushy salt and pepper mustache, wearing sergeant's stripes on his uniform, got out of the police car.

He took a last puff on his cigarette before dropping it to the pavement and crushing it.

Eddie greeted him with his hand out. "Hi, Sergeant, I'm Eddie Marshall with the CDC Enforcement Unit out of Atlanta."

"I'm Joe West," the sergeant said, guardedly shaking Eddie's hand. "Atlanta, huh? You fellas are a long way from home, aren't you?"

"You know it. Thanks for the help earlier. A couple of your guys were out here in case we needed them. I really appreciate it."

"You federal boys call and we come running. I hope you got who you were looking for. The FBI agent didn't tell us anything."

"Sorry about that. The agent in charge didn't get issued a personality when he went to work for them and, truthfully, we didn't give him much information, either. But, to answer your question, no, we didn't get who we were looking for. I can't tell you a lot either and I apologize for that. What I can tell you, though, is this is a really bad guy and if you've been watching the news you've seen some of his handiwork."

Eddie let that sink in. Sergeant West nodded slowly. "That helps a lot. Are we in danger of a terrorist attack here? What do you need me to do?"

"I don't know about a terror attack here. My gut feeling is 'no.' I'd guess he's heading north for DC or New York or another one of the big targets. Virginia Beach and the naval base are only two hours away, but again, we just don't know.

"The bad guy left his car behind. What I need to know is if your department's had any reports of stolen vehicles in the last twenty-four hours? I need whatever you can get me as soon as possible.

"He left some other evidence behind that's about to get taken to the FBI's lab. That may give us some ideas. Until then, we're working the transportation angle.

"If we get lucky and he stole a car and if there was a witness, let me give you the physical on the guy we're after. He's a thin black male, about six foot three. He's got long dreadlocks and is in his mid-twenties."

The sergeant looked surprised. "I thought these terrorists were all foreigners? Iranians and Somalians are what the news is saying."

"The vast majority are foreigners, but this perp got recruited while he was in prison for armed robbery. Apparently he's got a chip on his shoulder."

Sergeant West grunted. "It'll take us a little while but I should be able to give you what we have in the next hour or so."

"Thanks, Sarge. I knew you'd be able to help us."

West started for his car and then turned back to Eddie. "Agent Marshall, you don't strike me as the typical federal cop. Are all the CDC agents like you?"

Eddie smiled. "I appreciate that. We all have local law enforcement or a military background or both. I was with Chicago PD for fifteen years. The bottom line is that we never forget that when there's a crisis like the zombie virus or anything else that you can imagine, you guys are the first ones there. That thin blue line is still strong."

Fifty-five minutes later, Sergeant West pulled his cruiser back into the parking lot. He exited, extinguished his cigarette, and approached the group of CDC agents. They were all kitted out like a SWAT team with heavy body armor and rifles slung across their chests. They look like they're ready to kill some terrorists, West thought. The circle opened at his approach.

"Hey, Sarge," Eddie greeted him warmly. "Did you have any luck?"

"I think so," he said, smiling. "It looks like your boy got himself a new ride. There's a Planet Fitness, one of those twenty-four hour gyms, a half a mile from here. Yesterday, about 1500 hours, a BMW X4 was stolen from one of the members.

"They've got one of those baskets on the counter where everybody throws their car keys while they work out. A guy fitting the description you gave me came in and was asking about gym rates. The girl working the desk got called away while your suspect was reading a brochure. When she came back, he was gone.

"Thirty minutes later, the BMW owner went to leave but she couldn't find her keys. She thought maybe she'd left them in the car by mistake so she walked out in the parking lot and realized her car was gone."

"Sounds like him," said Jimmy. "Do they have security cameras in the gym, Sarge?"

"They do. Our detectives haven't followed up on the case yet. If y'all want to go up there, I'm sure we could get them to pull the video for you."

The forensics team was almost done with the motel room. To process a crime scene correctly takes time and even a small motel room would take at least an hour. They would photograph it, dust for fingerprints, attempt to collect DNA evidence, and collect any physical evidence that was left behind. The stolen Ford Explorer would be impounded to their lot where it would be processed, as well.

One of the crime scene supervisors, a curvaceous African-American girl, walked up to the men. She was holding a plastic bag and a clipboard.

"Well, hello Sergeant West. How'd you get dragged into all this?" she asked with a smile.

"Hi, Ginny. You know, duty calling and all that."

Ginny turned her attention to Eddie. "Agent Marshall, here's that cell phone you wanted bagged up." She laid her hand on his arm and continued, "Now, it's unusual to break the chain of custody like this, but since you asked so nicely…," she almost purred the last few words.

"But, we're not really breaking the chain of custody," Eddie answered. "We're signing for it and it's going straight to the FBI lab. I know your team is amazing but I need this phone broken into ASAP and I think the FBI will be able to do that for us."

"And there are some things that the FBI is really good at.

Forensics is one of them," she agreed. "But, if you need anything else from me, Agent Marshall, anything at all, please don't hesitate to ask." She put special emphasis on the 'anything,' and the 'anything at all.'

Eddie heard the snickers of his men. He was grateful for his dark skin or his blush would have been evident.

"Thanks for all your help, Ginny. That FBI agent over there, standing against his truck, he's the one who's going to sign for the phone and take it to the lab."

"That fella who looks like he has a stick up his…" she asked.

"That's Supervisory Special Agent Daniel Ward and he could probably use a little of your special charm, Ginny," said Eddie.

Ginny made eye contact with Eddie and held it for a moment. She smiled at Sergeant West and the CDC officers and then strolled over to Ward, handing him the evidence bag containing Terrell Hill's cell phone. She pointed to the place where he was supposed to sign. When he was finished, Daniel gave a half salute to the group of CDC officers and started towards Washington, D.C.

Petersburg, Virginia, Thursday, 1745 hours

Sergeant West led the two Suburbans up to Planet Fitness. It would have been an easy walk from the motel for Hill, Eddie realized. When they arrived, West noted that the CDC officers had removed their tactical equipment and looked much more like regular cops now. Gray cargo pants, black polo shirts with their sewn-on CDC badge and black boots.

Their nylon duty belts contained their pistols, handcuffs, extra ammo, and radios. And those guys from Atlanta had something else on their belts. Was that a suppressor? the sergeant wondered. That wasn't something you saw everyday on a police officer's duty belt.

Within minutes, the CDC agents were looking at printouts of images taken from the security cameras. West heard Eddie say,

"That's him. Now, we just need to know where he's going," as he looked at the terrorist. Terrell Hill was wearing a ball cap but the dreadlocks gave him away. In the photo, his hand was in the car key basket. The next picture was of his back sauntering out the door.

Eddie thanked the gym's manager and the officers met up at their vehicles in the parking lot. Marshall turned to the police officer and said, "Sergeant West, thanks for your help. Knowing what Hill is driving may be the break that helps us find him. Do you have a card? I'll call you if it looks like there's any threat in your area."

West and Marshall exchanged business cards and shook hands. "Good luck catching this scumbag. Let me know if there's anything else we can do," West said.

After the sergeant left, Jay asked what everyone was thinking, "What now?"

"Sergeant West said the stolen BMW is listed on NCIC so maybe we'll get lucky and a state trooper will run across him. For now, let me update the man in Atlanta and then let's find some place to eat? All this police work is making me hungry."

Eddie composed a text and sent it to Chuck. *'Motel room empty. Ford Explorer still in parking lot. Cell phone left in room. The FBI is transporting phone to their lab for immediate processing. Local police advise and we have confirmed that Hill probably stole a silver BMW X4 yesterday at 1500 hours. Local forensics processing Explorer at their PD. Nothing further at this time.'*

As he hit send, Marshall saw that Jay's silent man, Terry Hunt, had walked over. "I own an X5. One of the features they offer is BMW Assist. It's a fancy GPS roadside assistance program, perfect if the driver is in an accident or broken down and doesn't know their exact location. Or, if a terrorist has stolen your car and you want to know where they're at."

"I didn't even think of that," confessed Eddie. "Let me make a couple of phone calls and see if we can find out where this car is."

McCain answered on the first ring. "Hey, Eddie, I just got your text. What's the plan?"

Marshall told him what Hunt had relayed about BMW Assist. "We're going to call BMW and see if they'll help us but they probably won't without a warrant. I may need you to talk to our friends at one of the other government agencies and see if they can hack into BMW's system. We need to find Hill before he strikes again. We don't need another Athens, Georgia."

"No, we don't," agreed Chuck, thinking quickly. "Me, Andy, and Scotty are getting ready to head back to the office. We've been out on a pretty serious incident in Atlanta."

"You guys OK?"

"Yeah, we're fine. We killed fifty something Zs and rescued around thirty survivors. As soon as we leave, I'll see if I can get the NSA to help us out."

"Sounds like you guys have had an eventful day. I wish I could say the same. Thanks for the help."

"Text me that vehicle info so I can give it to one of the alphabet agencies."

When they disconnected, Eddie sent Chuck a text with the stolen BMW's tag and vehicle identification number. He glanced over and saw that his and the DC agents were gathered around a laptop set up on the hood of one of the Suburbans. They were intently watching news footage of the incident McCain had just told him about.

Jay nodded at him. "It looks like your guys in Atlanta had a little action today. Fox is saying that it was just Atlanta PD's SWAT team but Jimmy pointed out three guys from your office."

Marshall watched the video for a few minutes, observing the three assault teams expertly taking down infected people. There was no mistaking Scotty Smith, especially when he looked up at the news chopper and scratched the top of his head with a middle finger salute. The officers watching the computer all laughed out loud.

Ten minutes of the earlier incident were shown as the news anchor commented on what they were showing. Eddie pointed out

Chuck on the screen.

"That's our boss. I just talked to him on the phone and he said they killed over fifty zombies and rescued a bunch of people."

"Your boss gets out and fights? That's my kind of guy," observed Jay. Walker did not say anything else, but it was clear that he was making a point about their own officer-in-charge at the DC office.

"He's as tough as they come and usually leads from the front," Marshall agreed. "Terry, thanks for the heads up on BMW's GPS system. Since you've probably dealt with them before, would you mind calling and giving them the VIN and see if they'll track it for us?"

Eddie handed him the copy of the stolen vehicle report and Hunt stepped to the side to make the call.

"While we're waiting to hear something, I still think we need to go eat," Marshall said to Walker.

"Sounds good. Looks like it's going to be a late night. Okay, ladies, let's saddle up," Jay said to the all the CDC officers.

Marshall was an expert at tracking people. He had done it during his time with the Chicago Police Department and then with the Federal Marshals. Most fugitives were not that difficult to track. They almost always returned to the familiar. A list of family, friends, and acquaintances was the first thing Eddie pulled when he was looking for someone.

Terrell Hill was not going to be that easy. All his known friends and family were in Georgia or South Carolina but he had just been in southern Virginia. Now where was he going? Who did he know up this way? Or, instead of running away, was he on another terror assignment?

Their only other lead was the Imam Ruhollah Ali Bukhari in Alexandria. Maybe the other DC team could go do a surveillance on him and see if Hill showed up. Eddie had a feeling that it would not be that easy.

Petersburg, Virginia, Thursday, 1830 hours

The CDC officers went to the McDonald's across the street from the Planet Fitness and stuffed themselves with hamburgers and French fries. Terry had gotten nowhere with BMW Assist. They politely but firmly told him that they would not release any information to him without a warrant. Now, all they could do is wait to see if Chuck had had better success with the 'other government agency.'

Eddie and Jay listened to their men swapping war stories from the different zombie terror attacks they had all been involved in.

"Jay, I'm sorry you and your men got dragged into this."

"Don't worry about it, Eddie. We need to find this guy, Hill. I'm kind of worried we might already be too late to stop another attack. He has such a big jump on us and we have no idea where he's gone."

Marshall's phone vibrated with an incoming call. He punched the speaker button and answered.

"Hi, Chuck. I've got you on speaker with Jay Walker and his team from Washington."

"Okay, Eddie. No problem," said McCain. "DHS was able to pull some strings and get things cracking at that other government agency. They found the BMW. It's parked at the Springfield Town Center Mall, in Springfield, Virginia. How far away is that, Jay?"

Eddie made a circling motion with his hand to let the men know they needed to move.

"Wow, that's at least two to two and a half hours away from us. Have there been any reported attacks or infections there?" Walker asked.

"No, nothing at all. Maybe he just dumped the car there. Maybe he's waiting. Jay, can you call your OIC and ask him to send your other team over there? I've left him a voice mail, sent him a text, and an email but he hasn't responded."

Walker sighed. "Sorry about that. I'll make it happen and we'll be on the road in just a couple of minutes."

Chapter Four

Good versus Evil

Annandale, Virginia, Thursday, 1845 hours

Bob Murray, the Supervisory Agent of the Washington, D.C., office of the CDC Enforcement Unit, had been home from work for less than an hour and was already well on the way to drunk. His third tumbler of Maker's Mark bourbon was almost empty. SportsCenter was playing on the television. Bob had five hundred dollars riding on the NFL game that night between Dallas and Green Bay. He had been losing a lot lately. He had that feeling, though, that tonight was the beginning of a new winning streak.

Murray had worked for the Central Intelligence Agency for twenty-eight years. His last foreign field assignment was Afghanistan. Oh, how he had hated that place. He hated the locals. He hated the weather. He hated most of the people he had worked with. But what he hated the most was how hard it was to get a drink.

He had always been a heavy drinker and prided himself on how well he handled the booze. Bob had gotten some of his best intelligence gems from contacts who did not handle the drink as well as Bob Murray. Afghanistan, however, was rough for a guy who liked to take a sip every day.

When he finally transferred home, Bob's boozing had gotten progressively worse. His new supervisor at the Agency was a young guy who just didn't understand the intelligence game. Having a few drinks at lunch had never interfered with how he did his job, but

Jason, the new boss, did not agree and after smelling alcohol on his breath had written him up for drinking on duty.

Bob didn't even bother appealing the letter of reprimand that went into his file. He could retire soon and leave all this foolishness behind. A month later, though, Jason smelled alcohol on Bob's breath again and required him to submit to an immediate breath test. When it registered .09 grams, Murray knew he was in trouble. That was over the legal limit and he had just driven his issued CIA vehicle to and from his lunch meeting.

Jason wrote him up again, this time recommending termination. Bob felt as though he had been punched in the stomach. He was only two years away from retiring and drawing his pension. There had to be something that he could do. Two days later, Murray was summoned to the office of the Assistant Director of Operations, Admiral Williams.

The door was ajar and Bob was about to knock but he heard a female voice speaking. "I don't think he can handle it, Admiral. He was undependable in Afghanistan and I think this position is too critical to give to someone with a drinking problem."

Someone was coming down the hall and Bob did not want to appear to be eavesdropping. He knocked on the door.

"Come in."

"I'm Bob Murray, Admiral. You requested to see me?"

The admiral was seated behind his desk. Rebecca Johnson was sitting in one of the leather chairs in front of it. Johnson. I should have known, he thought. She had turned down his romantic advances in Afghanistan and had made all of the male agents look bad when she had discovered that the zombie virus was for real. And now, she's in here talking smack about me to the admiral.

"Please come in, Agent Murray. Agent Johnson was just leaving."

Rebecca got to her feet. "Hello, Bob," she said, without making eye contact with him. The woman nodded at the admiral and then left the room.

“Rebecca,” he acknowledged, nodding back to her. She was still hot, he thought. It’s too bad she turned me down every time I asked her out. She didn’t know what she was missing.

“Have a seat, Agent Murray,” the admiral ordered. “We have a lot to discuss.”

Admiral Williams had Murray’s file in front of him. He got right to the point and said that he was signing off on Jason’s investigation and Bob’s termination. Bob’s felt his heart almost stop beating. His throat constricted. He realized he was holding his breath.

The admiral was still talking but Murray was having trouble hearing and understanding what he was saying.

“I’m sorry, sir, I didn’t hear the last thing you said.”

“I said, Agent Murray,” the admiral’s voice stern, “that there might be a way for us to resolve this without terminating you.”

For the next half hour, Williams explained the idea behind creating the Centers for Disease Control Enforcement Unit. Experienced CIA agents were being installed as the officer-in-charge of each office. The sworn federal police officers working for them would not know that they were actually working for the CIA.

After reviewing the intelligence that the CIA had given him about the zombie bio-terror virus, the President signed an Executive Order calling for the CDC to have an enforcement branch. This would allow the Agency to covertly continue battling this new terror threat.

Bob might have some personal issues but he was a seasoned field agent with years of experience. He would be put in charge of the Washington D.C., CDC teams. Williams made it clear that there were no second chances. If Murray screwed up one time, he would be gone and he would lose his pension.

“If you have a drinking problem, get some help, Agent Murray. I need you to support the federal officers that are going to be working for you. Make sure they have everything they need and take care of them."

That had been almost two years earlier. Now, he had less than six months to go and he could retire. And, he'd outlived that woman who thought she was better than him. The details around her death had been a little sketchy. She and one of her officers had gotten into a shootout with one of the Iranian terrorists who had infected so many people at the University of Georgia. That was all he knew.

Bob held up his glass in a mock toast. "Rebecca Johnson. Too bad you're dead." He drained the last of the bourbon.

His team leaders, Jay Walker and Tu Trang Donaldson, despised him. He could see it in their eyes. He had never been out on an operation with them. When they were all in the office, he preferred to stay locked in his, unless he needed to pass information to them.

Murray forwarded every piece of intelligence that came in to Walker and Trang and he handled all the administrative duties. If Williams wanted him to be a manager, he would be a manager, for just a few more months. Plus, staying in his office allowed him to monitor his favorite gambling website open all day on his computer.

Bob had stopped drinking during the day. He could not afford to lose his pension. The gambling, though, had become his newest obsession. He needed to pad his retirement account and what better way than making a little money on sports? When he got home, though, Murray would always have a few drinks as he relaxed in front of the television.

Murray stumbled into the kitchen to refill his glass. His phone, keys, and wallet were all laying on the counter where he had dropped them. The smart phone vibrated. Bob picked it up and saw that he had missed several text messages and voice mails.

He put the glass down and sat in a chair at his kitchen table so he could focus, slipping on his reading glasses. The first text was from a number he didn't recognize. Someone saying he was the OIC at the Atlanta office and something about a possible terror attack at the

Springfield Town Center Mall in Northern Virginia.

The next text message was from Jay Walker. He repeated what the first message said but told Murray that he had taken it upon himself to activate Trang and his men to start for the mall. Walker was only a team leader and did not have the authority to do that but those Navy SEALs thought they were God's gift to the world. And Trang wasn't much better. At least the Green Berets tended to be a little more tactful in how they dealt with problems.

The voice mails from Chuck McCain and Walker reiterated what was in the texts. The voice mail from Shaun Taylor, Admiral Williams' aide, was more problematic. It had come in forty-five minutes earlier and was asking for an update. An update on what? Had there been an actual attack? Bob needed to clear his head. He pulled up Walker's phone number and tapped the screen to dial.

"Hey, Boss," Jay answered. "Did you get my text and voice mail?"

"Yeah, Walker. I got them. What's really going on? Is this an active incident at the mall or are we just chasing our tails?"

"It doesn't appear to be an active incident yet but the guy who was behind that big attack at the University of Georgia parked his stolen car at Springfield Mall. We don't know how long it's been there and since I couldn't reach you, I asked Tu and his guys to roll that way. They should be there within the hour. Me and my guys, and the team from Atlanta, are still about two hours away."

Something clicked in Murray's head. Springfield? That was only ten minutes from his apartment. He could be there long before his teams. This might be the chance to get back in the good graces of the brass over at Langley.

"Which mall was that, Walker?"

"The Springfield Town Center Mall. Do you know it?"

"I live less then fifteen minutes from there. Where's the car parked? I'll leave right now," Bob slurred, rising unsteadily to his feet.

There was a pause on the other end. "Are you sure you're OK,

Boss?" Jay asked.

Murray knew what he was really asking. 'How drunk are you tonight, Boss?'

"I'm fine, Agent Walker. Send me all the information and I'll go get eyes on the suspect vehicle."

Bob was actually excited and felt the familiar tingle of adrenaline. This was the real deal. He had a chance to prevent a terrorist attack. He might be able to stop something bad from happening and go out on top. This would be the way to retire. It was much better to go out as a hero than with the stigma of being a drunk.

Murray refused to wear a uniform like his officers did, preferring the suit and tie, cloak and dagger look. He left his tie off and slid the holster onto his belt. He checked the 9mm Glock 19 and made sure there was a round in the chamber, dropped it into the holster, and slipped on his jacket.

The gray Chevrolet Impala jumped out of the parking space as Bob pressed down the accelerator, almost running over his neighbor walking across the parking lot, carrying a bag of groceries in each hand. He slammed on the brakes, mouthed that he was sorry and then lurched out of the parking lot.

It was a straight shot to Springfield. Virginia Highway 617 or Backlick Road, as it was commonly known, would take him right to the mall. Traffic was still heavy but Murray knew he would be there in ten minutes. His phone beeped, letting him know he had a text. It was from Walker and gave him the description of the stolen BMW, the tag number, and said it was parked near the main entrance.

The big, black Ford F-350 pickup in front of him stopped for the traffic light. Murray was busy reading the text and slammed into the back of the truck at forty-five miles an hour. The airbags deployed and the cell phone was knocked into the floorboard. Bob was stunned and disoriented. He looked around, trying to figure out what had happened.

Someone was tapping on his window. An angry looking Hispanic man was pointing at him and cursing him in Spanish. Why is he mad at me? Murray wondered.

Bob waved at the guy and tried to steer around the big truck parked in front of him. Then he realized that his Impala was dead as steam was rising from the front of the car. He turned the key to restart it but nothing happened.

The man at Bob's window tried to open the driver's door but it was jammed. Blue lights appeared in Murray's rear view mirror. I need to get out of here, he thought. They're going to think I was driving and that I was at fault.

He laid over in the passenger seat and used his legs to force open the driver's door. The angry guy was back yelling at him some more. Bob saw that the man was bleeding from several cuts on the face. I wonder how he got hurt?

A police officer gently pulled the injured man away as a second officer approached Bob, carefully watching him exit the wrecked vehicle.

"Thank God, you're here officer," Murray mumbled, putting his hand on the side of the Impala to keep from falling over. "I have a situation involving national security and I need a ride to the Springfield Mall."

He held out his ID packet for the cop to examine. He felt himself sway as he extended his arm.

After looking at Bob's ID, the officer asked, "Agent Murray, how much have you had to drink tonight?"

"You don't understand, officer," Bob stammered. "This is a national emergency."

"I don't think you getting to the mall tonight qualifies as an emergency. I'm going to need you to take a test so we can see what the alcohol content is in your system. You're under arrest for Driving Under the Influence and Following too Closely. Please, turn around and put your hands behind your back."

No, I can't do that, Bob thought. I can't get arrested, but I could borrow your police car. Murray acted like he was going to comply with the officer's commands and then tried to sprint around the uniformed policeman to his cruiser.

As the intoxicated CIA agent went around him, the police officer calmly drew his taser and shot him in the back. Murray felt a pain like he had never felt before go through his body and heard himself squealing. He landed hard, face first on the asphalt. The second police officer moved in, quickly handcuffing and searching him, removing Bob's pistol from the holster.

As the two officers lifted Agent Murray to his feet, they discovered that he had urinated and defecated on himself when the taser hit him. He had broken his nose and chipped two teeth when his face impacted with the roadway. The breath test would later show Bob's blood alcohol content to be .16 grams, twice the legal limit. Fortunately, the other driver's injuries were minor, but both vehicles and Murray's career were totaled.

The Springfield Town Center Mall, Springfield, Virginia, Thursday, 1930 hours

Tu Trang Donaldson had just gotten home from work when Jay Walker called him. He was looking forward to a relaxing evening with his wife, Gi, and their one-year old son, Robert. When Jay told him what was going on, though, Tu never hesitated. He kissed Gi and Robert and rushed back out to his vehicle.

His first call was to his assistant team leader, Jason Lewis, to notify the other two team members. Tu lived the closest to the mall and he instructed Lewis to have everyone meet there. Trang slipped his body armor on over his shirt, attached his web gear, and put his M4 rifle in the passenger seat, with the muzzle pointing towards the floor of his Suburban.

Tu's second phone call was to the Fairfax County Police

Department. They handled the police services for the area and he requested two marked units and a sergeant meet him at the mall until they could determine the scope of the incident. He was making good time down Virginia Highway 617 until he saw blue lights ahead, indicating a traffic accident. Tu made a quick left turn onto Commerce Street and took it down to the Springfield Mall.

Tu was born in South Vietnam. His mother had met and fallen in love with an American Special Forces soldier towards the end of the United State's involvement in Southeast Asia. Mai, his mother, did not know she was pregnant with him until his father had deployed back to America.

Mai realized that she would probably never see Bobby Donaldson again. She persisted in trying to get a message to him, both by mail and by pestering the small contingent of Americans left in South Vietnam to get a message to the Green Beret staff sergeant. After not hearing anything for months, Mai gave up and focused on having her baby and trying to survive under the communist regime.

Over the years, Tu's mother loved to tell the story about how one night, after a year and a half had passed, a stranger had shown up at their small apartment. He told Mai that he was one of the South Vietnamese soldiers that Donaldson had trained. He had a message for her from Bobby. She was to pack a few belongings and show up at the port the next evening with her toddler son.

Mai followed the mysterious man's instructions and reported to the port of Ho Chi Minh City. Another stranger approached her there and told her to follow him. He led her and her son to a medium sized cargo ship that was bearing a French flag. They were secured aboard in a small cabin and told to stay out of sight.

This messenger let her know that when they docked at Cherbourg, France, the next week, someone would meet her. Mai was scared for herself and for Tu but she trusted Bobby and followed the instructions without question. An American man with passable Vietnamese had met her in Cherbourg and driven them to the United

States Embassy. As they drove through the gate and Mai saw the American flag waving in the breeze she started crying, knowing that her son was going to grow up under that flag rather than in Vietnam.

Bobby Donaldson had received several of Mai's messages in Fayetteville, North Carolina and had begun working immediately to get his girlfriend and son to America. It was not an easy process and he spent his entire savings and then some to pay off the right people. He utilized the network in Vietnam that he had developed while serving there, training their special forces. Both of the messengers he had used were South Vietnamese Green Berets and were devoted to him.

Donaldson had also worked closely with CIA agents in Southeast Asia and had performed many missions for them. He had no problem calling in favors with the Agency. They greased a number of palms, using Bobby's money, of course, but the CIA had made things happen. The agent who had met Mai and Tu at the French port had American passports waiting for them.

When they arrived in North Carolina a few days later, Bobby was at the airport in Fayetteville in civilian clothes. One of Tu's favorite framed photos was of his parents crying on the tarmac that day, with himself squished in the middle of their tearful embrace. His mother and father were wed in the chapel at Fort Bragg the next week.

Tu followed in his father's footsteps and joined the army, becoming an Airborne Ranger and then a Green Beret. The young man's proudest moment was at his graduation ceremony when his father had placed the green beret on his head, saluted him, shook his hand, and then grabbed him in a bear hug.

After fifteen years in the army, Trang met Gi. She was a second generation Korean who worked as a nurse at Fort Bragg. When they decided to get married, he knew it was time to get out of the army. He had had a wonderful time but he wanted to be a good husband and eventually, a good father.

Tu applied to the Federal Bureau of Investigation but, without a college degree, they weren't interested. He then applied to the Secret Service and was quickly offered a job. After almost five years there, working a variety of assignments and protection details, he heard that his friend, Luis García, was going to work for the newly created CDC enforcement unit.

Trang knew that something was up. He had heard of how Luis had been shafted by the Secret Service brass for something he had had no control over. If García was going to work for the new agency, this was worth taking a closer look at. Tu called Luis and asked him about his new job. Before long, he was working for the CDC as well, just out of a different office.

The silver BMW X4 was parked in the front parking lot, surrounded by the cars of mall customers. Tu did not see anyone in the vehicle but realized they could be lying down. He called the Fairfax County Police Department and gave them his location at the mall, his description, his vehicle's description, and asked the officers to join him. Trang did not want the police to mistake him for a terrorist.

The former Special Forces soldier approached the stolen vehicle cautiously. He drew his Glock and holding it at a low-ready stance, used the flashlight attached to his pistol to illuminate the interior. After confirming the vehicle was unoccupied, he holstered his gun and sent Walker a quick text. The three marked police cars pulled to a stop nearby.

Trang briefed the police on what he had. He requested someone from the PD's Explosive Ordinance Disposal Unit respond to make sure the vehicle wasn't rigged with any devices. It would be up to the sergeant to decide what the police should do in the mall.

The sergeant got on the phone and within minutes let him know their SWAT Team was on the way. Better safe than sorry. When the other CDC officers arrived, they would request to see surveillance camera video in the mall security office.

After an EOD officer checked the car for booby traps, Tu asked the local police impound it and he called one of CDC Clean Up Teams to process the vehicle. Trang had been as shocked as anyone at the death and devastation that this suspect had caused at the University of Georgia. They had to get this guy.

Fifteen minutes later, another marked Fairfax County Police car pulled up. The officer approached Tu holding a piece of paper.

"I heard that you guys were here over the radio. You're with the CDC Enforcement Unit?"

Tu held out his hand. "I am. Tu Trang Donaldson. I'm one of the team leaders."

The officer shook his hand. "Officer Davis. I have some bad news for you. Do you know Bob Murray? Does he work for you guys?"

"Yeah, he's the officer-in-charge of the DC office. He's my boss. Why?"

"I just arrested him for Driving Under the Influence. He was in a vehicle accident just up the road from here. He blew a .16 grams on the Breathalyzer. The other driver he hit had minor injuries. Then, your boss tried to flee on foot.

"Actually, I think he was going to try and steal my police car but he was so drunk, I could see it coming. He got tazed and a little banged up himself when he fell down. Both cars are totaled."

Trang shrugged and shook his head. "Yep, that sounds like Bob. Sorry you had to deal with that, Officer."

"You don't seem surprised?"

"No, everybody knows that Bob has a drinking problem. I just thought he was smart enough to drink at home and stay off the road."

The Fairfax officer sighed. "He told me he was on his way down here to the mall to deal with an incident involving national security. Have you talked to him tonight?"

"No, our other team leader notified him of what they were dealing with. We're working a case here and a few of your other guys are helping us. I guess Bob wanted to come and supervise."

"That's too bad. Are you going to bail him out?"

Tu laughed. "Not hardly. We're dealing with something pretty big here. I'll let the chain of command at the CDC know and somebody else can go deal with Bob."

Alexandria, Virginia, Thursday, 2000 hours

Terrell Hill lay on the small bed with his hands behind his head in the sparsely decorated room. The room gave him flashbacks to his cell at the Reidsville State Penitentiary. He had spent almost six years in that maximum-security prison. There were some really bad people in that place. I guess that includes me, he thought. How many thousands of people did I kill last week?

He had converted to Islam in prison because those were the coolest guys in the place and nobody messed with them. He did not understand the tenets of the Muslim faith, nor did he care. As a Muslim, no one bothered him for the entire time he was incarcerated.

Today had been an interesting day. Usama had found Hill in the food court inside The Springfield Town Center Mall. The guy was good. He slipped right up on me, Terrell thought, and was sitting across from me in that booth before I even knew he was there. I wonder how long he'd been watching me?

Terrell had spent the night before at a Day's Inn in Alexandria. The dude he had talked to on the phone had instructed him to go to the mall and eat lunch at 1215 hours on Thursday and someone would meet him. The food court was packed at that time and Terrell immediately understood the wisdom of meeting in such a crowded place.

Usama had short, dark hair and a salt and pepper beard. He was smaller than Hill but he had intense eyes. Terrell had the same feeling with Usama that he'd had with Amir al-Razi. This was a dangerous man.

"We have a safe house near here. We would like you to come

there and tell us everything about the attack last week in Georgia and discuss other operations."

Terrell looked into the Middle Eastern man's eyes. The accented voice sounded like the same one he had talked to on the phone.

"Okay. That would be good. I want you know, though, I can't work for free. I'm sure we can make some kind of deal and help each other out."

"Of course," nodded Usama. "We want to debrief you on what you and Amir did and then decide the next best attack. We will pay you well."

Hill smiled. That was what he wanted to hear. "Sounds like a plan."

"One more thing," Usama said. "When we get to the house, you have to give me your gun. I will give it back to you or give you a better one when you leave."

"Man, I don't want to give up my piece."

"I'm sorry. This is non-negotiable. The man in charge does not allow any guns in the house. But, we have access to many weapons and can give you anything you want when you leave."

The carrot on a stick approach worked and Terrell nodded. "Alright, man. No problem."

Today, he and Usama had talked for hours. He had been asked to describe every detail of the attacks in Athens. Of course, Hill only knew what his role was. Al-Razi had kept him in the dark about what parts other people had played. Since it appeared that Amir was out of the picture, though, Terrell played up his own role and made it sound like he had helped Amir plan everything out.

Another black guy had come to the house in the afternoon. Haseem was the only name Terrell had gotten. He had not wanted to talk but Hill had seen the jailhouse tattoos. Maybe he was going to be working, too. Or, maybe he was some extra muscle to make sure Terrell did not try to leave.

Usama had worked in the garage for several hours on something after the debriefing. He told Terrell they had another car for him to drive, another SUV, but it wasn't quite ready yet. It made Hill feel good that they already had a vehicle for him. They needed him enough to pay him and to give him another ride.

Usama had eventually retired to one of the other bedrooms but had told Terrell that tomorrow the imam was coming to talk to him. This must be the guy, Hill thought. He'll be the one to offer me a mission. This holy war stuff might end up making Terrell Hill one wealthy man.

The Springfield Town Center Mall, Thursday, 2215 hours

The security office wasn't big enough to hold everyone. Eddie, Jay, Tu, and Fairfax County police sergeant, Paul Moore, were all crowded around a computer monitor as mall security officer, Mike Jenkins, searched through video footage from the last thirty-six hours. The Fairfax County SWAT Team was patrolling the mall in their full tactical gear. The CDC officers walked the mall, as well, looking for any indication that the zombie virus had been released.

After hearing of the incident with Bob Murray, Admiral Williams had acted quickly. Tu was now the acting OIC of the Washington, D.C., office. Now that Eddie had been briefed on who the CDC was really working for and being supported by, he could appreciate why the CIA had recruited the caliber of men surrounding him. Tu and Jay both had an extensive special operations background in the military and Trang also had some federal law enforcement experience. These guys knew what needed to be done and having Agent Murray out of the picture did not slow them down at all.

Security Officer Jenkins started with the camera facing the front parking lot and finally found the footage of the stolen BMW pulling into the mall the previous day. They all watched Terrell Hill saunter inside, his ball cap cocked to the side, his pants tugged low, gangster style. Everyone was surprised he had not chopped off the dreadlocks to try and disguise his appearance.

Jenkins marked the time and then changed to the camera inside the front door. It picked up Hill as he continued towards the food court. Another camera change and Terrell was observed buying his lunch at the Burger King kiosk and seating himself at a table in the middle of the dining area to eat his Whopper and fries. The officers all studied the terrorist and waited to see what he would do next.

After a few minutes, a bearded man who looked Middle Eastern came from the periphery of the dining area and slipped into the booth across from Hill, startling him. He was wearing a ball cap, as well, but his was pulled down low onto his forehead. They had a conversation and then left together, exiting on the other side of the mall. The security officer was able to track them out of the building and into the parking lot.

They climbed into a white Chevrolet Astrovan and drove out of the parking lot, heading north towards Franconia Road, a highway running east and west. Jenkins zoomed in and was able to get the license plate. Sergeant Moore called his dispatcher over the phone to get the registration information on the tag.

"Can you print out some stills of those two guys together?" Eddie asked Jenkins.

"Sure, no problem," Jenkins quickly answered, glad to help out. He had no idea what these two men had done but with the Fairfax County SWAT Team walking the mall and the CDC Enforcement Unit in his small office, it was clearly bigger than anything else he had done as a mall cop.

Walker looked at Marshall. "Any ideas for IDing that second guy? He looks Middle Eastern and might be one of the big players in all of this. I've got a feeling I've seen him somewhere before, maybe in Iraq."

"That's the problem with dealing with stuff this time of night," said Trang. "I can call the DHS switchboard and see if they can point me in the right direction."

"Let me make a phone call," said Eddie. "My boss in Atlanta is pretty persuasive."

By 2300 hours, the mystery man who met with Terrell Hill had been identified as Usama Husan Zayad. Chuck had texted the pictures to Admiral William's aide, Shaun Taylor, and told him they needed to know who he was ASAP. Taylor got to work and McCain soon had a name and a bio, which put him in The Who's Who of the terrorist world. The CDC officers and the police sergeant were in the hallway outside the security office as Eddie told them what they had found out.

"Usama Husan Zayad is the worst of the worst. His specialty is explosives, specifically car bombs, suicide vests, and IEDs. He was a suspect in multiple assassinations of business people and politicians in Baghdad who were trying to work with the Americans. He was one of the guys who had his own playing card but they were never able to find him. And, now it sounds like the powers that be had no clue that he was in America."

For several years during the war in Iraq, high-value targets were listed in a deck of playing cards. Fifty-two of the most notorious terrorists, including Saddam Hussein and his sons were contained in the cards. The goal was to help the American soldiers memorize the terrorist's faces as they played poker.

Walker nodded. "I thought he looked familiar. We went looking for him a couple of times over there and came up empty. We met several of his associates, who are no longer with us, but we never could track him down."

Eddie and Tu both understood the implication of what Jay had just said. If SEAL Team Six had been given the assignment of tracking down Usama Husan Zayad, he was even more dangerous than they had first thought. Team Six only went after the most notorious terrorists.

"Sarge," asked Trang, turning back to the county officer who was listening intently, "what did you find out about that car registration?

"It comes back to an address a few miles from here. It's registered to an Islamic charity but the street address is a residence. I've already sent an officer to do a drive-by in an unmarked car to see what he can see."

"That's good work. Thanks for that," Tu told the sergeant.

"What now, Eddie?" asked Jay.

"If we can confirm that the vehicle we saw them leave in is at that address, I say we get a search warrant and hit the house. Hill is wanted and Zayad is a known terrorist. There's no telling what else we might find in there."

Trang and Walker both smiled. "Sounds like we're just getting started tonight," said Jay.

Chapter Five

Layers of the Onion

Springfield, Virginia, Friday, 0130 hours

The CDC officers and the SWAT Team relocated to the elementary school on Franconia Road, less than a mile from their target location on Higham Drive. A Fairfax County officer had radioed in that the white van was parked in the driveway next to an identical Astrovan. The tag on the second vehicle was registered to the same Islamic charity. There were no lights on at the residence.

Eddie and Sergeant Moore had gone to the Fairfax County Courthouse to get the search warrant from the on-call judge. The police officers at the school talked quietly and checked their equipment as they waited. The local SWAT officers knew that their role would be to support the federal officers but they were fine with that. Four SWAT snipers were already in place, watching the front and rear of the residence through their night-vision scopes.

Sergeant Moore's police cruiser turned into the parking lot of the school and drove around to the rear where the officers waited. Eddie got out of the passenger door holding some papers. Everyone circled around the former linebacker, ready to get briefed and go to work.

At 0215 hours, it was time. Tu and his team were in place at the rear of the house. They had driven in with their lights off and parked on Elm Street, the next street over from the target location. They then quietly made their way through the neighboring yards and into position. Walker's and Marshall's CDC teams loaded into a white box truck with the rest of the SWAT force at the elementary school. When Trang radioed and said that they were in position in the backyard, Eddie gave the order to move.

In less than two minutes, the unmarked truck pulled up and stopped one house shy of the suspect address. Jay rolled the door up as softly as he could and the heavily armed men exited, walking quickly towards the residence. The SWAT officers fanned out and assumed cover positions around the house. Both the front and the rear CDC elements had a SWAT breacher with them. Both men were carrying heavy metal door battering rams that would assure a fast entrance.

The goal was for both the front and rear teams to enter the house at the same time. Sensor lights prevented that from happening. As Eddie and his team approached the front door, they were suddenly bathed in light as two spotlights were activated.

Without hesitating, Eddie hit transmit on his radio. "We're compromised. Make entry now!"

Inside the safe house, Usama Husan Zayad was awake instantly, reaching for the 9mm Browning Hi-Power pistol he kept beside the bed. He used the room at the front of the house because the imam often spent the night there and used a rear bedroom. Zayad could react faster to protect him if he was in the front bedroom. Now, he realized that it was he who needed to be protected.

His senses had been trained by years of fighting and fleeing American forces. Zayad listened. It could have just been a neighborhood dog setting the sensor lights off. No. He heard footsteps. Muffled voices and then, "We're compromised. Make entry now!"

Haseem was sleeping on the couch in the living room. He was another prison convert but had proven faithful and loyal. His primary job was to make sure that Terrell Hill did not leave before the imam allowed it.

Once Hill had been given a job, Haseem would make sure that Terrell completed his assignment. He also provided security for the safe house. Maybe he can slow them down, Usama thought.

A loud crashing came from the front of the residence and then another from the rear. Two explosions rocked the residence. Flash bang grenades, the terrorist recognized. The Americans loved to use those. He was shielded from the full effects of the blasts inside his bedroom. Haseem might not be so lucky out in the living room.

Usama instinctively knew that he was surrounded. Even escape through the window would be futile, as he guessed that more law enforcement was surrounding the house, watching and waiting. This was Allah's will. He had fought the infidels for many years. Maybe he could kill a few more before they killed him.

The SWAT breacher with Eddie's and Jay's teams slammed the metal battering ram into the front door, shattering the frame and opening the door on the first strike. Every breacher's goal was a one-strike entry. Eddie tossed the flash bang inside and then turned away from the entrance.

As soon as it exploded, he was in, the muzzle of his suppressed M4 leading the way, the gun-mounted flashlight illuminating the hallway in front of him. Marshall could see another hallway up to the left and what was probably the living room straight ahead. The flash and crack of another grenade went off in that area.

"Police officers! Search warrant!" he yelled, putting those inside the residence on notice as the law required.

To their right was a dining area and another doorway that appeared to lead into the kitchen. Jay and his three officers peeled off to the right and cleared the kitchen, circling around towards the living room. The deafening blast of a shotgun rang out from just in front of Walker in the living room.

Tu had thrown his stun grenade through the back door after it was smashed open. It had exploded on the opposite side of the room from Haseem and only slowed him down momentarily. Trang and his team burst into the living room from the rear door just as Haseem fired his Mossberg twelve gauge shotgun down the front hallway towards Eddie and his team. Trang heard a grunt from that direction and brought his rifle up. Movement to his left. He recognized Jay coming into the living room from the kitchen.

The big black man with the shotgun racked the slide, ejecting the spent shell and loading another one. He tried to swing the Mossberg towards the new threats behind him. Before he could get off a second shot, though, Jay and Tu both fired, striking Haseem in the torso and head with 5.56mm rounds. As Walker's and Trang's teams kept moving forward, Trang fired one more shot into the downed gunman's head. Smoke and the smell of cordite filled the air.

Eddie had felt the heat of the shotgun blast go by him and heard Jimmy groan in pain. More shots exploded from the living room as the muzzle flashes lit up the dark house. Marshall peeked down the hallway to his left and saw a figure sticking his head out of a doorway ten feet down and then a pistol rising towards him.

Everything slowed down but Eddie felt like he had to move faster. The gun was almost pointed at him. Marshall sighted on the man's forehead and fired two shots. A red mist hung in the air as Usama Hasan Zayad fell to the floor, dead.

Marshall kept his rifle pointed down the hallway. There were three more closed doors that would have to be checked.

"Status report?" he called over his shoulder.

"One tango down in the living room," Walker answered.

"And I've got one down in a doorway, first room on the left. I think it's Usama," said Eddie. "Jimmy, are you OK?"

"I'm hit. My vest stopped most of it, but I may have a cracked rib," the assistant team leader answered, the pain evident in his voice.

"Go out and get the SWAT medic to check you."

"I'm fine, Eddie."

"That's an order, Jimmy. We've got plenty of officers to clear the rest of the house. Go!"

Jimmy turned and left the residence.

The crashing sounds, the explosions, the loud voices announcing the presence of the police, and then the sound of gunfire woke Terrell up. He threw himself off the bed and ducked behind it, between the bed and the wall. He didn't have a weapon and his bedroom was an interior one without any windows. Oh, man, they're coming to get me!

What should he do? he wondered. If he gave himself up, they would give him the death penalty. He would go back to prison for ten years before they finally strapped him to a gurney and killed him.

Maybe I can get the police to kill me, he thought. He had never thought about suicide before. At least this way, he said to himself, I can go out as a warrior. Anything was better than going back to prison and being executed like an animal.

Estrada and Rogers quickly cleared the room that Usama had come out of and then the one across the hall from it. Eddie, with Hollywood and Chris behind him, was about to turn the doorknob of the next room when the door was suddenly flung open and Terrell Hill threw himself out into the hallway. A less experienced officer would have shot Hill then and there, but taking him alive was important if they could do it.

Marshall saw that the terrorist did not have anything in his hands and was not an immediate threat. He swung the stock of his rifle into Hill's face, snapping his head back and ripping open his cheek. Terrell staggered but did not go down. He drew back his right hand to punch the big federal officer, but Eddie was faster, stepping in with an elbow strike that impacted the bridge of his nose, breaking it, and knocking him into the wall.

As a bloody Terrell Hill slid down the wall to a sitting position, Marshall drove a knee into his face to make sure that he stayed down, the terrorist's head smashing through the sheetrock of the hallway wall. Alejandro and Chris grabbed the unconscious man, handcuffed him, and searched him. They dragged him towards the front door. Jay and his team moved up to help Eddie finish clearing the house.

Springfield, Virginia, Friday, 0300 hours

The full-size black Ford van was there within thirty minutes of Eddie calling Chuck and giving him a status update. Terrell Hill was handcuffed and secured in a police car with a SWAT officer guarding him. A paramedic had already checked Hill and said that his nose was broken, he probably had a few other broken bones on his face, and had likely suffered a concussion. The paramedic had cleaned the cut on Terrell's cheek as best he could and put a bandage onto it.

Two muscular white men, both sporting thick beards, got out of the van and approached the CDC officers. They were wearing black t-shirts and jeans. Their pistols were only partially covered by their shirts.

Eddie, Jay, and Tu walked over to the newcomers. One of them was holding a clipboard. "Which one of you guys is Marshall?" he asked.

"That's me," Eddie answered. "You guys here for Hill?"

"Please sign here," he said, handing Marshall the clipboard. Eddie shone his light on the paperwork to see what he was signing. He scribbled his name on the form and handed the clipboard back.

The other bearded man glanced at Jay Walker and his face registered surprise. Jay had recognized him, too, but the newcomer shook his head slightly before Walker could say anything.

The two men took Terrell out of the police car and secured his hands and feet with restraints, attaching them to a belly chain around his waist. As they moved him towards the van, the terrorist found his voice.

"I need a doctor. I want to go to the hospital. And I want to press charges on all of those officers who beat me up."

One of the bearded men opened the back of the van to reveal a secure metal cage, tall enough for someone to sit inside. He opened the cage door and motioned for Terrell to get in.

"Where are you taking me? I'm not getting in there. I need medical attention," the prisoner demanded and tried to back away.

The transport men grabbed Hill, picked him up, slid him into the cage, and secured the door. They then got into the van and drove off without looking back.

"Well, that was strange," said Tu.

"You're telling me," agreed Jay. "I know that guy who was driving the van. He was a SEAL. He was on Team Six just as I was getting there and then he left. The rumor was that he was going to go work for the CIA."

Trang nodded. "And the other guy was a Delta operator, the last I knew. He was in Special Forces and then one day he was gone. We heard he had gone to Delta. And now they're doing prisoner transports? But who are they transporting for?"

"If anybody asks," Eddie injected, "Hill was taken for questioning by officials of the DHS."

"What was on the clipboard you signed?" asked Tru.

Eddie smiled. "Nothing really. Just a piece of paper with Hill's name, this address, and a place for me to sign."

The Asian man shook his head. "Sounds kind of shady to me. Is that even legal?"

Marshall wasn't sure what to say. He wasn't authorized to discuss anything about the CIA's involvement in what they were doing.

"Well, guys, we just killed two dangerous terrorists and arrested the worst mass murderer in American history. If I had to guess, other government agencies want to have a chat with Mr. Hill to see what he knows. It might not fit nicely into our law enforcement framework, but good riddance to him."

Jimmy's wound was not serious but was painful. His body armor had stopped most of the blast of buckshot that Haseem had fired. One .30 caliber pellet had hit him in the side panel of the vest but had not penetrated all the way. It felt like he might have a broken rib. Jones had been transported to the closest hospital to be tended to, with Chris Rogers riding with him for moral support.

The FBI's Supervisory Special Agent Daniel Ward had not wanted to respond to a shooting scene involving CDC agents in the middle of the night. He especially did not want to deal with Walker or Marshall again. He alerted his team, however, and got there at 0400 hours. When the CDC supervisors walked him through the scene, the FBI agent realized quickly that this was going to be scrutinized at the highest levels. How had this Usama guy even gotten into the country and what was he up to? Ward wondered.

The garage at the Islamic "charity house" appeared to have been Usama's workshop. There were explosives, detonators, vests, and a refrigerator that contained several half-liter bottles of a clear liquid. A Nissan Pathfinder SUV was parked in the garage with its rear cargo door open. Usama had been installing explosives in this one but it appeared to be a work in progress. The officers kept the garage door shut to prevent nosey neighbors or reporters from seeing what they were working on.

A Fairfax County Police Explosives Ordinance Disposal expert made sure there were no live devices present in the garage. The bomb in the Pathfinder looked like it was almost complete but still needed a few more elements. The EOD officer saw something in the corner of the room that made him stop suddenly.

"Why don't you guys step out of the garage and wait outside. I need to check something."

They followed him out of the house while he retrieved a small electronic item from the SWAT truck. He disappeared into the garage again but was back within a minute.

"There's radioactive material, maybe nuclear waste, in a yellow bucket in the garage. They were building dirty bombs," the bomb expert said.

Northeast of Atlanta, Friday, 0430 hours

McCain couldn't sleep after Eddie's call, updating him on their shootout and what they had discovered, and finally got up and made a pot of coffee. He was planning to fly up to Virginia later in the morning on the Department of Homeland Security's corporate jet. Thankfully, with the exception of Jimmy's minor wound, Eddie and his team were fine. The Nuclear Regulatory Commission would be advised about the discovery of nuclear materials, but not until later.

They did not need the dirty bomb story to hit the news yet. With the terrorism element involved, it was important that only minimal information be released to the public. The zombie virus had spread panic nation-wide, causing thousands of people to flee from the various targeted cities. In many cases, however, they had taken the virus with them into the nation's interior.

If the terrorists were now creating dirty bombs, it could easily create the worst panic the United States had ever known. And, at this point, no one knew if any of these bombs had been deployed yet. The presence of radioactive materials and explosives together was an ominous find, though. Chuck was especially curious as to what the clear liquid was that was found in the refrigerator. He had a feeling he wasn't going to like the answer.

McCain was also apprehensive that Andy and Scotty were heading for their stakeout in North Georgia by themselves. They had briefed him on their mission the previous evening. Chuck's only concern was that they were so far from backup. They would be almost two hours north of Atlanta and the local law enforcement in that area was spread very thin and lacked the training of the metro Atlanta police agencies. At the same time, if there were ever two men who could hold their own against terrorists, zombies, or any other threats, it was Fleming and Smith.

As he sipped his third cup of coffee, McCain opened his Bible and read a few Psalms and a chapter out of Proverbs. He prayed for wisdom and protection for his daughter, his men and himself. He asked for courage for all of them and prayed that the plans of the wicked would be exposed. When he was finished, Chuck took a deep breath and closed his Bible.

I wish I could talk to Rebecca about all this stuff, he thought. Her years as a CIA agent had honed her ability to know which paths were worth pursuing and which ones weren't. A sudden sadness wrapped itself around him and the image of her opening her eyes and looking at him right before she died flashed across his mind.

"I'm so sorry, Rebecca," he muttered, holding his head in his hands. "God, why did you allow that to happen? Why did it have to be her?"

The big man climbed to his feet, understanding that he needed to keep moving. He had not had any nightmares last night, but knew that they could return at any point. I might as well go on in to the office, he thought.

As he drove to CDC HQ, Chuck dialed Shaun Taylor's number. If I'm awake, he can wake up, too, Chuck thought. The groggy voice of Admiral Williams' assistant answered and McCain said he had some important new information for their boss. When he was sure that Taylor was awake, Chuck told him about the radioactive materials in the bomb maker's workshop.

There was a long silence on the other end of the phone. Taylor finally found his voice.

"Thanks, Chuck. I'll pass this on to the admiral."

Chuck got to HQ, worked out, showered, and was at his desk by 0630 hours. He had gotten a text that Andy and Scotty were in position and watching their target location. They suspected that the two buildings and the large gravel parking area were being used as a terrorist training camp. Andy said there were seven cars and two vans there. No one was stirring yet.

At 0645 hours, McCain heard their office door open. Their administrative aide, Vanessa, did not normally report until 0800 hours and the rest of his men were out on assignments. Chuck walked to his door and peered down the hallway. Luis García was limping towards him, wearing a stiff walking cast on his injured ankle.

"Hey, Luis! Good to see you. I thought you weren't coming back until next week. How're you feeling?"

"Hey, Boss. I took a few days off but I was bored out of my mind at home and figured I could do something here."

Chuck smiled broadly. "It's great to have you back. Come on in here and let me give you a run down on everything that's going on."

Gilmer County, North Georgia, Friday, 0500 hours

Andy and Scotty had been on the road since 0300 hours and were finally nearing their destination. After studying the satellite imagery provided by the NSA, as well poring over Google maps, they both felt that they had discovered a terrorist training camp. Some of the photos were just a week old and showed around twenty men training in hand-to-hand combat. One of the latest images showed the gravel parking area, packed with multiple vehicles, that wrapped around two buildings. One of the structures was bigger and looked like a small house or dormitory with the other possibly being used as a storage facility.

This area of North Georgia was very rural and it was not hard to find secluded areas to grow and manufacture drugs or to train terrorists. The closest town was Elijay and it was almost twenty miles northeast of the suspect location. The officers located the address in the intel folder that Chuck had given Andy to dig through and a little investigation revealed that the one thousand acre tract of land was owned by an Islamic non-profit organization. They could find no specific information on this particular NPO, however, which indicated that it was probably a charity in name only.

Fleming and Smith planned to hike in under the cover of darkness and conduct a surveillance of the site. Their GPS indicated that they were there. Andy turned the SUV onto a dirt drive that led off of Georgia Highway 136.

The turnoff was a short dead end where people had dumped plastic bags of trash, appliances, and yard debris. There were no streetlights or any homes nearby. Their vehicle was hidden from sight from the road.

The men exited the Suburban, stretched, and began to put on all of their equipment. The aroma of the trash all around them assailed their nostrils. The silence of the night was only broken by the two warriors going through the same rituals that they had performed hundreds of times before. They applied cammo makeup to their faces, checked their weapons for a second and third time, verified that their radios were working, and then activated their hand-held GPS devices, pre-programed with the coordinates for the suspected training camp. It was a hike of almost two miles through the woods.

"You sure you're up to this, Andy?" Scotty, the former Army Ranger, asked, smiling.

"Big Boy, I can keep up with you any day of the week," the former Marine special operator answered, also smiling.

There was no traffic this time of morning and the federal officers crossed to the other side of Highway 136 and slipped into the woods. They used their flashlights and kept a fast pace for the first mile. After that, they went into patrol mode and moved slowly and deliberately for the second mile.

In other settings, they would be equipped with night vision

goggles but that was a piece of equipment that they did not have. Most of their other operations had been during the day. Since the biggest part of the action they had been involved in as CDC officers was against zombies, they worked during daylight hours. Now, they both wished that they had night vision capability.

When they got close to their target location, Scotty set up on an incline a hundred yards away from the two buildings. He could see the front of the structures and the gravel parking area. Nine vehicles were parked there, all on the front side of the buildings. Smith had not had many opportunities to utilize his Ranger sniper skills as a CDC officer. He quietly pulled a few branches up next to him to break up his outline for anyone who might look in his direction later.

Andy moved two hundred yards farther down the ridge, overlooking the rear of the location. They both had earpieces in and quietly conducted another radio check. The sky was just starting to lighten up and the woods slowly came to life around them.

At 0655 hours, Andy observed four Middle Eastern-looking males step out of the rear door, stretching and talking quietly. They all walked to the edge of the small gravel parking area in the rear and urinated. A few minutes later, three other dark-skinned young men repeated the same procedure on the edge of the front parking lot.

Fleming and Smith noticed that all of the men were wearing the long white traditional Muslim garment. Scotty couldn't help but think of the thawb as a nightgown. They were also wearing a taqiyah, the Islamic skullcap.

Smith pushed the transmit button on his radio. "Why are they dressed up so early in the morning?" he quietly asked Fleming.

"I bet they're about to have their morning prayers," came the answer.

Sure enough, the men went back inside and the sound of Arabic chanting from many voices soon was heard from the open windows. After ten minutes, only one voice was heard, also speaking in Arabic. Andy, who had had multiple deployments to the Middle

East, understood some of what he was hearing.

"I'm going to ease down the ridge, a little closer to the house to try and listen," Andy told Scotty over the radio. "Move down this way a hundred yards so you can cover me. I'm going to set up behind that biggest tree at the left corner of the rear parking area."

"10-4."

Smith began slithering through the woods. Fleming had already begun moving from his perch down to the edge of the wooded area. The undergrowth was very thick here. That made it uncomfortable to maneuver through but provided the concealment that Andy needed.

The former SpecOp Marine stopped at the edge of the woods and crouched behind a large tree. He was only forty yards from the building where the men were having their service. Scotty repositioned himself so he could cover the rear of the building. Even with the optics on his rifle, he could not see Andy, hidden in the foliage below.

The rear door of the building opened and a man strode purposefully down the steps and over to the edge of the gravel. He stopped and relieved himself, facing Fleming's tree. Smith had the red cross in his EOTech sight on the back of the man's head.

If the suspected terrorist saw Andy, Scotty would have to decide whether or not to kill him. Smith did not see a weapon on the Muslim but he also did not want him shouting an alarm. The CDC agent continued to cover him but knew he could not shoot unless he presented a threat to Andy or himself.

After thirty seconds, the man finished his business and looked around. No one had followed him outside. He pulled out a pack of cigarettes, shook one out and lit it. He stepped off the gravel and walked to the edge of the woods in the direction of Andy.

Scotty had his finger on the trigger still ready to fire if the guy pulled a weapon. The smoker peered into the trees as he finished his cigarette. He finally flicked the butt into the foliage and turned around, walking back into the building. Smith realized he had been holding his breath.

Ten minutes later, Fleming's voice came through his earpiece. "I'm back up on the ridge. I was able to hear a lot of the sermon and it sounds like he's prepping these guys to go on suicide missions for Allah. Stay where you're at and I'll come to you."

A few minutes later Andy appeared next to his teammate.

He put his mouth to Scotty's ear and said in a low voice, "The imam, or whoever was talking, was getting them pumped up about becoming martyrs and striking a blow against the Great Satan. He said that their attacks would be an important part of this Holy War and that their families would honor their memories forever."

"So, you want to let's go kill 'em all?" Smith whispered. "I mean, if they want to become martyrs, I don't want to hold them back. And, out here in the middle of nowhere is much better than downtown."

Andy nodded. "For sure, but I don't think we can do that. Just talking about becoming a martyr isn't illegal in America and we're cops now."

The muscular man sighed. "Right. How do you want to handle it, then?"

"Let me check in with the boss and see if there are any other assets we can pull in. I think you and me could take them all out if we needed to. Easy. But, if they go mobile, it'll be another story."

Gilmer County, North Georgia, Friday, 0840 hours

Andy slipped a little deeper into the woods to call Chuck. One of the things that Fleming appreciated about McCain's leadership was that he wasn't afraid to make a decision. After hearing his team leader's assessment of the situation, Chuck's instructions had been clear.

"Andy, you're right. We can't shoot these people just for talking about becoming martyrs. If you guys see any evidence to back up what they're saying, though, deal with it. If you see any weapons, explosives, or if it looks like they're going to follow through on their threats, do everything you can to stop them.

"I trust you guys and we absolutely cannot have a repeat of the terror attacks that we've seen. Keep me in the loop and I'm going to have some local law enforcement back you up. I was getting ready to leave for the airport to fly up to be with Eddie's team but I'll put that on hold until I hear back from you."

At 0855 hours, the two CDC officers were lying side-by-side on the ridge, near Scotty's original spot, overlooking the buildings and the front parking area. The vehicles in the lot ranged from small to mid-size cars to SUVs to a pair of vans. Andy and Scotty were waiting and watching, softly discussing their options.

They had nixed the idea of having one of them run back through the woods to bring their vehicle closer. There was no good place to park where it would be hidden. The driveway that led up to this compound was several hundred yards off of the main road. And, if things got ugly while one of them was gone, a lone officer, no matter how well trained, would be in over his head against the much larger number of terrorists.

The front door of the main building opened and Middle Eastern men started pouring into the parking lot. They seemed subdued with little talking among themselves. Most of them were carrying what looked like a white garment of some sort.

Andy counted twenty-two men, all wearing the traditional Muslim clothing. As he looked through the magnifying optics on his rifle, he saw that only twenty of the men were holding the white object. Two older men began helping the younger men put the garment on.

"Dude, those are suicide vests," Fleming said, out of the side of his mouth, as he recognized what was happening. "Looks like it's game on."

He and Smith had seen those on many occasions in the Middle East. On one mission, Andy and his MARSOC team had raided a home in which suicide vests were being manufactured. They looked just like what he was seeing today.

"I really love killing terrorists," Smith whispered, already plotting his shots. "Just say when."

Andy watched as the older men assisted the would-be martyrs in strapping on and arming the bomb-laden clothing, then covering their torsos with loose-hanging shirts. The officers decided to wait until everyone had their vests on. That would indicate more of an intention to use them. As soon as the twenty young men were suited up, they all paused to listen to one of their elders, who appeared to be sharing some parting words of wisdom.

"You start left and work to the right. I'll start right and work to the left," said Andy.

"Clear."

Fleming's first shot blew off the top of a young terrorist's head. His second pull of the trigger hit another in the temple. Scotty shot the far left bomber in the back of the head and then swung the muzzle slightly to get his second one with a round to the throat. Four down.

As the shooting began, mayhem quickly ensued. Now, all the terrorists were moving, ducking, and yelling. The man who had been giving the speech crouched and ran to a nearby Nissan Altima. He reached into his pocket for his key fob, mashing a button and opening the trunk as he ducked behind it. He grabbed an AK-47 rifle and started firing blindly towards the wooded area on the other side of the parking lot, where he suspected the shots were coming from.

The federal officers shot three more of the terrorists before they started receiving return fire. As bullets started impacting trees and the ground around them they separated, Scotty going left and Andy moving right, each man crawling twenty yards further along the ridge. The AK fire was not well aimed and still had not pinpointed them so they quickly set up in their new locations and continued picking off the potential bombers.

Smith could see AK man clearly from his new vantage point. He was still crouching behind the Altima and firing over the top of his car, in their general direction. The older terrorist realized he had been in one place for too long and stood up to run to a brown Dodge Caravan. Scotty put a 5.56mm round into his chest and another into his head sending him sprawling onto the gravel.

Movement. A white mini-van and a black compact car were in motion, trying to get out of the kill zone. Scotty swung his rifle towards the vehicles racing down the dirt driveway. He got off one shot and then the entire parking lot erupted.

One of the martyrs had turned and started running toward the main building they all exited just moments before. Andy fired and missed twice, trying to hit the running target. His third round caught him in the ribcage, setting off the vest in a powerful explosion and obliterating the young man. The front of the building collapsed and started to burn. The detonation ignited two more armed vests on the bodies of previously shot terrorists and caused another, larger blast.

The second building, a large storage shed, was only twenty-five feet to the far side of the first building. As things and people started blowing up, the door and windows were blown inward. Without warning, the shed erupted in a fiery roar, sending its roof skyward and fiery debris outward. Several other detonations came from within the remains of this structure.

These multiple concussions triggered the vests on the terrorists who were still alive. As their bomb clothing went off, fuel tanks in the seven remaining parked cars ignited, sending several fireballs high into the sky. Car parts, body parts, and pieces of the two buildings rained down throughout the area.

Both of the structures at the terrorist's training camp were destroyed. The larger building was on fire and the roof had completely caved in. The second building, the storage shed, was gone. The concrete slab and a pile of debris were all that was left.

At the first explosion, Scotty and Andy backed up over the edge of the ridge and buried their faces in the ground, keeping the top of their kevlar helmets towards the blast. As the detonations finally subsided, they looked at each other with stunned expressions and automatically reloaded their rifles. Then Scotty started laughing.

"That was awesome! Can we do it again?"

An hour and a half later, the Department of Homeland Security Blackhawk helicopter assigned to the Atlanta CDC team circled and then landed in an open field sixty yards from the blast site. Chuck, Luis, FBI Supervisory Special Agent Thomas Burns, Clean Up Crew supervisor Nancy Long, and two Bureau of Alcohol, Tobacco, and Firearms agents got off. Andy and Scotty were there to greet them.

Burns had not made a very good impression on Scotty the last time the men had crossed paths. Today, though, Agent Burns shook both his and Andy's hands and congratulated them on a job well done. The FBI agent did not always approve of the way that the CDC did things but he could not argue with results. And these guys got results.

Luis greeted his friends by calling them some off-color names in Spanish. "Right. I see how it is. You guys wait until I get hurt and then you go out and kill a bunch of terrorists and blow a bunch of stuff up."

"Luis, chill, man," said Scotty. "There were only twenty-two of them. That was barely enough for me and Andy. You're going to have to find your own bad guys."

Behind them, the scene still burned and black smoke filled the air. It took almost forty-five minutes for the first volunteer firefighters to arrive. This was like nothing any of them had ever seen.

One building was gutted and the other one was gone. Seven vehicles had exploded and burned up, leaving the smoking frames behind. And there were body parts scattered over a radius of a hundred and fifty yards.

The Gilmer County Sheriff's Department had sent a sergeant and a deputy. By the expression on their faces, this was clearly the biggest call that either of them had been on. Fleming had asked the deputies to go down to the end of the driveway to the main road and to keep reporters and nosey people out.

Andy and Scotty briefed Chuck and the other federal agents on what had happened. Fleming pointed out where he and Smith had been and talked about why they had done what they had done. They would give more detailed statements to the FBI later, but for now, Andy provided a snapshot of the incident.

"Based on the magnitude of the explosions," Fleming concluded, "it looks like the storage shed was where they kept their bomb-making supplies. I'm sure you ATF agents will be able to sort all that out once you start sifting through the debris."

There were a few questions from McCain, Burns, and the ATF. The older of the ATF agents asked Andy, "Did you challenge them before you started shooting? Did you even try to arrest them?"

Scotty's nostrils flared and his eyes immediately narrowed. He began thinking of all the ways he could express the stupidity of that question without losing his job. Before he could reply, however, FBI agent Burns stepped in front of him and Andy and spoke to the ATF man.

"These two officers just took out almost an entire terrorist cell. That's close to twenty suicide bombers who aren't going to be blowing themselves up in our malls, churches, schools, or anywhere else. We'll do our investigation and they'll give us statements but I don't want to hear any more questions like that until we start doing our interviews. There's no telling how many lives these CDC agents saved today."

Standing behind Burns, Smith smiled at the ATF agent. "Yeah, what he said."

The other ATF agent spoke up. "I'm just curious to know how you knew this place was even here? Where did you get your intelligence?"

McCain answered that question. "We can't tell you that. Sorry. What we will say is that Agents Fleming and Smith were following up on a lead that turned out to be a good one. When they realized that they were training and arming suicide bombers here, they were forced to engage them to save the lives of innocent people.

"Agents Fleming and Smith caught them in the act of putting suicide vests on twenty young Middle Eastern males. At great risk to their own lives, and while being shot at by one of the terrorists, they engaged these suicide bombers, killing most of them. That will be how the story reads."

Burns looked at Chuck, almost spoke, and then just nodded his head. He had other agents, currently en route to the site, who would lead this investigation, along with input from these ATF fellows, and yet McCain had just told him how the report was going to read. And, Burns realized he was right. That was exactly what the report would say.

From what he had seen and heard, Chuck was an excellent cop and tactical leader. After Rebecca Johnson's murder and McCain's subsequent promotion, Burns wasn't sure if the big man was up to running the Atlanta office of the CDC Enforcement Unit. Thomas had felt that the former street cop did not have the political know-how to understand the way things ran in a large government institution like the CDC. The more he was around McCain, though, the more he realized just how intelligent and savvy he really was.

Chuck looked back at Andy. "How many do you think escaped?"

"It's hard to say. There were twenty bombers and two older guys who were helping them suit up. We probably shot ten outright before things starting blowing up. A white mini-van and a black compact car got away. Scotty and I both think two or three bombers and one of the older guys slipped out on us."

"It was kind of a no-win situation," said Chuck, shrugging. "If you'd done nothing, all twenty-two terrorists would have gotten away. Another question: did any of the dead guys turn into zombies?"

Scotty shook his head. "No, but we were making head shots and after the explosions, there wasn't much left to reanimate."

McCain looked as if he was thinking about how much he should say. He decided to share it all and looked at the other federal agents.

"The reason I was asking about zombies is that one of our teams is in the DC area tracking one of the tangos from the UGA attack. They hit a house early this morning and got into a shoot out. They arrested the UGA terrorist and killed two others. One of them happened to be a really bad guy. He was a professional bomb maker who had killed a lot of Americans in Iraq.

"He's dead now but at the house they found radioactive materials and a liquid that I'm almost positive is going to be the zombie virus. It looked like he'd been turning out some suicide vests of his own. Small dirty bombs laced with the zombie virus. Oh, and he was making car bombs and doing the same thing with them."

Agent Burns and the ATF agents all looked pale. This was news to them and they questioned what else they hadn't heard. Burns wondered again about Chuck McCain. He had intelligence and sources that the FBI did not. There was much more to him than met the eye.

"I'm sure by now our guys up in DC have notified the ATF to come and process the scene and the FBI has been there helping, as well. As we get our forensics people working on this mess," he motioned with his hand towards the scene behind them, "let's check closely to see if we can find any traces of radioactive material or the zombie virus."

Clean Up Crew supervisor, Nancy Long, had already started walking the scene and making notes on a clipboard. She had a camera around her neck and was snapping photo after photo of the carnage. Both of the Clean Up Crews were on their way to the location, along with a team from the FBI and the ATF. It was going to be a long day.

Chapter Six

East Coast Destruction

37,000 feet, Friday, 1430 hours

Luis García was glad to be back at work. His ankle still hurt but as a Brazilian Jiu-Jitsu black belt and instructor, he had a high tolerance for pain. He glanced at Chuck sitting across the small aisle from him in the Lear jet, tapping away on his laptop.

Luis knew that he and Rebecca had loved each other, no matter how much they had downplayed it. He couldn't imagine how horrible it must have been for McCain to watch her die in front of his eyes. Right after they had taken off, he had watched Chuck staring out the window, a pained expression on his face.

Rebecca Johnson had been a friend, as well as a boss, and she had always treated Luis well. Johnson had really given him a fresh start and he would always be grateful to her for that. His law enforcement career had begun as a City of Miami police officer. The son of Cuban immigrants, García worked hard to make his parents proud.

He had worked as a bouncer at a few of the nicer Cuban clubs but always aspired to make a difference with his life. Miami police officers often worked part-time jobs as security at these establishments and Luis became friends with several. They had encouraged him to apply to join the police department.

After twelve years as a local police officer, Luis began thinking about going federal. The only agency that would even talk to him, since he didn't have a college degree, was the Secret Service. He found out later they were being told that they had to hire more minorities. When García heard that, he was angry. He didn't want to be anyone's token anything.

His friend and fellow agent, Tu Trang, had calmed him down and given him some fresh perspective.

"Don't worry about why they hired you, Luis. You're here now and doing a great job. Make them respect you because of who you are and for your work ethic."

When he had first started with the Secret Service he realized it was not what he had envisioned. Because of his law enforcement background, his first assignment was as an investigative agent. The Secret Service has jurisdiction over counterfeit money, cyber-crimes, and many other forms of financial fraud.

These investigators were also called upon to follow up on threats made towards the President, Vice-President, and other protectees. Usually, these were mentally unbalanced people who had not thought through the results of sending a threatening letter or email to the White House. The last thing that they expected was Secret Service Special Agent García and his partner knocking on their door. In most cases, it was obvious that these people were not a legitimate threat and knowing they were now on the Secret Service's radar was enough to keep them walking the straight and narrow.

After three years as an investigator, Luis applied to get on a protection detail. His dream was to get on the counter assault team but he knew he had to pay his dues. He was assigned to protect an elderly former President. It wasn't exciting work but the aging man and the former First Lady were beautiful people and treated the protective detail like members of their family.

When he was finally approved to try out for the counter assault team, García was thrilled. Even though he was one of the older guys in his group at thirty-eight, his lifetime regimen of martial arts training and fitness kept him in the front of the pack. Being older also allowed him to handle the mental games and the stress that the instructors put on the applicants.

One hundred and ten men started the six-week CAT course. At the end, only twenty-two were left. The instructors seemed surprised that the, "little, old, Hispanic guy" had made it. Not only had García passed the course, he was ranked number three in his class. After sweating thru the grueling application process, the real learning had started.

Luis was assigned to a team where he spent three more months training with his new teammates. The protective details in the Secret Service are designed to remove the President or other protectee out of a hostile environment as quickly as possible. Protection details are not trained to go after the threat unless it is in close proximity to the person they are protecting.

The counter assault team, however, is trained to respond with overwhelming force to suppress and neutralize attackers. The CAT is also responsible for the logistics of Presidential trips. These agents arrive a week ahead of the President or Vice-President and coordinate all the security details with local and other federal law enforcement agencies.

After joining his team, García realized that unless they were on a mission, they were training. They practiced every possible scenario that they might encounter. The CAT agents also focused on their weapons skills, shooting hundreds of rounds every week.

When Luis' team was given an assignment, he was excited. This was what it was all about. His group was being sent to Amsterdam as an advance team for a Presidential visit as he made a European tour. The President and his entourage would be staying in a five star hotel and the CAT was sent to set up security arrangements.

During the day, the agents met with law enforcement officials to discuss and set up protective measures for the President's trip. They looked at each building the President would be visiting, marking entrances, exits, and possible safe rooms. Motorcade routes were planned in conjunction with the local police so that they could make sure the roads were clear and side streets were blocked.

In the evenings, after the day's work was done, however, Luis found out that his teammates drank and partied. He had never been much of a drinker, but he was the junior guy on his five-man team. Even though he was older than all but one of his fellow CAT agents, he was new to the unit. For the first two nights, García nursed a single beer while his friends drank themselves into a stupor and tried to pick up women in the hotel bar.

On the third night, after sitting with his teammates at the bar for an hour, Luis excused himself and went to the hotel fitness center. He worked out and stretched for an hour, showered, and went to bed. At 0330 hours, his phone rang. He answered it on the first ring, wide-awake.

"Hello?"

An accented voice said, "Are you with the American Secret Service detail?"

"Who is this?"

"I am sergeant with the Amsterdam Police. I need you to come down to the bar. Your friends are drunk and causing big problems."

"I'll be right down."

When he got off the elevator in the lobby, he could hear the yelling. Mike, his team leader, was poking a uniformed police officer in the chest and screaming profanities at him. Larry, a teammate, was handcuffed and sitting on the floor, staring at his feet. Luis' other two teammates were standing just behind Mike, looking like they were ready to start fighting the local police officers.

Three other Dutch police were staring apprehensively at the scene, not sure how to proceed. Two female waitresses were standing nearby, one of them crying. The other had her arm wrapped protectively around her friend's shoulders.

Mike yelled at the sergeant, "You need to take those handcuffs off of him right now and walk out of here and go back to writing parking tickets. You don't know who you're messing with."

Luis shook his head. This was not going to end well, he thought. He stepped in front of Mike, between him and the police officer. Mike's breath reeked of alcohol.

"I got this, Mike. Let me talk to the officers."

Even though Luis was the junior man, Mike had already come to like and respect him. He knew Luis had years of law enforcement experience and was cool under pressure.

Mike took a step backwards, took a deep breath, and nodded. García turned back to the Dutch officers, smiling in an effort to diffuse the situation.

"I'm sorry for all of this, officers. What can we do to resolve it?"

The sergeant, who had been getting poked in the chest, motioned for Luis to step away from the group. The other three Dutch officers watched Larry and his cohorts warily.

"Your friends are very drunk and caused a bad situation," the sergeant explained.

"I'm really sorry about that. I tried to keep an eye on them but then I went to bed. I'm not much of a drinker," Luis shrugged. "What did Larry do? He's the one you have handcuffed."

The sergeant sighed. "He tried to kiss that girl who is crying. He asked her to go to his room but she said no and he grabbed her and put his hands all over her. Hotel security called us.

"When we got here, Larry was passed out at the table. The girl pointed him out and told us what he did so we handcuffed him. The other men acted like they wanted to fight us."

No, this is not going to end well, Luis told himself again.

"Okay, are you going to arrest him? I was a City of Miami cop before I went to work for the Secret Service. I understand you have a job to do, but I'll need to know what to tell my superiors."

"You seemed to have calmed your other friends down," the officer observed. "Maybe, I can talk to the girl and see if she will not prosecute? I can try and if you will give me your word that this will not happen again, I will go back to 'writing parking tickets' as your friend said."

"Hey, I know you guys do a lot more than that and we need to stay friends. Mike's just had a little bit too much to drink and didn't really mean that. We need your department's help when our President visits in a few days. Why don't you talk to her and I'll talk to my guys and make sure they aren't going to cause any more problems?"

In the end, the waitress declined to prosecute Larry but the hotel management forbade them from entering the bar or hotel restaurant during the rest of their stay. The Amsterdam police sergeant documented the incident and turned the report in at the end of his shift. When the Chief Commissioner of the district police in Amsterdam reviewed the report the next day, he picked up the phone and called the American Embassy to lodge a formal complaint.

Luis was hoping the incident was over and that his teammates would learn from their close call with the local authorities. Later that day, however, Mike received a call from their Supervisory Special Agent in Washington, D.C., ordering them home immediately. Another CAT would be arriving within a few hours to take their place.

All of the men were interviewed by internal affairs when they returned to Washington. Within a week of the incident, the investigation was complete. Garcia's four teammates were transferred out of CAT to the Uniformed Division. This was as far down as they could be demoted without being fired. Larry and Mike were given two-week suspensions and the other two were suspended for one week.

The Supervisory Special Agent met with Luis last and told him that he, too, was being transferred out of CAT but not being suspended.

"I'm sorry, García. Your teammates all said you weren't involved and actually got things calmed down without Larry, or anyone else, getting arrested."

"So, why am I being kicked out of CAT?" Luis asked,

incredulously.

"That was the Deputy Director's call. He said you should have been watching over your friends and kept this from happening."

Luis opened his mouth to protest, but the supervisory agent cut him off with a wave of his hand.

"It's done, Luis. There's no arguing with the man. He wants to be able to say that all of the agents have been disciplined and reassigned.

"What I will do, though, is give you your pick of assignments. If you want to go back to protection, there is an opening on the VP's detail. That's a good slot. If you want to do something else, I'll make it happen."

García had a lot of vacation time built up and asked for a week off to think about his options. He knew he would probably take the slot on the Vice-President's detail. That was a prestigious position and would put him in line for the Presidential detail at some point. If he performed well, maybe he could get back on the counter assault team, he thought.

Luis had also considered taking a corporate security job. He had done quite a bit of bodyguard work over the years when he had been a local cop and as a federal cop. When a client needed him, he would take vacation for the week or two that the particular job required.

All his training and traveling with the Secret Service had taken a toll on his jiu-jitsu training. A week of good, hard rolling was what he needed to clear his head. When he was in town in DC, he always went to his Brazilian friend's school to train and sometimes teach.

The following Tuesday night, a very attractive, tall, blonde woman was waiting for him at the martial arts school, wearing a pink gi. He noted her purple belt and caught himself staring at her. Luis had been divorced twice. His first wife left him when he became a police officer in Miami. His second wife divorced him when he went to work for the Secret Service. Now, he figured he would be single for life.

“Hi, are you Luis García? I’m Rebecca Johnson. I was hoping to get a private lesson with you tonight if you can work me in. I called ahead and got the price. I’ve been a little sporadic in my training and I was thinking that private instruction might be the way to go.”

“For sure,” Luis said, a little too eagerly. “Private instruction is the best way to progress quickly. I see you’ve gotten your purple belt, so you’re at an advanced level. With private lessons, if you train hard, you could probably earn your black belt in two years.”

Her eyes lit up. “Really? That’d be great.”

García took Johnson through a warm-up, stretching, and then an intermediate workout. She was technically solid, just a little rusty. As the professional instructor that he was, he had forgotten for a moment how attractive she was and was thinking of how he could help her improve in her jiu-jitsu.

After an hour of rolling and working intermediate and some advanced techniques, Luis and Rebecca sat with their backs against the wall, cooling down, and sipping water. There were no other students around them. Luis was about to ask her about herself. He wanted to know a little more about this beautiful woman sitting beside him.

Without making eye contact, Rebecca spoke first. “I’m sorry about what happened to you in Amsterdam.”

Luis’s head shot around. “What did you say?” he demanded.

“I said, ‘I’m sorry about what happened to you in Amsterdam.’ You got shafted.”

No one knew about that incident outside of the upper levels of the Secret Service. It had not hit the news yet, thankfully. She must be a reporter, he quickly surmised.

García angrily started to push himself to his feet. “No comment. Class is over.”

“Luis, please sit down. I work for another branch of the government and I have a job offer for you. I promise that’s all. Just listen to what I have to say. If you aren’t interested, no problem. I’ll still be back Thursday for my next lesson."

He eyed her suspiciously but sat back down. "You want to offer me a job? What kind of job?"

For the next twenty minutes, Rebecca told him about the CDC's new federal law enforcement agency that the President had created by Executive Order. When she was done, he stared at her without saying anything. Was this what he was looking for? Who was he fooling? Of course it was.

Even if he took the position on the VP's detail, he was always going to be that agent who got kicked off the counter assault team for partying in Amsterdam. The Secret Service would never put him back on CAT. Once blackballed, always blackballed. This was the chance for a fresh start, and to be on the cutting edge of the war on terrorism was a great opportunity for him to really make a difference.

"Why the charade? Why not just call me?" he asked.

Rebecca laughed. "This was no charade. I love jiu-jitsu and heard that you're a pretty good instructor. I figured I'd multi-task. Get some training in and try to recruit you."

García shook his head. Wow, she has a beautiful smile, he realized.

"How did you hear about me? I didn't realize the CDC had such good intel and that thing in Amsterdam is not public knowledge."

She laughed again. "Oh, you'd be surprised at how good our intel is."

When Rebecca came for her Thursday night lesson, Luis told her that he would take the job.

New York, Washington, D. C., and Atlanta, Friday, 1515 hours

Ali drove the non-descript, silver Nissan Sentra to Brooklyn, New York, arriving just before midnight on Wednesday. Usama had programmed the location of a parking garage into the car's built-in

GPS unit. He had also given Ali the address for a small hotel two blocks from the garage, run by a sympathetic Muslim, who simply handed Ali a key when he mentioned Usama's name.

The Pakistani brought the young martyr his meals because Usama had made it clear he was not to leave his room for any reason until his mission. On Thursday, Ali studied the street and subway maps that he had been given. He also read his Quran and prayed.

On Friday morning he repeated the process. After lunch, he bathed, purifying himself with the ritual washing before strapping the white explosive vest around his body. His traditional long shirt went on next, concealing the deadly device.

The detonator went into his right front pocket. Usama had rigged it with a metal cotter pin to act as a safety. It would not go off until the suicide bomber removed the pin and then squeezed the handles together. Ali slipped the Quran into his pants pocket and walked out of the room, leaving his few possessions behind.

When he went to retrieve the car, the Muslim attendant did not charge him for parking, giving Ali a knowing nod. The next destination that Usama had programmed into the GPS was the 9/11 Memorial. As Ali drove across the Brooklyn Bridge into Manhattan, he felt his sense of anticipation rising.

The first phase of his orders were simply to park as close as he could to the memorial, lock the car, and then walk away to the nearest subway station. The challenge was that there were very few places to park. The bomb in the trunk was set to go off at 1700 hours. Ali needed to make sure the police did not have an opportunity to tow the car away to their impound lot before it exploded.

He had allotted himself plenty of time and drove around for over an hour, looking for the best place to park the car bomb. He finally decided on abandoning the vehicle behind St. Paul's Chapel of Trinity Church on Church Street. It was only a block from the 9/11 Memorial, the streets were packed with infidels, and the blast should do substantial damage to the church. The St. Peter Roman Catholic

Church was also nearby and would be affected as well.

Ali circled the block several times, hoping a parking space would open up. He finally saw an opening in front of the large post office building at Church Street and Vesey Street. The car bomb was now between the two churches, a block from the 9/11 Memorial, in a densely populated area. Praise Allah, he thought.

As he parked, he activated the emergency flashers on the car and put the handwritten note that Usama had given him on the dashboard where it could be seen from the outside. "Car trouble. Coming back with tow truck. Sorry."

He locked the doors, pocketed the keys, and started walking. The Chambers Street subway station was less than half a block away. A voice stopped him.

"You can't park there. That space is for loading and unloading only."

Ali glanced over. The words came from a young black man who was pointing at him. He did not have a uniform on and Ali did not know if he should stop and talk to him or not. There was no sign prohibiting parking there but Ali did not understand American laws.

"I'm very sorry but my car is broken. I have to go call my friend to come and look at it."

"Well, you're going to have to pay me to watch it while you go call him."

"I…I don't have any money with me. I will bring some back and give to you." He rushed across the street towards the subway station.

"I'll be waiting right here," the voice called after him, the tone threatening.

Ali glanced at his watch. 1635 hours, 4:35 in the afternoon. You wait there, my friend, he thought. Yes. You wait there for me. He entered the subway station and was soon on the northbound train.

Since his target was in America's capital, Hassan did not have to travel very far and had the most time on his hands. His GPS sent him to another safe house in the northern part of Washington, D.C., near the George Washington University. An Iranian-born lecturer in Islamic Studies would house him for two days and give him a place to park his car.

They spent hours in the evening discussing the Quran and the need to destroy the Great Satan, America, and their lapdog, Israel. Both agreed that after the United States was destroyed, Israel would be an easy target. Of course, after Iran's recent devastation at the hands of the infidel American military, it would require other nations uniting against the Zionists.

On Friday, Hassan washed and purified himself. He read his Quran and performed his prayers. His new Iranian friend did not have to teach on Fridays and stayed home, preparing him a special meal and encouraging him in his mission. Hassan had not shared any details with the professor but he seemed to understand that his houseguest would not be returning.

At 1500 hours Hassan dressed, carefully put the explosive vest on, told his friend goodbye, and began driving towards the heart of the city. The GPS in Hassan's black Ford Focus took him towards some of America's most sacred landmarks.

Ramzi had never seen so much traffic in his life. He was glad that he had followed Usama's instructions to the letter and started for his target at 1500 hours. By allotting him two hours to reach the target, Usama assured him he would be there with plenty of time to park the car and to make his escape to another part of the city. The closer Ramzi got to Atlanta, though, he was not sure that he had left early enough.

As the terrorist drove his explosive-laden Toyota Corolla south on Interstate 85 into Atlanta, he felt his stress and anxiety rising. An overturned tractor-trailer blocked the middle two lanes, creating a nightmare for commuters. He was losing time.

The clock on the dashboard read 4:05pm. The GPS unit indicated he should be at his target by 4:40pm, but with this accident, he was not so sure. Usama had set the timer on the large bomb in the trunk for detonation at 5:00pm.

He had driven all night on Wednesday, arriving at 0400 hours on Thursday morning. The elderly Muslim cleric was waiting for him and raised his garage door so that Ramzi could pull inside. A guest bedroom had been prepared and the future martyr was soon asleep.

When Ramzi had risen, food was waiting on him. The imam did not say much to the young man, leaving him to himself. He studied the maps that master-bomber Usama had provided, paying special attention to the different approaches towards his target. On Friday, however, the cleric read the Quran with him after he had bathed. They prayed together, had lunch, and then it was time for Ramzi to leave.

The suicide vest was uncomfortable and he felt the sweat pooling beneath it. Not much longer, he thought. Traffic finally began to move after he got past the wrecked eighteen-wheeler. After a few miles, however, Ramzi was forced to slow again because of a three-car accident blocking the two left lanes. 4:36pm. Now the GPS was showing an arrival at 4:55pm.

Ramzi did not know Atlanta. He had studied the maps but now he suddenly felt trapped, surrounded by stopped cars. Interstate 85 and Interstate 75 merged a half mile in front of him, continuing south through the city.

With so many lanes, traffic was still stop and go. 4:45pm. Estimated arrival time now was 5:05pm. He wasn't going to make it. Even with the air conditioning turned on high, the sweat dripped off of the terrorist's face.

The primary target for his car bomb was Centennial Olympic Park in the heart of the city. As the two interstates merged, Ramzi could see even more gridlock moving deeper into Atlanta. He knew he was going to have to abandon the car but if he just walked away from it on the highway, there was no place for him to escape to. He was not afraid to die but he did want to complete his mission.

In front of him, Ramzi saw the exit ramp leading off the interstate to 17th Street. He maneuvered the car over, almost striking a work van in the lane next to him, as he drove onto the exit ramp. The van's driver, a large black man, honked the horn and screamed profanities at Ramzi. 4:50pm. A long line of cars were stopped in front of him on the exit ramp. The traffic signal ahead where the ramp intersected with 17th Street helped Ramzi to decide his course of action.

A large, electronic sign indicated that the Atlantic Station Mall was on his right, visible from where he was sitting. This was not his primary target but it would have to do. A tall office building loomed in front of him. The blast here would throw shrapnel at the mall and it's surrounding buildings. The packed exit ramp would also assure that many vehicles were destroyed and their occupants killed or even worse.

Horns blared again as Ramzi pulled onto the narrow shoulder of the off-ramp. He activated his emergency flashers, exited the Toyota, locked the doors and started running. He had to get as far away as he could before the bomb went off. 4:52pm.

Atlanta police officer Tracy Sparks exited onto the ramp for 17th Street, as well. She was responding to a call of a car accident in the parking lot at Atlantic Station. A witness had just recontacted the police and said that the two female drivers were now engaged in a fight. The caller said they were punching each other and trying to rip each other's hair out. Job security, Sparks thought.

In front of her, a few cars up, Sparks saw a Middle Eastern-looking man hurriedly exit a Toyota Corolla and start running. That doesn't look right, she thought. He's running away from that car like it is about to blow up or something. It must be stolen, she concluded.

Tracy turned on her blue strobe lights and used her horn and siren to get around the stopped traffic and catch up to him. The exit ramp was full of stopped vehicles but the flashing blue lights and the siren motivated people to move to the right just enough so that Sparks could maneuver through. The fleeing man was almost to the top of the ramp, over a hundred yards from where he had left his vehicle, and had not slowed his pace yet. Officer Sparks pulled up behind the runner and stopped her cruiser, turning the police car slightly to the left to keep the engine block between her and the suspicious man.

The siren had startled Ramzi and he almost fell down as he glanced over his shoulder and saw the police car with its blue strobe lights flashing. Without thinking, he reached for the pistol tucked into the front of his pants.

A female voice challenged him. “Police officer! Stop! Get your hands up where I can see them! Now!”

Sparks was standing behind her open driver’s door and she saw the man’s hand reach for his midsection. Tracy drew her pistol without any conscious thought. She was less than ten yards from the man, her gun held in a solid two-handed grip.

Tracy challenged him again. “Put your hands up!”

Motorists watched the drama unfold in the heavy rush hour commute. The traffic on the exit ramp was still stopped because of the red light at 17th Street where they would all have to turn right or left. A few people had their cellphones out and began to video the scene of the police officer pointing her pistol at the Middle Eastern man, hoping to see something newsworthy. Three male motorists who were stopped behind the Atlanta officer got out of their cars to get a better look at what was transpiring, holding their phones up to get the best footage.

The man wearing traditional Muslim clothing quickly spun around with a Makarov pistol in his hand, firing at the infidel woman who had challenged him. Officer Sparks pointed her pistol at him as he turned but she had to be sure that the man was an actual threat and not just holding a cellphone. She saw fire come out of the muzzle of the suspect’s gun, the round impacting the grill of the police car.

Tracy fired back, her first 9mm round catching him in the lower abdomen. The suspect’s second shot struck the windshield next to the officer’s face. Sparks kept firing, her second round missing, hitting the concrete wall on the side of the ramp. Her third shot, however, caught Ramzi center-mass, piercing his heart.

The police officer's bullet also triggered the explosive vest the terrorist was wearing. Usama had packed the vest to create maximum damage. Nails, screws, and ball bearings were used as shrapnel. The bomb maker had attached a thick glass container of radioactive waste and another of the zombie virus into both the front and back panels of the suicide garment.

The explosion shattered the glass containers, blowing the bio-terror virus outward in multiple directions, along with the nuclear materials. Shrapnel ripped through the air, shattering car windows and ripping people apart. Officer Tracy Sparks was less than thirty feet from the suspect and was blown backwards by the concussion. Several pieces of shrapnel were stopped by her ballistic vest, but a ball bearing punched through her forehead, killing her instantly.

The cars closest to Ramzi took the brunt of his explosion but the blast radius threw shrapnel and deadly materials over a hundred feet. The three men taking video were knocked to the ground and almost instantly became infected with the zombie virus. Within minutes, they had reanimated and were on their feet looking for victims.

The initial explosion killed nineteen motorists and wounded another forty-seven on the exit ramp. Shrapnel was blown through the large glass windows of several floors of the Wells Fargo building less than a hundred feet off of the interstate, wounding twenty-six people and infecting them with the zombie virus, now mixed with radioactive waste. Within minutes, the wounded people in the office building had succumbed to the virus as their co-workers tried to help them. Those friends and co-workers who tried to be of assistance were the first to get bitten when the bio-terror compound turned those who were bleeding out into death machines.

Within a minute of the detonation of the suicide bomber, two cars near the initial blast erupted as their fuel tanks ignited. A Toyota 4 Runner's gas tank exploded and the SUV flew into the air, landing on the Volvo wagon that was stopped next to it. A Honda Civic also blew up, sending the small car onto its side. The fireball from the secondary explosions rose over the scene as another six people died.

Motorists who were further down the exit ramp panicked and left their cars to run to safety. The three first zombies who had been out shooting video of the police officer's encounter with the terrorist chased down three more victims and killed them. Others who had been hit by poisoned shrapnel in their vehicles were struggling to get free of their seat belts. The concussion knocked open the doors of several older cars and new zombies stumbled out.

The radioactive waste combined with the zombie virus was giving some of the infected almost supernatural strength. Some of those held captive by their seatbelt were able to rip them off and then force their way out of their vehicles to begin their search for new victims.

When a human being is exposed to high doses of radioactive materials, the potential for serious health issues including death or cancer is greatly increased. For a human who was dead, however, the effects were completely different. The radioactive materials, working in conjunction with the bio-terror virus produced a change in the victim's DNA that enhanced their natural strength, speed, and power.

The ramp was now completely blocked and drivers further away from the blast continued to attempt their escape by abandoning their cars and fleeing on foot. People ran in both directions looking for an exit. Those who had been infected by the zombie virus did not have to look far for their next victims.

Since Ramzi had exploded near the top of the ramp, traffic on 17th Street was also affected. Eight motorists died and twenty-one were wounded near the bridge leading back over the interstate. Within minutes dozens more infected people climbed out of their damaged vehicles. Cars and SUVs slammed into each other in their haste to get away. The 17th Street Bridge over I-85 and the exit ramp were both completely blocked. The time was 4:59pm.

CDC Enforcement Office, Washington, D.C., 1630 hours

The new acting Supervisor for the Washington office of the CDC Enforcement Unit, Tu Trang, and new acting team leader, Jason Lewis, picked Chuck and Luis up from the Ronald Reagan Washington National Airport. They drove them back to their office, where all the CDC officers had assembled to be interviewed by the FBI and go through a thorough debriefing session. The shooting scene in Springfield was still being processed with Fairfax County police officers providing security.

When they arrived, the interviews with the FBI were wrapping up and Chuck congratulated his guys from Atlanta on a successful operation. McCain saw Jimmy Jones and put an arm around his shoulder.

"How you feeling, Marine?"

"Nothing to it, Chuck. I went to the hospital this morning and the doc said he hadn't seen such a fine specimen of manhood in a long time. I've got a bruised sternum and some damage to the cartilage on the right side of my rib cage but nothing's broken. The AK bullet I took to the vest in Iraq was worse. You know us Marines are hard to kill."

Jimmy had been a rifle platoon leader in the Marine Corps and had two combat tours in Iraq. The first had been as a lieutenant, the second as a captain. Jones had left the Marines after eight years of service to be with his mother when she was diagnosed with terminal cancer. After she had succumbed to the disease a year later he had gone to work for the Alabama State Patrol. After a very successful five years as a trooper, he had been recruited to work for the new CDC Enforcement Unit.

"Well, a blast of OO buck to the chest is nothing to sneeze at," said Chuck, with a smile, "but you'll be feeling it every time you sneeze for a while."

After meeting all the DC agents, McCain asked Marshall,

Walker, and Trang if they could talk privately. Tu led them into Bob Murray's former office, soon to be his own. Eddie and the two DC supervisors took McCain through the entire scenario of locating and capturing Hill and the subsequent shootout. Trang also filled him in about the unfortunate arrest of Bob Murray.

"And, we just heard back from the FBI lab before you got here," said Jay. "Those containers of clear liquid in that fridge at the terrorist's house were positive for the zombie virus. They were loading up car bombs and suicide vests with radioactive materials and the virus."

Chuck sighed. "That's what I figured. Let me tell you what some of our other guys got into today."

He recounted Fleming's and Smith's adventures in the North Georgia foothills. The three men were surprised at this turn of events and sensed that these were not isolated incidents.

"How many of these terrorist cells are out there?" Jay asked rhetorically.

"Who knows?" answered McCain. "Thankfully, Andy and Scotty were able to eliminate most of the terrorists, but two or three got away. I'm sure we'll be hearing from them soon. The preliminary report from forensics is that there were no traces of the virus or nuclear waste in the debris at that scene in North Georgia."

"Yeah, who would've thought we'd look forward to the day of just a normal suicide bomber armed with conventional explosives?" asked Eddie.

There were nods and grunts of assent to Marshall's observation.

"Chuck, do you have any idea who those dudes were who took Hill? Who they worked for or where they might have been headed?" asked Tu. "I mean we had him under arrest and they just came and whisked him away.

"Jay knew one of them and I knew the other. The guy that was driving the van was a Seal Team Sixer who went to work for the CIA. The one that I knew was Army SF and got recruited by Delta. That was the last I heard of him."

McCain glanced at Marshall, wondering what he had told them when Terrell Hill had taken away. Eddie's face was impassive. He merely raised an eyebrow towards Chuck.

Without answering Trang's question, McCain reached into his bag and pulled out two disclosure forms. He handed one to each of the DC CDC officers.

"You guys have seen these before. Sign them and I'll enlighten you."

Chuck didn't know if he was authorized to brief Walker and Trang on the CIA's involvement in the CDC Enforcement Unit or not, and sometimes, it was just easier to ask for forgiveness than permission. Both men, however, had extensive special operations experience and had worked with the CIA in the Middle East. These guys were sharp and it would be better for them to have accurate information about what was going on.

Jay and Tu merely nodded and grunted as Chuck explained the CIA's ongoing operation on American soil to combat the Muslim terrorists. When he finished, Jay just shrugged.

"Pretty slick. That explains why the intel we get is so good and why we don't have a problem with funding. The Agency has pretty deep pockets. And I really like the idea of Terrell Hill in the hands of one of their special interrogation teams."

"I know all of your guys are trustworthy but you can't tell them any of this," said McCain. "Loose lips sink ships and all that stuff. We just can't take a chance on a leak that could hit the media and get us shut down."

At that moment, all of their phones began to vibrate with incoming texts. McCain's also kept vibrating with an incoming call. Chuck looked at his screen and realized Shaun Taylor, Admiral William's Assistant, was calling. He noted the time. 1710 hours.

New York City, Friday, 1715 hours

In Manhattan, the Nissan Sentra exploded, killing one hundred and twenty-seven people. Most of these were pedestrians, construction workers at the site adjacent to the post office building where the car bomb had been parked, or were in passing vehicles. Others were killed inside nearby buildings from the force of the blast and the incoming shrapnel. The powerful car bomb also set off the fuel tanks of six nearby cars, creating devastating secondary explosions.

Windows were blown out of buildings three blocks away, with nails, screws, and ball bearings claiming victims hundreds of feet away. Those closest to the explosion were obliterated. Victims further back were killed or wounded and infected with the mixture of nuclear waste and the zombie virus.

Overturned cars and trucks blocked the intersection of Church Street and Vesey Street. Within minutes, victims became predators as the bio-terror chemical did its work. Some of the infected were grotesquely wounded but still began hunting for fresh meat to feed on.

A bloody woman with one arm blown off at the shoulder shuffled north on Church Street, away from the devastation. A man who was missing both of his arms followed her. Before long, growling figures were moving in both directions through the fire, smoke, and carnage. A teenage boy, who had lost his legs in the blast and bled to death, was now dragging his torso up the sidewalk, growling and snapping his mouth open and closed.

Zombies who were still inside their vehicles began forcing their way out. The mixture of nuclear materials and the virus was having an interesting effect on the newly reanimated. One businessman who had been struck and killed by shrapnel was trapped inside his car a half block away.

When the radioactive version of the virus took effect, he was able to kick open the passenger door, almost ripping it from the car. The infected man, wearing an expensive suit and tie, smelled a survivor in the white Audi behind him. The German car was heavily damaged but the zombie easily forced open the jammed door and pulled a screaming woman into the street where he held her down and ripped out her jugular with his teeth.

Sirens drew closer as police and fire units responded to 911 calls. The first fire truck pulled up next to the woman with one arm. She had walked almost a block, not finding a victim yet. As the firemen jumped off their truck to help her, she used her one hand to grab the closest first responder and, with almost supernatural strength, pull his face to her mouth. The fireman screamed in pain and tried to push the crazy woman away. Her teeth sunk into his cheek and then ripped at his neck.

One of his companions attempted pull the bloody female attacker off his friend. The zombie turned on the second fireman, biting his forearm. The bite didn't penetrate his heavy protective jacket, but the infected woman threw him to the ground and straddled him, sinking her teeth into his Adam's apple.

As the third fireman grabbed the back of the zombie's jacket and tried to pull her off, the infected man who was missing both arms slammed into him, biting at his back. His jacket also protected the fireman, but the attacking woman quickly turned on him and together, the two zombies knocked him down and began to chew on his face and throat.

The first NYPD cruiser skidded to a stop behind the fire truck and the two officers jumped out, surveying the carnage all around them. Smoke hung in the air and burning cars filled the street for almost a block. Incredulous, they watched as a one-armed, bloodied woman and crazed man without any arms were assaulting some of their FDNY counterparts.

The two officers rushed to the aide of their fire department brethren. As they got to where the struggle was taking place they both froze at what they saw. Two bloody firemen were struggling to get to their feet. The injured woman and man turned towards their newest victims, growling and snapping their teeth together in anticipation. A growl suddenly came from the third prone fireman and he clambered to his feet, as well.

Both police officers realized at the same time that New York had been infected again. They drew their pistols and started backing towards their cruiser, thirty feet away. The woman leapt towards the police, her legs stronger than they had been in life. She landed in front of the closest policeman and grabbed for his neck. He fired a single shot under her chin, the 9mm round penetrating her brain and sending her to the pavement.

The second officer managed to get to the police car and was standing behind the open passenger door. He raised his pistol and sighted in on the armless man's forehead, dropping him instantly and permanently. The first officer ran and dove into the driver's seat. His partner got in and they locked the doors. The officer in the passenger seat called the dispatcher and tried to give a status update.

The three infected firemen reached the police car, however, and without hesitation punched through the passenger window, reached in, and dragged the officer out. The driver tried to grab his friend's gun belt to keep him in the car but two of the zombie firemen were already ripping at the officer's flesh as he hung screaming, halfway out of the car.

The first officer never saw the third fireman smash through his window and snatch him out by the head. By this time, other newly infected people joined the firefighters as they ripped the police officers apart. The sound of sirens got closer as other emergency vehicles closed in on the scene.

Ali stood uncomfortably on the packed subway train as it started north. He felt that every infidel's eyes were on him and he knew that at any moment someone would shout an alarm. The sweat dripped off of him. The explosive vest was not made for comfort. On the plus side, if someone did try to apprehend him on the subway, he could easily activate the suicide garment and kill many of Allah's enemies.

He grasped the dangling strap with his left hand to hold him steady as the train sped along. His kept his right hand near his waistline where he could either reach for his pistol or the detonator in his pocket. Ali decided he would try and use the pistol first if he was detected. To set off the vest, he would need to take the detonator out of his pocket, remove the safety pin, and then squeeze the two handles together.

This was New York, however, and no one paid any attention to the sweaty Muslim man wearing traditional Islamic clothing. New Yorkers saw these everyday and Ali had not done anything to draw attention to himself. In ten minutes, he was climbing the steps and exiting at the City Hall metro station.

He glanced at the map that Usama had provided for him, checked his surroundings, and then hurried down City Hall Park Path. Ali checked his watch. 1655 hours. Perfect. It would take him ten or fifteen minutes to reach his last target. By that time, the car bomb would have detonated with police and fire personnel rushing to the scene. 1 Police Plaza Path, NYPD Headquarters would soon feel the wrath of Allah.

Washington, D.C., Friday, 1720 hours

The nation's capital was just starting to get back to normal. Most of the zombies from previous attacks had been eliminated. The local police, alongside the CDC officers, and the National Guard had been working hard on making the city safe again. The Guard troops had finally been recalled and the police were getting very few 911 calls about infected people. Tonight's busy rush hour was reminiscent of the way that life had been before the bio-terror weapon had been unleashed two months earlier.

Hassan had parked his car bomb in front of the Rayburn House office building on Independence Avenue. It is located behind the United States Capitol and housed the offices for the U.S. House of Representatives. He could not park his car within three hundred yards of the Capitol or within five hundred yards of the White House, but here, he was able to stop directly in front of the large structure. The unloading lane was only a hundred feet from the six large columns that marked the entrance.

He activated the emergency flashers, placed his note claiming car trouble on the dash, and left the vehicle, darting across the four lanes of Independence Avenue at 1646 hours. By this time, most congressmen and congresswomen had clocked out for the day. Many, representatives, however, were inside working late, meeting with constituents, discussing strategy with their teams, and a few having romantic encounters with one of their staff. Even if the explosion did not kill many of the elected officials, it would still slaughter hundreds of infidels as heavy traffic inched slowly by the building and the parked car bomb.

Once he had crossed the street, Hassan turned left and hurried down the sidewalk. His next target was five blocks in front of him. He walked as fast as he could without running to get clear of the blast zone. At 1658 hours, he arrived at the large building housing the Smithsonian National Air and Space Museum. Now, he just had to walk the length of the building, about a block, and turn right to get to the main entrance.

When the terrorist was halfway down the block, the car bomb exploded. Hassan felt the concussion hit him in the back and he started running towards the front entrance of the Air and Space Museum. Closing time was 1730 hours but people were already pouring out the doors to try and get a head start on the heavy DC traffic.

The detonation from the car bomb and then the secondary explosions of gas tanks going off made the throng of pedestrians pause outside the museum. Several hundred people stopped on the large museum entrance landing, wondering what the explosions meant. The sidewalks were packed as people hurried to their nearby apartments, to where they had parked their cars, or to the Metro entrance.

Hassan pulled the detonator out of his pocket with his right hand and snatched the cotter pin out with his left. The terrorist rushed to where the biggest groups of people were gathered, listening to the detonations from down the street. He glanced up and saw that he was directly in front of the museum, only seventy-five feet from the entrance.

Hassan paused momentarily and took a deep breath.

He yelled, "Allahu Akbar," and then squeezed the handles of the detonator together.

Nothing happened. The people closest to Hassan sensed something was amiss and began walking quickly away from him. He looked down at the detonator he was holding, squeezing it again.

This time, Hassan disappeared in a thunderclap of an explosion. Eighty-two people were killed instantly. The blast radius for the suicide vest was over a hundred feet but shrapnel was thrown much further than that. The toxic mixture of the zombie virus and the radioactive materials was flung outward in every direction.

Pedestrians and motorists driving down both 7th Street and Independence Avenue were affected. Some victims felt a sting as a particle of glass hit them, infecting them with the bio-terror chemical blend. Within minutes, people collapsed and died. After the virus spread through their systems, they were soon climbing to their feet and looking for fresh meat.

The explosion from the terrorist's vest also blasted out the front doors of the museum, wounding many inside. There were still several hundred people inside the Smithsonian but when the doors blew inward, people started screaming and rushing to get out of the building. Only a few of those escaping had been infected, but as they rushed outside, the new zombies fell on them and quickly killed over a hundred more people.

Chaos ensued as others, seeing what was happening, were madly scrambling back inside the museum with hungry zombies pursuing them. Many of those who had remained inside were knocked down and trampled as the crowd rushed back into the museum, with zombies right behind them. Many other survivors attempted to flee down the sidewalks, scattering as a larger group of infected gave chase.

When the car bomb exploded in front of the Rayburn House Office Building, over two hundred people were killed outright, many blown apart by the powerful blast. The four lanes of Independence Avenue were packed with traffic and over one hundred cars were damaged.

The fuel tanks of nineteen cars erupted in secondary explosions within a minute of the initial blast. Depending on how much gas was in their fuel tanks, some vehicles were blown into the air and others flipped over on top of the cars next to them. Vehicle debris and parts were sent flying in every direction as these fireballs shot into the sky.

The windows of the Rayburn House were blown inwards, with nails, screws, and ball bearings cutting down people inside and infecting them with the virus. Sixteen staffers, two congressman, two US Capitol police officers, and four reporters were killed in the lobby. As the debris settled, twenty-four new zombies got to their feet and started shuffling deeper into the building, looking for those who had been spared.

In front of the building, Independence Avenue was littered with burning cars, burning people, body parts, and other debris. The road was completely blocked. Nothing survived inside five hundred feet of the explosion. Usama's car device contained seven hundred and fifty pounds of explosives, shrapnel, zombie virus, and radioactive materials.

Even over two blocks away, people were struck by debris, shrapnel, and the nuclear bio-terror virus. Beyond three blocks, people began exiting their cars to get a better look at what was happening. They had all heard and felt the explosions and could see black smoke billowing into the air.

Emergency vehicles from several nearby fire stations responded to the 911 calls but were having a slow go of it. Even with flashing lights and sirens, there was no place for traffic to go to let the fire trucks, ambulances, and police cars get around them.

People from all walks of life abandoned their vehicles and began running towards the explosions to see if they could be of assistance. Infected people closer to the scene climbed out of their vehicles, attacking the Good Samaritans. When the first police and fire personnel finally managed to get to the Rayburn House, these brave men and women, who had pledged to serve the public, were all overwhelmed by these zombies. Within minutes, new Zs were spreading out in every direction, going deeper into the heart of the city.

Chapter Seven

Video Games or Reality?

The Wells Fargo Building, Atlanta, Friday, 1730 hours

Paul Kowalski sat against the wall with his arms wrapped around his knees, shaking uncontrollably in the small storage room filled with office supplies. Earlier, he had been looking forward to an exciting night of playing his new video game, "The Return of the Dead," a first-person shooter involving zombies. He had even laughed at himself.

What a loser I am, he'd thought. You're thirty-three years old, it's Friday night in the big city, and you're going home to kill zombies on the screen. Now, zombies or something like them were actually outside the door of his hiding place.

Paul was the supervisor of a team that provided IT support to several different businesses. His company, StartUp Solutions, provided a host of services for startups to midsize companies, who preferred to outsource at a reasonable price. StartUp Solutions also provided marketing and human resource support but Kowalski and his team only handled the internet technology part of the equation. It was a good job and he managed a great team of engineers and specialists.

As he was packing up his Mac Book Pro and getting ready to

head home for the weekend, Paul heard the initial explosion, even on the other side of the building. His company occupied half of the 18th floor of the Wells Fargo building at the corner of 17th Street and I-85. The front entrance to the large, modern skyscraper was on 17th Street. The IT offices were on the left side of the building, opposite of the interstate. That fact saved Paul's life.

Kowalski and two of his team members met in the hallway after hearing the loud boom and then the subsequent detonations. The marketing and HR support teams had their workspace and cubicles on the right side of the office building overlooking I-85, with fantastic views of the Atlanta skyline, of course. The IT crew got to enjoy a view of trendy Atlantic Station, an upscale outdoor mall near Turner Broadcasting and the urban Georgia Tech campus. Today, however, Paul was glad to be on the far side of the building.

When he and his two engineers approached the marketing and HR section, they could hear people crying out in pain as the street sounds and smell of smoke from outside carried in through the shattered glass. The blast had blown out several large plate glass windows right where eight employees, four men and four women from both sectors, had their cubicles. These eight people and several others had been hurt.

Paul took in the bloody scene in front of him but could not comprehend what had happened. What kind of car accident could have caused an explosion of that magnitude? he wondered. He walked over to the gaping hole where the windows had been and looked down.

Kowalski tried not to look at his bleeding co-workers. Heights did not bother him but blood did. He had always been squeamish when he saw blood and was known to faint whenever his doctor needed to draw some.

The scene below was like something out of a video game or an apocalyptic movie. Cars were on fire and a couple of them were on their sides. People were scurrying around and traffic was completely shutdown on the exit ramp and on 17th Street. Smoke made it difficult to see everything that was happening.

"Paul, can you get me some paper towels?"

Brian, one of his team members, was trying to staunch the blood flowing out of Terri, the cute brunette who helped clients with their social media presence. She was on the floor beside her desk, bleeding from several gaping wounds to her face and arm.

Kowalski glanced over at Terri and immediately became light-headed at the sight of so much blood. He realized the danger he was in standing close to the shattered window and forced himself to take a step back.

"Yeah, sure," he answered, trying to will himself not to pass out. "I'll be right back."

He rushed to the restrooms in the center of their office space to get the paper towels. Without warning, another, much more powerful, explosion shook the building and shattered the rest of the glass windows, spraying slivers through the air. Six additional employees were cut down by the flying glass and infected shrapnel from the massive car bomb.

Paul was knocked to the floor by the concussion, even inside the men's room. He climbed back to his feet and stood there for a moment, breathing hard and feeling his heart pounding inside of him. Grabbing a handful of paper towels, he rushed back out to see what else had happened.

The smoke from the street below swirled through the now completely open-air facility. Kowalski saw the fireball from the car bomb hanging hundreds of feet in the air. Additional bodies were scattered across the office floor after the last explosion.

When he returned to Terri's cubicle, he was surprised to find the petite girl straddling the balding, middle-aged man. She was biting his face, her teeth digging into his cheek, with strange growling sounds emanating from her throat. Paul felt his legs getting weak as he gazed at the gaping wound on the side of Brian's neck, his blood still pumping out of it onto the floor. The IT engineer wasn't moving. Was he dead? Paul wondered, feeling light-headed again.

A young black man, Paul couldn't remember his name, stood up from behind a desk ten feet to his right. Heyward, Kowalski remembered. Heyward with HR. That was how he remembered names.

Something was wrong with Heyward. His face was covered with blood and his sharply pressed button down shirt was stained red. He was making a funny noise. It almost sounded like he was growling, too.

Paul's eyes scanned the area, trying to take it all in and decide what he should do, when he noticed a pair of brown legs extending out from behind the desk Heyward was at. They began twitching and a young woman pulled herself up using the desk for help. Her throat had been ripped open and she was also covered in blood and gore. Her glazed eyes settled on Paul. Heyward was already walking his way. What was this? What do I do now? Kowalski dropped the paper towels on the floor and looked for a way out.

Someone was now moving to his left. Paul looked over and saw Mary growling and stumbling towards him. Her white slacks were bloody and both of her legs were injured, yet somehow she was shuffling in his direction.

Mary was like everyone's second mom. She made birthday cakes for people and brought in homemade muffins and cookies at least twice a week. That was part of the reason Paul was a bit on the chubby side. Oh my God, he thought, what's wrong with Mary?

Kowalski turned and ran. He needed to find a way out of this bizarre nightmare, get to somewhere safe, and call the police. Making his way quickly to the other side of the offices, he realized that it was too late. They were already there at the entrance, as well.

Four zombie-creatures were on top of Candi, the receptionist, loudly ripping her apart in their feeding frenzy. The crunching of bones and the sound of the creature's chewing sent a wave of nausea through Paul. He had always had a secret crush on Candi, but had also known that he had no chance with her. And now she was dead.

Paul was trapped. The infected surrounded him, causing him to nearly lose his mind with panic. Think, Paul, think, where can you go? He remembered passing the storage closet when he exited the men's room and rushed back down the short hallway. He dove inside the closet and locked the heavy wooden door. He was safe. For the moment.

CDC HQ, Washington, D.C., Friday, 1730 hours

The large television screen on the wall was tuned to FOX news. The station was cutting back and forth between New York, DC, and Atlanta. Large computer monitors were displaying a live feed from Department of Homeland Security drones flying over each location.

The Washington CDC officers were all putting their equipment on and checking their weapons. The Atlanta team was waiting to hear from Chuck about what their next move would be. Would they assist in Washington or would they head back to Atlanta? The pressing question was, could they actually leave the capital? If the FAA shut the airports down, they might be stranded amidst the chaos in DC.

McCain was holed up in one of the offices making phone calls to his DHS contact and to Shaun Taylor, getting the latest intel from the CIA. Trang and Walker were going over a satellite map of the affected areas around the Rayburn House Office Building and the Smithsonian Institute, trying to calculate the best way to respond. Traffic was gridlocked in the entire area and emergency vehicles were still unable to reach the epicenter of the blast, or even break the periphery at this point. The first responders who had managed to get close to the scene transmitted that they were being attacked and then contact had been lost.

The federal officers were being updated moment-by-moment by the Department of Homeland Security, and it sounded like the numbers of infected were increasing exponentially and spreading out in every direction of the city. A group of over one hundred zombies were moving in the direction of the White House. Upon being advised of this imminent danger, the Secret Service sprang into action. The First Family was on Marine One within minutes and evacuated to Camp David. The Vice-President and his family were transported to Andrews Air Force Base in nearby Maryland.

The office door opened and Chuck joined all the CDC officers in the briefing room. Tu and Jay, along with their entire squad, were prepared to move out and attempt to bring the situation under control. Eddie and his team were ready to jump in and help the Washington officers if they couldn't get back to Atlanta.

Trang was finishing up his briefing.

"This is going to be a rescue mission. DHS wants us to start at the Rayburn House and secure it. We'll kill all the Zs that we can, but our main goal is locating and rescuing survivors. The reports are indicating that there could already be close to a thousand or more infected moving through the city. I'm guessing that number is going to go a lot higher before we're done.

"So, let's find the people that are hiding in the building. If they're in a safe place, we'll leave them there and radio the location in to the Metro Police. If we find survivors and it's not a defensible location, we'll have to play it by ear. We don't have the manpower to protect large groups of people out in the open."

Jay spoke up. "I just got off of the phone with the Department of Homeland Security. Everybody's jumping in to help. The Metro PD's SWAT Team is on the way, the FBI's Hostage Response Team has been mobilized, and the ATF's and DEA's tactical teams are also going to be out there. Metro SWAT is going to start at the Air and Space Museum and the FBI's HRT will start at the Capitol.

"Other than that, the DHS didn't have any specifics of where these other teams are going to be or what they were going to be doing. All they could tell me was that the President ordered every federal agency with an enforcement branch to do their part. Let's be very careful and try not to shoot any other cops. This is what we do but these other guys have stayed out of the zombie fighting business until today. We don't need any blue on blue shooting."

Tu nodded to Chuck. "What are you guys going to do?"

McCain motioned to Marshall. "Eddie, we're heading south. The FAA has grounded all flights but we got a special dispensation to fly. Tu, we've got a Blackhawk that's going to land on your roof and take us to Reagan National. The DHS was kind enough to arrange that for us. Y'all want a lift? It sounds like traffic is pretty rough and an air insertion would save you a lot of time and be safer than trying to fight your way inside that big building."

"Yeah, Chuck, that would be great," Trang answered.

"Just figure out where you want him to drop you off. Their ETA is fifteen minutes."

"I was kind of hoping you guys would be grounded so you could help us," said Jay, with a smile.

"Sorry, Jay. Two officers from our other team are about to get started without us. If we don't hurry and get home, there won't be any left for the rest of us to kill."

"So, what are Andy and Scotty up to?" asked Luis.

"There's a skyscraper right next to where the bombs went off. The windows were blown out, the virus was blown in. Now, the entire twenty-three floors are crawling with zombies. There are a lot of trapped survivors and Atlanta PD can't get to them right now."

"Two guys clearing twenty-three floors?" asked LeMarcus, incredulously.

"Yeah, but you don't have to worry about them," answered Jimmy. "I'm a Marine and all Marines are badasses, but Andy is one of those MARSOC Marines. They're extra special badasses. And Scotty was an Army Ranger. That boy ain't happy unless he's shooting somebody or blowing something up. At the end of the day, there's going to be a lot of dead zombies and some people rescued."

The Wells Fargo Building, Atlanta, Georgia, 1745 hours

For the moment, he could not hear anything outside the supply closet he was hiding in. It sounded like Paul's co-workers turned zombies had migrated to the other side of the offices. There had been some terrible shrieks and screams and that awful, incessant growling. But now, there was silence. Paul Kowalski continued to sit frozen, his back against the wall, his cell phone to his ear.

Finally, after fifteen minutes, someone at the 911 Call Center answered. He told the dispatcher what was happening and where he was located. She could not give him any indication of when or even if he would be rescued. All she could tell him was that other survivors were also hiding in the building and to sit tight and wait.

Paul was having trouble thinking clearly. In a video game, you could always locate a better weapon, more ammo, grenades, and first-aid kits. Here, he was surrounded by toner, envelopes, printer paper, and staples.

There was a tapping at the door. Softly, but then a little louder, followed by a voice. "Please, let me in."

He got to his feet and stood next to the door. What if it's a trap? Zombies can't talk or can they?

"Who is it?" he asked quietly.

"It's Maggie, from Social Media. Please open the door."

Paul took a deep breath and opened it a crack. A tear-streaked face, framed with black hair, was looking back at him. He pulled the door open and Maggie rushed inside. She grabbed him and hugged him, sobbing into his shoulder.

Kowalski wasn't sure what to do. He didn't know Maggie other than the occasional "Hi" in the hallway. He awkwardly put one arm around her and patted her back, using his other hand to shut the door.

They stood that way in the supply room for a couple of minutes. He put his other arm around the girl and felt her sobs. It had been a while since he had had a girlfriend and the way things were shaping up outside, he might never have another one. The human contact was comforting and he began to feel better.

Finally, Maggie pulled away, wiping her face with both hands. “I’m sorry,” she said, with an embarrassed laugh. “We’ve never really talked and I just threw myself at you.”

Paul forced a smile. “Don’t worry about it. I was crying earlier but I didn’t have anybody to hold me. Let’s sit down,” he suggested, and they slumped to the floor, the gravity of their situation weighing heavily on both of them.

“So, what do we do now?” she asked.

“We could introduce ourselves and then I could ask you out? I’m Paul Kowalski,” he said, sticking out his hand.

“What? No, I mean about this…everything that’s going on. How do we get out of here?”

Paul smiled again. “I was just kidding and trying to lighten the mood a little. I’m not sure. Do you have any ideas?”

She sighed. “No, and I’m Maggie Warren,” she said, extending her hand. “It’s nice to meet you, Paul Kowalski.”

“How’d you escape?” he asked. “I saw some really bad stuff. I was going to try and get out the front entrance but the doors were blocked. They had the receptionist, Candi, on the floor and…well, I knew I was trapped. They were behind me and in front of me so I ducked in here just in time.”

“Call it fate, luck, or God. I don’t know,” replied Maggie. “I was in the break room, getting a cup of coffee, when the first explosion hit. I tried to do what I could but things got crazy fast. One of the men from HR was lying on the floor near my cubicle with blood pouring out of him.

“I ran back into the break room and grabbed a handful of paper towels and rushed over to him. But then I heard a guy groaning really loud and I saw Terri grab the man who was trying to help her. He was twice her size but she slammed him down on the floor and start biting his neck.

“And Heyward! Heyward jumped on that new girl and bit her to death. This was all going on at the same time. It was awful so I jumped up and ran around to the other side of the offices. I was thinking the same thing you were. Get out, but like you said, that was a no go. I saw you duck in here but I didn't think I'd make it to the closet before they got to me.

"I thought I was trapped, too, but I ran back and saw that most of them had moved to the front, where Candi was. I managed to slip behind them and get into the women's room. It locks from the inside. But, I knew you were here and I didn't want to be alone. I don't even have my phone. Maybe we'll have a better chance together?"

"I hope so," he answered. "The police weren't very reassuring. I had just spoken with a 911 operator when you knocked. She said that there are a lot of people in the building calling in but she couldn't tell me when the police would be here. She just said stay put in a safe place.

"I don't know if you were able to look outside after the first explosion. I did and it was a mess. All the roads look like they're shut down. Want to see if we can get online and find out what's happening?"

Paul pulled his large screen smart phone out of its belt holster and opened the web browser. Maggie sat next to him against the wall. The internet was abuzz with stories and videos. They stared in disbelief at the video footage coming out of Atlanta, New York, and Washington, D.C. No law enforcement agency or media outlet had a clear picture yet of exactly how the bombings had transpired or how many had occurred. Casualties were already estimated in the thousands with even more newly infected zombies making their way through the city streets.

Unconfirmed reports were saying that all of the explosive devices were dirty bombs with a twist. The zombie virus and radioactive materials had been mixed and were endowing these latest infected with almost superhuman strength. A cell phone video from New York showed a zombie going after a family trapped in a van. He ripped open the side door of their minivan and killed everyone inside. Another clip, this one from DC, showed a teenage boy run down a muscular man in his thirties, tackling him. The boy easily controlled the bigger man, ripping his stomach open with his hands.

"Superhuman strength?" commented Maggie, pointing at a news report on the screen. "I wonder if that was why Terri was able to body slam that big guy who was trying to help her?"

"That was Brian, one of my team members," Paul said, sadly, remembering that his friend and co-worker was dead.

"I'm sorry," said Maggie, leaning against Paul. "I wonder if anyone got out of here or if we're the only two still alive from our company?"

Kowalski turned the phone off and put it back in the holder on his belt. They didn't speak for a few minutes, both lost in their thoughts. Paul was a good manager. His people loved him because he was always positive and knew how to say the right thing to encourage them. But, what could he possibly say to make Maggie feel better about their hopeless situation?

"You want to hear something funny?" he asked.

She looked at her new friend but didn't answer. Funny? she thought. What could possibly be funny right now?

"I was going to go home tonight and play a zombie video game," he said.

Maggie smiled, in spite of herself. "Oh, yeah? Which one?"

"The Return of the Dead."

"No way," she said, excited. "That's my new favorite game! I've been stuck on level three for two days and I was going to go online over the weekend and try to find a walkthrough."

Paul glanced over at his dark-haired companion with new respect.

"Yeah, level three is almost impossible without the grenade launcher. Did you find it at the end of level two?"

Maggie shook her head. "No, but that helps. I'll go back and do level two again and look for it. That is, if we don't get eaten by real zombies first."

Paul nodded. It would be nice to have a real grenade launcher about now, he thought.

Atlanta, Friday, 1805 hours

The Blackhawk circled the scenes of destruction caused by a car bomb, a suicide bomber, multiple secondary explosions, and now, an unknown number of zombies unleashed upon an unsuspecting city. Andy and Scotty peered down through the smoke and tried to get an idea of what had happened. The large crater where the car bomb had detonated was easy to see.

A hundred yards further up the exit ramp, several charred vehicles marked the spot where the suicide bomber himself had exploded. The entire interstate was shut down because of the devastation at the 17th Street exit. The officers also saw that 17th Street itself was completely gridlocked and the bridge going back over I-75/I-85 into the city was blocked by vehicles, bodies, and zombies.

Fleming and Smith watched hundreds, maybe thousands of Zs shuffling, walking, or running in every direction. Many were crouching and chewing on dead bodies. Others were hunting survivors still trapped in their cars or chasing down those who had decided to abandon their vehicles, trying to escape on foot.

"At least we've got a target rich environment," Scotty commented over his headset to Andy, a wide grin on the bearded man's face.

An hour earlier, Smith was driving their black Suburban south on Interstate 75 towards Atlanta. The FBI and ATF had a command post at their scene in Gilmer County, almost two hours north of Atlanta, where earlier that morning they had engaged the suicide bombers. The two CDC officers had been there all day, assisting with the investigation, and were happy to finally be heading back to the office to drop off the company car before calling it a day.

"You and Emily going out this weekend?" Andy asked Scotty.

"Yep, we're having dinner with her parents tomorrow night. Some nice French restaurant. She told me that I need to wear a blazer."

"That sounds serious."

"Yeah, I don't think I've ever eaten at a place where I needed to wear a jacket."

"Not that," said Fleming. "The whole having dinner with her parents thing. That sounds very serious."

The big man tilted his head sideways and shrugged his shoulders. "I really like her and it's not like I can tell her I don't want to meet her folks. At least, not if I want to keep seeing her."

Andy patted his friend on the shoulder. "I've got first dibs on being your best man."

"Dude, we've only been out a few times. I'm not planning on getting married any time soon."

"You may not be, but Emily wants to run you by mom and dad to see what they think. A couple of pieces of advice. Close your mouth if you have to burp. Sip your wine, don't gulp it. And try not to spend too much time talking about shooting zombies in the head."

Both of their smartphones started vibrating at the same time. Andy called in to their contact at the DHS and got the notice that Atlanta, New York City and Washington, D.C., were being attacked again. By 1715 hours, traffic had started backing up and they got off of the interstate near the SunTrust Atlanta Braves stadium, still ten miles from downtown.

For many years, the Atlanta baseball team had played in one of the worst areas of the city. Recently, a state of the art stadium had been built north of downtown in a much safer area. There was no game tonight and one of the parking lots would serve their purpose.

Andy's phone vibrated again, this time with an incoming call. He put it on speaker so Chuck could speak with both of them. McCain needed to send them to a skyscraper adjacent to where the bombs had gone off. People were trapped inside and reporting that Zs were killing everyone in sight.

Survivors were hiding in offices, closets, and restrooms. A few brave souls had managed to get to the lobby but soon realized their mistake. Besides the many infected that were already in the lobby waiting for some more victims to show up, the area outside the building was swarming with zombies. There was no place to go.

The Atlanta Police Department was trying to formulate a response to the incident but, with the infected wandering around and creating more zombies, the scene still wasn't safe. The first two fire trucks and ambulance onscene lost their entire crews.

Four responding police officers could not get their patrol cars any closer than three blocks from the scene of the explosions. Not knowing the scope of the destruction, the sergeant and his three patrol officers approached on foot with the intention of rendering aid to those injured in the blasts. The sergeant was soon calling for help over the radio. He said they were being attacked by a mob of zombies and were trying to get back to their police cars. Every other officer on their radio channel could hear the gunshots, the screams, and the fear in the supervisor's voice. Within two minutes, there was no response from the sergeant or the other three officers.

The SWAT Team was enroute in their truck but was not sure how long it was going to take to get there or even how close they could get. APD dispatch requested the CDC's help in securing the Wells Fargo building. Since the interstate was impassable, McCain had their Blackhawk helicopter on the way to pick Fleming and Smith up in the stadium parking lot. Their insertion point would be the roof of the building. After getting off the phone with McCain and while waiting on their ride, they pulled up the building specs on Andy's laptop and tried to memorize as much of the floor plan as they could.

"Isn't your apartment near Atlantic Station?" Andy asked Scotty.

"Yeah, it's probably half a mile from where all the excitement is today. You know, this is the nicest place I've ever lived. We have a security guy in the lobby who calls me 'Mister Smith.' Can you believe that? Looks like I'm going to be in the market for a new home."

The warriors reloaded from the extra ammo they kept in all of their SUVs. Both men also shoved a few extra rifle and pistol magazines into their cargo pockets. When the helicopter touched down, they rushed to board.

Scotty stopped suddenly, holding up one finger to Andy and the Blackhawk crewman and ran back to their SUV. He opened the rear door and lifted up the backseat to reveal a Remington Model 870 pump action shotgun, secured in a special case under the seat. Smith retrieved the shotgun and a bandolier of shells. He slung them both over his shoulder, locked the vehicle and jogged back to the aircraft.

The crewman of the Blackhawk had attached his mini-gun to a side mount, pointing out the left side of the helicopter. The six-barrel rotary machine gun was capable of firing over two thousand rounds a minute of 7.62mm bullets. This powerful weapon covered Chuck and the CDC agents in their recent fight on the University of Georgia campus, cutting down hundreds of zombies.

The Blackhawk and their crew would provide air support for Andy and Scotty as best they could and help with evacuating survivors. The copilot monitored the radios for the latest information from the Atlanta Police and the FBI. After circling the Wells Fargo building twice to confirm the landing zone was clear, the pilot touched down to let the two warriors out.

"Be careful, gentleman, and we'll be in the area to provide assistance," the pilot said.

Andy and Scotty threw salutes to the aircrew, ducked under the spinning rotors, and ran to the door on the other side of the roof. Smith clutched a pry bar he had brought from the helicopter. The big man used it to force the locked metal door open. They did not want to start shooting yet and needed to stay as quiet as possible. After listening at the open door for three full minutes, the two men entered the unknown.

The Wells Fargo Building, Atlanta, Friday, 1830 hours

Paul Kowalski and Maggie Warren had quietly worked through the entire supply closet to see if they could find anything useful. Each now had a pair of scissors in their back pockets. They had also found a flashlight, a small first aid kit, a roll of duct tape, and a metal letter opener. Since they did not really know exactly how their co-workers had been infected, they also used a couple of bottles of hand sanitizer to wipe down all exposed skin.

While better weapons were a definite priority, they would also eventually need some food. There was a case of two-dozen Dasani water bottles in the closet so they could at least stay hydrated. A plastic trash can would serve as their toilet. Paul tried to reassure Maggie that it was just a matter of time before the police came to their rescue, but they both realized that spending an awkward night in the closet was highly likely.

Kowalski had attempted several more times to speak with a 911 operator, but now none of his calls were going through. The recording advised him that his call was important but all operators were busy and that he should stay on line. Paul and Maggie, even though they were together in the closet, felt a growing sense of isolation. They were cut off from the outside world and couldn't even reach 911. Another problem they were facing was that the battery in Paul's phone was down to nineteen percent so he could not really afford to sit on hold for thirty minutes.

From time to time they heard a growling zombie wander by their hiding place. Up till now, they had been able to remain undetected. The looming question was: how long would that last?

Chapter Eight

Two Against the World

Staging Area near the Braves Stadium, North of Atlanta, Friday, 1845 hours

Emily Clark sat in the passenger seat of her blue and white West Metro Ambulance Service ambulance in the big parking lot that was quickly filling with emergency vehicles from multiple Metro Atlanta agencies. The Atlanta Police Department had picked this large parking area just across Interstate 75 from the SunTrust Stadium, next to the northbound lanes for easy access. The command post was set up at the rear of the lot with federal and local police and fire commanders trying to coordinate a response. The attacks in downtown Atlanta were almost two hours old, but after losing several police officers and firemen already, the authorities were unsure how to proceed.

Emily and her partner, Darnell Washington, had been glued to their smart phones, watching the events unfold. When they had pulled into the staging area, Emily immediately recognized a black Suburban, parked off to the side, as one of the CDC Enforcement Unit's. Of course, other government agencies used those kinds of vehicles, as well, but Emily somehow knew that Scotty, or one of his colleagues, had parked it there.

Emily and Scotty hadn't spoken since the night before. She had seen him on the news, however, the previous day in video captured by the local news helicopter, leading other officers in terminating a large group of zombies in Virginia Highlands, near where the two of them had had their first date. The part of the video that kept being replayed showed Scotty and his team of SWAT officers standing in the middle of the street as a group of Zs charged them.

The officers had calmly dropped all of the infected. It was the first time the young woman had seen her boyfriend in action and it had terrified her. Smith had called her when he had gotten home and they had talked for an hour.

In typical Scotty fashion, he had asked her all about her day. When she asked him about his, he was nonchalant.

"You know. Work is work. Same old, same old," he answered.

"I saw you on the news, Scotty," her voice rising. "I watched all those things running at you. And why did you flip off the news chopper?"

Emily heard him laughing.

"Did you see that?" he asked. "I've never liked reporters. As far as work goes, that's what we do. We shoot the zombies and save people."

"It scared me," she admitted softly. "I'm glad you're OK. I…I know what you do but this was the first time I've seen you doing it," her voice broke. "I started crying when those zombies ran towards you."

Scotty heard her trying not to sob into the phone. He had a sudden epiphany that what was just a normal day at the office for him had created a terror-filled few moments for someone he cared about deeply.

"Emily, its OK. Really, I'm sorry. Please don't cry. I'm fine. I promise. I'm always careful and I work with some of the best operators in the world."

There was a long silence but he could still hear her sniffling. "Say something, Emily. I'm so sorry I made you cry."

She sniffed and laughed. "You didn't make me cry, you big goofball. I just, I was worried, that's all. I'm sorry I lost it."

After they hung up, she realized that the reason she was crying was that she had fallen in love with the big goofball. She texted him earlier Friday morning. He sent a short reply saying he was involved in another situation and would call her tonight.

Emily looked out her window at the police, fire, and ambulances assembling for the moment they would be needed. Scotty is already out there, she thought. The CDC officers did not wait until the scene was secure. They moved in and were the ones who tried to secure the scene. She felt the hot tears again running down her face as she closed her eyes, saying a silent prayer for her boyfriend and for all the other warriors who were already in harm's way.

The Wells Fargo Building, Atlanta, Friday, 1845 hours

Fleming and Smith listened at the stairwell door for the 19th floor. Each floor plan was identical, office space on both sides of a marble corridor running the length of the building. Glass-encased elevators anchored each end of the hallway, built to run along the outside of the structure. On any other day, the views of the city would be spectacular.

The staircases at either end of each floor acted as emergency exits. Some of the bigger tenants rented out an entire floor, while other, smaller businesses only needed a quarter or half a floor.

The elevator on the north side of the building had just started climbing towards the 19th floor when Ramzi's vest went off. The lift contained a four man and one woman Japanese delegation on their way to meet with their biggest American client. Infected ball bearings and screws punched through the thick glass on the elevator. All four people were struck by shrapnel and knocked to the floor. When the elevator doors opened, five Japanese zombies lunged for the smiling CEO, CFO, and COO.

The first floor that the two officers had cleared was the 23rd and only housed a few infected. A large law firm occupied the top level of the building and by the time the bombs had gone off, most of the lawyers and paralegals had left for their weekend. Sixteen secretaries and administrative personnel were still working late on a Friday afternoon.

Four had been injured and infected from the first blast and they quickly reanimated, attacking five of their co-workers. Andy and Scotty had easily eliminated those nine Zs and helped the seven survivors find a secure place to wait until they could be rescued. Those they left behind all wanted to come along with the two heavily armed police officers.

"We've got twenty-two more floors to clear and the reports are that the lower levels are crawling with Zs," Andy told them. "You guys sit tight. It might be a few hours, but your floor is secure now and you'll just have to wait it out."

One young law clerk, who barely looked old enough to drive, asked them, "Where's the rest of your team? The internet says that there are thousands of those things outside."

Scotty looked at him disdainfully. "Son, I'm not a very religious man, but the Good Book tells us that one warrior can put a thousand enemies to flight and two warriors can handle ten thousand. And we aren't putting them to flight. We're shooting them in the head. But thanks for your concern."

The 22nd floor had no infected at all because the offices on the side of the explosions were unoccupied. The business on the other side was a twenty-four hour call center offering customer service for a satellite TV provider. Scotty instructed the operators in no uncertain terms to stay put and wait to be rescued.

"You have no chance against the zombies if you leave this area," the bearded man told them. "Please wait for law enforcement no matter how long it takes."

The next two floors contained a total of twelve infected and a handful of survivors. When the CDC officers got to the 19th floor, though, they could hear the distinctive zombie growl of a large pack of the creatures from the other side of the stairwell exit. The small window on the door did not allow Fleming or Smith to see the length of the corridor.

They could hear them growling and banging on something but could not see any of the infected. Andy eased the door open to peer down the walkway. After surveying the scene for a few seconds, he motioned for Scotty to have a look at the group of Zs clustered further down the hall.

They quietly shut the door and spoke softly. "I figure roughly thirty in the hallway," Andy whispered. "It looks they were having a reception or something and some Zs decided to crash the party."

"Looks like it. You want to just start shooting them?" asked Scotty. "I think we can drop all of them before they know what happened."

"Let's do it. Just be ready to duck back into the stairwell if they get too close."

Most of the infected had been in the corridor waiting to welcome the Japanese delegation. They had tables set up with refreshments and drinks. The group in the hallway had actually been much larger but when the infected visitors got off the elevator and started attacking people, some employees had fled to the safety of their offices. Others, who had tried to help, ended up becoming zombies themselves.

Now, the zombies were pounding on the heavy wooden doors on either side of the corridor, trying to get to the living people inside. Fleming and Smith stepped into the walkway and began engaging targets. Even suppressed, the M4s were loud in the corridor. Their 5.56mm rounds punched through the heads of the closest zombies, blood spraying their infected comrades.

The horde immediately turned and began surging towards the two men. Several of the creatures tripped over the fallen bodies of their zombie friends. Andy and Scotty sighted and shot as fast as they could but the large group was quickly racing towards them.

"Back into the stairwell," Fleming ordered.

Just as they got inside and shut the door, the fourteen remaining Zs slammed against it. The two men had eliminated eighteen of their attackers, but those remaining would also need to be dealt with before they could check the offices for survivors.

"So, upstairs, down the hall, downstairs, shoot 'em from the other stairwell door?" Scotty asked, swapping the magazine in his rifle for a fresh one.

Andy nodded, also reloading his M4. "Good plan."

They sprinted up to the safely cleared 20th floor, rushed down the corridor and down the stairs to the opposite end of the 19th floor. All of the remaining infected were still congregated at other end of the hallway, shoving against the stairwell door. In seconds, the two officers had put bullets into each zombie head.

After another reload, it was time to clear the business. From inside the offices on the explosion side of the building, they heard growling and then a heavy pounding on the solid wooden door. Suddenly, the thick wood began to crack under heavy blows.

Fleming and Smith backed down the corridor towards the stairwell to give themselves some room to work.

"Those doors are two inches of solid hardwood," Andy commented.

"Maybe the Zs have learned how to use fire axes?" Scotty wondered.

The door continued to splinter under an unrelenting pounding.

"I'm getting a bad feeling about this," Andy commented.

Wood suddenly exploded outward as the door came apart. Bodies began to push their way through the opening. The first one to make it into the hallway was a large African-American zombie, about the same size as Scotty, at least six foot five and two hundred and fifty pounds. He was wearing khakis and a navy blue polo shirt. The officers saw that his muscular forearms had been ripped open, probably by an infected co-worker's teeth.

A loud roar burst from his throat and he charged. For a man his size, his speed was amazing. In an instant, he was almost on top of the two officers. They both fired at the same time, hitting him in the head, snapping it back, and dropping him at their feet.

Those who had escaped the massacre in the corridor had escaped to a massacre in the offices. When the bombs went off, six people had been injured and infected inside the business from infected shrapnel blown through their windows. They had turned on their work colleagues and killed all of them. There were no survivors, just thirteen more zombies that wanted to kill and eat the two federal officers.

The infected rushed down the hallway into a hail of bullets. Twelve of them were cut down but the last one had run behind an obese girl and got within five feet of Scotty without being hit. When her heavy friend went down, the surviving Z launched herself through the air at the big man. He quickly sidestepped to his right and swung the stock of his rifle into the creature's head as she went by.

The folding stock of the M4 rifle knocked her to the ground and ripped open her cheek but she quickly recovered, pushing herself to her feet. Smith shot her in the side of the head, sending her back to the floor.

"What was up with them?" wondered Andy. "That big guy and that chick you just shot were like zombies on steroids?"

"That's a scary thought. But, yeah, he busted through that door like it was nothing and she was like a track star zombie competing in the high jump."

They cleared the side of the building from which the infected had just escaped. Three more were inside, still eating their dead victims. Quick head shots eliminated them.

The offices on the opposite side of the corridor contained twelve survivors locked in a back office. They were given the same command. Stay where they were at until they were rescued. This did not go over well with the terrified officer workers.

"Please don't leave us here," a middle-aged white woman begged. "We saw what happened. They just started killing people."

A young African-American girl started crying, also pleading for the CDC officers to protect them.

"I've got a baby, officers. I don't want my baby to grow up without me."

"I know you're scared," Andy said, trying to get everyone calmed down. "This floor is clear now. The zombies are all dead. The rest of this building has other scared people who are hiding, too. We've got to try and save them, as well. I promise, we'll send someone to come and get you."

Fleming pulled out a small notebook and wrote down which floor they were on and the number of survivors. Scotty and Andy paused to drink some water in the break room. They had both been going since before dawn and were starting to tire. Their spec ops backgrounds, though, had equipped them to push through the fatigue barrier. They just needed to take a couple of minutes and recharge their batteries.

Smith opened the refrigerator to see what was inside. A Firehouse sub sandwich, still in its wrapper, was too much to resist. He ripped it open and started devouring it.

Andy shook his head. "Man, that's low, eating somebody's food."

"Maybe, but the percentages are pretty good that we've already shot the owner of this sandwich in the head."

Fleming grunted. "That's probably true."

He pulled out a Domino's pizza box from the bottom shelf of the fridge and opened it. Half of a pepperoni pizza stared out at him. He tore off several slices and joined his partner in a meager dinner.

After a ten-minute break to catch their breath, rehydrate, and down some food, they were ready to go back to work. They checked their weapons and did an ammo check. They made sure they had full magazines in their rifles as they prepared to clear the 18th floor.

The Islamic Center of North Georgia, Marietta, Georgia, Friday, 1900 hours

Hakeem sat transfixed in front of the TV in the imam's small dwelling. The Islamic Center contained a mosque, the house, and a multi-purpose community building and had a fence that went around the entire compound. The leader's home was set in the back corner of the property, behind the mosque and hidden from view from the street.

When the shooting had started at their North Georgia base early that morning, Hakeem and Abdul had dived into the Chevrolet van. Omar had managed to get into the Volkswagen Jetta. Alhamdulillah, thank Allah, Hakeem had had the foresight to order that all keys stay in their vehicle's ignitions in case a quick getaway became necessary.

Sadly, only the three of them had escaped. Khaled had bravely engaged the many gunmen who had attacked them. Khaled's courage was what allowed Hakeem, Abdul, and Omar to escape. They would make sure that Khaled and their brothers had not died in vain.

Who were the gunmen who had attacked them? American police? Normally, the soft Americans tried to arrest you first. Not today. What he couldn't wrap his head around was, what sort of agency would just start shooting his men with no warning, cutting down the young soldiers of Allah?

Maybe it was the FBI's SWAT team. But they, too, would always try to get their targets to surrender instead of just opening fire. The American police had so many rules that they had to abide by.

Hakeem had fought against the Americans in Iraq and in Afghanistan. What he'd seen today was much more indicative of the manner in which SEALS and Special Forces engaged in warfare. Set up an ambush and then shoot everything in the kill zone.

But, the American military did not operate on their own soil, did they? No matter, Hakeem estimated that it had to have been fifteen or twenty gunmen who had engaged them this morning. Allah had spared himself and his two young soldiers for a reason.

On the television, the news channels did not know what to cover. Three simultaneous, large-scale attacks in three major cities were almost overwhelming for the news anchors. For obvious reasons, Hakeem was especially interested in what was happening in Atlanta.

A Channel 2 news helicopter showed the absolute chaos and devastation where a suicide bomber and a car bomb had detonated downtown at the 17th Street exit from I-85. Both sides of the Atlanta interstate and 17th Street itself were now shut down with packs of zombies roaming freely through the area.

The anchorwoman, with an eye for the obvious, said that this appeared to be a new wave of attacks using the zombie virus. The eye in the sky helicopter cameras showed hundreds of infected people filling the streets. Hakeem was mesmerized by the clip of a large, blood-covered African-American woman punching out the driver's side window of a passenger car that was stopped with all the other traffic on the southbound side of the interstate. The infected woman reached in and dragged a petite Asian woman out by the hair. They cut the clip as the zombie pulled the screaming woman up to her mouth.

The orders that Hakeem and his cell had received, before his men were brutally cut down, were to unleash their twenty suicide bombers on Friday. They had selected targets all over the northwest side of Atlanta. They were planning to strike malls, schools, restaurants, and other places where the infidels congregated.

Of course, Hakeem had not known about these other attacks. Each cell leader was only given the information they needed to carry out their part of the mission. After escaping with Abdul and Omar, they had driven to the Islamic Center of North Georgia. The imam was a true believer and the compound was one of their safe locations.

When they had arrived, he had carefully disarmed the suicide vests that Abdul and Omar wore and set them aside. As the news footage continued to play out, a new plan began to formulate in Hakeem's mind. His two young soldiers would still get their chance of becoming martyrs. And, Inshallah, God willing, so would Hakeem.

The Wells Fargo Building, Atlanta, Friday, 1915 hours

Paul and Maggie sat silently against the wall in the closest, clutching their scissors tightly. Paul held that weapon in his left hand and the metal letter opener in his right. The sounds of movement and the incessant growling outside their hiding place had them both terrified. They didn't think that the zombies knew they were inside but there was no way for the two survivors to make their escape, either. They were trapped in the small room.

As they sat staring at the door, willing the creatures to go somewhere else, Paul saw another weapon right in front of him. A fire extinguisher was hanging from the wall, next to the door. He had played enough zombie video games to know that you had to damage the brain to put them down for good. The heavy fire extinguisher would be much more useful than the scissors and letter opener.

He whispered to Maggie what he was going to do. She looked over at the red extinguisher and nodded at him. He quietly got to his feet and approached the door. For the moment, there were no sounds from the other side and the two survivors hoped the infected had wandered off to another area of the business.

The device was held to the wall by two metal brackets. Kowalski got the top open without a sound. The bottom one, however, would not budge and he had force it. Suddenly, the bracket popped open with a loud snap and recoiled into the wall.

He glanced over at Maggie who jumped at the loud noise, her

eyes open wide with fear. Paul mouthed, "I'm sorry," and pulled the fire extinguisher free.

Without warning, a body slammed into their door, and then another. Groaning and growling zombies were now congregating outside the supply closet. Suddenly, a powerful blow shook the doorframe. It sounded like one of the Zs was using a battering ram.

On the other side of the supply room stood sixteen of the creatures. In front of the group was Matt. Matt had a muscular five foot eleven frame and, in life, had been a CrossFit instructor in his spare time. He had survived the initial explosion, hidden under his desk while his colleagues had been infected, turned, and started attacking people.

When the Zs moved to the other side of the offices to look for fresh victims, he had climbed out from his hiding place to be greeted by the car bomb going off. Matt was struck by flying glass and several pieces of shrapnel. The potent mixture of the virus and the radioactive waste turned his natural strength into something much more lethal than a normal zombie.

His third punch to the supply closet door broke most of the bones in his hand. Feeling no pain, he used both fists to pound the door. Even after destroying all the bones in his both hands, he continued smashing the wood, trying to get to the people inside. He craved human flesh and he could now smell fresh victims on the other side of the door. The wood finally began to crack.

Maggie was crying hysterically standing behind Paul. "They're going to kill us! We're trapped and we're going to die in here!"

Paul agreed with her assessment. He didn't think he would be playing any video games tonight or ever again. This was it. He was terrified.

"No, we're OK," he told his companion. "When they get the door open, I'm going to rush through them in melee mode with the fire extinguisher. I'll clear a path so you can run for the front door. I'll be right behind you. If they get too close to you, stab them in the eye with your scissors."

His reference to "melee mode" made her smile and shake her head, even as she wiped the tears from her eyes so she could see. Most first-person shooter video games have this function in which the character one is playing can go on the attack with a contact weapon when the enemies get too close.

Paul's positive attitude calmed her down a little and she took a deep breath. The door was splintering and Maggie knew they only had seconds before they would meet their fate. The growling got louder as the Zs anticipated another meal. The weakened door finally collapsed inward.

Fleming and Smith paused at the stairwell door leading to the 18th floor. They could not see or hear anything. This time, Scotty eased the door open and peered out into the corridor.

He quietly closed it, a disgusted look on his face. "Three Zs eating somebody about halfway down. They've ripped them apart. There's no way that victim's going to turn. There isn't enough left. They have their backs to us so we can take them out before they know what happened."

Andy nodded and they quietly stepped through the doorway into the hall. As Fleming raised his rifle, he saw what Scotty was talking about. An arm and a leg had been ripped off of the victim and blood had sprayed the walls and coated the floor.

"This job isn't for the faint of heart," he commented to his partner.

Three shots eliminated the three infected. The men moved to the office doors on their right. There was no question as to whether or not there were zombies inside. The loud banging and growling noises carried into the hallway.

"It sounds like they're busy for the moment so maybe we can get in without them knowing it," Fleming said.

He turned the handle and pushed the door open. Another dismembered corpse was just inside. This was unlike anything they had encountered so far in their dealings with the zombie virus.

They had come across bodies that had been eaten or partially eaten by the infected. Some of the dead that they were finding here, though, looked like the Incredible Hulk had ripped them apart, limb from limb. What was going on?

The officers found themselves in a reception area. Thirty feet down the hallway to their left, a large group of zombies were clustered around a door, trying to smash it open. They stepped over what was left of the blonde receptionist and raised their rifles.

As the door of the supply closet cracked and came open under the onslaught of the zombies, Paul Kowalski raised the fire extinguisher. Maggie Warren stood behind him, clutching her scissors in one hand and the letter opener that Paul had given her in the other. Matt, the former CrossFit instructor-turned-zombie, saw the two people inside and rushed towards them with a loud snarl, his muscular arms outstretched.

Paul swung the extinguisher and hit Matt full in the face, knocking him backwards. He stumbled into two other infected who were trying to get into the closet, knocking them back into the hall. Matt stayed on his feet, though, and his growl sounded like a roar as he charged again.

Kowalski was ready and this time the red canister hit Matt on the left side of his head and knocked him to the floor. Gunshots erupted from around the corner and the Zs in the hallway started collapsing.

A voice boomed, "Hey, dead people, you want a bite of something sweet? I'm right here!"

The distraction caused the zombies to quickly lose interest in Paul and Maggie and turn towards the new people. The shots continued to explode heads and stack the hallway with bodies. Movement caught Kowalski's attention and he saw Matt trying to push himself to his feet. Paul saw that the left side of his skull was caved in from the fire extinguisher. He swung it again before the muscular zombie could stand, this time fracturing the back of his skull. Matt fell facedown and was still.

Andy and Scotty shot six of the infected before the rest of the mob registered that there was more fresh meat only thirty feet away. Scotty yelled at them to turn their attention away from whoever was hiding behind the door they had just smashed open.

Smith placed the red dot of his EOTech scope on an older white woman's forehead. Her eyes were glazed over and her face was covered with blood. She was walking quickly towards the two officers. When he pulled the trigger of the M4 rifle, nothing happened.

Police officers and soldiers are taught to perform an immediate action drill if their weapon ever fails to fire. They drill over and over so that it becomes second nature. Scotty tapped the bottom of the thirty round magazine, making sure that it was seated in the rifle. He then pulled the charging handle to the rear and let it slam forward.

This simple drill clears ninety-five percent of all weapon malfunctions. It did not clear his. He saw that the bolt would not go all the way forward which probably meant he had a double feed. For the moment, his rifle was useless.

Andy shot the woman and was still engaging targets. The last six infected were less than ten feet away now. Scotty let the rifle drop across his chest to hang by its sling, drew his Glock pistol, and started firing. In seconds, the last Z fell dead at their feet.

"CDC police officers," Fleming called. "Is anybody in there?" He moved down the hallway to the closet, stepping over the zombie bodies, his rifle at a low ready.

"Yeah, thank God you guys are here," a man called.

Scotty watched their backs as Andy peered into the closest and saw a heavyset man with a goatee and a dark haired woman. She was clutching scissors and a letter opener and the guy was holding a fire extinguisher, dripping with blood and brain matter. A muscular zombie lay facedown in the closet, the damage to his head evident.

"Are y'all OK? Did either of you get bit?"

Fleming kept his rifle pointed in the direction of the couple but aimed at the floor. He was not taking any chances. The man with the goatee set the fire extinguisher on the floor.

"No, sir," he answered, breathing hard. "We hid in here after everything started. This guy broke in right before you got here. I took him out with the fire extinguisher."

"What are your names?"

"I'm Paul and this is Maggie."

Fleming stepped inside the supply room to look at the dead man with the crushed skull. It looked like it had taken at least two blows to put him down.

"Good work. We'll clear the rest of the offices and be right back."

Suddenly, something grabbed at Andy's leg. Matt was awake again, trying to use his shattered hands to pull Fleming's leg toward his snapping teeth. The woman screamed as Andy kicked the zombie in the face and took a step backwards. He snapped off a shot that drilled through Matt's temple, finally stopping him for good.

"Scotty, let's finish clearing these offices so we don't have any more surprises. What's wrong with your rifle?"

"I've got a double-feed so it's probably a broken extractor. I'll check it after we finish in here," he answered, screwing the suppressor onto the threaded barrel of his pistol.

As the officers moved out of the closet, Maggie and Paul moved with them. Andy stopped and the woman ran into him.

"Sorry," Maggie said.

"I meant for you guys to wait here," said Fleming, "and my partner and I'll check the rest of your offices. We'll be right back."

"I'm not staying in there with the guy who doesn't want to die," Maggie said, firmly, motioning to Matt lying on the floor of the closet. "I'm going with you."

Andy sighed but knew he wasn't going to win this one.

"Okay. Stay between me and the big guy and we'll try to protect you. Scotty, I'll take point. Put these two between us and let's try to keep them from getting eaten."

A few minutes later, they circled back around. They had not found any other infected people. Andy turned to Paul and Maggie. "In a few minutes, we're going to take you up to the 19th floor. There are some more survivors hiding there in a safe place. We need to keep clearing the building and trying to save people."

Scotty unslung his rifle and pulled the flashlight off of his belt. He removed the magazine and locked the bolt to the rear. A live round fell out but he could see a spent casing lodged in the chamber. He shone his light onto the face of the bolt and confirmed that his extractor was broken. The Colt M4 was now useless.

Without an extractor, the weapon would not eject the empty brass after a shot had been fired. He didn't have any spare parts with him so he couldn't fix it. He did, however, have the Remington 870 pump shotgun that he had brought from the Suburban. He had had it slung over his back, thinking that in a densely packed office building it might come in handy.

"How many rounds do you have for the shotgun?" Fleming asked.

"The bandolier holds fifty-six and I have five in the gun. So, sixty-one if I counted right. I'll use my Glock with the suppressor as my primary, but the shotgun should come in handy."

Smith worked the action on the pump shotgun to put a round in the chamber. He pushed the safety on, pulled a single twelve gauge shotgun shell from the bandolier, and inserted it into the loading tube of the weapon. He was ready.

He and Andy walked over to the shattered windows of the office space and looked down on the scene below them. Cars still burned while smoke hung over the whole area making it hard to see the ground from their height. As the wind shifted the dark smoke around, they could see hundreds of infected moving around. The sound of nearby gunshots from outside carried up to them.

The interstate was a parking lot. No cars were moving in either direction but they could see the zombies shuffling among the vehicles, looking for someone to eat. There was also no traffic moving on the exit ramp or 17th Street. They could see more Zs crossing the bridge over the highway and heading deeper into the city.

More gunshots echoed from behind their building. "I wonder if that's APD's SWAT team?" Scotty wondered. "It would be nice to have a little help here."

"CDC One to Team One Alpha," Chuck's voice transmitted over their radios as if reading their minds.

"Team One Alpha, go ahead CDC One."

"Are you guys OK?" McCain asked, clearly relieved at making contact.

Andy gave him a quick rundown of what they had accomplished so far.

"Sounds good. We're in the air and should be with you in an hour or so. Eddie's guys have been on the go for over twenty-four hours and they're all grabbing an hour nap in the back of the plane. The chopper's going to meet us at PDK airport and bring us to you.

"I finally managed to get someone from APD on the phone and they told me that they have no idea where to start. They weren't able to get any emergency vehicles there after the explosions. Their SWAT is near you guys in two of the high-rise apartment buildings doing the same thing you are.

"The bombs evidently threw a lot of that stuff hundreds of feet and the Zs are running rampant everywhere. SWAT is securing buildings and rescuing people. It sounds like that's gonna be our job for the time being, too."

DeKalb-Peachtree Airport, Chamblee, Georgia, Friday, 2010 hours

Eddie and the men of Team Two were exhausted. They had

flown to Virginia the previous day and had not slowed down much at all in their pursuit and eventual capture of Terrell Hill. And they had been involved in a shootout.

A couple of the guys had grabbed a catnap in the DC offices before all the bombs started going off. Chuck had ordered them to try and get at least an hour's sleep on the plane. He had awakened them fifteen minutes before landing.

After the bombs went off in New York, Washington, and Atlanta, the FAA had grounded all flights except military and law enforcement. DeKalb-Peachtree Airport is normally one of the busiest of the smaller airports in Georgia but was strangely quiet as the Department of Homeland Security Lear jet landed and taxied over to where their Blackhawk helicopter was waiting. The CDC officers were suited up and ready to go back to work, trying to contain the damage from these latest terrorist attacks.

McCain pulled Jimmy aside as they walked to the helicopter. "How you feeling, Jimmy? How are the ribs?"

"I'm fine, Chuck," the former Marine officer answered, dismissively. "The doc said nothing was broken so I'm good to go. Hopefully, none of the Zs have learned to use a shotgun. I sure don't want to go through that again!"

Chuck smiled. "As long as you can function."

"No problem. I just popped a couple of those pills he gave me for pain and I'm ready to roll."

As they started to board, Chuck noted Bobby Walsh, the Blackhawk crewman, had already mounted his mini gun in the left doorway of the helicopter. Daniel Campbell was their pilot and Jessica "Jessie" Webb was their co-pilot. McCain assumed they worked for the CIA, even though their cover story was that they flew for the DHS.

The crew's black BDUs did not have any markings but Chuck had seen the small Night Stalkers pin on Campbell's lapel. Night Stalkers was the name of the famous 160th Special Operations Aviation Regiment or SOAR. These were the Army's Special Forces of the air. Their pilots and crews were the best of the best and McCain always felt safe knowing a Night Stalker was flying them into battle.

"Evening, Mr. McCain," Daniel said.

"Were you a captain or a major, Daniel?"

There was a slight pause from the pilot. "I was a major, sir."

"Well, good evening, Major. Let's get going," Chuck said. "First, I'd like to fly over the scene a few times and get a feel for what happened so I'll have something to report to Washington. Then, please insert us on top of the same building where you dropped off Fleming and Smith. Agent García will stay on board and monitor our radio traffic."

"Yes, sir."

Luis wasn't happy at being left behind but he understood. His ankle was still injured and he did not want to slow his teammates down. He was professional enough to know that he would be a liability on a mission like this.

In less than fifteen minutes, the helicopter was circling the area where the two bombs had detonated. The officers all peered down through the darkness to the burning vehicles that partially illuminated the scene. At a thousand feet, they could smell the smoke. Co-pilot Webb activated the spotlight and lit up the scene below them.

"Whoa!" exclaimed Jimmy. "It looks like somebody kicked over an anthill."

The people who had been infected that afternoon and evening in Atlanta now numbered in the thousands. The sound of the helicopter had all of them looking upward, with some even reaching out as if they could grab the flying machine. The area around the bomb blasts was covered with Zs but they could also see groups of them walking in every direction. The Wells Fargo building was surrounded.

Chuck quickly did the math in his head. Three hours after the explosions, it was conceivable that infected people could have walked five or six miles, spreading the virus along their path.

“How do we control this and how do you evacuate a city this size?” McCain wondered out loud.

The Wells Fargo Building, Atlanta, Friday, 2015 hours

After speaking with Chuck on the radio, Andy and Scotty cleared three more levels. There were no zombies or survivors on the 17th floor. The 16th contained two businesses. The one on the explosion side had been completely decimated as infected shrapnel had blown through the windows. The remains of a body were lying in the office doorway, blocking it open.

Fleming did a quick peek from the stairwell door and motioned for Smith to follow him. They stepped out into the hallway and started moving towards the open door, thirty yards away. After only moving ten yards, however, the growling sound of a large group came from just inside the business. Andy stopped and raised his rifle and Scotty his pistol. Twenty-two zombies burst into the corridor and rushed towards the two officers.

Andy and Scotty were too far away from the stairwell to retreat and were going to have to stand and fight. Fleming started firing as fast as he could pull the trigger. Smith shoved the Glock into his cargo pocket. With the suppressor attached, it would not fit into the holster.

The big man quickly brought the shotgun up to his shoulder and started firing into the group of infected. The shotgun was loaded with alternating double 00 and number four buckshot. Double 00 buckshot contains eight .30 caliber pellets and number four contains twenty-seven .25 caliber pellets. At twenty yards, the buckshot has around a ten-inch spread pattern.

Scotty sighted in on the closest target, a large white man with his throat ripped open and one of his eyeballs ripped out of the socket, bouncing against his face. The shot took him down along with two others, as the buckshot impacted them, as well. He racked the slide and fired again, killing two more.

He and Andy continued to fire as they slowly retreated towards the stairwell. The shotgun took down at least two zombies with each shot and by the time they reached the door, all of the Zs were sprawled on the floor. Fleming fed a full magazine into his rifle.

"That shotgun is so loud," commented Andy, raising his voice.

"Huh? My ears are ringing and I can't really hear you," Scotty said, pushing shotgun shells into the feeding tube of the weapon. "That shotgun is really loud. But it sure did a number on those guys. Two and three at a time! How about that?"

"Yeah, pretty impressive."

The offices that the creatures had just exited contained the familiar scenes of bodies ripped apart with blood splatter throughout. There were no survivors on the entire floor. The other business on the 16th level was empty but had clearly been occupied earlier. Andy hoped they hadn't taken the elevator down to the lobby, otherwise those poor people were probably all infected or devoured by now.

As Smith and Fleming walked down the stairs to the 15th floor, they could hear the growling and snarling outside the stairwell door. They could see through the window that the corridor was packed. The two officers backed up the stairs to the 16th floor and walked the length of the hallway and went down the other set of stairs.

It was no better on that end of the building. The infected were congregated on this end of the corridor as well. They could see the closest three standing motionless five feet away. Two white men wearing dark suits and a black woman in a blue dress. All of them had open wounds on their arms, faces, and torsos. Fleming and Smith looked at each other and smiled. They were both tired but knew that there could be survivors hiding on the floor who needed to be rescued.

"What do you think?" Andy whispered.

"Crack the door and I'll pop those three with the pistol. That should be loud enough to get the attention of the ones down the hall and bring them down here. Then we can go to the other end. I don't really want to shoot the shotgun in this small place. We'll both go deaf."

"Okay, sounds good."

Andy eased the door open. Scotty raised the suppressed 9mm Glock and fired three quick shots into the heads of the three professionally dressed zombies. Fleming pushed the door closed as a body slammed against it. Sure enough, the crowd from the other end of the corridor rushed down to see what was going on.

The officers retreated up the stairs and quickly retraced their steps to the other end of the building. They could not see any infected now when they peered out the window onto the 15th floor. Smith opened the door slightly and looked out.

After closing the door, he said, "The good news is that they are all on the other end of the hall. The bad news is that there are a lot of them."

"Define a lot."

"I wasn't real good in math but I'd figure close to forty."

"Same drill. Let's thin out as many as we can and then duck back into here and go to the other end and do the same thing."

They stepped into the corridor to start their attack. Most of the infected were clustered around the stairwell door on the far end, close to seventy-five yards away. This was beyond the effective range for Scotty's shotgun or pistol.

Andy quickly shot four before they realized what was happening. The remaining thirty-seven rushed down the corridor towards the two men. Scotty began firing the shotgun when they were fifty yards away. The shot pattern was very wide at this distance and his first blast knocked four to the floor. The number four buckshot was especially devastating as the twenty-seven pellets spread out taking down multiple zombies at a time.

"Back inside!" Fleming ordered when they advancing Zs got to within twenty yards.

"Really nice," Andy commented as they reloaded. "You're knocking them down in waves."

When they got back over to the other end of the building and peered out into the corridor, there were only eleven zombies remaining upright. Fleming dropped three before they turned and started running at them. The bodies of their comrades created an obstacle, however, and they all tripped in their haste for a meal of fresh flesh.

The blast of the shotgun began to take its toll as the Zs tried to get back to their feet. Within a minute, the hallway was clear. Both men fed ammo into their weapons and prepared to check the offices. Smith let the shotgun hang from its sling, pulling his pistol out and loading it with a full magazine.

Something was smacking the other side of the door. It wasn't hitting it hard but it was clear they needed to be cautious as they made entry. Andy pushed the door open while Scotty covered the opening with his Glock.

On the floor just inside the doorway, a woman in a skirt reached up for them from where she was lying. Her left leg was missing from the knee down, the stump bloody and jagged. She tried to push herself up with her hands and almost managed to get up on her one leg. A 9mm hollow point hit her in the face and she collapsed to the carpet.

As they cleared the business, the familiar scenes of death were all around them. They killed two more infected that had been so mangled they could only crawl. There were two closed offices that they saved until last. After the officers were certain they had eliminated all the Zs, Andy tapped on one of the doors.

"CDC Police. Anybody in there?"

The door opened to seven people who had managed to survive the onslaught. As they were describing how they all thought they were going to die, the other office door opened and a stocky, middle-aged man came out. He was wearing a tan suit and a brown tie.

"Thank God you're here. I need you to get me out of here right now," he said.

Scotty turned his back on the man and spoke to one of the other survivors, a hipster in his twenties. "Who's this guy?"

"That's our manager, Stanley Poole."

Andy addressed the eight survivors. "We'll take you up to one of the top floors that has already been cleared. There are other survivors there. After we secure the rest of the building, we'll figure out a way to get everyone out of here.

"The lower floors are supposed to be even worse than what we've seen so far. The area outside, around the building, isn't even close to being safe. The rest of our team will be inserting by helicopter in a little while and then we'll be able to clear the other floors."

"A helicopter?" repeated Stanley. "That's wonderful. You can fly us out when they arrive. I demand that you get us out of here."

Scotty stepped over to the manager, looming over the smaller man, placing a meaty palm on his shoulder.

"Stanley. Is it OK if I call you, 'Stanley,' Stanley? My partner and I've had a long day. We dealt with suicide bombers this morning and we've been shooting zombies in the head for the last two hours. I'm really not in the mood to listen to a little short, fat man telling us what to do."

Poole's face grew red but the nearness of the big bearded man kept him from saying anything.

"So," Smith continued, "let's have a little understanding. You're not in charge here. We'll take you upstairs to a safe place where you can wait with all these other wonderful people. But, if you get on my nerves again, Stanley, I'll feed you to the zombies."

Scotty patted Poole on the shoulder. "It was nice having this little chat, Stanley."

The other seven survivors were all trying not to snicker as their obnoxious boss was put in his place. Andy lined them up. This time, Smith took the point and Fleming brought up the rear. The climb from the 15th to the 23rd floor had all the survivors huffing and puffing. Stanley Poole was in bad shape, having to stop and catch his breath several times.

"You know, Stanley," Scotty said, matter-of-factly, "it would probably do you some good to take the stairs a little more often."

The manager glared at him but was smart enough to keep his thoughts to himself. As they worked their way to the top floor, Andy and Scotty stopped at each floor where they had left survivors and added them to the group, escorting them all to the 23rd floor. When they got ready to start evacuating, it would be better to have them all together. For the moment, thirty-eight people would wait together on the top floor.

Chapter Nine

Floor after Floor

The Wells Fargo Building, Atlanta, Friday, 2030 hours

As the helicopter lifted off the roof, Andy and Scotty led the rest of their teammates to the stairwell. Gunfire suddenly sounded from one of the nearby apartment buildings.

Chuck pointed in the direction of the shots.

"APD SWAT is over there trying to rescue people in those apartment buildings. I heard on the radio, right before we landed, that one of their teams lost an officer. The sergeant said they were about to get overrun and one of the guys stepped out in front of his teammates and sacrificed himself. That gave the other officers just enough time to waste the Zs."

The CDC officers stood silently for a moment, digesting this information.

"There's no greater love than to lay your life down for your friends," said Chris Rogers.

"Yeah," replied Scotty, "but let's try not to play that game over here."

They took the stairs down to the last floor that Fleming and Smith had cleared, the 15th, where they could meet and discuss how they wanted to proceed. The officers had to step over several bodies as they entered one of the empty offices the survivors had just vacated.

"Looks like you guys have had a time," commented Eddie, nodding at Andy and Scotty.

"You know, winning hearts and minds," Fleming replied.

As everyone grabbed a chair and sat down, Andy and Scotty gave them a quick briefing.

When they were finished, Eddie asked, "How many survivors upstairs?"

"Close to forty," said Andy. "From here to the roof, all the floors are secure. As we find more people hiding, we can keep sending them to the top."

When they got up to go back to work, Estrada asked Smith, "How'd you tear your rifle up?"

Scotty shook his head. "A broken extractor. The good news is that this shotgun works great. At least, until I run out of shells."

He had put his broken M4 on the Blackhawk when they met the others on the roof. He still had over forty shotgun shells.

"What do you guys think about splitting into two groups?" Chuck asked. "Eddie, you and your guys and I'll go with these two," pointing at Andy and Scotty. "That way we can clear two floors at a time. Let's stay in close contact on the radio. If one team gets in trouble, we'll only be one floor apart."

Marshall nodded and glanced around at his men. They were all ready to go. Everyone was tired and emotionally drained from the last two days but their job was to rescue as many people as they possibly could.

"Perfect," said Eddie. "How about if we go ahead and start evacuating the survivors that are upstairs? Luis could coordinate that. From what we saw on the flight in, it doesn't look like anyone is going to be driving out of here anytime soon. The roads are gridlocked and the Zs are everywhere. Maybe our pilot, the good Major Campbell, could even put some other air assets into play."

"Good idea," said Chuck. "I'll call Air One and Luis to get that happening."

Andy, Scotty, and Chuck started with the 14th floor. There was one large marketing business on the floor. The corridor was clear but they could hear the familiar sound of zombies coming from the open office doors. The officers moved quietly but they knew from previous experience that the infected used their sense of smell to track their victims.

Suddenly, twelve bloody, former marketing professionals burst out into the hallway, running straight for them. Andy's and Chuck's suppressed rifles and Scotty's suppressed pistol coughed out their rounds. The last one, a tall black woman, fell at McCain's feet. His shot had hit her in the face and she went down hard. Her arms were still moving, however, grabbing at Chuck's leg. He put two more 5.56mm rounds into her head and she was finally still.

"That was different," he said.

"Let's finish clearing this floor and we'll tell you what me and Scotty saw earlier," said Andy.

Eddie and Team Two went down to the 13th floor. An accounting firm and another law firm shared the level. The CPA firm was on the side of the building where the explosions took place. Eddie motioned that they would start there.

Normally, Jimmy would take the point position but Eddie had insisted that he stay in the middle of the stack. The blast of 00 buckshot that had hit him less than twenty-four hours earlier had left Jones with some severely bruised ribs. Hollywood moved up to point, with Eddie number two, Jimmy number three, and Chris securing the rear.

The doors were closed and the business sounded quiet. Maybe this one was empty, Estrada thought as he slowly pulled the door open. Suddenly, a bloody, snarling face pushed into the doorway, inches from Hollywood's own face. Several of the creatures were right inside the opening and started growling loudly, shoving against the partially opened door.

"Contact," said Hollywood. "Need some help here."

One of the former CPAs ran and threw himself into the group of infected who were trying to get to the officers. The combined impact knocked Hollywood backwards as the door flew open, sending the officer to the floor. Marshall, Jones, and Rogers all began firing into the group of seven zombies that blasted through the opening.

All of the infected accountants wore blood-saturated white shirts with standard issue ties. The gunfire exploded several heads as they burst out into the hallway. An Indian-looking zombie threw himself onto Alejandro Estrada, still prone on the slick marble corridor, his teeth aiming for the officer's throat. Hollywood managed to get his rifle up and catch the infected man under the chin. Estrada felt the almost supernatural strength of the creature but was able to turn to the right and use the rifle as leverage to knock the creature off of him.

As soon as the zombie was clear of his teammate, Chris fired a quick double tap that struck the Indian Z in the forehead, dumping him onto his back.

"How you doing, Hollywood?" Jimmy asked. "That was a little too much drama, if you ask me."

"I'm good but I don't need a repeat of that. Thanks, Chris."

There were no survivors inside the CPA firm, just a number of torn and ripped apart bodies. Eddie assumed the point as they moved through the offices and shot two infected women who were feeding on a large, middle-aged man. The doors to the law firm on the other side of the floor were locked tight and no one responded to their knocking.

"Maybe everybody left before it got nasty," said Jimmy.

"Let's hope so," said Eddie, "otherwise they got eaten in the lobby on their way out."

Roof of the Wells Fargo Building, Atlanta, Friday, 2100 hours

Luis García was glad that he had a role to play. He could move well enough on his injured ankle to help the survivors get to the roof and onto the helicopter. To evacuate the current thirty-eight survivors would require three trips by the Blackhawk crew. Of course, the rescuers all hoped that number would increase dramatically as the team cleared the remainder of the building.

Co-pilot and former army captain Jessie Webb had told McCain that they would transport the people to the Atlanta Braves stadium where the local police, the CDC, the FBI, and other EMS personnel had established their command post. Now that night had set in, the authorities were even more in the dark as to how to proceed. Since the infected were mobile and had spread out into the city, they were not even sure that setting up a large perimeter was the answer.

Of course, the FBI was now calling the shots but they had no idea where to start either. With all the roads shut down around ground zero and since the virus had spread so quickly, there was still the possibility of survivors trapped in cars. Other than the CDC Response Teams and the Atlanta Police SWAT Team, however, no first responders had ventured into the area.

When the helicopter touched down, García and crewman Bobby Walsh exited the big bird, both heavily armed, and cautiously descended from the roof to the 23rd floor, following the directions they had been given by Fleming. Luis knocked at the door for Berenstein and Associates Attorneys-at-law.

"Police officers," García called out.

A minute later, he and Walsh were inside the large reception area, dividing the survivors into three groups. Stanley Poole positioned himself in front of several women, hoping to get out first.

"Go to end of the line," Luis told him. "The women go first."

“You can’t make me do that,” he replied. “I have a heart condition and I need to be on that first helicopter.”

He had not dared stand up to Scotty, but the narcissistic manager was a little taller and much bigger around than García. Stanley poked a finger into the chest plate of Luis’ body armor.

“I’m leaving in the first group and you can’t stop me.”

Suddenly, the stocky, middle-aged accounts manager found himself face down on the carpet, with the smaller Hispanic officer jamming a knee into his back, handcuffing him. Luis stood, grabbing Stanley by the collar of his brown blazer, dragging him off to the side.

Poole immediately began to scream, “This is police brutality and excessive force! I’ve got witnesses. You’ll pay for this!”

By now he was red-faced and breathing heavily. “I have a bad heart and I need my medicine!” His voice rose to a fevered pitch.

García knelt beside him. “I don’t know who you are, amigo, and I don’t really care. At this point, you might want to worry about how you’re getting home. I’m not putting you on that helicopter. I think you’re mentally unstable and a danger to these nice, calm people.”

Poole’s face went white at the idea of being left behind. “You can’t do that to me. You’re a police officer and you have to protect and serve.”

Luis smiled. “Si, jefe, and right now I’m protecting all these other people from a selfish, crazy man. Buenas noches.”

The first thirteen, all women, were escorted up to the roof. The remaining twenty-four had to wait and endure Stanley pleading for help and not to be left behind. All wondered secretly if Officer García would really leave the crying, handcuffed man in the abandoned skyscraper.

Twenty-five minutes later, Luis was notified that Air One was inbound for the last group. Walsh started to lead them out the door. Stanley Poole was now in tears, begging not to be left there. García paused and walked over to the man.

"So, if I let you go, are you going to cause any problems or are you just going to sit quietly on the helicopter and be a good boy?"

"I promise I won't cause problems. Please, just don't leave me here."

"Before I take those handcuffs off, I think you owe everyone here an apology for your behavior."

"Yes, yes, I'm very sorry for my actions. There's no excuse for the way I was acting. Please, forgive me, everyone," the now contrite man begged.

Luis took the handcuffs off and helped Stanley to his feet. "Okay, let's get you guys out of here."

The Wells Fargo Building, Atlanta, Saturday, 0225 hours

The floors all began to blur together but finally, they were almost finished. Over one hundred survivors had been sent to the top floor, where Luis waited. He would babysit them until transport could be arranged. The CDC's helicopter had left to refuel but Major Campbell said there were two Air Force Pave Hawks enroute from Dobbins Air Force base, located north of Atlanta.

The two teams met up on the 4th floor after it had been cleared. They needed a breather before finishing the last three. They sipped water, sitting with their backs to the wall, quietly sharing what they had encountered.

"Let's stay together for these last few floors," Chuck ordered. "We're all exhausted and I think we'll be better together. We're almost done but we need to stay sharp."

Team Two led the way as they entered the 3rd floor. This level contained the corporate gym on the side closest to the explosions and the management and security offices for the building on the other side. The fitness center had floor-to-ceiling glass walls and they could see movement inside. The glass appeared to have an opaque finish.

In the corridor, four infected people were bent over a prone body. The zombies, three men and a woman, were all wearing workout attire. Their victim had been an older African-American woman wearing a beige pants suit, although, by now, there was barely enough left to recognize her race or gender. As the door opened from the stairwell, one of the infected men turned and got to his feet, staring towards the opening. Chris was leading the way this time and quickly brought his rifle up, engaging the zombies.

Rogers' quick and accurate gunfire brought down three of the fitness zombies and Marshall shot the last one. Both teams were in the hallway now, listening. They could hear growling coming from the direction of the gym. Suddenly, a large figure slammed into the glass wall, cracking it. A second try and the zombie crashed into the corridor. The broken glass ripped him up but did not slow him down. The muscular white man, wearing a tank top and shorts, sprinted towards the officers.

Several other figures darted through the opening he had made, following him. The CDC officers fired quickly, making good head shots on the zombies, stopping all of them. Hours before, these twelve people had chosen to exercise after work before starting for home. They had found that normally, after they trained for an hour or so, traffic died down enough to make their commute a little easier.

Today, however, the suicide bomber and the car bomb had blasted infected shrapnel through the fitness center as they had trained. After the second explosion, the woman in the pants suit had walked across the hall from the management office to see if everyone in the gym was OK. When she opened the door, the first four dove onto her, knocking her back into the corridor and killing her.

The officers listened for any other zombies that might be on the floor. Everything was quiet. Chris led the way towards the fitness center. The glass wasn't opaque. Blood splatter from two other victims coated the glass.

"Check this out!" exclaimed Rogers. "This glass is at least half an inch thick and that guy was able to break through it like it was nothing."

"Scotty," said Chuck, "can you take a mouth swab or two from some of these infected? Do one on that big guy who smashed through the glass and maybe one more. We'll get them to the lab to see what's going on. I'm wondering if these bombs came from DC, where Team Two found the radioactive materials and the zombie virus side-by-side."

Three women were hiding in the management offices. They had seen their friend and supervisor killed and partially eaten as they had watched through their window. The zombies had not realized they were nearby or they would have probably become victims also.

One of the survivors was a very obese woman who had to walk with a cane. Andy directed the three women that they needed to take the stairs to the top floor so they could be evacuated. The big woman balked at this.

"I can't climb those stairs. I have knee problems."

"Your choice, lady," answered Fleming, clearly agitated. "Climb the stairs or stay here and become zombie food."

"But, you don't understand. I need help. Can't I take the elevator?"

"The elevators are off-limits. They've been infected with the virus and were possibly damaged in the explosions. They're not safe. We still have a few floors left to clear so you better start climbing now."

Eddie spoke to the other two women. "There's another officer on the top floor who'll get you on a helicopter that'll fly you out of here. This building is overrun and it's not safe to leave through the lobby.

"You ladies can try and help your friend but you need to get going. Go straight to the top. Don't open the doors for any other levels. We think we've killed them all but we could've missed some.

The stairwell is safe all the way to the top."

Chuck stopped the women as they were leaving for the stairwell. "I see the security office," pointing to a closed door. "What happened to the security officers?"

A petite Asian lady replied, "Normally, there's always one of them in that office, monitoring the cameras. A few minutes after the explosions, he ran out saying the officer in the lobby needed help. He never came back."

The door to the security office was locked. It was made of wood and the top half was frosted glass. McCain pulled the metal expandable baton off of his utility belt and flicked it open. One strike broke the window and gave them access to the office.

A bank of nine television monitors were hanging on the wall above the desk. Andy Fleming was the closest thing the enforcement unit had to a computer expert, having worked for an IT company in the year between getting out of the Marines and coming to work for the CDC. The camera feed for the lobby had all the officers looking on in disbelief. There appeared to be over a hundred Zs milling around the lobby of the skyscraper. The doors had a sensor-opening device, and they could see the infected wandering in and out.

"Do they have outside cameras?" Chuck asked. "It would be good to get a real-time feel for what's going on out there."

Andy played with the system for a few minutes and then four of the screens started showing the four sides of the building. Streetlights illuminated the area to show that the infected were everywhere. Many were standing motionless in the street in front of the building.

Others were walking quickly towards the downtown area. Another large group was congregating near the entrance to the apartment building next to the Wells Fargo building. That was the one that Atlanta SWAT had been clearing.

"Can you back it up to 1700 hours, when the bombs went off?" Eddie queried.

The angle was not the best and did not show the car when it exploded. The result of the explosion, however, was caught on video. Debris, flaming shrapnel, smoke, and the effects on all the surrounding vehicles were clearly seen at the moment of detonation.

Fleming backed it up further and the confrontation between the female Atlanta police officer and the suicide bomber was played out in front of them. The CDC officers saw her challenge him, bringing her pistol up. The terrorist turning and firing. The officer returning fire and striking him, setting the bomb off.

"That's what happened in New York and in DC, also," Chuck said. "A terrorist parks a car bomb somewhere dense and then leaves on foot to blow himself up in another part of the city. Here, a good cop just happened up on the scene and stopped him before he could get very far."

Andy rummaged around the office and found a memory stick. He inserted it into the computer and started downloading the videos that had been recorded. They would be evidence later on and might give the FBI something to work with.

The Wells Fargo Building, Atlanta, Saturday, 0320 hours

The last two floors were part of the Georgia Institute of Technology's Research facility. The 2nd floor was a research and development lab for robotics. Unfortunately, there were no survivors to give the officers a tour.

There were, however, thirteen Ph.D. students in white lab coats who had been infected when the suicide bomber detonated. A young Asian woman had been killed by a ball bearing to the head. Her decimated and mostly eaten body lay in the middle of the floor.

Three other students had been injured and infected in the blast. They quickly turned and started attacking their friends, who were trying to administer first-aid. Within minutes, the only people left in the lab were zombies.

The officers stood outside the door listening to the growling and snarling inside. Scotty had point on this one but the door was locked. There was a keypad on the wall next to the entrance.

"Let's see how strong these tech students are," said Smith with a smile. "You guys back down the corridor and get ready. I'll see if I can't stir them up a little, kind of like a hornet's nest."

After his teammates were in position, the big man slapped the wooden door twice with his open hand.

"I've got two hundred and fifty pounds of white meat waiting for you," he yelled. "Come and eat me!"

He then ran to join his mates.

They formed a skirmish line thirty yards from the door.

"You need professional help," Jimmy grinned at Scotty as he took his place in line.

Smith just flashed him a big grin and raised the shotgun. A body crashed into the door and then another. This was repeated over and over for five minutes. A cracking sound was finally heard as the door started to give. The bodies continued to ram the door until it popped open.

The infected students poured into the hallway and rushed towards the federal police officers. Their white lab jackets were bloody and the officers could see open, jagged wounds on all of them. Each of the students was Indian, Korean, or Taiwanese. This explained why it took them so long to smash the door open. Not a single one of the tech students weighed over one hundred and thirty pounds.

The suppressed M4s and Scotty's unsuppressed shotgun quickly cut down the zombies. The officers paused to reload and cautiously moved into the lab to clear and check it for survivors. There were dried pools of blood and the familiar smell of smoke drifting in through the shattered windows but no living people.

The 1st floor contained a large computer lab. Surprisingly, no one had been infected on this level. The way that the lab was configured, banks of large computer servers had protected the students from infection.

Flying shrapnel destroyed several of the servers but the eleven survivors were fine. They told the officers that six of their friends had gone down to the lobby to investigate and had never come back. After the explosions, the survivors started following the coverage online and had decided to stay put.

Eddie, Chuck, and Andy stood by the windows, looking down at the destruction below them. The growl of the infected carried up to them. From their vantage point, McCain estimated they could see around two thousand. And that was just on one side of the building.

"Well, it's been fun but I think it's time to get these people to the roof and call it a day," Chuck said.

"What's next?" asked Eddie.

"I don't know. We'll go check in at the CP at the Braves Stadium and then I think we'll all take thirty-six hours to rest and recover. My best guess is that we'll be doing a lot more of this. I also need to call over to our HQ and see if they've seen any Zs. I alerted the powers-that-be earlier that they might need to evacuate the night shift. That's only five miles from here. We may need new offices come Monday morning."

The roof of the Wells Fargo Building, Atlanta, Saturday, 0445 hours

"This is our ride," said Luis, as the helicopter materialized and began its descent.

All the people they had rescued had been air lifted to the staging area near the Atlanta Braves Stadium. As they waited, the officers had sat on the roof talking quietly or dozing. McCain and García kept watch as their exhausted teammates waited for the Blackhawk.

The Centers for Disease Control Headquarters had been evacuated almost five hours earlier. The security officers helped the third shift of scientists and specialists get some of their gear packed up and loaded into their vehicles. The director had been following the event and decided to err on the side of caution.

The men stirred at the noise of the rotors and got to their feet. Chuck let everyone board before he joined them. Crewman Bobby Walsh handed him a headset as he snapped on the seatbelt.

"Welcome aboard, Mr. McCain. Congratulations on rescuing all those people. It sounded pretty chaotic inside. Where can we take you gentlemen?" Major Daniel Campbell's voice came through Chuck's headphones.

"Thanks for the ride, Major. You can drop some of the guys off at the staging area. We have one of our SUVs there. Please take the rest of us to DeKalb-Peachtree airport. We've got another vehicle there. After that, we're done until Monday morning unless I get other orders."

"Very good, sir. Let's get going."

In seconds the helicopter lifted into the air, turned north, and pulled away from the abandoned skyscraper.

"Major, as we head towards the evac and staging area, can you turn the FLIR on and let me know how far the Zs have traveled up the interstate? We need to know how fast they're moving and if they're going to need to move the CP."

"The FLIR won't do us any good," Campbell answered. "These things are dead and don't put out much of a heat signature. We dropped down on our way to pick you up and illuminated them with the spotlight.

"The lead element is a several hundred strong. They're five miles from the staging area and moving steadily that way. A group of about three hundred is less than a mile behind them. Another six hundred are bringing up the rear, half a mile back. One of the news choppers said they are spreading out like that in every direction. We could take some of them down, or at least thin them out with Bobby's mini gun but the DHS told us not to go that route."

"What? There are thousands of Zs loose in the city. Let's kill as many of them as we can, any way we can."

"Yes, sir, I agree, but those were our orders."

Idiots!" McCain said, angrily. "An entire city is about to be lost. What was their rationale?"

"They said they didn't want to turn an urban area into a war zone. And, that was coming straight from the White House. At this point, they think the Zs can be contained by conventional measures without resorting to military hardware.

"The President or his advisors feel that if we use the military we'll be somehow admitting defeat. Our military has pretty much destroyed Iran but we don't want to give them any reason to gloat by having to use the American military on US soil."

"Idiots!" Chuck repeated. "I'll make some phone calls and see if I can get you guys weapons free when we land."

McCain passed the information on to his men. They just shook their heads in disbelief. It was the zombie apocalypse and Washington wanted to play politics and not ruffle any feathers.

Chapter Ten

Waiting for the Tsunami

Staging Area, Braves Stadium Parking Lot, Saturday, 0515 hours

Scotty leaned back against the bulkhead of the helicopter for the short flight and pulled out his smart phone. He had not checked it for hours and saw that he had multiple texts from Emily asking if he was OK. She said she was still at the staging area waiting to be given an assignment. She also texted that no one at the command post seemed to have any idea what to do.

He sent her a quick note saying that he was fine and that he'd be there in ten minutes. Smith looked up to see McCain carrying on an animated conversation with their pilot. Chuck looked upset. That's not good. It took a lot to make McCain angry. After years in the military and now working as a federal police officer, Smith wasn't surprised by any of the stupid decisions that came out of Washington.

It's been a long two days, Scotty thought. He looked around the helicopter at his exhausted teammates. Thank God, everybody is

OK. These guys had become his family. Them and Emily.

Emily Clark was really a special girl. He thought back to their conversation two nights ago. Or was that a week ago? She had started crying because she was worried about him. He didn't think anyone had ever cried for him before.

His mother might have but he didn't even remember what she looked like. Scotty's father told him and his two brothers that he had come home from work one day and she had disappeared. She had packed her stuff after her three young boys had gotten on the school bus and was gone when they all got home.

But Emily had cried and called him a 'big goofball.' That made him smile. Actually, every time he thought of Emily he smiled.

The Blackhawk flared and made a soft landing. The officers felt and heard the engines shutting down. Something must be going on, Smith thought, if Major Campbell and the helicopter crew were going to be staying for a while. McCain was out the door and ducking under the slowing rotors, rushing towards the command post.

Two firemen wearing all of their protective gear, including their breathers, appeared holding Geiger-Mueller detectors. One of them waved it over Chuck as he passed by. They then checked each of the officers as they exited the aircraft.

Scotty was the third man off of the helicopter. After getting an all clear from the fireman who waved the radiation detection device over him, the muscular man looked around, wondering where Emily might be. There were rows of ambulances, fire trucks, and both marked and unmarked police cars. Three SWAT trucks sat off to the side, as well.

Decontamination tents were set up near the fire trucks and ambulances. Each of the survivors had registered on the GM detector and had been stripped, decontaminated, and then given fresh clothes. They had all been in the detonation zones when the radioactive material in the dirty bomb was blasted outward. The CDC officers, however, barely registered at all because the nuclear waste had settled to the ground by the time they got to the scene.

Scotty, not seeing his paramedic girlfriend, reached for his phone to send her a text. Something hit him and almost knocked him to the ground. Emily grabbed him and hugged him hard.

"I was so worried about you, Scotty."

She had told herself she wasn't going to start crying. Emily was not a crier. In spite of herself, though, the tears came as she and Scotty held each other.

Smith's teammates walked around the couple, heading towards the CP. "That's right," commented Jimmy, not slowing his pace. "You hold onto that man. He's had a rough couple of days."

The couple kissed, their first one since they had started dating, standing next to a Blackhawk helicopter, surrounded by armed first responders and emergency vehicles.

"I'd hoped to take you out some place really nice before we had our first kiss. Sorry about that," Scotty whispered, when they came up for air.

"It's fine," said Emily, smiling up at him. "The main thing is that you're safe. They're saying that the entire city is overrun."

Smith continued to hold her. "That's only part of it. The Zs are marching this way. That was why Chuck was the first one off the helicopter. He's going to go try and shake some things loose."

"How long do we have before they get here?" Clark asked, the alarm evident in her voice.

"Probably three or four hours. This helicopter's got a machine gun on it. They could take out hundreds of those things but Washington doesn't want them using military weapons in the city. If Chuck can't talk some sense into them, you guys are going to have to evacuate and soon."

"What are you going to do? Is your team going to stay and fight? And what about your apartment? How are you going to get home?"

"Yeah, well, there's not much I can do about it. The army taught me to live a simple life. I'll probably go home with Chuck. He's got an extra bedroom."

"My couch is pretty comfortable if you need another place to stay," she offered, a shy smile on her face.

Scotty smiled and kissed her again. "I may take you up on that, eventually. I have a feeling the next few days are going to be intense."

FBI Supervisory Special Agent Thomas Burns stood in the command post with representatives of most of the metro-Atlanta police departments, the Department of Homeland Security, the Atlanta CDC Director, and various other federal agencies. A single upper level FBI director and his assistant had arrived an hour before. The fire department had set up portable lights so the personnel in the CP could work.

Normally, by now, Burns would have had all of the Washington brass breathing down his neck on an incident of this size. Washington, D.C., however, was in the midst of its own crisis and they could only afford to send the Deputy Director of the Weapons of Mass Destruction Directorate, Charles E. Trimble, III. Trimble's assistant, Special Agent Mir Turani, was thankful to get out of DC for a little while.

Burns saw the big man in dark tactical clothing approaching the command post. He was wearing a black helmet, web gear, and had a suppressed M4 slung from his chest. If I didn't know better, Burns thought, I'd almost swear that's Chuck McCain. But the last time I saw McCain was yesterday and he was leaving for Washington.

There were multiple conversations taking place in the CP. As the heavily armed man walked up, the talking died down and every eye was on him. He unsnapped the kevlar helmet and removed it from his head, looking around at the assembled federal and local law enforcement and EMS brass.

"McCain? I thought you were in DC?" Burns walked over to Chuck with an incredulous look on his face.

"Hey, Burns. I was, but we flew right down when the bombs

started going off."

"Were you with your guys in the Wells Fargo Building?"

McCain nodded, wiping the sweat off of his face and sighing. "Yeah, I was in there. We cleared the building but on the flight up here, I heard about some stupid orders not allowing us to use any heavy weapons?"

The FBI agent looked uncomfortable and lowered his voice. "Yeah, I'm not sure where that came from. I mean I know it came from the White House, but it doesn't sound like something the President would push."

Chuck was angry and wanted to lash out. Not at Burns but at the politics behind not allowing them to utilize the military resources they had at their disposal. He had seen the thousands of Zs spreading out in every direction. He knew military air power could not kill them all but he also knew that the police officers here at this staging area had no chance of stopping the oncoming zombies.

McCain was a professional, though. He knew he needed to brief the brass here on what they had seen and done. Maybe he could convince them to withdraw all the officers if Washington would not let them use their heavy firepower. But, withdraw to where? If they did not eliminate these infected, their numbers would continue to grow. How many other cities would be lost?

Chuck nodded at Burns. "Why don't you gather everyone around and I'll give a quick briefing on what we did and what I saw on the flight out of the city?"

Trimble and Turani had not said anything to McCain. They listened closely to everything the CDC Supervisory Agent in Charge said. Turani, especially, took everything in. This was his first time to see the famous Chuck McCain in person and he did not want to miss anything.

"We rescued close to two hundred people," Chuck concluded, "and probably killed three hundred or so Zs. That entire area of the city is overrun. I saw thousands of them around the skyscraper we just cleared.

"On our flight up here, we saw over a thousand coming this way. They'll be here in a few hours and Washington isn't allowing us to use any heavy weapons. Our Blackhawk is equipped with a mini gun that could put a serious dent in the Zs but for some reason we aren't being allowed to use it."

"I take it that you disagree with that order, Mr. McCain?" asked Deputy Director of the Weapons of Mass Destruction Directorate Trimble.

"Who's that?" Chuck asked, looking at Thomas. Burns introduced the two men.

"And this is his assistant, Special Agent Mir Turani."

McCain nodded at the two men, fixing his gaze on Turani. "Iranian? he asked.

Mir bristled, "Is that any of your business?"

"No offense, Special Agent. Just curious. I've always had a thing for trying to figure out where different names come from."

"My parents emigrated here when the Shah was overthrown in 1979."

Chuck nodded and looked at Trimble.

"Yes, sir. I do disagree with that order. This staging area will be overrun. If you can get the National Guard here, we might have a chance of holding it, but the hundred or so officers here can't do it. And even if, by some miracle, we manage to kill all the zombies, we're going to take casualties. A few helicopter gunships could eliminate the bulk of the Zs and then the SWAT teams could mop up the stragglers."

"So, you're the expert now, Mr. McCain?" Turani asked.

Careful, Chuck, he told himself. He's trying to bait you. He took a deep breath and held it, slowly exhaling, and letting a smile come to his face.

"Yes, I'm the expert or at least one of them. My men and I, along with the other CDC officers in different cities, have been leading the way since our enemies deployed this bio-terror virus. My officers took out a group of suicide bombers yesterday, a couple of hours from here. Also yesterday, one of my other teams took down one of the most wanted bomb-makers in the world and apprehended one of the terrorists responsible for the attack at the University of Georgia.

"I was there in the middle of that attack at UGA and if it wasn't for the mini gun on that Blackhawk, we would have all been killed and there would have been no survivors."

Trimble smirked and nodded. "Oh, I've been following all of your exploits. Your men got some of the suicide bombers but I understand a few got away. And, yes, your team did shoot and kill a notorious bomb maker and terrorist in Virginia, after he had already dispatched his men to New York, Washington, and Atlanta. It seems like you and your men are always just a little late to the party."

McCain realized he was staring at the deputy director's throat. No, you can't kill him, he told himself.

Chuck lowered his voice and looked into the man's eyes.

"And what have you done, Mr. Deputy Director? We haven't received a single piece of actionable intelligence from your office. I didn't even know the FBI had a Weapons of Mass Destruction Directorate until five minutes ago. It would seem to a simple street cop like me that the zombie virus would be your primary mission."

Trimble quickly looked away, cleared his throat, and acted as if he had not heard anything McCain had just said.

"Well, sir, this is clearly a policy decision that is over both of our pay grades. I think these fine policemen and women will be able to bring these infected people down and show the world that we do not need to unleash our military weapons on our homeland.

"The President wants to let Americans know that we are winning this war and that our local and federal law enforcement officers can handle this crisis without military intervention. This is a good place to stop the onslaught and I'm sure that these fine local officers, FBI agents, and your agents from the CDC will keep these infected people from going any further north."

"Are you going to stay and help us fight, Mr. Deputy Director?" Chuck asked, looking into both Trimble's and Turani's eyes.

Trimble gave a small smile and said, "No, I'll leave that to you, Mr. McCain. After all, you are the expert."

With that, Trimble and Turani turned and walked to the other side of the CP. Burns shook his head.

"I'm sorry, Chuck. He's no cop. This is just a stepping-stone for him to get a bigger and better job in the Department of Justice and then run for some office. He has no idea what he's doing.

"Before you got here, I had the same conversation with them. A few gunships could engage the Zs on some of the long, deserted stretches of interstate. There would be no collateral damage and no civilians would be in danger. He just told me that if I wanted to 'climb the ladder' at the Bureau, I needed to see the Big Picture."

"Yeah," said Chuck, "but considering where he has his head, I'm surprised he can see anything."

Staging Area, Braves Stadium Parking Lot, Saturday, 0730 hours

At 0600 hours, the FAA grounded all news helicopters. The previous evening, and even into the early morning of the next day, the feds had waived the non-flying exemptions for them and allowed them to keep broadcasting from the air. With the President's order not to utilize the military to stop the zombies, however, the administration wanted to control what was being released to the public.

The media was being kept in another of the stadium parking lots a quarter mile north, off of Stadium Parkway. This road ran parallel to I-75 and meant that the press was also in path of the zombies. The Atlanta Police Liaison Officer gave an updated briefing at 0700 hours. The officer encouraged the reporters to leave and let them know that the police could not protect them. Every available officer was going to be needed to fight the oncoming Zs.

At 0545 hours, Chuck had briefed his men on the situation and let them know that they were still needed. No rest for the weary. A big fight was on the horizon. The Zs were coming straight towards them, the interstate funneling them directly towards the staging area. He told the CDC officers to check their weapons, reload their magazines, find some food, and to get a nap. He would wake them before the fun started.

Major Campbell agreed to stay airborne, providing updates on the progress of the zombie horde. Campbell now estimated at least two thousand Zs were heading north, in the direction of the command post. Air Force helicopters were monitoring other groups moving in different directions out of the city.

Earlier, at 0600 hours, McCain had called Shaun Taylor, Admiral Williams' assistant. There was no answer so he left a voice mail asking for a call. At 0630, McCain's phone vibrated. The caller ID showed it was the admiral himself calling.

"Good morning, sir," Chuck answered.

"Good morning, Mr. McCain. I understand you've had an eventful few days."

"Yes, sir. You could say that."

"Well, first of all, congratulations to you and your men for tracking down Terrell Hill and Usama Zayad. I had no idea you'd be able to find Hill so quickly. And, taking out Zayad was even more good news."

"Thank you, Admiral, but that was all the doing of Eddie Marshall, one of my team leaders. He worked for the US Marshals Service before he came to work for us. I'd heard he was pretty good at tracking down fugitives. He and his men did an exceptional job."

"They certainly did. Hill is spilling his guts, even as we speak. To have done as much damage as he did, he knows surprisingly little. We did get one important piece of intel from him that has helped us tie up at least one loose end. Your colleagues in DC will be getting a visit from my assistant, Mr. Taylor, in the very near future, and giving them a very special mission."

"Walker and Trang both know about the Agency's involvement, sir," Chuck confessed. "I told them."

There was a pause and a deep breath on the other end of the phone. "Why did you feel a need to tell them, Mr. McCain?"

Chuck almost laughed. "Well, sir, you guys weren't very subtle when you sent the van to take custody of Hill. Jay was on Seal Team Six and Tu was a Green Beret. They knew both of the contractors who came and got him. Jay and Tu started asking Eddie questions. He was able to deflect them until I arrived.

"Trang and Walker are two high level operators. They knew something was up, so I had them sign a disclosure form and told them everything. I figured it was better to go ahead and tell them rather than having them trying to figure it out on their own and getting their other officers involved. Honestly, they couldn't care less since they had a lot of contact with the Agency when they were spec ops warriors."

"That might actually be better," admitted the admiral. "I was going to have to come up with an elaborate DHS cover story for Shaun to use when he meets with them. Now, the cards are on the table. So, please tell me, what's happening in Atlanta?"

McCain told him everything that he had observed and why it was absolutely necessary to bring some military assets into play if they were going to take the city back. He let the admiral know that the police staging area was in the path of a large group of infected. Other big groups, however, were moving in every direction, through the downtown area and out of the city, and on all the other highways. Additional law enforcement barricades were set up at different points in and around Atlanta. None of them had enough manpower or firepower to stop the mass of zombies coming their way.

"Admiral, do you know a deputy director with the FBI named Charles Trimble? They sent him down here to monitor what's happening."

"Charles Trimble, III. Oh yes. He probably wouldn't admit it but we're pretty sure the suggestion to not use the military came from his office. Is his young lapdog, Special Agent Turani, with him?"

"Yes, sir. That explains why Trimble got a little upset when I said this was a stupid decision."

Williams laughed. "That would do it. Trimble thinks a lot of himself but he's actually not that bright. He has political aspirations and his eyes set on the attorney general's office, but he's no cop and not even a very good lawyer.

"The idea for not using the military or any heavy weapons probably originated with Turani. He's smart and a pretty good attorney. He's been riding Trimble's coattails for a while now. He's also our prime suspect for some of the leaks they've been having over there. We've haven't been able to catch him with a smoking gun yet. If he's not a Muslim extremist and a traitor, I'll be very surprised.

"For now, do your best with what you have. You're a resourceful person. Try to eliminate as many of them as you can and then withdraw. I know this looks like a losing battle but the CIA Director and others in this crazy city are trying to get the President to listen to reason. The President seems to have bought into this idea that if we turn our military loose on American soil, we've somehow given our enemies a moral victory."

"Yes, sir. Thank you, Admiral. I'm just worried that by the time the President comes to his senses, it'll be too late."

When Chuck walked back to the command post, there was no sign of Charles E. Trimble, III or Mir Turani.

"Your buddies flee back to the safe confines of their DC offices?" he asked Burns.

"Not my buddies. Those two don't have many friends inside the agency. I have to admit, it did my heart good to watch you put both of them in their place. And you never raised your voice. Very impressive. And, yes, they'd seen enough and could report back that they put themselves in harm's way to make sure everything was being handled correctly."

“It’s easy to see why they don’t have any friends. And, speaking of friends, who’s in overall command of this scene?”

“Technically, I guess that would be me. That’s Atlanta’s Deputy Chief of Police over there, Beverly Cochran,” Burns said, pointing out a middle-age woman in an APD uniform on the other side of the CP. “She’s done a great job of getting all these assets in place. It’s just that none of us know where to start and we have a mass of Zs coming towards us. This is kind of starting to feel like the Alamo, McCain.”

“Okay,” said Chuck. “I don’t want to step on anybody’s toes but we have maybe two thousand of those things that’ll be here in an hour. We need to get organized and ready to fight. We can’t let them pass unopposed. Our orders are to make a stand. Marietta is just up the road and we have to try and stop them or at least thin the ranks some.”

Burns nodded. “Let’s go talk to the Chief and see if she has anything in mind.”

“It’s a pleasure to meet you, Mr. McCain,” said Deputy Chief Cochran, as they shook hands. “I spoke to a few of our SWAT team after the incident the other night in Virginia Highlands. They said that you and your men were the ‘real deal.’ Coming from our SWAT officers, that’s high praise.”

“Thank you, ma’am. They’re all quick learners and did a great job.”

Cochran was a short, stocky, fifty-something African-American woman. She had earned her position the old-fashioned way- she had worked for it. Cochran came up through the ranks, tackling a variety of positions. Her favorite job had been as a homicide investigator and she had been known as one of the best detectives in the country.

Standing in the command post, however, Cochran knew that she was in over her head. They all were. How many hundreds or thousands of zombies were coming their way? And she was supposed to stop them with a hundred cops? With the exception of the SWAT officers and the CDC agents on the scene, none of them were ready for this.

When she had first arrived at the CP a few hours earlier, the deputy chief had directed some of her officers to drive south in the northbound lanes of the interstate. With traffic gridlocked around the incident location, nothing was driving out of the city. They had managed to rescue over a hundred people. The last group of officers had gone too far south, though, encountering the front elements of the zombies. Six of her officers were lost. The chief cancelled any further rescue efforts.

One of the things that Deputy Chief Cochran's officers loved about her was that she didn't think she had all the answers. In reality, her job and the job of the other executive leaders at the police department was to make decisions to keep the police agency moving forward. The best ideas did not always come from her. They often came from her people, the ones out in the field doing the work.

"Mr. McCain, we need some help. Agent Burns and I have been talking but we're both not really sure what we should be doing. What do you think?"

Chuck quickly outlined what he thought they needed to do, if Agent Burns and Chief Cochran would allow him. She quickly told McCain that he was in tactical control of every police officer at the staging area. Burns nodded in agreement. This was not the time for egos or jurisdiction squabbles. They needed someone to take charge and get them ready to fight.

North of Atlanta, Saturday, 0800 hours

Hakeem and Abdul were in the white Chevrolet van. Omar drove the black Volkswagen Jetta. Before they left the Islamic Center, Hakeem had briefed the two men and helped them put their suicide vests back on and armed them. Thanks to the local news coverage, he knew exactly where the closest police staging area and command post was set up.

The news channel had shown aerial footage from the previous day of large groups of zombies moving throughout the city, up the interstates, and now closing in on the location near the Braves Stadium where the police and first responders waited. That was where Hakeem and his two soldiers would attack. While the infected attacked the police from the front, the soldiers of Allah would hit them from the rear.

Hakeem did not have a suicide vest of his own. He did have his AK-47, however, and several magazines of 7.62x39mm ammo. Today would be a day of vengeance. Hakeem had lost many friends over the years to the infidel soldiers. Today, he would shed some American blood on American soil.

Staging Area, Braves Stadium Parking Lot, Saturday, 0815 hours

Chuck had gone right to work. He had his seven men, twelve SWAT officers, sixty-five patrol officers, and eight FBI agents. Not quite a hundred officers to stop two thousand hungry zombies. Two of the three SWAT teams previously at the staging area had been sent back to their own counties. Both of those teams been pulled an hour before to protect their own jurisdictions as the infected moved in every direction out of Atlanta.

Deputy Chief Cochran had sent out a help call for additional officers from her own department and some of the surrounding police agencies. Supposedly, there were officers on the way. Several of the other departments, however, saw the news as well, and knew that the zombies would eventually be in their neighborhoods and were hesitant to send away their manpower when they might soon be needed there.

Along with not having enough shooters, another challenge was that Interstate 285 was half a mile south of the staging area. Chuck wanted to prevent the zombies from getting on that highway. I-285 is the Atlanta loop and would give the Zs even more access to other parts of the city. They needed to keep the infected moving north on Interstate 75 so they could kill as many of them as possible before the police would be forced to retreat.

Before the I-285 intersection, however, there were two other exits that the police needed to prevent the infected from using. Cumberland Boulevard was the first one and Akers Mill Road was half a mile further north. Chuck quickly developed a plan to keep the zombies moving north on I-75.

Of the sixty-five patrol officers on scene, only thirty-two were equipped with rifles. Another thirteen had pump action shotguns. The other twenty were armed with their handguns. Chuck shook his head when he found this out.

The effective range of a pistol and a shotgun loaded with buckshot was twenty-five to thirty yards. And the idea of making head shots at that range with those weapons was not realistic. The sad fact is that most police officers are, at best, average shots.

Chuck asked Scotty to take charge of the two APD SWAT snipers and to take out as many Zs as they could from distance. Smith borrowed an extra sniper rifle, a Remington Model 700 in .300 Winchester Magnum, from the tactical team. The CDC officer was also able to repair the extractor on his M4 rifle. The Atlanta SWAT truck had a number of gun parts stored on board and within a few minutes, the rifle was functional again.

As an Army Ranger sniper, Scotty had engaged and killed targets at distances of over a thousand yards in Iraq. The average American police sniper shot was around seventy yards. The two SWAT snipers had both trained at long distances, however, and the three of them would start engaging zombies very soon.

McCain had Jimmy and Andy putting the police officers in good fighting positions near the command post. Jimmy had been a Marine infantry officer and had led young Marines into battle on two combat tours in Iraq. Andy had had multiple deployments as a special operations Marine in Afghanistan, Iraq, and other hotspots throughout the world. They both knew what needed to be done.

South of the Staging Area, Braves Stadium Parking Lot, Saturday, 0845 hours

The Blackhawk touched down on the overpass where Cumberland Boulevard crossed I-75. Major Campbell landed about fifty yards from the center of the bridge. That would be where the three snipers, Andy, Jimmy, and seven other SWAT officers would start engaging the horde of zombies. The heavily armed men exited quickly and took positions facing south.

Before picking up the officers at the staging area, Campbell had done a flyover of the mass of infected steadily moving north. Chuck had run up to the helicopter to hear the latest from the pilot in person.

"It looks like about two thousand now, coming straight for us. And they're moving fast. The lead group of six or seven hundred is about five minutes in front of the others. When I drop these guys off on the bridge, the Zs should just be coming into view."

"Okay," replied McCain. "I've briefed them to be ready to pull out when the Zs get inside a hundred yards. The rabbit will be under the bridge. When you take off, the rabbit will haul ass down to the next bridge, making enough noise to keep them all coming this way. Repeat the same thing on the Akers Mill overpass and then again on 285. After that, bring the guys back here and then, can you monitor everything from the air?"

"Yes, sir. We can do that. We're here to support you. We could support you a lot better with our mini-gun, though."

McCain nodded, patting the pilot on the shoulder. Chuck would have preferred to be on the helicopter with the officers. Since he had been given tactical command of the scene, however, he knew that he needed to stay in the command post. This would allow him to monitor all the radio traffic and move officers around as needed. He knew that with the number of zombies coming their way, though, he would be in the fight eventually.

Scotty peered through the range finder scope mounted on the Remington bolt-action rifle in .300 Win Mag. The first of the infected had just come around the bend, about five hundred yards south of the Chattahoochee River. When they reached the river, they would be a thousand yards from the Cumberland Boulevard Bridge. For now, they were roughly fifteen hundred yards from the shooters.

Smith would have preferred a prone position from which to shoot. The bridge had a two-foot high solid concrete wall, with a four-foot chain link on top of that, to discourage people from committing suicide or throwing things onto the traffic below. A support pole ran the length of the fence. He would have to shoot standing, using the pole as his base. Not the best position to shoot long distance from, but it would have to do.

He laid the muzzle of the rifle on top of the fence and cinched the sling tight around his left arm. The stock of the gun rested on the horizontal metal pole. He pulled a hand towel out of a cargo pocket, rolled it up, and slid it under the stock. According to the rangefinder on his scope, the Zs were now at one thousand three hundred and eighty yards.

The lead zombie was a stocky white male wearing a red and white Atlanta Falcons jersey. The zoom on the optic allowed Smith see his bloody face and the man's mouth opening and closing. The right side of his neck was torn open with blood covering the zombie's jersey and right arm.

Behind the Falcons fan, hundreds of other infected people had come into view. The virus was no respecter of persons. Black, white, Asian, Hispanic, male, female, young and old. They all were moving north as if on a group mission.

"I need a spotter," Smith said. "I'm going to start engaging but I need to know where I'm hitting for the first shot or two."

He had not shot this borrowed rifle yet, although he had used one like it on many occasions in Iraq. The SWAT snipers had zeroed it at a hundred yards, common practice for police sharpshooters and military snipers. Scotty still needed to fire a couple of shots to see where the rounds would be impacting on his targets.

One of tactical snipers with a scoped rifle set up next to Smith as his spotter to help him get the .300 Win Mag zeroed. The other SWAT sniper also settled into a shooting position on the other side of Smith and asked, "When do you want us to start shooting?"

"Let's wait until they get closer. I used to shoot at this distance a lot when I was in the army. I think I can put a few down. Who knows, maybe if I hit a couple, the rest will get scared and run off."

Jimmy laughed. "Big Guy, if you can do that, you'll have my undying affection."

Without looking up, Scotty grinned, "Bro, you told me I already had it."

To his spotter, Smith said, "Front Z wearing a Falcon's jersey. They sucked this year anyway."

The sound of the shot echoed over the empty interstate. Two seconds later, the spotter reported, "Miss, no, wait, you hit the big black girl on his left. She's still moving but the round hit her in the right shoulder. Man, that pretty much blew her arm off at the shoulder. I'd bring it to your left about a foot and up about six inches."

Scotty made two adjustments to the scope. He sighted on the same man and squeezed the trigger again.

"Hit!" the sniper yelled. "Holy crap, that round took the top of his head off and hit the Z behind him in the chest."

"Okay, I'm dialed in now. Let's see what we can do," the bearded man said.

By the time the zombies crossed the Chattahoochee River, Smith had taken out fourteen. Two of his shots had dropped four of the creatures. The .300 Win Mag is a powerful cartridge and he desperately needed to use that to his advantage by taking out multiple targets with one round.

Only head shots would stop someone who had been infected with the virus. The densely packed mob meant that most of Smith's shots had punched through the first target and also hit another zombie behind them. Even if the shot did not find the second Z's head, Scotty hoped the big rounds did enough damage as they penetrated to at least slow the creatures down.

As the mob surged over the river, the two SWAT snipers started engaging with their Remington Model 700's in .308 caliber. This is a traditional sniper round and also performs well at long distances. Within seconds, they were adding to the kill count.

At around five hundred yards, Andy and Jimmy began firing their Colt M4s. While not configured as sniper rifles, they did have EOTech optics on them with a distance magnifier for longer-range shots. And, they were both Marines.

Of all the services, the Marines place the most emphasis on marksmanship. "Every Marine a rifleman" is their mantra. The other SWAT officers also fired into the ranks of the infected, just not as accurately.

Below them, from under the bridge, the officers could hear additional shooting. The 'rabbit,' Emily's ambulance, was parked on the interstate below the overpass, facing north. Her partner, Darnell Washington, had volunteered to act as bait to a flesh hungry multitude of zombies. Emily had wanted to drive but Scotty had threatened to handcuff her to a fire truck if she even tried.

In the back of the ambulance, Marshall, Estrada, and Rogers began shooting at the oncoming threats out the open back door. Eddie and Hollywood fired from a prone position on the floor of the vehicle, while the smaller framed Chris stretched out on the stretcher and picked off Zs. No one was rushing as they fired. At this distance, it was much more important to focus on the fundamentals and make good, quality shots.

"Team One Alpha to Team Two Alpha," Andy called Eddie.

"Team Two Alpha, go ahead."

"Can you have Darnell turn the lights and siren on now?"

"10-4, will do."

In seconds, the siren on the ambulance was blaring from the stationary vehicle. The red and white strobe lights were flashing and it was the perfect draw for the oncoming zombies. They had no understanding that their zombie comrades were being shot around them. The virus caused their bodies to respond only to stimuli. The loud noise with the flashing lights got their attention and they continued to move forward.

Both sets of officers, those on the bridge and those under it, were still firing as the infected closed to within three hundred yards. It did not seem that they had made any kind of a dent in the mass of creatures although they had killed at least seventy-five. Over the noise of the idling helicopter, the growl of over two thousand infected was clear. When the Zs passed inside a hundred yards, it was time to go.

"Wrap it up, guys, and let's get out of here," Fleming ordered. The men made their weapons safe and trotted towards the helicopter.

He called Eddie on the radio and told him it was time for them to head to the next interchange. The zombies were clearly agitated by the siren and flashing lights, with many starting to run towards the loud noise. Darnell began driving north at thirty-five miles an hour and stopped under the Akers Mill Bridge.

Major Campbell made a perfect landing on top of the Akers Mill Bridge and the shooters quickly moved into position along the top of that overpass. The Zs were already inside seven hundred yards when the bullets began tearing into them. At this distance, Scotty was able to take two heads off with one shot a few times.

The SWAT snipers and the other officers were also doing their part, dropping one infected after the other. The problem was that nothing slowed the pack down. They just kept coming.

Eddie and the CDC agents in the ambulance accounted for a number of kills themselves. Darnell left the siren and flashing strobe lights on, trying to keep the infected on the interstate rather than getting off the exit ramps. As bullets tore into the ranks of the Zs, those behind them often tripped over their bodies, causing others to trip as well. It did not matter, though. They continued to get to their feet and push onward.

Within minutes, it was time to move again. Fleming directed the men on the bridge to the helicopter and ordered the ambulance to pull back to the I-285 interchange. This would be the last overpass before they got to Windy Ridge Parkway and the staging area and command post. They would try to hold that position as long as they could and kill as many Zs as they could before they had to fall back.

Andy estimated that the twelve shooters on the bridge and the three in the ambulance killed close to two hundred at the first two bridges. That was not enough to stop the onslaught of two thousand. The staging area was looking more and more like it was only going to be a speed bump for the surging zombies.

Chapter Eleven

Broken Arrow

Cobb County Chamber of Commerce, Saturday, 0915 hours

Hakeem thanked Allah that the parking lot of the Chamber of Commerce was mostly empty. Just up ahead, he could see the police cruiser parked in the middle of the intersection with its strobe lights flashing. Hakeem turned into the big parking area of the C of C before getting to the officer's location.

His research earlier on the imam's computer had led him here. He and Omar parked their vehicles on the far end of the building. A few cars were scattered across the parking lot but the three terrorists did not see any other people as they prepared to attack the Americans.

All they had to do was walk through a small wooded area and they would be across the street from the staging area. The command post was on the far side of the parking lot but Hakeem knew that he, Abdul, and Omar would do much damage here. The police were focused on the large group of infected people coming towards them on the interstate. They had no idea that they were about to be attacked from the rear.

The zombie virus was a masterpiece, Hakeem thought. Hopefully, Allah would reward those who had created such a powerful weapon. The news broadcasts he had watched earlier showed thousands of these zombies in Atlanta, New York, and Washington, D.C. According to a police spokesperson, law enforcement had staging areas set up in strategic locations along all of the interstates in Atlanta. The police were spread very thin as they attempted to kill the infected.

As far as Hakeem could tell, only local and some federal police were manning these positions. He could not understand why the United States military was not bringing their incredible might to bear. As good as the American police were, they had no chance of stopping these creatures. This was another blessing from Allah.

The older terrorist led the way through the trees, his AK-47 held at a low ready. He did not have any web gear but he did have a magazine holder hung around his neck. It contained three thirty round mags, while Hakeem had one in the rifle and a fifth tucked into his rear pants pocket.

In minutes, the terrorists were at the edge of the wood line, looking across the street to where the police were preparing their defense. The staging area was a scene of people and vehicles in motion. Fire trucks and ambulances were being turned and positioned for quick getaways. Heavily armed police ran towards the bridge to get into position.

Marked and unmarked law enforcement vehicles were parked on the right side of the large parking area, closest to the interstate. The largest group of officers was in position on the Windy Ridge Parkway overpass. Around thirty nervous-looking police were facing south down I-75, waiting for their turn to fight. Another twenty were on the exit ramp. The two groups of officers formed an L ambush, Hakeem noticed.

The exit ramp was where the fight was going to get nasty. Officers clutched their rifles, shotguns, or pistols tightly. The news anchor had said that law enforcement officers had been ordered to stand and fight as long as they could. No one really knew what that meant. "As long as they could?"

On the left side of the large parking lot, the fire trucks and ambulances were standing by. The fire fighters and paramedics huddled close to their vehicles. They were close enough to render aid but far enough away that they could escape if it looked like the CP was going to be overrun. Several large tents were set up near the fire trucks. Another tent was set up on the backside of the staging area between the police and the EMS personnel.

That must be the command post, Hakeem thought. Uniformed and plain-clothes police officers were talking on their radios or cell phones. A man wearing an FBI windbreaker spoke to two men wearing black and carrying assault rifles.

The sound of rotor blades filled the air and a Blackhawk helicopter suddenly appeared over the three terrorists concealed in the woods. Hakeem felt a surge of panic, knowing that the helicopter was about to kill him. Many of his friends had been killed by the air power of the infidels and now they had come for him. He raised the AK-47 to his shoulder.

Staging Area, Braves Stadium Parking Lot, Saturday, 0920 hours

Chuck stood next to the CP, having just gotten off the phone with his daughter, Melanie. He had not spoken to her in a couple of days and wasn't sure how today was going to end. He hoped the assembled law enforcement firepower would kill all of the zombies. At the very least, he hoped they could eliminate the majority and then pull everyone back before engaging the Zs again.

Maybe the walking dead would just stay on the interstate and keep moving north. The officers could just keep shooting them from the overpasses. Once the zombies started exiting, however, it was going to be bad.

From here north, the metro Atlanta area was still densely populated and had not been evacuated. The local TV stations had been broadcasting an emergency message for the last few hours to those who lived in the Metro Atlanta area. People were being told to stay inside their homes and not try to flee the city. They were also told that the police had the situation under control.

In his heart, McCain knew that there were too many infected and not enough people with guns to stop them. For the moment, Melanie was still safe with her boyfriend, Brian Mitchell, and his parents who lived up near the South Carolina line. If the zombies continued unchecked, though, they would be in her neighborhood in less than forty-eight hours.

After talking with his daughter, Chuck asked to speak with Brian's dad, Tommy, and told him a little of what was going on. Chuck let him know that it was time to head for their relatives' farm in the mountains of North Carolina.

"But the news coverage says that you guys have this under control," said Tommy.

"Not even close," McCain replied. "The President has tied our hands and the zombies are going to keep marching and killing, eating and infecting everyone they come in contact with. Please get out of there and take care of my daughter for me. I can't worry about her and focus on what I have to do here."

The two men had never met but there was a feeling of connection.

"Don't worry, Chuck. We'll take care of Mel. We're going to start packing right now and be on the road in a few hours. Hopefully, you and your guys can handle this and you can come visit us. We look forward to meeting you in person and we're praying for you."

As he disconnected the call, McCain heard the Blackhawk coming in for a landing. Burns and García watched with Chuck as the helicopter went into a hover, preparing to land on the far side of the parking lot, near the fire trucks.

Scotty watched the staging area come into view out the right side window of the helicopter. A line of officers was in position on the bridge and another group was waiting on the exit ramp. Smith estimated that they had eliminated over two hundred and fifty Zs from the three overpasses, around ten percent of the infected. The rest were coming straight towards them. Yep, it was about to get ugly. He had just eighteen rounds of .300 Win Mag ammo left and then he would have to start engaging them with his M4.

After clearing the I-285 interchange, the rabbit vehicle had kept its lights and siren on until most of the mob had followed them under the bridge. Darnell then shut the emergency equipment off and accelerated back to the staging area. He stopped at the top of the ramp to let the officers out of the back of his vehicle.

Sirens suddenly filled the air and ten police cars with their emergency lights flashing came into view. They had been sent by the neighboring jurisdiction of Dekalb County. Each car had at least two officers in them and some had more. As they entered the large parking lot, they turned their emergency equipment off.

The Blackhawk was descending, now fifty feet off the ground, as McCain tried to count how many officers had just arrived in the line of police cars. At least twenty-five, he thought. I hope they all have rifles.

Luis had stayed by Chuck's side in the CP. He could move on his injured ankle, just not very well. He had been helping his boss keep up with the radio traffic and logistics.

"Luis, can you go meet those new officers and get them in position? Put most of them on the bridge and the rest on the exit ramp. Tell them to take all their ammo with them and get ready to start shooting. I think we only have about five minutes…"

Out of his peripheral vision, McCain saw two figures run out of the woods from across the street. One was charging straight for the helicopter that was about to touch down. The other was rushing towards the CP.

García turned to see what Chuck was looking at, immediately recognizing the threat. He started running as fast as his injured ankle would allow him towards the helicopter. The sound of gunfire carried over the sound of the helicopter's rotors.

"CDC One to Air One," McCain yelled into the radio. "Abort landing, I repeat abort landing!"

The Blackhawk touched down as co-pilot Captain Jessie Webb answered, "Air One to CDC One, repeat your last. I think we're taking ground fire."

The helicopter was now between Luis and the running figure. He swung to his left and saw him, a Middle Eastern-looking male, now only fifty yards from the aircraft. Luis saw that he was holding something in his right hand. It has to be a detonator, he thought. García raised his M4 and started to squeeze the trigger.

A sledgehammer blow struck his left side and Luis found himself lying on his back on the pavement. He tried to roll to his stomach and push himself up but only his right arm was working. He heard the popping of more shots just as he managed to get to his feet.

Who was shooting? he wondered, trying to raise his rifle with one arm. Another AK-47 round ripped through García's left leg, sending him back to the ground. An explosion turned everything to darkness.

Chuck saw Luis go down and got a glimpse of the shooter around a hundred and fifty yards away, next to a tree on the other side of the street. The other male was now running next to the line of police cars that had just turned into the staging area, continuing his trajectory towards the CP. McCain raised his rifle and fired. The terrorist saw Chuck pointing his gun at him and instinctively knew that he was about to get shot. He squeezed his detonator just as McCain's 5.56mm round punched through his head.

Omar's suicide vest exploded about seventy yards from the command post. The blast killed eight newly arrived Dekalb County police officers and injured twelve more. The closest police car was knocked onto its side and the others were all heavily damaged, with the windows blown out of them, sending glass spray across the parking lot. The concussion knocked Chuck backwards and onto his back. Shrapnel from the terrorist's ballistic vest was blown outward, wounding another eleven officers who were in position on the exit ramp.

Abdul had gotten to within fifteen yards of the helicopter when Omar blew himself up. Abdul was inside the blast radius and was wounded by shrapnel that knocked him to the pavement. He was stunned but looked up to see the pilot pointing a pistol at him. Abdul activated his detonator.

The three CDC officers on the Blackhawk heard Chuck over their headsets telling the pilot to abort. Several AK bullets struck the helicopter, one of them penetrating and striking crewman Bobby Walsh in the head, killing him instantly. The first explosion rocked the aircraft just as it touched down.

Scotty ripped the side door open, unsnapped his harness, and was about to jump out when Abdul's bomb went off. Both the pilot and the copilot of the Blackhawk died in the blast, along with six of the police officers and one of the snipers who were on board. Shrapnel shredded the left side of the helicopter and the aircraft was blown to the right.

The spinning rotors smashed into the pavement with two of the four blades breaking off and flying across the parking lot. One of the loose rotors struck a fire truck, damaging it heavily. The other loose rotor bounced and flew over the command post.

Smith was knocked out the open door by the concussion and landed on his face in the parking lot, just feet from where the aircraft's large blades had impacted. Andy and Jimmy had both hesitated before unhooking their safety harnesses. They had heard the abort command and thought the aircraft might lift back off. Now, they were both dazed and bleeding, trapped inside the crippled, smoking helicopter.

McCain heard and felt the second explosion but was on the opposite side of the helicopter from the bomber. Chuck found himself being pulled to his feet. He opened his eyes and saw Thomas

Burns helping him.

"There's a gunman across the street," he yelled at Chuck.

The explosions had disoriented McCain but now he could hear the steady popping of an AK-47. He would know that sound anywhere. He nodded at Burns and looked for some cover. They were exposed out in the middle of the parking lot. Thomas was holding his Glock pistol at his side as he pulled Chuck towards an Atlanta Police cruiser parked to their right.

McCain felt the agent jerk, stumble, and then fall to the ground. Chuck swung his rifle in the direction of the shooter and squeezed off a few shots. He then reached down and grabbed Burns by the collar, dragging him twenty yards to the cover of the police car.

Gunfire erupted from the bridge over the interstate. The police officers there had seen the drama unfolding in the area around the command post. The shooters on the overpass had been mostly screened from the flying shrapnel by two rows of parked police vehicles.

They could see that the mass of infected people on I-75 was now inside three hundred yards. The explosions and gunfire seemed to make them move faster. Their growling got louder the closer they came.

The officers on the overpass with rifles began firing, trying to make head shots. A few of the zombies were hit but there were a lot of misses. The sounds of combat from near the CP on the officers' left was distracting. They kept glancing over, not sure if they were in danger from that direction, as well.

A few of the zombies were now rushing up the exit ramp and soon hundreds were moving straight towards the staging area. All of the waiting police officers, even most of those who had been wounded by shrapnel from the suicide vests, began to shoot. Handguns, shotguns, and pistols fired into the horde of zombies advancing towards them.

They had been ordered to fight until given the order to

disengage. Shrapnel from the suicide bombers, however, had mortally wounded Chief Cochran, and that order never came. When the zombies closed to within seventy-five yards the officers began to break contact and run, knowing that they had failed.

Gunfire continued to sound as the men and women in blue retreated to their vehicles, only to find that the two explosions had taken their toll. Tires were flattened, engines were damaged, and windows had been blown out of so many of the police cars. The growling zombies were now only fifty yards away.

Scotty smelled smoke and his face throbbed with pain. Their humvee had hit an IED. Again. Where were Alex and TJ? He had to get them out of there. The dazed man climbed to his feet.

When he turned around and saw the smoking Blackhawk, tilted to its side but held up by the two remaining rotors, he snapped back to reality. He wasn't in Iraq. This wasn't a humvee, it was a helicopter. It wasn't Alex and TJ, now it was Andy and Jimmy. Smith reached in and unsnapped Andy, pulling his semi-conscious partner out.

Where was he going to take him? They were in the middle of a parking lot and someone was still shooting at them. He turned and saw the fire trucks about fifty yards behind him. He'd be exposed for part of the way but that was the closest safe position. Smoke continued to pour out of the aircraft.

"I'll be right back, Jimmy."

Scotty tossed Andy over his shoulder and ran towards the cover of the big red truck. He heard the whiz of bullets going by him, some striking the pavement, and others pinging into the metal of the fire truck. When he got behind it, he gently laid Andy down.

Two firemen had seen him coming and immediately started checking Fleming for injuries. A paramedic reached up to check the damage to Smith's face. Scotty pushed the hand away.

Smith raised his M4 and set the selector to 'Auto,' ran back towards the helicopter, firing several bursts into the tree line. He had not seen the shooter but hoped he could at least get him to keep his head down.

Jimmy had managed to undo his harness and was trying to stand up. Blood poured down his face from a gash on his scalp. Scotty grabbed his teammate, telling him, "I've got you, buddy. Let me help you."

Jones went over his shoulder and Smith started running for the fire truck again.

Darnell had stopped the ambulance about a hundred feet from the top of the exit ramp, adjacent to the staging area and across the bridge from the stadium. Eddie, Hollywood, and Chris got out of the back to take their positions for fighting the oncoming zombie horde. They watched as the helicopter started to descend and then heard Chuck telling them to abort.

When the first suicide bomber detonated his vest, the three CDC officers instinctively threw themselves to the pavement. There was a line of police vehicles parked at the edge of the staging area, closest to the exit ramp. The row of cars and a slight hill protected the ambulance from damage. The shrapnel shattered patrol car windows and injured some of the standing policemen and women, waiting for the zombies steadily coming towards them.

Untouched, Eddie and his men started to get back to their feet. When the second bomber blew himself up, the CDC officers dove to the ground again. After that explosion, the steady popping of an AK could be heard over everything else. Additional gunfire started behind them as the officers on the bridge and the exit ramp began engaging the Zs.

"CDC One to any available units," McCain radioed out. His voice was slurred and his speech was slow. "There's at least one gunner armed with an AK across from the staging area. I'm pinned down behind a police car near the CP. I'm with Burns, who's been shot. Luis is also down and needs medical help."

"Team Two Alpha to CDC One," answered Eddie. "We're

moving to intercept the gunner now."

"Hollywood," Marshall ordered, looking at Estrada, "Rogers and I are going to advance and lay down suppressing fire. Flank them and take them out. We don't have much time."

Estrada nodded and was immediately on his feet running for the opposite side of the street. Marshall and Rogers stood, raised their rifles to their shoulders and began advancing on the area they heard the shots coming from. They saw movement as Hakeem popped out from behind his tree and fired another burst towards the Blackhawk.

The two agents moved towards him, firing slow, steady bursts at the terrorist. The gunfire drove him back behind the tree for cover. Eddie and Chris started jogging, aiming at the tree they had seen the gunman duck behind.

As Smith carried Jones to safety behind the big vehicle, three other fire trucks raced across the parking lot to the smoking helicopter. Two of the engines parked long ways next to the aircraft, blocking it from the shooter. The other red truck stopped nearer the Blackhawk and the firemen from all the trucks rushed over with fire extinguishers, hosing it down before it could catch fire.

Once the threat of fire was gone, the firemen began looking for survivors. Two of the SWAT officers were still alive and the firefighters gently pulled them out of the aircraft. A pair of ambulances drove over and parked nearby, ready to have the injured loaded aboard.

As soon as the fire trucks had stopped near the Blackhawk, a small figure carrying a large medical bag, jumped out of one of them and rushed towards Luis, still lying motionless on the pavement in a large pool of blood. Two bullets struck the asphalt near Emily as she gently felt for a pulse from the CDC officer. There was none. She tried again but he was clearly dead. She saw movement out of the corner of her eye. Two of Scotty's teammates, Eddie and Chris, were advancing towards the tree line across the street, shooting as they moved.

The paramedic observed the gunshot wound to the outside of García's left shoulder, the area unprotected by his body armor. That bullet probably went right through into his chest cavity, she thought. The round that had struck his leg penetrated above the left knee and appeared to have severed the femoral artery. Either of those two rounds could have killed him.

Emily gently laid Luis' head back on the pavement and grabbed her medic bag. She rushed across the parking lot to the car she had seen Chuck duck behind. He was bent over a man with a hole at the top of his sternum.

McCain had grabbed his own individual first-aid kit and was applying a chest seal to the hole. Chuck's hands were covered in blood as he worked to save the FBI agent's life. Burns' eyes were open but unfocused and blood trickled out the side of his mouth.

"I'm here," she told McCain. "Let me in there."

Estrada ran as fast as he could across the street and into the wood line. The pine trees were spaced several feet apart and he was able to move quickly. The AK had gone silent but Hollywood could hear Eddie and Chris firing steadily as they moved towards the shooter's position.

Hakeem felt trapped. He had gotten a glimpse of the two men firing and advancing on his position. A big black man and a small white man who looked very young. If he stayed in this position, they would easily kill him. He had to move. He wanted to slaughter some more infidels before they managed to kill him.

The terrorist swung the muzzle out from behind the tree and squeezed off three rounds towards the two officers coming towards him. He jumped to his feet, running in the direction of his car. Hakeem only had one full magazine of ammo left. As he ran, he tried to swap out the partial mag for the full one.

Something slammed into Hakeem's face, knocking him to his

back. He thought that he had run into a tree limb, until the dark skinned man leaned over him, pointing a rifle at his head. The terrorist realized that he had dropped his own gun and felt for it with his right arm.

Hakeem reached for the man's leg with his left arm in a feeble attempt to trip him. Estrada kicked him in the face, snapping the terrorist's head back. Hollywood let the M4 hang from his chest, reaching for his handcuffs.

Chuck's voice came over the radio, "CDC One to all units, Broken Arrow. I repeat Broken Arrow. Break contact immediately."

"Well, amigo, that changes everything," muttered Estrada, taking a step back. He raised his rifle and fired two rounds into Hakeem's head.

Staging Area, Braves Stadium Parking Lot, Saturday, 0932 hours

Chuck was only too happy to let Emily in to work on Burns. As he started to get to his feet, she grabbed his left arm and looked into his eyes.

"I checked Luis. He's gone. There was nothing I could do."

McCain sighed and nodded. Somehow, he had suspected that when he'd seen his friend fall. The gunfire from the bridge began to slow down. He looked over as the police officers started to flee from their positions. The few on the exit ramp still shooting were aiming down the ramp and not towards the interstate.

An ambulance came roaring over to where they crouched behind the police car. The remaining officers on the exit ramp and the bridge began to retreat, as well, running for their police cars. The growl of hundreds of zombies sounded close. Darnell ran to the rear and helped Emily load Burns into the back of the emergency vehicle.

The first wave of zombies came into view, moving up the exit ramp. They were less than a hundred yards away. Chuck looked behind him at the command post. The body of an FBI agent was lying face down with a gunshot wound to her head. Chief Cochran was on her back, her dead eyes staring into the sky, several wounds visible to her torso and head. A fire commander was lying beside her, his white shirt bloody where shrapnel had ripped through his body.

"Get out of here!" he commanded Emily.

She pointed towards the far side of the parking lot.

"Scotty and two of your guys need a pick-up, that's where we're heading now."

"Go get them," he said, "and I'll meet you there."

McCain pushed the transmit button on his radio, "CDC One to all units, Broken Arrow. I repeat Broken Arrow. Break contact immediately."

"Broken Arrow" is the call sign the American military uses when it's units are in danger of being overrun. That's exactly what's happening here, Chuck thought. We're about to be overrun by an enemy that wants to kill and eat us. He raised his rifle, firing into the pack of oncoming Zs.

Eddie and Chris heard the shots and cautiously made their way to where Hollywood was standing over the dead Middle Eastern man. Marshall looked at the terrorist with blood dripping out of his ventilated head and then at Estrada questioningly. Hollywood shrugged.

"I was going to try and take him alive 'til that 'Broken Arrow' came over the radio."

To shoot and kill a prisoner who could have and should have been arrested went against everything that Hollywood stood for as a police officer. The rules had changed, however, in this war on terror. And since their position was about to be overrun, there was no way they were going to drag a hostile prisoner along with them as they tried to escape. They didn't even have transportation.

Marshall nodded. "We can't go back up there. Those Zs were right behind us and with all the explosions and this idiot shooting," he said, pointing at the dead terrorist, "the officers were already starting to break when we came after him."

"What about Chuck and the rest of the guys?" Hollywood asked, the concern evident in his voice.

"I don't know, man," said Eddie, somberly. "I don't know."

A few shots still came from the staging area above them, but the shooting was definitely tapering off. Chris rolled the dead man over and searched him, carefully, not knowing if he was wired to explode. The only thing he was carrying were two sets of keys.

"Grab his rifle," ordered Eddie, "and let's see if they parked around here."

"Team Two Alpha to CDC One."

"CDC One," Chuck answered, sounding out of breath.

"Hey, Boss, the shooter's down," said Eddie. "We found their rides. They parked over here at the Chamber of Commerce and we're going to take both of their cars. Do you need us to come get you?"

"Negative, I've got a ride. Get out of the area ASAP. Meet over at Northside Hospital."

"10-4."

They quickly but thoroughly checked the Astro Van and the Jetta to make sure they weren't wired to blow up. When they were satisfied the vehicles were safe, Eddie took the van and Hollywood and Chris jumped into the VW. They accelerated towards the exit just as a group of infected came over the hill, saw them, and started running towards the two vehicles. Marshall and Estrada turned right out of the parking lot and sped away.

Now that he knew his other officers were safe, Chuck could focus on trying to get away. He saw Scotty and Emily helping Andy and Jimmy into the back of the ambulance. McCain stood his ground, rifle to his shoulder, picking the Zs off, one-by-one, giving the escaping police officers and firemen a few more seconds.

Many of the cops who had parked near the exit ramp had found out too late that their patrol cars had sustained heavy damage. Zombies rushed these officers, reaching through the shattered windows and pulling the struggling figures out of the car. In several cases, the police were able to shoot the attacking zombie, only to be bitten and ripped apart by others from the pack.

Other officers abandoned any idea of fleeing in their police cars, desperately running across the parking lot to where the ambulances and fire trucks were getting ready to leave. The big red trucks raced away with both firemen and police officers hanging from the rear. Chuck continued to fire his M4 until the ambulance pulled up next to him.

Darnell waved him into the front seat. Growling zombies were running across the parking lot, only fifty feet away, chasing an FBI agent who had been on the bridge. Chuck shot the closest Zs as the agent closed the distance. Emily opened the back door and the young man fell inside, breathing hard.

McCain dove into the front passenger seat as the ambulance pulled away. A middle-aged African-American man, wearing an expensive suit, threw himself, growling and snarling, at the big vehicle. Darnell smashed into the infected man, knocking him down, and then running over him. The ambulance's tires crushed two more infected as they left the parking lot behind.

As Chuck looked in the rear view mirror, he saw several groups of Zs bent over their uniformed victims, chewing on their throats, faces, or any other exposed skin. He hated leaving police officers to their fate but he knew that a number of them had been able to escape. He thought of Luis' broken body lying on the asphalt and closed his eyes. This should not have happened, he thought. And, God help him, someone was going to be held accountable.

Northside Hospital, Atlanta, Saturday, 1200 hours

FBI Agent Thomas Burns was taken to Northside Hospital. It wasn't the closest to the Braves Stadium but it was out of the path of the oncoming zombies, at least for the moment. Emily and Scotty had worked on Burns all the way to the hospital. He was still alive, but just barely.

Both Jimmy and Andy had suffered concussions from the explosion of the suicide bomber. Fortunately for them, they had been on the right side of the helicopter, closest to the exit and had been shielded by the other officers, who had taken the brunt of the blast from the suicide vest. Jones also had a large laceration on his scalp from flying glass, but fifteen stitches took care of that.

Scotty had a severe case of road rash from where his face had planted on the asphalt. A nurse cleaned his wounds and bandaged him up. Chuck was also suffering from a concussion from the explosion of the second suicide bomber. The ER staff found several pieces of shrapnel embedded in his body armor and embedded in him.

McCain didn't realize until he got to the hospital that his right arm and left leg were really hurting him. A doctor anesthetized the area around the wounds and dug several small pieces of metal out. Chuck shuddered and thanked God that these bombers had not had access to the zombie virus or he would have turned into one of those creatures. After his wounds were cleansed and bandaged, Chuck went to check on his men.

McCain could hear loud voices coming from the examination room that contained both Fleming and Jones. Jimmy was clearly not happy about something.

"No, sir," Jimmy's voice boomed, "we don't need to stay for evaluation. You might want to turn on the news and look at what's going on. I'd suggest you guys start thinking about what you're going to do when dead people start showing up at your door."

Andy chimed in. "Yeah, thanks for patching us up and all, but we'll be heading out as soon as they finish plugging the holes in our boss."

Chuck walked into the examining room and saw that Fleming and Jones were already up and getting dressed.

The emergency room doctor saw him and said, "Sir, your men need to have an MRI and a CAT Scan, but they're insisting on leaving. They could have serious brain injuries."

"Yeah, Doc, they're like that. They don't listen to me much, either. And for what it's worth, I thought they were both brain damaged long before today. They can fight, though, so I keep 'em around. How's that FBI agent we brought in?"

The doctor sighed. "He's in surgery now. I don't know. He's in bad shape. Mr. McCain, I saw your chart, as well. You need to have an MRI and a CAT Scan, too."

"Ain't happening, Doc. We've got people to rescue and zombies to kill."

"I had CNN on earlier," the doctor replied, "and they were saying that, despite some reports, local law enforcement had things under control in Atlanta, DC, and New York."

"First mistake," Chuck replied, "is to believe anything CNN says. We were there and I watched one of my men die. We couldn't even recover his body. Our helicopter and crew were lost. We saw a lot of police officers get killed.

"When we unassed the area, there were at least two thousand Zs heading north on I-75 or getting off the exit over where we were across from the Braves Stadium. And, we heard from Atlanta PD that the same thing was going on all over the city. Like Jimmy said, you guys probably want to start thinking about an exit strategy."

Chapter Twelve

Picking Up the Pieces

District Heights, Maryland, Saturday, 1230 hours

Special Agent Mir Turani could not have been any happier. His boss, Deputy Director of the Weapons of Mass Destruction Directorate, Charles E. Trimble, III, had loved his suggestion that this current zombie threat be handled only by federal and local law enforcement. They had worked on the wording and then sent it up the chain-of-command.

Trimble was easy to manipulate and usually did whatever Turani suggested. It helped that his assistant knew all about Trimble's young girlfriend, Natalia. Mir even had some "insurance" pictures and video tucked away on a portable hard drive of Trimble in compromising positions. That bit of information kept the deputy director on a short leash. Trimble knew that if his wife found out about his infidelity, she would divorce him in a heartbeat.

And, that would be a bad thing all around. Turani knew that their marriage was one of convenience. Mrs. Trimble came from money and a well-connected family in New York City. Her husband's political connections meant she was invited to all the right parties and social gatherings in Washington. Trimble enjoyed spending his wife's money, especially on young Natalia.

A messy divorce would hurt Trimble's chances of running for office in a few years or possibly being named as the Attorney General. So, Turani would guide Trimble's decision-making and policy suggestions. The deputy director normally went along with whatever his assistant put in front of him.

Their idea had somehow made its way to the White House and the President of the United States had swallowed it, hook, line, and sinker. The President had responded forcefully earlier in the year after seeing evidence of Iran's involvement in developing and spreading the zombie virus. The bio-terror attacks in the United States had led to war between the two nations.

It had not been much of a war, though, as the US military had destroyed Iran's military and infrastructure, leaving Mir's home country a pile of rubble. The American people had supported the war and had no sympathy for the nation that had initiated zombie terror attacks on US soil and had killed thousands of their citizens. It would be years before Iran recovered from the destruction they had endured at the hands of the Americans.

The Supreme Leader of Iran had severely underestimated the response of the American President. The previous administration had been weak and inept. The current President had shown himself to be decisive and willing to act, even when world opinion said America should respond with sanctions or even very limited military action.

Instead, the President had ordered his generals, "Level the entire country. Do everything short of going nuclear to make sure that Iran never poses a threat again."

Mir had watched the coverage of the short war on television and knew that his relatives in Tehran were probably dead. Insha Allah, he thought. God wills it.

Now that the American President had destroyed the nation that had caused so much damage to the United States, he wanted to assure the citizens that everything was getting back to normal. Federal and local law enforcement were winning the war against bio-terrorism and the zombie virus. The FBI had made some arrests and the CDC police had recently prevented a bio-terror terror attack near Georgia State University and had killed or arrested a number of terrorists involved in spreading the deadly virus.

When the policy suggestion came across his desk not to use military forces or weapons on American soil, it sounded like a good idea. His advisors assured him, law enforcement officials had the zombie war well under control. And in reality, they had- until yesterday, that is. When the double bombings occurred in the three cities, the war quickly lost whatever ground law enforcement had previously attained.

The number of infected was now in the tens of thousands and all three cities were in danger of being completely overrun. The mayor of Atlanta was aired briefly on CNN asking for the National Guard and other military help. He said that he had issued an unprecedented evacuation order to the people of Atlanta. The danger, however, was with zombies spreading quickly throughout the entire downtown area and beyond, evacuation was now almost impossible. The interview with the Atlanta mayor was cut short by "Technical Difficulties."

New York City was encountering similar problems. There were reports of thousands of zombies wandering the streets of Manhattan and Brooklyn. In the densely packed city, the infected were multiplying exponentially. When Ali had blown himself up in front of 1 Police Plaza Path, NYPD headquarters, twelve police officers and nine civilians had been killed. The explosion had also blasted infected materials through shattered windows of surrounding buildings, into passing vehicles, and down the sidewalks infecting many more.

The close proximity of the Brooklyn Bridge made it easy for the zombies to carry the virus into Brooklyn, Queens, and eventually, Long Island. The New York City Police Department had taken eighteen casualties in responding to the two explosions. Now, they were being cautious as they tried to develop a strategy to contain the quickly spreading virus.

In DC, the FBI was working with the Secret Service and the Capitol Police to evacuate elected officials. Because so many people had been infected in the initial explosions, the number of Zs continued to increase with every passing hour. Over a hundred zombies rushed the capitol building, killing and infecting police, staffers, and even a few congresspersons and senators. Because of his position as Trimble's assistant, Special Agent Turani had not been assigned to evacuation and rescue duty.

The J. Edgar Hoover building, the FBI's headquarters was only a few blocks from the Smithsonian Air and Space Museum where Hassan had blown himself up. The order had been given late Friday night to relocate to Andrews Air Force Base in Maryland. Mir lived in nearby District Heights so this was actually better for him. There was a mandatory meeting with the FBI Director on Monday morning at one of the auditoriums on the base.

The question for Turani now, was "What next?" He had passed much sensitive information on to Imam Ruhollah Ali Bukhari and other cell leaders using coded language on a Farsi internet bulletin board. So far, Mir had not seen anything to make him think that he was under suspicion. If anything, the politically correct bureau went out of their way not to offend their Muslim employees.

For now, he decided, he would lay low and watch things unfold. The President would eventually realize that he had been given bad advice and would want to know where it came from. Heads would roll. Not Mir's, of course. He was only Charles Trimble, III's assistant. Trimble might be out of a job, though, and that would probably be the time when Turani would need to disappear.

Chuck's house, Northeast of Atlanta, Sunday morning, 0700 hours

McCain sat on the edge of the bed. He had slept almost twelve hours. His wounds ached, his head throbbed, and the big man felt the dark cloud of depression hovering over him. He walked into his bathroom, filled a glass with water, and swallowed four extra strength Tylenol.

Chuck did a quick search on his smart phone for the latest on the zombie crisis. The news was now reporting that over eight thousand infected were working their way out of Atlanta on all of the interstates, in every direction. Another several thousand were wandering around the streets of the city, attacking anyone foolish enough to venture outside.

As McCain walked by his first guest room, he could hear Scotty snoring. Sorry, Jimmy, Chuck thought. That has to suck sharing a room with that chainsaw. The other guest room served as his home office but did not contain a bed. Rogers and Estrada were sharing the floor using two of McCain's sleeping bags.

In the living room, McCain saw that Emily was still asleep on the couch, covered with a comforter. They had tried to get her to take one of the bedrooms but she wouldn't hear of it. Darnell was sleeping in Chuck's recliner, covered with his paramedic jacket.

Andy and Eddie had both gone home, Eddie driving the Astro Van and Andy taking the Jetta. They were the only two married men on the team and both lived near Chuck. McCain had asked them to come back to his house at noon on Sunday so they could discuss their next moves as a team. Emily and Darnell had volunteered to go to the store for groceries and clothes for Scotty, Chris, and Hollywood, as well as themselves. Their apartments were all either in the city or in the path of the zombies.

After they had arrived at his house the previous afternoon, Chuck had updated Admiral Williams. While everyone had taken showers, McCain sat on his deck and spoke to the CIA's Deputy Director for Operations, briefing him on everything that had happened since their last conversation. When he finished, there was a sigh from the other end of the phone.

"I'm very sorry about Agent García. He sounded like a true warrior."

"Yes, sir, he was," Chuck said, softly.

"And I'm sorry about the Blackhawk crew. Of course, they worked for us. They were good people."

Jonathan Williams understood combat and what it meant to lose friends in battle. He had been a Navy SEAL in Vietnam. On his second tour of duty, he had been wounded and forced out of the SEALs. He had chosen to stay in the Navy but, even now, well into his seventies, he still had the mind of a warrior.

"So, what are your orders now, sir?" Chuck asked.

"Rest and recuperate for a couple of days. I'm thinking the best use of your team will be for rescue missions inside the infected areas. I'll work on getting another helicopter assigned to you. Shaun will call you Tuesday with further details."

"I haven't spoken to Tu or Jay in DC. Are they OK?"

Another sigh. "They lost two agents. KIA. They've all pulled back, out of the city, and are in the same situation that you're in. They'll be doing some rescue operations, also.

"The New York CDC office took the worst damage. We lost an entire team of four in Manhattan. They got overrun trying to get to the scene. Zombies surrounded their SUVs and they were all killed trying to fight their way out. Our second team there lost another agent down in Brooklyn trying to rescue some kids trapped on a school bus."

"I'm so sorry to hear that," said McCain.

"Were you still thinking of bringing on another officer?" Williams asked.

"I was. He was actually scheduled to report on Monday."

"If you think he has what it takes, go ahead and bring him in. Use the company credit card to equip him and replace anything your team lost in the fight. Rent vehicles and talk with Dr. Martin at the CDC about the best place for you to set up shop. You and your officers are still in this fight and we have a long way to go."

Chuck got a pot of coffee going and sat down at his kitchen table, thinking over the events of the past couple of days. The image of Luis going down was frozen in his mind, quickly replaced by another picture: Rebecca's eyes staring into his as she died. How many more lives would be lost before this war was over?

The smell of the brewing coffee woke Emily up and she joined Chuck in the kitchen. They sat quietly at the table sipping from their mugs. Even in her gray sweat pants and blue t-shirt, she was an attractive girl. It wasn't hard to see why Scotty had been drawn to her.

"I'm really sorry about Luis," she finally said, not meeting his eyes. "There was nothing I could do. There was no pulse and it looked like he'd already bled out."

"I know," Chuck answered. "It's not your fault. I appreciate you checking him. You're a brave girl, Emily."

"Thanks, Chuck. I just wished I could've saved him."

"Well, you did a great job working on Burns. You gave him a chance. Hopefully, the doctors were able to save him. So, what's next for you? Have you talked to your parents or any of your people at the ambulance service?"

Emily nodded. "Mom and dad are fine. They live up I-75 near Rome. I spoke to them yesterday and they were going to leave this morning and head up to my brother's house in Tennessee.

"I called and left messages at the office but no one has returned my call. Our ambulance service is based off I-20, just west of the city, so I guess the Zs could have gotten there by now. My apartment's over there, too, but I don't guess I'll be going home anytime soon." Tears began to run down her face.

"Plan on staying here as long as you need to. I just hope you don't mind being the only girl hanging out with us savages."

She laughed and wiped her eyes. "Thanks, Chuck. I really appreciate that. You know Scotty really likes you. He also said you're the only guy to ever knock him out. He laughed about it," she said, shaking her head.

Chuck smiled at that memory. "Scotty's one of the best that I've ever worked with. He's one of a kind."

"He is that," she smiled. "He is that."

"And," Chuck added, lowering his voice to a conspiratorial level, "he talks about you all the time. I think you're civilizing him."

Emily felt herself blushing and took a drink of coffee.

"I checked the news this morning," McCain said, changing the subject, "and as far as I can tell, we're far enough out of the city and far enough away from the interstate that we should be OK for a while. There's no doubt in my mind that they'll eventually come out here, too, but for the moment, we're clear."

Chuck's house, Northeast of Atlanta, Sunday, 1330 hours

The sound of plates being scraped and water running came from the kitchen. Emily had cooked up a big pot of spaghetti and had directed Scotty in putting a salad together. When Eddie and Andy arrived at noon, they had all eaten, devouring the meal and not leaving any leftovers. Ice-cold beer made the spaghetti go down even better.

Marshall leaned over to Estrada as they ate and asked quietly, "Have you heard from Isabella?"

A cloud crossed Hollywood's face. "I called her Friday evening right before we left DC and left her a voice mail. She texted me later that night and said her flight back to New York had been diverted to Chicago. She's safe but she can't make contact with her family in Brooklyn."

Isabella Rodriguez was the flight attendant that Alejandro had met a few weeks earlier traveling from New York to Atlanta. A man had become infected in the air and Hollywood had been forced to kill the zombie with his knife to protect the rest of the passengers. Isabella and Hollywood had been on several dates, whenever they could coordinate their schedules.

"Thank God she's out of the city," Eddie said. "Hopefully, her family's safe, riding this thing out until we can kill all the zombies."

"Yeah, thanks for asking, Eddie."

After everyone had complimented Emily on a great meal, Chuck made sure they all had a fresh beer before adjourning to his living room. After they got settled, Emily and Darnell went to work on the dishes.

Chuck raised his bottle. "The first order of business is to remember a fallen comrade."

A hush fell over the room. "Luis was one of the toughest guys I've ever known. He was a badass in every sense of the word. As a fighter, he beat up guys who were twice his size and he never ran from a fight. It was an honor to serve with him," McCain said, toasting their fallen friend.

"I never told you guys about the time Luis choked me out," Scotty confessed, looking around sheepishly.

"Oh, this is going to be good," Jimmy laughed, taking a drink.

Smith smiled a sad smile. "Yeah, after Chuck knocked me out, I began to focus more on my hand-to-hand skills. Chuck coached me a little and I was feeling pretty confident after a few months of training with him.

"One day, Luis and I were in the gym lifting and I said I'd like to roll with him. I knew he was a black belt and a really dangerous guy but I thought I could take him. I never had any jiu-jitsu training but I'd wrestled and the boss had been training me. Plus, I was like twice his size."

Scotty took a big swallow from his bottle.

"So, we went over to the mats and I thought I'd just grab him and pin him. Easy. When I went for the grab, he caught me in a flying arm bar and almost hyper-extended my elbow. I was so embarrassed because he made me tap.

"I said, 'Come on, Luis, you got lucky. Let's go again. He shrugged and said, 'Okay, if that's what you want.' He was so fast. He swept my leg and when I tried to get up, he was on my back and sunk a rear naked choke. I thought I could muscle out of it but the next thing I knew, Luis was standing over me, slapping me in the face, trying to wake me up."

Everybody laughed at the story. "How did we not hear about this?" Eddie asked.

When Scotty looked around at his friends, they could see the tears pouring down his face. "That was one of the things that made him such a great guy. He didn't want to embarrass me so he never said anything."

Everyone wiped the tears from their eyes.

Andy spoke up, his voice angry. "I want some payback," he said.

The other men nodded. Fleming had voiced what they were all feeling. McCain felt the same way but, for the moment, he had to keep them focused.

"Definitely," agreed Chuck. "Luis, the Blackhawk crew, all those police officers, they died in vain. That was some Washington stupidity. Hopefully, a few of the idiots responsible had an up close and personal with a zombie.

"For now, though, we have orders. We're going to be tasked with rescue operations. They're going to get us another helicopter, I hope, and we'll be working with local PDs and whatever feds are still functional to try and save some people in the city or wherever.

"We have until Tuesday to rest and heal up. We'll be getting some more specific orders then. Terrence Matthews is starting tomorrow, if he can get here from Douglasville. He's the SWAT officer who helped me and Luis when we had the big incident out at Six Flags. He called me last week and told me that his little sister was inside Sanford Stadium when all hell broke loose. He hasn't heard from her so you can imagine that he's ready to do his part.

"Tomorrow we'll go rent some vehicles and buy equipment for Terrence. If you guys need anything let me know and I'll buy it. We'll hit up Bass Pro Shops and Target Time gun store."

"I don't know about a new guy starting in the middle of all this," stated Jimmy, the surprise evident in his voice.

"Yeah, I know but we need him and he'll fit right in. He's a solid operator and is going to be a quick learner."

Everybody nodded or shrugged. It was always a different dynamic when someone new joined the team. But, they did need him and Chuck had seen him in action.

"Anything else?" Chuck asked.

Eddie spoke up. "Jimmy's going to come home with me. I've got an extra room and he said sleeping with Scotty was worse than fighting the zombies."

Everybody laughed.

Andy spoke up. "I can take Chris. Plus, he and my son probably wear the same size clothes."

More laughter. It was good to release some steam, Chuck thought.

"Okay. Everybody be here at 1000 hours tomorrow and we'll go spend some of the government's money."

Chuck's house, Northeast of Atlanta, Monday, 1100 hours

McCain's wounds still pulsed with pain and his head was still sore, but they had a lot to do today. Plus, staying busy kept the black cloud at bay. Terrence had driven the back roads, avoiding the interstates and other areas where Zs had been spotted. It had taken him over four hours to get from the west side of Atlanta to Chuck's house at 1000 hours.

A federal district judge swore Terrence in over Skype as a CDC Enforcement Agent. He was a twenty-nine year old, muscular, African-American who was both nervous and excited. The week before, Terrence Matthews was a local police officer who served on the SWAT team. Now, he was a federal police officer, working for the CDC, being sworn in over the computer in his boss' living room.

Now McCain and his men sat around the kitchen table, sipping coffee and compiling a list of equipment that they needed. All of their supplies and extra weapons were locked up in their offices in the basement of the CDC headquarters downtown. With the city overrun by Zs, it made no sense trying to drive downtown until they absolutely had to. The first order of business was to rent vehicles. Andy had his computer in front of him, searching rental car companies.

Chuck's phone vibrated. The caller ID showed that it was Dr. Charles Martin, the Assistant Director of the Office of Public Health Preparedness and Response at the CDC. McCain pulled the company credit card out of his wallet and handed it to Andy.

"Go online and rent four big SUVs. Get all the extra insurance and I'll be right back."

McCain stepped out onto his deck and answered the phone. "Hello, Dr. Martin. How are you, sir?"

"Chuck, thanks for taking my call. I heard about Agent García. I'm very sorry. I heard some of your other officers were injured. I hope nothing serious?"

Dr. Martin knew of the arrangement and the backing that the CIA provided for the CDC enforcement agents. On paper, they reported to him but he understood that Admiral Williams was really the man to whom Chuck answered. It was no surprise that he was in the loop and knew about Luis' death. In the chaos of the combat on Friday and Saturday, Chuck had not even thought about calling him.

"Yes, sir. Thank you for that. No other serious injuries and I apologize for not calling and giving you an update. It was a crazy couple of days."

"Don't worry about that. Because of your quick notification on Friday of the new attacks we were able to evacuate headquarters without any casualties. But, we may have lost a couple of people."

"What happened?" asked McCain.

"Do you know Dr. Nicole Edwards? She's one of our top epidemiologists."

"Isn't she the one who's heading up the team which has been trying to develop a vaccine?"

"That's her. She and her team did develop that solution that kills the virus on contact but they haven't made much progress with a vaccine. Anyway, she's missing, along with one of her lab assistants, and one of the security supervisors, Darrell Parker. I got a call yesterday from Nicole's boss, Dr. Patel. Her family hasn't heard from her since Friday. Same story on the lab assistant.

"They were logged into the computer system and appeared to be working late Friday night/Saturday morning when all hell broke loose. We gave the evacuation order and had security check the building to make sure everyone was gone but now it looks like they may still be inside. Darrell was working at that time, as well, and his family hasn't seen him. They got a call from him about 1:00am Saturday morning saying they were evacuating and that he'd be leaving as soon as he could, but it doesn't look like he ever left the building.

"I spoke to the Director of Security and he had his people remotely view the security camera footage. There was no sign of our missing people but there were a lot of infected people wandering around the outside of the building and even into the lobby. There are some gaps in the video because it looks like there was a power outage in the area to go along with everything else."

Chuck sighed. "And you heard about this on Saturday?"

"I did," Martin answered. "Look, I heard about what you guys were involved in. I knew you'd lost Luis and had several agents injured. I actually spoke to our mutual friend in Washington and he recommended trying to find someone else who could help us since you guys had been kind of beat up.

"Atlanta Police said they were going to send some of their people over there but it hasn't happened yet. The FBI took a number of casualties on Saturday and said 'no.' I've called the Atlanta offices for the Federal Marshals, the DEA, the ATF. They're cops, for crying out loud! They've all said that they're very sorry but they're focusing their assets in other locations."

McCain did not say anything as his mind was already spinning into action.

"I'm sorry, Chuck. If you can't do anything, I understand. This is the worst crisis that I've ever dealt with. I just hate the idea of some of our people trapped downtown."

"We'll handle it, sir. I'll get right to work. It may take us a few hours to develop a plan and to get mobilized, but we'll do everything we can to find them."

"Are you sure? Thank you so much," Martin said, the relief evident in his voice.

East of Atlanta, Monday, 1500 hours

There were no air assets available, so that drive into the city was about to happen. Andy rented four Nissan Armadas that were delivered to Chuck's house within the hour. Chris pulled up Google maps on McCain's smart TV so the team could look at different routes to their headquarters in Atlanta.

Chuck told Andy and Jimmy that they could sit this one out. They had been busted up pretty good in the explosion just two days before and Jimmy had been shot the day before that. The two warriors just laughed at him.

"Come on, Boss," said Jimmy, smiling broadly. "Me and Andy are Marines. Jarheads. Devil Dogs. I've had worse training injuries than this. I survived Paris Island, Iraq, and a bunch of zombie terrorists. We're good to go."

Andy nodded. "I think you're going to need every available gun on this one, Chuck." He nodded at Terrence. "Even the rookie gets thrown into the deep end today."

Traffic was surprisingly sparse. People had already fled or were holed up in their homes. The four big SUVs stayed off the interstate, using Georgia Highway 29 to get them close to their destination. They didn't see any infected for most of the trip south.

Chuck had decided to take all four of their newly rented vehicles.

His reasoning was three-fold. They had no idea what they were going to run into and he would rather have too many vehicles than not enough if one or more of them got disabled. Second, he was planning on rescuing three people but there was always the possibility they might encounter others who needed help. And, third, he intended to gather as much of their equipment, weapons, computers, and gear as they could from their offices.

Thankfully, Terrence had some basic equipment. He'd had to purchase most of his gear when he had joined his former police department's SWAT team. He was wearing black BDUs, body armor, and web gear. He had a 9mm Beretta 92F in a tactical thigh holster. For this operation, Chuck had loaned him one of his own personal rifles, a Colt AR-15 Sporter with a collapsible stock.

After driving for an hour, McCain pulled into the parking lot of a big Baptist Church in the little town of Tucker. They were about two miles outside of the perimeter, I-285. The area looked clear and the parking lot was large enough for the men to see anything approaching them. The Nissans lined up and Chuck put Chris, Hollywood, and Terrence on first watch, scanning the area for threats.

Andy pulled out a laptop and set it up on the hood of his Armada. In minutes, they were watching a real-time feed from a drone flying over the area they were going into. At first, everything looked peaceful from thousands of feet in the air.

As Fleming zoomed in, however, they saw figures moving all around the CDC headquarters and the surrounding area on Clifton Road. The roadways in the area were full of cars but none of them were moving. Zombies gathered around a few of them, looking inside or slapping the windows.

For several minutes, they watched the Zs walking out in the middle of the street or down the sidewalk. Occasionally, one or two would stop in front of one of the nearby businesses.

"Look at that," Eddie said, pointing at the screen.

They saw several figures shuffling out the front entrance of the

CDC. Two others passed them, walking inside.

"How'd they get in? The front gate should be closed. They act like they own the place," commented Jimmy.

"I guess they do now," said Chuck.

A fence surrounded the CDC compound that took up close to a city block. An electric metal gate protected the front entrance. Normally, security had to let visitors in. The rear driveway led to the employee parking decks. CDC employees could swipe their ID cards to gain entry. Both entrances were standing opening and the infected were wandering around the buildings.

"What about the parking decks, Andy? If we can get in there undetected, we can slip in the back door, do our thing, and then get back out."

"I'll zoom in on the rear and we can take a look," answered Andy.

"I like your optimism, Boss," said Scotty with a smile and then a laugh. "I think this is going to be a lot of fun. It kind of feels like an Iraq mission, riding dirty in a convoy, looking for the bad guys."

Terrence stared at the large, bearded man. His face looked like he had been dragged behind a car. There were stains on his black uniform that looked a lot like blood. The last time he had seen Scotty and Andy was that day a couple of months before when they had stopped a van load of terrorists on the interstate west of Atlanta in his jurisdiction.

The two CDC agents had gotten into a shootout with the terrorists and both officers were wounded. Scotty had still managed to wreck and disable the suspect's van against the median wall. Fleming and Smith had then taken down the bad guys before seeking medical help for themselves.

Smith saw Matthews looking at him and winked at the new officer. "Good times, huh?"

Terrence could not help but smile. "Sure, man. Good times."

Scotty slapped him on the shoulder, almost knocking him over. "You're going to love working with us."

“Well, good news and bad news,” reported Fleming. “The bad news is that there are Zs in the back, too. The good news is that there aren’t many, at least that we can see. There might be some inside the parking deck, hidden from view. That’s probably our best bet. Any way we go, we’re going to be in contact.”

Chapter Thirteen

Back into the Belly of the Beast

Security office, CDC HQ, Monday, 1500 hours

Dr. Nicole Edwards was beyond scared. In the dark office, however, she had prayed for the first time in years and made peace with God. Nicole had accepted the fact that she was going to die in this small, windowless room.

The last few days had been a blur. Friday night, she and her lab assistant, Salman Kumar, were working late again. She was pushing her team and herself to find a vaccine for the bio-terror virus.

They had been so engrossed in their experiments that they had not even heard about the explosions a few miles away. As her team started trickling out of their lab for home by 6:00pm, one of her epidemiologists called Nicole and told her about the chaos that was taking place in Atlanta, Washington, and New York. She said that traffic was a nightmare as people were taking surface streets instead of the interstate, hoping to avoid the chaos near downtown Atlanta.

Edwards and Kumar decided to keep working, but they did turn on the television that hung on the lab's wall, to monitor what was happening. Edwards felt like they were finally making progress on a vaccine. It appeared that they had found a compound that seemed to slow down infection times in their lab mice. In some cases, the mice were not turning into zombies for several hours as opposed to the minutes that it had been. It wasn't much but it was a start.

She and Salman kept getting distracted by what they were seeing on television. The video from the news helicopters and from reporters who had managed to get into the area, as well as from citizens shooting video on their phones, was terrifying. This was worse than anything she had ever seen. What was it going to take to contain this attack?

By 10:00pm, the two scientists finally gave up trying to work and went to the break room down the hall. Many of the third shift workers were glued to the TV there, also watching events unfold. Nicole had a sudden realization that Chuck McCain and the other CDC officers were out there somewhere, trying to help wherever they could.

Edwards had known and been friends with Rebecca Johnson. They hadn't been close, but the two women had worked well together and shared a mutual respect. Nicole knew that Rebecca and Chuck had feelings for each other. It was hard to miss, even from a distance. On more than one occasion, Nicole had thought to herself, 'You're one lucky girl, Rebecca. That is a good looking man.'

In reality, the attractive brunette researcher had never even spoken to Chuck McCain. A girl could hope, though, she told herself. For now, Edwards said a silent prayer for his protection and for the protection of the men who were with him.

At 1:00am, the word came from the CDC Director that they needed to pack up and leave. They were to take whatever they needed to work in another location for a few days. Darrell Parker was the security supervisor on duty and he sent his four officers to make sure the building was evacuated.

Nicole and Salman were almost packed up and ready to go by 1:30am. She hated to leave because she felt they were so close to a breakthrough. She carefully placed ten vials of their current project securely in her padded briefcase.

"What about the mice?" asked Kumar.

"I forgot about them. I guess we need to euthanize all of them. It may be several days before they let us back into the building."

"Okay, I'll do it while you finish up in here," the assistant offered.

The room with the test animals was adjacent to their lab, separated by one door. As Salman went to take care of the unpleasant task, Nicole stuck a memory stick into her desktop computer to save her work and then began shutting the computer down. A gasp came from the adjoining room and then the sound of a mouse squealing.

"Salman, are you OK?"

There was no answer. She walked over, opened the door, and saw her assistant standing on the dead body of one of the small rodents. His brown face looked pale.

"What happened?" she asked, concern in her voice.

"I…I must've messed up and not secured one of the cages. This little guy escaped and I was trying to find him. He snuck up behind me and nipped me on the ankle. I had to step on him. Sorry. I know, not the most ethical way to euthanize a lab animal."

He tried to smile. "I'm fine, though. I don't think it broke the skin."

"Come back in here and let's check you out," Nicole said.

Kumar walked slowly back into the lab. His steps were unsteady and his boss guided him into a chair. She grabbed a pair of rubber gloves and slipped them on before slowly pulling the young man's pants leg up. A drop of blood dripped onto the white laboratory floor. There were four small holes just above his ankle. More blood oozed out of the wounds.

"You're bleeding. It did break the skin. Let me get the first-aid kit."

"Oh, that's not good." He was having trouble breathing now, trying to suck oxygen in.

Edwards returned and opened the kit, pulling out several antiseptic wipes. She looked up and saw Salman had his eyes closed and his breathing had become shallow. She needed to call for help.

Nicole dropped the wipes and rushed over to her desk and dialed the number for the security office. There was no answer. They were probably helping everybody get out. She dialed 911. There was a fire station less than a block away but every call had to be routed through the 911 Center.

As the phone rang, she looked at Salman. His eyes were still closed and he was slouched over in the chair. Suddenly, he gasped loudly and his head slumped to his chest.

"Somebody, please answer the phone," she pleaded.

There was a click on the other end of the line and a recording letting her know that her call was very important but all of the 911 operators were busy and would be with her as soon as possible. The bombings, she thought. That's why no one is answering. All of the police and fire units are busy. Nicole hung the phone up.

I'm on my own but what do I do? Could he be infected? Several of those mice had received injections of the virus and the experimental vaccine. How did that work? Would it be possible to get infected from the bite of an infected test mouse? Yes, that was very possible, she realized.

Nicole walked back over to her assistant and watched him. He did not appear to be breathing. She placed her fingers on his carotid artery to check for a pulse. There was none. Oh, my God! she thought. What now?

Dr. Edwards eased Kumar to the floor and onto his back. She started chest compressions on him, feeling a couple of his ribs crack under the pressure. It had been a while since her last CPR certification but she remembered that they were now teaching that chest compressions were more important than the rescue breathing. That's good, because there's no way I am blowing into his mouth.

After several minutes, her arms began to tire. Nicole remembered that there was a portable defibrillator in every break room. She got to her feet and rushed for the exit. Before she got there, the door to her lab opened.

Security supervisor, Darrell Parker, was in the doorway. "Hi, Dr. Edwards. You guys packed up? We need to get y'all out of here."

"Please, I need help. Salman is on the floor over there. He got bit by a lab rat. I was doing CPR but he's unresponsive. I was going to get the defibrillator."

Parker walked over to where the inert form was lying on the

floor. He had retired from the City of Baltimore Police Department as a sergeant. After twenty-seven years of service, there was nothing he had not seen and this did not look good.

"I'll go get the defib if you want to keep doing CPR," Darrell said.

He rushed out the door, down the hallway to the break room. When he got back to the lab, Darrell heard a loud growling sound coming from inside and then a woman's scream. He placed the device on the floor and drew his revolver.

Parker had never converted over to semi-automatic pistols. His Smith & Wesson Model 10 in .38 Special had always treated him right. He had been in two shootings in his police career and his wheel gun had not let him down.

"Salman, no!" Dr. Edward's voice carried through the door. "Help!" she yelled.

Darrell pushed open the door and rushed in. Dr. Edwards was on the floor, fighting for her life. Kumar held a handful of her long, brown hair with his left hand and was trying to pull her face to his mouth. Her right hand was under his chin, trying to keep his mouth closed. Her left hand was pushing against his right arm as it tried to wrap her in a deadly embrace.

Parker was sixty-two years old but a lifetime of law enforcement experience propelled him into action. He placed his right boot over Salman's face, pinning his head to the floor. Nicole threw herself backwards, leaving a handful of her tresses in Kumar's hand. She scrambled away, gasping.

"Now Dr. Kumar, you need to stop that and calm down," the security supervisor ordered.

Salman wasn't a doctor but Darrell promoted everyone, calling them doctor or director. That was one of the reasons why everyone loved him. The only answer he received was a growl and hands reaching for his legs.

"Darrell, I think he's infected with the virus. Don't let him bite you."

Parker's friend, Chuck McCain, had told him to always shoot them in the head. This was his first time dealing with an infected person but he was thankful for Chuck's advice. He stepped back quickly, removing his foot from Kumar's head.

Darrell fired a single round into the infected man's forehead. The shot was loud in the enclosed room and blood splattered several inches into the air but Salman now lay still.

"I'm sorry about that, Dr. Edwards. Mr. McCain says that's the only way stop one after they've turned into a zombie."

"I know, Darrell. I'm sorry, too." Tears streamed down her face as she watched blood and brain matter run out of the hole in her former assistant's head.

Darrell and Nicole were the only two left in the building after the incident with Salman. After helping the rest of the staff leave, Parker had ordered his men to start for home themselves. He had been planning on doing the same after getting Edwards and Kumar out.

Now, he helped Dr. Edwards carry some of her things to the elevator and rode with her to the second floor parking deck. The lights in the elevator started flickering. He would walk her out to her car and make sure she got away safely.

I guess I need to report that shooting, he thought, but who do I report it to? Everybody is kind of busy right now. What do we do with that body? I'll need to call somebody. We can't just leave a dead body in that lab.

The lights in the hallway went out just as Nicole opened the door and stepped outside onto the parking deck. Darrell was carrying two of her bags, a padded bag of samples and experiments, as well as her laptop bag. When the door shut behind them, they realized they were in trouble. Nine bloody, shuffling figures were scattered throughout the parking area.

The noise of the exit door closing got their attention and they all started growling. Darrell dropped the bags and drew his gun as the group advanced towards their newest victims. A small gold Toyota

Corolla was parked alone on the left side of the deck and Dr. Edwards' Honda Accord was parked on the right. The zombies had to walk around the cars to get to their victims.

"Back inside. Open the door," Darrell directed.

Nicole fumbled, trying to get her ID card out of her purse. A gunshot echoed across the parking deck and then another. The growling got louder and closer. Darrell's first shot struck the closest zombie in the chest. Old habits, he thought. He raised the sights and his second .38 Special round hit the Z in the face.

Another one rushed towards him. Parker fired and missed but his next shot hit the infected Hispanic woman in the nose. Edwards finally got her card out and swiped it but nothing happened. She ran it through again. The green light showing access did not come on. Another shot dropped a third zombie.

"Something's wrong, Darrell. It won't open," she said.

"Here, take my keys," he said, grabbing at the keys on his belt. "That big one's the master key."

He sighted in on a young black man who was only fifteen feet away. The young man's loose pants had slipped below his waist and were slowing him down. The gun clicked empty. Rookie mistake, Old Man, Darrell told himself. You didn't reload after shooting Kumar.

Parker popped open the revolver's cylinder, quickly dumped the empty brass onto the ground, and grabbed a speed loader off of his belt. With a practiced fluidity he loaded the six bullets, slammed the cylinder shut, and put one hollow point into the fashion-challenged zombie's forehead. He heard the keys jingling behind him as Dr. Edwards unlocked the door.

Suddenly, a tall, white woman with half of her face chewed away was grabbing for him. Darrell fired, the round entering under her chin and carrying on into the brain, sending her to the pavement.

"We're in," Nicole said.

The security officer backed towards the door. The last four were still ten yards away and he held his fire. Edwards pulled him inside into a darkened hallway.

"Are you OK?" she asked him.

Parker realized he was panting. He holstered his revolver and felt for the light switch. Nothing happened when he flipped it. They both jumped when the remaining Zs slammed into the other side of the door they had just rushed through.

"That was close, but I'm fine," he said.

"Why are the lights off?" the doctor asked.

"I don't know, ma'am," he answered, pulling a small flashlight from his belt and turning it on.

He led her down one flight of stairs to the main level where the security office was located. It was just off of the lobby. Once he got in there, he could call for help, he hoped. It was a good secure location and he would feel safer there.

"We'll go to the security office. We'll be OK in there until we can figure out what to do," Darrell told the woman.

"Oh, no, my bags! They're outside. They have samples of the vaccine that I'm working on! And my computer is out there, too."

"Well, I'm sorry about that, Dr. Edwards, but I'm not going back out there. We'll worry about it later. Let's go someplace safe.

When they got to the lobby, there was enough light that they could see a few figures shuffling around the front entrance of the building. Darrell kept his flashlight off but had his revolver ready to go. He had reloaded his cylinder this time.

They only needed to cross the lobby, about thirty feet, and they would be at the security office. They moved slowly, not wanting to attract the attention of the infected. Halfway there, Nicole slammed into one of the leather chairs that are scattered around the large atrium. The noise did not go undetected.

Growling figures threw themselves into the large glass doors. For the moment, the two survivors were safe and got to the security office, locking themselves inside. A few minutes later, they could hear glass breaking as the front doors gave way and twenty infected rushed into the lobby, looking for their prey.

Darrell and Nicole sat quietly in the dark office, not wanting to alert the Zs to their hiding place. The windowless room did appear to be safe for the moment. Parker had shone his light around the security office so Edwards would know the layout in case they had to move.

There were several cubicles, each containing a computer. The door was a solid, heavy metal construction. It would take some work to get through it. The small restroom in the back of the office would be their last stand if the creatures got through the main door.

They both checked their phones but were unable to get any service. With the power out, the only light they had was from their phones and Darrell's flashlight. The desk phones did not have a ring tone and the power outage had also eliminated their access to wifi. They were completely cut off and surrounded by hostile creatures. They were safe but sitting in the dark was not Nicole's idea of a long-term solution to their problem.

Nicole and Darrell were now two and half days into their ordeal. They sound of the infected moving around the lobby had been almost non-stop. They spoke very quietly and tried to move as little as possible. There was a small couch in the back of the security office and they took turns napping.

A small refrigerator contained five bottles of water, which they were trying to stretch out. Several of the security officers had leftover food in the fridge that sustained the two survivors.

Parker leaned over to Edwards and whispered into her ear, "I'm sorry about this, Dr. Edwards. I thought this was the best place to go. I guess I didn't think it through."

"It's OK," she told him. "I don't know what else we could have done. There was no way that we were leaving and I don't know if I would want to be wandering around this big building in the dark. Someone will eventually come looking for us. We just have to sit in the dark a little longer."

"That's right," Darrell said, responding to her optimism. "Somebody will come get us."

They sat quietly for a moment and then Parker spoke again. "I just hope we're still alive when they get here."

CDC HQ, Monday, 1600 hours

It took almost an hour to cover the last few miles. Inside the perimeter, more and more cars were abandoned on the roadway and they started to encounter groups of infected. They only shot the ones they absolutely had to shoot to keep moving.

Andy and Scotty were now in the lead vehicle. Fleming plotted the best course using the live drone feed on his laptop. Smith drove following his partner's directions. Just south of the CDC is Emory University. The school had reportedly been evacuated late Friday night but they didn't want to take any chances of running into large groups of infected university students.

The area around the CDC's headquarters contained restaurants, hotels, and neighborhoods. All of the federal officers had their heads on swivels and their weapons ready as they got closer to their destination. When they got to Clifton Road, their senses went into hyper drive as they saw the big building they were heading for sitting one block up on their right. The traffic light hanging in the intersection was not working.

"Looks like the power's out in the area," said Andy.

There were no Zs close so they paused before continuing straight on Houston Mill Road. This would take them behind the CDC compound to the parking decks. Suddenly, a group of about twenty stepped out into the roadway two hundred yards away. They started moving towards the four SUVs.

Scotty gunned it across Clifton Road with the other three vehicles following. When they got to the employee parking entrance, they saw that the metal gate was standing open. The parking deck had five levels to accommodate the many scientists, researchers, administrators, support staff, and now, enforcement branch. The enforcement agents normally parked on the lower level, nearest to their offices.

As they sped down the driveway to the parking decks, two large women, one African-American and the other white, jumped out in front of the lead vehicle. There was no time to stop so Smith accelerated, hitting both of them. The black zombie flew off to the side while the other bounced up on the hood, her red, glazed-over eyes making eye contact with Andy as her faced smashed into the windshield, cracking it. She fell off of the vehicle as Scotty jerked the steering wheel to the left.

They could see several infected on the first level parking deck, along with several bodies sprawled on the pavement. The entrance dipped down into the dark, basement access parking. Their headlights illuminated four figures next to a compact car with the driver's door standing open. The Zs huddled over a uniformed body, ripping it apart.

The sound of engines caused the zombies to lose interest in the dead CDC security guard and move in the direction of their new prey. Andy's suppressed M4 spoke as he fired from his open window and an older white male's head exploded. The rifle fired again and a waitress from the cafe across the street collapsed to the pavement. Jimmy and Eddie were riding shotgun in their vehicles and they shot the last two.

Chuck had briefed them on how he wanted their vehicles positioned and each driver turned their SUV and backed into position. The four cars were set up in an inverted V around their door. Those in the two left cars would have to exit on the passenger side and those in the two right cars would have to get out on the driver's side. Parking in this way created a safety zone for the agents to get in and out of their vehicles in a hostile environment.

The two rear Armadas backed up until they were touching the wall on either side of the door and the other two backed up until they were touching the other vehicles. At this point, McCain wasn't worried about dinging up the rental cars. He just wanted to be able to get out of this alive.

As they clambered out of the Armadas, Chuck shone his flashlight on the hood and windshield of Andy and Scotty's car and shook his head.

"You just had to put a scratch on the rental didn't you, Scotty?"

"I put more than a scratch on it, boss," Smith answered, smiling. "I'm just glad that windshield held or Andy would've been getting some big girl zombie love."

"We've got a problem," announced Eddie, standing next to the door, holding his ID card. "The scanner isn't working."

He swiped his card a second and a third time but the door was still locked. Chuck pulled out his own ID card and swiped it, but nothing happened.

"The green light isn't coming on. The power must be off here, too."

"Well, anybody have any ideas?" asked Eddie. "The only other option is a frontal approach and that drone video showed the front was crawling with Zs."

Andy walked over to the door and slipped a key into the lock, opening the door.

"Once again, the Marines to the rescue," he announced, as his teammates rushed through the doorway.

"Where did you get a key?" Chuck asked him after they were safely inside.

"In spec ops they taught us to always plan on the power grid failing and to never get locked out of a place that you needed to be inside. I just told Darrell I needed a key and he gave me one."

Chuck nodded. "Lesson learned. Okay, Dr. Edward's lab is on the fifth floor. Let's check it first. Hopefully, she's just hiding in there and waiting for us."

The stairwell was dark but the men had flashlights attached to their rifles that allowed them to move quickly. CDC headquarters was quiet for now and they prayed not to have a repeat of the Wells Fargo building. Chuck led the way up the stairs and stopped at the fifth floor landing.

Silence greeted them but they knew that Zs could be waiting on the other side of the door. The small window on the stairwell entrance allowed them to see a small section of the hallway. Thankfully, ambient light from office and lab windows spilled out into the corridor, illuminating it.

After listening for three minutes, McCain had Terrence ease the door open and Chuck stepped slowly out into the hall, his M4 tucked tightly into his shoulder. He swept the flashlight around and said, softly, "Clear, let's move."

The lab they were looking for was right in the middle of the floor. They paused at the door, listening. Nothing. Chuck turned the knob and found that it was unlocked. He pushed it open and stepped into the room. Daylight poured through the large windows, illuminating Salman Kumar lying motionless in the center of the large lab.

"Body lying on the floor. Let's clear the room first."

Half the officers went left, the other half went right, checking the lab for any threats. After they had cleared the room, Eddie pointed at another door on the side of the lab.

Jimmy slowly pulled the door open and Eddie went in first, followed by the rest of his team. After clearing the room, they paused to look at all of the dead mice.

"This is pretty nasty," commented Chris, softly. "And look at this." He shone his flashlight onto the dead body of a white mouse laying on the floor. There was blood all around it.

"This place gives me the creeps," said Jimmy, going back into the laboratory.

They circled around the body on the floor. He was wearing a white lab coat and had a bullet hole in his head. Andy pulled the flashlight off of his belt and knelt down beside the body, shining his light around it.

"Check this out," he said, shining the light on the body's left hand. It was clutching a handful of long brown hair.

"How much you want to bet this guy turned and attacked the good doctor we're trying to find?" asked Eddie. "I wonder if he managed to infect her, as well? She could be waiting to try and make a meal out of one of us."

"But, who shot him?" wondered Hollywood. "Maybe one of the security guys? We could have a zombie security guard out there, as well."

"Hey, Boss," said Terrence, "do you think this is important?" He pointed to a memory stick poking out of a desktop computer.

"It might be. It looks like she cleaned out her desk so maybe she just forgot the memory stick. Grab it and take it with you."

Security office, CDC HQ, Monday, 1625 hours

The red eyes blazed in the dark room and moved towards her. How did he get in? Nicole pushed herself back against the wall. Somehow, she knew that he could see her, even in the darkness. Where was Darrell?

He was so close now that she could feel his hot breath on her face. She had to get away but there was no place to go. Even in the in pitch black room, she knew his teeth were about to bite into her flesh.

"No!" she yelled, pushing him away.

"Shh, you've got to be quiet, Dr. Edwards. You're havin' a bad dream," Darrell said, softly. She felt his hand on her shoulder, comforting her.

She was lying on the couch, breathing hard. The dream had been so real. The two survivors both had screwed up sleep schedules from sitting in the dark office for two and a half days. Edwards took a deep breath to calm herself.

A body slammed into the office door and then another one. Growling could now be heard outside the security office. Oh no! Nicole thought. Now they know for sure that we're in here. And I alerted them.

"I'm sorry, Darrell," she whispered. "It's my fault and I'm so sorry."

His hand was still on her shoulder. "Well, they know we're here now, ma'am. I just hope they can't break through that door."

The strikes on the door became more numerous as the infected who had been in the lobby began trying to get into the office. The Zs had heard Nicole's scream and now they wanted to eat the fresh victims.

Edwards patted Parker's hand. "Thank you for looking after me. No matter what happens, you've been my protector and friend, Darrell."

"You're a good person, Dr. Edwards. I think God's going to take care of us. Somehow."

The older man stood and flicked his light on briefly so he could find his way back across the room. His desk faced the door and he sat in his swivel chair and waited. That metal door is pretty stout but it sounds like a bunch of those things are banging into it, he thought.

Even if they don't get in, he wondered, how long can we hold out? For the moment, they were drinking the water from the bathroom sink, as it was still running. They would save the bottled water for later. The two of them found enough leftovers in the fridge and a few snack bars from rummaging through the other guy's desks to last a few more days, if they rationed them carefully.

The door and now the room itself were shaking under the heavy blows. A framed picture of the CDC Director fell to the floor and shattered. That loud noise got the Zs on the other side of the doorway even more agitated. It sure sounds like a lotta zombies out there, Parker thought.

He had reloaded both his revolver and his one remaining speed loader. His second speed loader was still on the parking deck upstairs from when he had to reload after shooting those Zs outside. Six rounds in the gun and six in the speed loader on his belt. He also had another twelve loose rounds of .38 Special from the box of ammo he taken out of his desk drawer.

I guess we could shut ourselves in the bathroom, he mused, but that door wouldn't keep them out. It was a just hollow wooden one that those monsters would rip right through. I'll send the doctor in there when it looks like they're coming, then I'll shoot as many as I can before they eat me. He chuckled. I hope they like tough, old, dark meat because that's what they're going to be getting.

Lobby, CDC HQ, Monday, 1630 hours

Chuck could see the big group of Zs clumped around the security office door. The loud growling and snarling carried into the stairwell. McCain had hoped they would find survivors in the security office. It looked like he was right.

"Let's go to work," he said, quietly, opening the door to the lobby.

The zombies were striking the door, over and over, now more than twenty of them. The infected crowded around, trying to knock the barrier out of the way. They knew their next meal was only a few feet away. Suddenly, one of the zombies' heads exploded, covering the three next to her with gore. The noise of their growling was so loud that it partially muffled the suppressed shots from the rifles.

The CDC officers took down twelve of the pack before the rest realized that there were closer victims to be had. They turned and charged the police officers, teeth bared. The front three were young Mexican men from the same lawn crew. They had been working in a residential area, just half a mile a way and were attacked and infected by Zs who had walked from ground zero.

Those three were quickly cut down along with seven others. The last two reached the skirmish line of officers, one reaching for

Chuck, the other grabbing Chris' arm. Rogers felt teeth sinking into his left forearm, his rifle pinned against his chest by the Z's body.

Suddenly, Terrence was there, plunging his knife into the base of the infected woman's skull. The dead zombie let go of Chris and fell to the floor. Thankfully, the kevlar-lined jacket had once again saved one of them. He would have a sore and bruised arm, but that was all.

The big male who reached for McCain clearly wanted to sink his teeth into Chuck's throat. Normally, McCain would step to the side and throw the attacker to the floor. He had teammates on both sides of him, however, and that would not work. Instead, Chuck quickly crouched and used a single leg take down, knocking the zombie onto its back.

As he disengaged to step back and shoot, he heard a shot from next to him. Scotty had stepped up and shot the infected man in the head.

"I had it," said Chuck, with a smile.

"I'm sure you did but I still need a couple more to hit my quota."

Everyone performed a tactical reload and Scotty stepped over to check Chris.

"How bad did he get you?"

"Thank God for kevlar," Chris answered, nodding at Terrence, "and for a rookie with a knife."

Rogers rolled up his sleeve to look. The area around the bite was reddish purple but the skin had not been broken. Smith nodded and pulled his bottle of solution out of his pack. He squirted it onto the sleeve of Chris' jacket, killing whatever residue of the virus that remained on the cloth.

The team cautiously approached the security office. For the moment, the lobby was clear and they did not see any more infected in front of the building. Hollywood, Andy, Scotty, and Chris provided security, training their rifles towards the front entrance. Chuck knocked softly on the door.

"Is anyone in there?" he asked, quietly.

"Who's there?" a male replied from the other side.

"Darrell? Is that you? It's Chuck. We're here to get you out."

The door opened and the older black man blinked at the sunlight flooding into the lobby. A figure rushed by him and grabbed Chuck.

"Agent McCain! I knew you'd come get us," Nicole gasped, hugging him tightly.

Chuck was surprised, as were his men. Jimmy cleared his throat. "Do we all get hugs, too, or is that just for the boss?"

Self-conscious, Edwards stepped backwards. "Sorry. Thank you all so much for coming for us."

"Just you two?" Eddie asked Darrell.

The security supervisor nodded. "That's right. Dr. Edwards' assistant, Dr. Kumar, turned into one of those things and I had to shoot him upstairs. The phones are dead, Mr. Marshall, so I haven't been able to report it to anyone."

"Was that the guy up in the lab? We checked there first and saw him," Marshall said. "Okay, Darrell, you've reported it. Now, let's get out of here."

Nicole grabbed her purse and briefcase and allowed herself to be placed in the middle of the line of CDC officers.

"Back to the basement," McCain ordered. "We'll grab our gear out of the offices and get out of here."

"We got attacked by zombies the other night when Darrell was escorting me to my car," Edwards said, looking at Chuck. "He had to shoot some of them on the second level parking deck. We dropped my computer bag and a bag with experimental samples of the vaccine we're working on.

"Could we get those? I hate to lose all of that work. I think we're close to a breakthrough. And, my car is out there. Can I get my car and drive out of here?"

Chuck glanced at Eddie and Andy, his two team leaders. They both shrugged.

"What kind of car do you drive, ma'am?" asked Andy.

"A Honda Accord."

Chuck shook his head. "We'll check for your bags but you'll

need to leave the car. It's too small. This area is crawling with Zs and if you hit one in an Accord, you'll be dead. Sorry. Okay, let's get moving. We don't want to get stuck down here after dark."

The door to the parking deck did not have any windows so they listened intently for several minutes. Finally, Terrence eased it open with Chris, Scotty, and Hollywood covering the opening with their guns. Matthews was tasked with keeping the door open so they could grab the bags and get back inside.

The bodies of the infected that Darrell had shot were still lying on the pavement but the leather computer bag and padded bag of samples were gone. There was no sign of them. The three officers did a quick scan of the area around the door and retreated back inside.

"There were no bags out there," Scotty told the scientist.

"But, they were right there, just outside the door," said Nicole, panic in her voice. "There were ten vials of different components that we had been experimenting with. They all contain the bio-terror virus."

"And that really sucks," commented Jimmy. "Like we need some more crazy people running around with the zombie virus."

Smith handed Parker his empty speed loader that he had picked up outside. The older man smiled and slipped it into his pocket.

"Thanks, Scotty. I was thinking that maybe it's finally time to retire my revolver and get me one of those semi-automatic pistols."

Chuck's house, Northeast of Atlanta, Monday, 1910 hours

The four Nissan Armadas had driven as fast as they could on the semi-deserted streets, escaping the city. The officers had killed seven more zombies that had either smelled them or heard them loading equipment and weapons into their vehicles. After leaving the CDC compound, they retraced their route out of the city. Thankfully, the team had not encountered anywhere near the numbers of infected that had overrun them on Saturday.

Dr. Edwards' apartment was in Buckhead, an upscale community right in the zombies' path, so for the moment anyway, she was homeless as well. Chuck kicked Scotty and Hollywood out of the guest bedroom and gave it to Emily and Nicole. Darrell's son and daughter-in-law lived twenty minutes away and picked him up from Chuck's home, after much hugging and hand shaking to thank McCain and the others for saving their father.

As the emotionally and physically drained officers, paramedics, and recently rescued scientist sat around McCain's living room drinking bottles of water, they conducted a debrief of the operation. Chuck, Andy, and Eddie were all happy with how smoothly this one had gone.

"Andy, call the rental car place tomorrow," Chuck ordered, "and have them come get the one Scotty tore up and bring us another one, if at all possible. If they don't want to rent us a replacement, find us another one with another company. We're going to be doing more rescue missions and we need cars with the windshield intact and preferably without zombie blood and guts strewn about," he said, winking at Smith.

"Boss, didn't you say we were getting another helicopter?" Jimmy wondered.

"That's what I was told," answered McCain, "but they said it might take a few days."

"I have a question," said Hollywood, staring at Matthews. "What's up with the rookie trying to one-up me with a knife kill on his first day?"

Up to that point, Alejandro had been the only CDC officer to kill a zombie with a knife, several weeks earlier. He had been on a packed airliner, thirty-five thousand feet in the air, and had had no choice. He could not take a chance on using his pistol in such a crowded environment.

Terrence looked uncomfortable. "I'm sorry, man. I didn't want to shoot so close to Chris' face. I was scared he might get some infected blood in his mouth or eyes. I don't really know how this virus works and I was trying to be careful. I wasn't trying to one-up anybody."

Hollywood stared at Matthews for a couple of seconds more and then broke into a big grin.

"I'm just messing with you, amigo. You did really good. That was nice blade work. Do you have any Latino blood in you?"

"No, I don't think so."

"That's too bad. Anyway, your first day on the job and you take out a Z with a knife. Pretty impressive. I'm renaming you: 'The Blade.'"

"Oh, I like that," said Jimmy. "The Black Blade. Kind of sounds like an urban superhero."

Everyone raised their bottles of water and said it in unison, "The Black Blade!"

Emily and Darnell had cooked a large pot of chili which everyone devoured after the debrief. Afterwards, Emily showed Dr. Edwards the upstairs area they were sharing, and Nicole took a long, hot shower. Chuck asked Emily to search through his closet to see if he had anything suitable for the tall, curvaceous scientist.

Edwards came back to a quiet living room wearing a much too-big pair of Chuck's sweatpants, a black t-shirt, and a University of Georgia sweatshirt. Her long brown hair was wrapped in a towel and she saw that Eddie, Jimmy, Andy, and Chris had left for the night.

Hollywood, Scotty, Terrence, Darnell, and Emily were seated on the leather couch and chairs, talking and sipping from bottles of beer. They smiled at Edwards as she walked into the room.

"How you feeling, Dr. Edwards?" Hollywood asked.

"Please, call me 'Nicole.' That shower was one of the best experiences of my life. Other than you amazing men saving my life today, of course. And thanks for finding me these clothes, Emily," she said, laughing. "They're just a little too big."

“Chuck says that we’re still safe out here,” Emily said. “Maybe tomorrow we can go to the mall and feel like normal women again and get you some new clothes?”

Nicole’s eyes lit up. “Really? You think we could do that?”

“Sure,” the young woman answered. “We’ll check with the boss and see what he has on tap but it shouldn’t be a problem at all.”

Terrence cleared his throat. “Ma’am, this was in the computer on your desk at the CDC,” he said, extending the memory stick to Nicole.

Her eyes registered surprise. “That’s right. With Salman getting infected and then turning, I forgot all about backing up my work. What’s your name? I haven’t met you.”

“I’m Terrence Matthews, ma’am. I just started with the CDC.”

“Well, Terrence, thank you for having the initiative to grab that memory stick. That’ll help me get back on track since I doubt we’ll be using that building anytime soon.”

Matthews smiled a shy smile, clearly pleased that he had done the right thing his first day on the job.

“Would you like a beer, Nicole?” Emily asked.

“No, thanks. You wouldn’t happen to have any wine around, would you?”

“As a matter of fact,” the paramedic smiled, “I think we do.”

Chuck sat on his back deck by himself, enjoying a few minutes of solitude. It was a warm fall evening and the woods behind his house were alive with the sounds of crickets, owls, and the small creek that ran through his back yard. He held a lit cigar in one hand, a tumbler of scotch in the other. The last week had been a blur of activity and missions. He marveled at how well his men had performed in a variety of different high-stress situations.

And according to Admiral Williams, they were just getting started. There would be other rescue missions and there could be more terrorists to track down. McCain couldn’t help but wonder, though, if their efforts were going to make a difference.

Of course, they would mean everything to the people whom they rescued. Dr. Edwards was living proof of that. But in the big scheme of things, were any of the federal and local police departments going to be able to stop the surging mass of zombies that were roaming through and pouring out of Atlanta, DC, and New York?

The back door opened and Nicole asked, "May I join you, Agent McCain?"

He really wasn't in the mood for company, the heaviness in his heart never far away. But he and Edwards had not had a chance to talk so McCain motioned to the deck chair next to him and said, "Please, call me 'Chuck.'"

After she sat down, he added, "I hope my cigar doesn't bother you."

"No, it's a nice smell," she answered, sipping her wine. "It's so peaceful out here. My apartment is in Buckhead, not too far from where the bombs went off. It's never this quiet there."

"I don't mind working in the city," Chuck said, "but I do enjoy coming home to this."

They sat in silence for a few minutes, enjoying the serenity. Edwards had left her hair towel inside and McCain took a moment to glance at her. She's really beautiful, he thought. Long brown hair, tall with a full figure, pretty eyes, inviting lips. Not that Chuck was looking for any romantic entanglements. His heart was still an open wound from Rebecca's death. Even the thought of her hurt.

Nicole glanced over and saw him looking at her. "Thank you, Chuck. That seems like such a small thing to say, but thank you and your men for coming and rescuing Darrell and I. As silly as it sounds, I was holding out hope that you'd come."

"We're on the same team," McCain said, smiling at her. "When Dr. Martin called and said you, Darrell, and your assistant were missing, we put the mission together as fast as we could. Thank God it went as smoothly as it did. How are you feeling now? I know it's been a traumatic few days."

The researcher nodded. "It really has. I think we are or were getting close to a breakthrough on a vaccine. We'd seen some promising results over the last week. When the word came to leave, Salman and I were packing everything up and he volunteered to euthanize all the lab mice. One of them managed to bite him and he died and turned into a zombie. It was horrible.

"I was performing CPR on him and his eyes opened and he started growling. We had worked together for over two years and now Salman was trying to bite me. He almost killed me but Darrell was able to shoot him."

Nicole wiped the tears from her eyes. "Your officer, Terrence, had the forethought to pull the memory stick out of my computer. That means I don't have to start from square one."

"But you said you lost your laptop and a bag of samples of the virus?"

She nodded. "Darrell was helping me carry things to my car. He had my computer bag and a padded medical bag with ten vials in it. When we got outside, there were zombies and he had to drop everything and start shooting. It's my fault. I should've been carrying them. Now, I'm going to need some samples of the virus before I can continue working."

Chuck nodded, sipping his scotch. "We might be able to help with that. I'm sure we'll be back in action in the next day or two and I can get Scotty to draw some zombie blood for you. Do you want DNA swabs, too?"

"Chuck," she responded, the relief evident in her voice, "that would be so helpful if you guys could do that. Please don't take any chances to get the samples, but I'll take whatever you can get me, blood and DNA."

McCain puffed his cigar and finished his drink. Nicole chuckled next to him.

"I forgot to thank you for the clothes. I'm sure I look pretty comical."

Chuck managed a laugh. "Yeah, sorry about that. I haven't been married for a long time and my daughter has a few clothes here, but she's closer to Emily's size."

"I'm just thankful to have something clean to put on. Emily told me that she'd take me to the mall tomorrow, if that's OK with you. She's such a nice person."

"She really is. Her and Scotty have a strange and wonderful relationship. He's strange and she's wonderful."

Nicole laughed at Chuck's attempt at humor and then said, "I'll try to make some other living arrangements as soon as I can and get out of your hair. Are there any decent hotels around here?"

"You're welcome to stay here as long as you need to. If you don't mind sharing a room with Emily and helping her with the cooking and shopping until the CDC sorts itself out, feel free to stay. I've got a good computer you can use until you replace yours. Plus, having you around, Emily has a little feminine support."

"Are you sure, Chuck? I don't want to impose on you and I don't mind staying in a hotel."

McCain looked at her. "Nicole, you're not imposing at all. I don't know how long it'll be before the Zs make it out this far. When they do, we'll all have to find some other place to live. Do what you want, but I'd suggest staying here for a few days until the CDC brass decides what they're going to do about giving you and everyone else a place to work."

She nodded, seeing the wisdom in his words. Plus, Nicole realized, she was in no rush to get away from Chuck McCain. Edwards caught herself yawning.

"I think I'm going to bed." Nicole stood but hesitated. "Chuck, I…I wanted to say I'm so sorry about Rebecca. We were friends and I had so much respect for her."

McCain looked at her and she saw the pain in his eyes. "Thanks, Nicole. That's a nice thing to say. She was a beautiful person and I miss her every day."

He turned away, staring into the darkness. Nicole touched his shoulder and then went into the house.

Chapter Fourteen

Payback

Near Hanover, Pennsylvania, the next Wednesday, 0330 hours

The two figures moved across the field under the moonless sky. Their night vision goggles gave everything a greenish tint but allowed them to move without fear of being seen. Unless their prey was scanning the area with night vision of their own, they would never detect the two intruders.

The small farmhouse sat over a hundred yards off the road, almost completely hidden by trees. The men had parked nearly a mile down the road, leaving their rented Toyota Highlander on a dirt driveway leading into a cornfield that spread along the highway. Now, only two hundred yards west of the house, they slowed their pace.

The intelligence that they had been given was that he had two bodyguards with him. Were the guards both in the house or were they patrolling the perimeter? When they were seventy-five yards from the target location, Jay Walker suddenly stopped and raised his fist over his head, slowly sinking to the ground. Tu Trang, following ten yards behind his partner, followed his lead.

There, in the carport on their side of the house. Tu saw it now, as well. The glowing tip of a cigarette. So at least one guard was outside, but he had just given his position away. After a couple of minutes, the cigarette was flicked out into the yard in an explosion of sparks.

The guard, a big black man, wearing a black stocking cap, was holding an AK-47 rifle. He walked behind the house. When he was out of sight, Trang slithered up next to Walker. Jay put his mouth next to his boss' ear.

"Slide up about twenty-five yards closer. I'll take care of him when he comes back around. Then we can make entry."

Tu nodded in acknowledgement. Both men had extensive special operations backgrounds. Jay had been with Seal Team Six, however, and sentry removal was one of the skills that they honed to perfection. Walker slipped his rifle off and left it with Trang. They were both wearing dark clothing and had black balaclavas covering their faces.

Jay drew his knife and crouch-walked to the edge of the field, near the house, kneeling behind a bush. In a few minutes, the AK-carrying sentry circled back around to the front of the residence, scanning the dark fields but oblivious to what awaited him. As the big man walked by Walker's hiding position, Tu saw Jay rise up, clamping his gloved hand over the guard's mouth, pulling him to the ground, while slicing his carotid artery. Trang heard the sentry grunt and saw the blood spurting into the air.

Tu moved up to where Jay had dragged the man behind the bush. Walker cleaned his blade on the man's clothes and searched him carefully. Trang quietly unloaded the AK-47 and took it apart, leaving the fieldstripped rifle laying next to the dead man. Jay pocketed the sentry's cell phone, his wallet, and a set of keys.

"Good job," whispered Tu. "Let's go finish this."

The previous Sunday morning, Shaun Taylor had called Tu Trang and said he needed to meet with him and Walker. Neither of the two Washington, D.C., CDC agents had ever met Taylor but

Chuck McCain had alerted Tu and told him to expect the call. Something about a special assignment. Like they needed another assignment.

They had lost two of their officers in the fighting after the bombs had gone off. Washington was a disaster. No one seemed to have any idea how they were going to clean the city out.

After the evacuation order was given to residents of the nation's capital, Tu had made some phone calls and gotten rooms for their officers in the Fort Belvoir bachelor quarters. The Zs had not made it that far south yet and Trang felt better about having his wife and son, along with his teammates and their families on the military base until the crisis was contained.

Shaun directed the two men to meet him at the Grist Mill Park, a few miles from the military base. Because of their spec ops backgrounds, both Tu and Jay recognized that Taylor was without a doubt, a CIA spook. They both had their guards up and were prepared to tell him to go pound sand. At this point, Tu figured that, within reason, he could pick and choose what he and his men did. He didn't intend to get screwed over by the CIA or any other alphabet soup organization in Washington.

When Taylor outlined what he needed done, however, Trang and Walker looked at each other and knew they would not be saying "no" to this mission. Imam Ruhollah Ali Bukhari was hiding at a farmhouse in Pennsylvania, biding his time until he could rebuild his terror cell network and get back to killing Americans. He had covertly run most of the cells along the east coast and had been responsible for thousands of lost lives, including Tu's and Jay's two agents.

"So, you guys know where he is. Why are you sending us to Pennsylvania to arrest him? That seems like a good use for the Bureau boys and girls," commented Trang.

Shaun looked out over the empty little league baseball diamond. He had never issued an order like this before, he thought. These two men were both federal police officers. Would they arrest him for what he was about to say?

He sighed. "Look, the rules have changed. We don't want him arrested. Chuck McCain briefed you about the Agency's involvement in the CDC. We're not even supposed to be active on US soil. As bad as all these bio-terror attacks have been, though, they would've been much, much worse without the work that you and your officers have done.

"Here's what we want. Eliminate his guards and then interview Bukhari thoroughly, using whatever tactics you feel are necessary. We need three major pieces of info from the imam: the name of his mole in the FBI, who his other cell leaders are, and their locations.

"We're pretty sure we know who his main man is at the Bureau but we'd like confirmation before we move. As for other cell leaders, there may not be any. He may have already activated everybody but it won't hurt to ask."

"And after we interview him, then what?" Jay asked, thinking he knew where this was going.

"We don't know how many more cells are out there or how many other homegrown Muslim terrorists are preparing to launch more attacks," Taylor answered, "but we want to send them all a message. We're not playing fair anymore. We'll hunt you down and kill you. You guys have performed missions like this before in the Middle East, and you know better than me what needs to be done."

Tu and Jay looked at each other. Trang nodded slightly to Shaun. "What kind of support do we get?"

Taylor opened the passenger door of his car and pulled out a large beige envelope, handing it to Tu.

"IDs and a credit card to rent a car and buy anything you feel is necessary. There's also a phone number in there to call for any equipment you might need, including weapons. The address for Bukhari's location and all the other information we have is in there.

"Obviously, if you get caught, you're on your own. So, don't get caught. This guy doesn't deserve a trial; he deserves exactly what you're going to give him."

Near Hanover, Pennsylvania, Wednesday, 0345 hours

The second bodyguard was snoozing on a leather recliner in the living room, facing the door leading to the carport. He woke up as Jay used the key from his dead partner to open the door. This guard was another black man, sporting a shaved head and full beard.

As his sleepy eyes tried to focus, he realized too late that two figures came through the carport door instead of just one. He fumbled with the Mossberg pump action shotgun laying across his lap. Tu's suppressed Sig Sauer P226 pistol coughed three times. The first two rounds struck the guard in the chest and a third 9mm hollow point hit him between the eyes. The dead man slumped back into the chair.

"Don't bother getting up," Jay whispered. "We'll let ourselves in."

They listened for any sign of other bodyguards. The sound of snoring came from down the hallway. Trang led the way, both men holding their suppressed pistols in a low ready stance.

The snoring got louder as they moved down the corridor, clearly coming from the last room on the right. Jay reached over and tried the doorknob. Locked. He motioned to himself and pointed to the door. Tu nodded and stepped back to cover his partner. Jay withdrew a lock pick set from a pouch on his belt. He slipped a long, thin pick into the cheap privacy lock and quietly turned the knob.

Through their night vision goggles, the two warriors saw the elderly man alone in the bed. He sensed someone was in his room and woke up, peering into the darkness.

"Who is there?" he asked in Persian, reaching for the Makarov pistol on the nightstand.

Jay crossed the room to the bed in two strides, bringing his Sig down on Imam Ruhollah Ali Bukhari's head before his hand could grab the gun. The blow stunned him and he fell onto his back, blood from his gashed head staining the white sheets. Walker flipped him onto his stomach and secured his hands and feet with flex cuffs. He pulled a precut piece of silver duct tape off of his belt and placed it over the imam's mouth.

Trang kept his pistol pointed at the other two closed bedroom doors. Jay joined him and they finished clearing the house. After confirming that it was empty, they went to work.

The first order of business was zip-tying Bukhari to a kitchen chair that they brought into his bedroom. They then dragged the dead terrorist from outside the house into the living room, dumping him on the floor next to his dead partner's recliner. The pieces of his AK were left beside him.

Tu pulled a leather pouch out of one of his cargo pockets. He unzipped it and removed a loaded syringe. He and Walker went back to where the terrorist sat, bound, and wide eyed. Blood trickled down the left side of his head from where Jay had struck him. Tu flicked open his knife and used it to cut away the long sleeve of Bukhari's nightshirt. He stuck the needle of the syringe into the man's arm and pressed the plunger.

After ten minutes, Walker ripped the duct tape off of the terrorist's mouth and they began to interview him. Tu turned two small digital recorders on to capture the interrogation. At first, the old man struggled to resist the effects of the sodium pentothal, also known as "the truth serum," with which he had been injected. Within thirty minutes, however, Trang and Walker were getting answers to their questions.

They asked him several things for which they already knew the answers and were pleasantly surprised that he answered truthfully. The two men began asking other, probing questions and recording the terrorist's answers. The interrogation took a little over an hour. That would have to do.

Tu and Jay needed to be gone before daylight. The Asian officer turned the recorders off and slipped one of them into a cargo pocket. The other was left on the nightstand, next to the terrorist's Makarov pistol.

Trang withdrew another, larger loaded syringe from his pouch. This one contained the two lethal drugs used to execute prisoners sentenced to death. Pancuronium bromide is designed to paralyze the person's diaphragm and induce respiratory failure. The other drug, potassium chloride, creates cardiac arrest.

Even in his already drug-induced haze, the imam sensed what was coming and struggled against his bindings. He started to yell at the two men in Farsi, Arabic, and even a few words of English, cursing them, their families, and promising the judgment of Allah on them. Jay shook his head and reached into his pack, pulling out a pack of raw bacon.

"You are now going to meet Allah smelling like a swine," Walker said in Farsi, smiling.

The imam's eyes bulged and a vein on his forehead was throbbing as he screamed at the officers. Jay shook out a few slices of the bacon and dropped them inside Bukhari's shirt, inside his pants, and used other pieces to wipe bacon grease on the condemned man's nose and mouth.

The imam tried to spit on Walker and Trang but his mouth was dry and nothing came out. Tu cut the other sleeve of the terrorist's shirt and held the needle above his arm, hesitating for a few seconds. He finally pushed the needle into the muscle and slowly pushed the plunger, sending the deadly cocktail of drugs into Bukhari's system. In less than five minutes, Ruhollah Ali Bukhari was dead.

The two officers had worn gloves for the entire operation, but double-checked the house to make sure they had not left any incriminating evidence behind or for any evidence that they could take with them.

As they started to leave, Jay asked, "Why'd you hesitate before you stuck him? Were you having second thoughts?"

Trang smiled. "No, I was thinking about saying something

dramatic about how he had been sentenced to die for crimes against the United States of America and humanity. But then I thought, 'Screw him.' I'm not wasting any more words on someone like him. The bacon was a nice touch, by the way. I guess the slices you placed down his pants should scare off his seventy-two virgins in the afterlife?"

Walker nodded. "That guy is responsible for twenty or thirty thousand dead Americans. I wanted his death to be as unpleasant as it could be, short of torturing him."

At 0515 hours, the two officers locked the door and left the house. By 0535 hours, they were back at their vehicle. Tu held out his hands for the keys. Jay shook his head and got into the driver's seat. He pulled out onto the road, heading south.

"Man, why won't you ever let me drive?" Tu asked.

Jay glanced at his boss with a smile. "Because you're Asian."

Walker's right arm hurt for several days from Trang's right cross.

CDC Research Facility, East of Atlanta, Wednesday, 0730 hours

Many of the displaced CDC scientists and epidemiologists, especially those working on a zombie virus vaccine, were given workspace at this rural location. While occupying over fifty acres, the buildings did not have enough room to house all of the CDC employees from downtown. Support staff had rented some offices within a mile of the research facility to allow administrative workers to keep the wheels of the organization turning.

Chuck's agents had been given two offices to share inside the sprawling compound. A week and a half after the car bombs and suicide bombers, they were still nowhere close to eliminating all of the zombies. When the President finally authorized the states to use National Guards troops, things had already been pushed beyond critical. The number of infected continued to increase as the Zs continued looking for fresh meat wherever they could find it.

The Atlanta Police Department had been devastated. They had lost over a hundred officers since the bombings near Atlantic Station. The downtown area was still controlled by the Zs and thousands remained trapped in their houses or apartments, hoping to be rescued. The police department was trying to respond to some of these requests for help but the problem now was that officers were steadily deserting their posts.

Policemen and policewomen had seen their friends die. In some cases, they'd had to shoot fellow officers who had become infected. APD and other Metro Atlanta departments were shrinking every day as police officers decided not to go to work, instead focusing on getting their own families to safety and out of the city.

With fewer and fewer cops on the street, fewer and fewer people were getting helped. Chuck and the CDC teams had been on twelve rescue missions over the last week. Most of these were VIPs, family members of government officials, or scientists from other government agencies or companies who were needed in the race to create a cure or a vaccine for the bio-terror threat. The CDC officers had also managed to get some infected blood samples and DNA swabs for Dr. Edwards' research.

This morning, however, McCain had received a one-word text from Tu Trang. The word was "Yes." Chuck knew exactly what it meant and what it would require of him. Shaun Taylor had flown down the previous Sunday and met with he and Andy, offering them an unsanctioned mission that could end their careers and even send them to prison. They had both accepted it without hesitation.

District Heights, Maryland, Wednesday, 1740 hours

Special Agent Mir Turani turned his gray Chevrolet Impala onto his street and accelerated towards his townhouse. Most of his neighbors had already fled to parts unknown with the advancing hordes of zombies leaving Washington and moving into Maryland. Mir was ready to flee, as well, but not just because of the infected.

At 1630 hours, two phone calls had come into the FBI's temporary HQ at Andrew's Air Force Base. The first came in on the general public line. It was answered by an operator who forwarded the information to her supervisor. The second call came in five minutes later to the Weapons of Mass Destruction Directorate where Turani worked as Deputy Director Trimble's assistant. Trimble was not in his office so the second call had been routed to Mir's desk.

Both calls had been recorded and Mir listened to each of them several times. The caller's voice was digitally distorted and had given identical information during each call- an address in Hanover, Pennsylvania where the FBI would find three dead terrorists. That was it. There was no chance to track the call nor identify the digitized voice.

Mir recognized the address immediately. It was the safe house in which Imam Ruhollah Ali Bukhari was hiding with his two bodyguards. Turani had helped make the arrangements for Bukhari to use the farmhouse. A Muslim sympathizer, who had made it available to Mir whenever he needed it, owned the residence and the land.

The FBI agent looked around the office. No one was paying any attention to him but he couldn't shake the feeling of being watched. Agents from the Weapons of Mass Destruction Directorate were sharing office space with agents from other sections until they all could return to their headquarters in Washington. Deputy Director Trimble had not come back from lunch, which meant he was spending the afternoon with his girlfriend. Mir had not advised his boss of the phone calls yet.

As soon as the anonymous messages came in, a supervisory agent from the Counter-Terrorism Division had contacted the Pennsylvania State Police, requesting that they secure the location, but not to enter until the FBI got there. A team was on the road within thirty minutes. Shortly thereafter, Mir stood, picked up his leather briefcase, and had headed for his car as well.

It was time for Special Agent Turani to disappear. The phone calls had shaken him up. Why had they called the Weapons of Mass Destruction Directorate and not the Counter-Terrorism Division? Did someone know of his connection to Bukhari? He wasn't going to stick around to find out.

There were three other radical Muslim agents whom Mir was aware of that worked for the Bureau. They had passed information to him and he had passed it, as well as his own intelligence, on to the imam. He would like to have warned them of what was coming but there was no time and Turani wasn't going to call anyone. He was sure they were listening in on all of his calls now.

Mir unlocked the front door of his townhouse and quickly stepped inside. He just needed to grab a few things and get back on the road to another safe house, this one in a more remote location. He stepped over to the alarm panel to deactivate his burglar alarm, but saw that it had already been disarmed. That can't be, he thought. I always set my alarm. Fear gripped the traitorous FBI agent as he realized something bad was about to happen.

He sensed movement to his left and reached for his holstered Glock. He whipped around to face the two figures in dark clothing, wearing black masks. The bigger of the two raised a gun and pointed it at his chest. Mir knew he had no chance but continued trying to draw his own pistol as the big man pulled the trigger on his weapon.

The taser fired two prongs that struck Turani in the chest. The prongs were connected to wires that fed back into the taser and released fifty thousand volts into the traitor's body. Mir stiffened and squealed as he fell to the floor. After the five-second burst was over, the smaller masked man knelt beside him, flipped him onto his stomach, and quickly secured his hands behind him with flex cuffs.

After a few seconds, Mir found his voice and started to protest. His attacker held a gloved left forefinger up to his lips and then slapped a piece of duct tape over the agent's mouth with his right hand. Turani's eyes got big as the man produced a black hood and pulled it over his head. He felt duct tape being wrapped around his ankles.

Hands expertly searched him, removing his pistol, wallet, and cell phone. They cleaned his pockets out, leaving nothing to identify him as a Special Agent of the Federal Bureau of Investigation. Turani still had not heard the men speak.

Five minutes later, a Ford van backed up to Mir's front door. Two more men wearing balaclavas got out of the vehicle and opened the rear of the van. The front door of the townhouse opened and they reached inside, grabbing the man lying on the floor. They checked to make sure the flex cuffs were secure, patted their prisoner down for weapons, and then unceremoniously tossed him into the cage in the back of the van. The two contractors for the CIA nodded at the two masked men inside the house, got back into the Ford Econoline, and drove away.

Inside Mir Turani's home, Chuck McCain and Andy Fleming pulled their masks off. Andy had bagged up the evidence they were taking with them. They had Turani's laptop, a hard drive that they had found hidden in the ceiling, several small notebooks, everything that was in his pockets, and three handguns. The handguns weren't actually evidence but Chuck wasn't going to leave them behind. The traitorous FBI agent would never be coming home.

As they were preparing to leave, McCain stopped Fleming and motioned towards the bar on the other side of the living room. An unopened bottle of Macallan Single Malt 21 Year Old Scotch sat next to several other bottles of different types of adult beverages. Chuck held the bottle up for Andy to see.

"Have you ever had a twenty-one year old scotch?" McCain asked. "This stuff is over five hundred dollars a bottle. I didn't know the FBI paid so well."

Chuck opened the bottle and poured a finger's worth into two tumblers, handing one to his partner. Andy sniffed the amber liquid and then took a sip.

"Very nice. And fitting. We break into an FBI's agent home, steal a bunch of his stuff, and then kidnap him. I guess drinking his expensive booze is the least of our worries."

"And, not just drink it," Chuck laughed. "This bottle's going home with me!"

Epilogue

Andrews Air Force Base, Maryland, Friday, 0930 hours

The email hit every single FBI agents' inbox at the same time. It also went to the White House, the Justice Department, all of the major media outlets, and, of course, Mrs. Charles E. Trimble, III. The email showed the sender to be her husband, the Deputy Director of the Weapons of Mass Destruction Directorate. In reality, it was sent from an undetectable server originating at one of the CIA's off-site locations.

When Mrs. Trimble clicked open the message purporting to come from her husband of twenty-three years, she saw explicit photos and videos of him engaging in a variety of sexual activities with a young woman whom Mrs. Trimble did not recognize. The pictures were all dated earlier in the year, and the email named Deputy Director Trimble, the young woman, Natalia, outlined their relationship, and provided the amount of money that he had spent paying her rent, credit card bill, and car lease.

The email also claimed that Trimble had been blackmailed by his assistant, Special Agent Mir Turani, and further stated that Turani was an Iranian intelligence agent who had managed to infiltrate the Bureau. For the FBI agents reading the email, this was easy enough to believe since Turani had gone missing two days earlier, right after the three dead terrorists were discovered in Pennsylvania.

At 0940 hours, a single gunshot rang out from Trimble's office.

Agents drew their weapons and cautiously approached the closed door. When they pushed the door open and peered inside, the deputy director was sitting at his desk, slumped back in his chair, the front of his white shirt red with blood.

Trimble's right arm hung down beside the chair, his issued Glock pistol laying on the floor where it had slipped from his fingers. The autopsy would later show that he had placed the gun in his mouth, angling it upwards, towards the top of his skull before pulling the trigger. The incriminating email had been sent to him, too, and was open on his desktop computer.

Coming Soon!

I hope you enjoyed *When the Stars Fell from the Sky*. If you did, could you do me two simple favors? First, would you leave a review on Amazon? Good reviews are life-blood for authors because they help push our work a little higher in the rankings and they let other readers know that a book is worth reading.

The second thing that you could do is tell a friend. People are really enjoying the Zombie Terror War Series and so many of them are discovering the books because a friend told them about the series. Thanks!

If you haven't read the first two books in the series, check them out:

When the Future Ended

The Darkest Part of the Night

Be on the lookout for the next installment, *Running Towards the Abyss*. It will be out later this year. If you would like to be added to my mailing list you can subscribe at DavidSpell.com. Feel free to email me your comments and suggestions at david@davidspell.com. I love staying in touch with my extended family!

Made in United States
North Haven, CT
03 September 2022